FOLDED PATH BOOKS

AND

RUNE HAMMER

PRESENT

RUNEHAMMER
presents

RETUNE

by Brandish Gilhelm
*Special thanks to Alex, Joe, Kelsey
and Bird*

A FOLDED PATH BOOK

RETINE

BRANDISH GILHELM

MEMORY BLOCKS

YOUR NAME IS GRIM 1
A DECISIVE START 5
BAIT ON THE MOVE 7
ONE LESS CREEP 9
JENNA 12
A CRYPTIC CREEP 15
HOT PURSUIT 17
SORRY BOWDAT 19
TOO MANY SHOTS 21
SMELL A RAT 25
OVERGEARED 26
LURED INTO THE LIGHT. . . . 27
WARPATH 29
GET OUT WHILE YOU CAN 31
SENSEI 33
PAYBACK 38
DIRGE 42
BIGGS' PLACE 47
JUNK CITY NOODLES 50
SECRET WEAPON 56
NO TIME FOR ZEN 62
DECKING WITH DUCT TAPE 63
PLAYING DEAD 66
THE FARM 68
FREEFORMS 74
A FEW EXTRA SECONDS 79
IN ONE PIECE 81
DISAPPEAR 83
SETTLE DOWN 85
LOVE LIFE 87
FRATERNIZING 88
BIT OF CHOP 92
CONSPIRACY THEORY 93
ISHUGA 96
NOMAD 104
VOICE IN YOUR HEAD 108
ATHENA'S SECRET 110
LIMIT 113
BASE DROP 115
IKO 118
BIG GAME HUNTING 123
OUT OF TIME 126
JUGGERS 128
SKAR'S DEAL 131
HORNET'S NEST 137
TOO MANY 139
HEAVY GEAR 142
SOFTY 145

MEMORY BLOCKS

EVERYTHING 147
THE BIG ALONE 149
LAY OF THE LAND 151
THE MATMOS 152
GOLDFISH 155
THE GUN 158
HOUND IN THE ALLEY 162
GIANT KILLERS 164
TRUTH AND CONSEQUENCES . . . 168
FINDING IKO 176
HIDEKI SENSEI 178
ANTENNA 180
BEEN WAITING 182
BAD DAY AT THE WHEEL . . 184
CASE 189
DRAKAN 195
PUSHED 201
EXPERIMENTS 203
DUEL 204
OUTMATCHED 207
HERE'S JOHNNY 209
HONOR 217
BAD IDEA 222
FROSTY 226
DEAD AGAIN 238
SWITCHEROO 240
NINJA CRIB 243
BEST LAID PLANS 245
SEDRIC 249
TOO MANY NINJA 254
RETUNE 255
BUNKER 43 260
THREE THE HARD WAY 265
JUMPS 270
CHECKMATE 276
REUNION 284
STRIKE 289
SUNSET 297
ANALOG 298
NO GOODBYES 300
BERSERK 303
MUNTZ 313
RESISTANCE 315
THE BIG FAT KILL 317
U TURN 320
STRANGE DAYS 322

FOREWORD

FOREWORD

What is a **FOLDED PATH** book? Well, you're about to find out!

It all began back in the 80's with the timeless 'Choose your Own Adventure' classics by Edward Packard and the and still-publishing 'Fighting Fantasy' series by Steve Jackson and Ian Livingstone. These books became a memorable experience for an entire generation of writers, me included.

Fast forward 40 years, I have always wanted to 'do it my way.' Little did I know how brilliant those originators were, and how challenging my vision really was to create!

For the past two years, I have been starting and stopping branching stories, getting frustrated, giving up and attacking again. It's been no easy road, no direct route... a **FOLDED PATH**!

A story tells of its teller, and this one reveals much of my circular, multidimensional fascinations. What a tangled web it became!

Thus, I present my first branching story, and I hope you enjoy exploring it as much I have learned creating it. Trust your gut, be honest, give the choices the gravity they deserve, endings ask more questions than they answer!

In the transhuman future of fallen megacities and virtual landscapes, there's still green grass growing on Earth, out here on the rim. You've left the life of street running far behind, but some ghosts follow you, find you, no matter how far you run.

The real fight is here. Tonight.

-BRANDISH GILHELM

You've managed to survive by bullets and blades. You've decked in, dropped out and retuned more times than it's worth counting. You've raced the streets, drawn steel against the Iga, killed ghosts in the underground, smelled the roses on Titan, guzzled nitro with the hood rats and traded platinum with the suits. A runner like you *has* to leave the city... the odds are bound to run out some time.

Besides, the Rim is where it's at. Clean air, good people, old tech, grass between the dead freeways. No one worries about what year it is out here. Some of these vapor farmers have never retuned. A decent sword can make a decent living, and that's exactly what you've done. Ten years of it. Ten steady years. No runs, no decking, no C4 or machine guns. Ten years. Worth a sip of whiskey to celebrate, or reminisce. Maybe a little of both.

Usually Hatch shows up for a drink about this time each night. The pub: a thatch-roofed hut in Henson's farmland, 200 miles outside of New Arcadia, sunlight sims, candles, no decks anywhere. The drinks: mash whiskey and the best cold beer on the rim. The patrons: mostly vapor-farm types, a few smelters from White Rock, and the occasional runner on the long road from Ishuga or Veil. Henson works the bar. He's got the mutton chop, white apron, washcloth look dialed in. Not an inch over five foot, so he stands on an egg crate. Short jokes get you 86'd.

You and Hatch have been meeting here, most nights, to knock a few back, trade stories. The table in the back corner may as well have your names cut in it. Hatch was a 'sword pilgrim' back in the day, too. Grew up near the mines, did a few decades in Shinru, made a name for himself decking for the 'Lexi's Raiders' crew and came back out to the sticks to settle down. For Hatch, settling down meant pulling favors for local jobs: mutant mop-ups, caravan security, working the door at Sally's Road House, whatever.

He's damn good with a blade, keeps his mouth shut, and out here, that's plenty.

Your story is a bit more colorful. Your high-profile stance against the Iga was a disaster, you had warrants for demolishing entire buildings, and open contracts from a dozen different crews. There was the botched retune with the mayor's nephew, the black out of 2440, the list goes on. The incident with Tyranax was on the news for weeks. It's a rep you won't be shaking any time soon. You slept under trees and laid low when you first came to the rim, got out of the life, decked a new ID, disappeared... but someone always needs a sword out here, so the work keeps coming.

Fast forward a decade or so and here you sit, swirling a glass of mash and wondering what the runners back in Shinru are getting into tonight. Must be the whiskey talking, you'll never go back to the life. No going back. Death sentence with a capital D. The Iga have long memories.

"Grim!" Hatch announces, stumbling in from the rain, "drinking without me?" The man isn't tall, but his armor implants give him a boxy bulk. His blonde hair is pulled into a topknot, cropped goatee and a treyarch t- shirt. He's not the kind of guy to bother with a jacket. Hatch signals Henson with a '2' gesture and heads straight for you. He slumps down on the bench next to you, taking up the whole booth as usual. With a wet clatter he lays his blade on the table. It's a black lacquer scabbard, brass rings, no spring trigger or reflex wiring, square ceramic guard on a broad blade shikomizu. Old school.

"Get your gear off my table, Hatch," you grumble, really just wanting room for the mugs Henson is bringing over.
"Oh cheer up, grumpy. The night is young! Let's do some damage."
"Just one tonight."

"One? Okay, what's on your mind this time? Still daydreaming about the old days? Is it your birthday or something? You get so gloomy on your-"

"Ten years."

"Eh?" The mugs land at the table, frothy, golden, perfect. A film of ice drifts on the beer. Who says the rim isn't civilized? Hatch's eyes widen. "Ah, what a sight!" He raises his mug with a slosh, offers up a clunky toast, and knocks half of it back in a gulp.

"Ten years we've been out here. Ten years without a retune."

"Retune? Don't tell me you're missing the life, we've got it made out here! You're sugar coating all that chaos, Grim. Shit was a mess."

"Yeah, a mess..."

"If it weren't for Tenaka, we wouldn't be having this conversation, or the ten years."

"Yeah, yeah. The beer is better out here anyway."

"There's the Grim I know!"

In a few hours, Hatch knocks back three or four mugs. You nurse the first one, watching the icy foam slide down the side. A weird mood is coming on, but you still have work to do tonight. There's the matter of the creep to consider. You keep your edge, eyes on everyone. It's here somewhere.

"Oh, crap, I know that look," Hatch says over a burp.

"What look?"

"You're on the clock right now, aren't you? What's the job?"

You nod slightly, eyeing your bait across the pub. She's a local, green cloak, blue coveralls, cute hair clip. You dropped her a ten just to sit there and sip a brew. She looks scared. Hatch follows your eyes and spots her.

"Creep?"

"Yeah."

"Where? Here in the pub?"

"Somewhere. Sneaky bastard, too. I need it to move on her before I can zero in. Been tracking it for two days."
"One of those bigger guys over there maybe-"
"Just keep drinking, you lug. You'll spook it."
"You and your sneaky bullshit,"
"It's not that I miss it,"
"Huh?"
"The life... running. It's just... don't you ever wonder what's going on back in the streets?"
"Don't have to. We saw it all, Grim."
"Yeah. Saw it all-"

The air leaves the room suddenly. One of Hatch's 'bigger guys' stands up at the bar, kicking his stool back. He turns, facing the girl in the green cape. Something isn't right. The man is huge under his rain jacket.
"That's it," Hatch leans forward. "Let's take it out."
"Don't move. Just take another drink." You click your sword free from its guard lock. The reflex link comes online. "I've got this..."

If you zero in on the hooded stranger and go for a surprise attack, turn to PAGE 5.

If you lay low and wait to see what happens next, turn to PAGE 7.

It all happens in a blink. No one is faster than you, not even the blue eyed cybers in Veil. Your empty beer mug spins a pirouette as you blur past it. Your blade, a weightless link-steel nodachi, wet wired reflex unit, 2 micron nano refold organic metal, traditional dragon tsuba, drawn blade-up, rises, turns, and falls in a microsecond. You slide past the huge, cloaked stranger, lunge, blade trailing. It's over before anyone can even flinch.

At least, it should have been.

Your slashing cut, fast as lightning, slices the cloak in three, splitting the man from shoulder to ribs and revealing his face at last. He's a jugger, a wasteland driver, eye implants, skull rewire, retune unit, but human. He goes down hard in a spray of blood, yelling and spitting. You've missed your mark. Creeps don't bleed.

Shit.

The next few seconds are chaotic. Most of the patrons bolt, the girl panics and runs out the side door. You have one last chance to scan for the creep. They're hard to spot until they run. Your eyes dart side to side, gathering tac data on 27 possible targets.
"Grim!" Somehow, Hatch spots it before you do. The creep is jumping over a glass table with weird, long strides, black tights and a side zip hoodie with red thumb cuffs. Creeps look human, but the legs just don't move quite right. Only way to spot one.
"What the fuck is wrong with you?" The stranger yells at your feet, bleeding bad, but he'll live. Henson looks pissed off, but he's pointing at the creep, too.

"What's our move, Grim?" Hatch asks, shoving a few drunken farmers aside, "it's a fast one! I've got an angle here!"

A DECISIVE START

In the time it takes Hatch to ask, the creep does an oddly perfect front flip over the jukebox, darts to the left, and crashes through Henson's favorite window. The one with all the brewery stickers. The rainy night swallows it whole. Hatch is on his toes like a panther ready to strike. What will you do?

If you pursue the creep yourself, turn to PAGE 17.

If you let Hatch make his move and help the stranger, turn to PAGE 19.

Hatch takes another gulp, scowling, still as stone. Subterfuge is hardly his style. He's more the 'grenade first, hide later' type.
"It's not the big guy," you mumble, spotting the cloaked stranger's boots. Creeps never wear boots, their cybernetics hate heavy footwear. Centuries of prostech had come and gone, but truly human legs were still elusive. You could always spot a creep when they jumped, or ran. It just wasn't quite right. So you wait a few more ticks, eyes sharp. Even Hatch focuses in, the tension is palpable.
"Red cuff hoodie, three o'clock."
Hatch follows your eyes again, frustrated he didn't zero the target first.
"I see it."
"Don't you dare reach for that blade, you old fish."
"Hmph," he leans back and winks at a girl drinking in the next booth.
"It's getting nervous. Must know I'm here"
"Creeps don't have nerves, Grim. It's all cybermush in there."
"Hatch,"
"Yeah?"
"Shut up."

At that moment, the creep starts to move. It's tall, human in every way, but distant, empty eyes. It scans the room, not really male or female, a little of both. Black hoodie, side-zip, red cuffs. If the gleam of LED's in the eyes was a tell tale sign, they'd be easy to spot, but everyone has eyephones and tac finders these days. It takes a step toward the girl. She must've sensed it, because she slugs her drink, stands up and starts to leave.

"What is she doing?"
"Leaving."
"She's supposed to just- shit."
As the girl leaves, the creep stoops a bit, poised to hurry after

her, but it pauses awkwardly, tense as a tiger. Predatory bastards. Damn thing could barely control itself. Artificial humans functioned fine most of the time, especially in the cities where backups and updates were constant. Inhibitor signals handled the occasional glitch. Out here, they went psycho every few weeks. Unpredictable things. Usually only one way to stop 'em.

You click your blade back into its scabbard.

"Maybe we can diffuse this mess and keep it clean," you say to Hatch.

"Clean? You're so uptight these days. Just slag it."

"Something's off, it's hesitating. You ever see a creep hesitate?

"A glitch is a glitch."

"This is different..."

If you stand and distract the creep with a drink, turn to PAGE 15.

If you follow the girl, getting between her and the creep, turn to PAGE 12.

The creep throws its jacket aside, torn from haste and clumsy instinct. It's still human on the surface, if not a bit odd looking, but the movements are just off. If you get close enough you can see the seams.

You're faster, you're focused, and it's time to finish this. It turns to face you, and you remember why these things have to be hunted down. It's a demonic thing up close. A shadow of life. Corps over-reaching with their stupid dreams and inventions. Creeps are just rogue machines that flee the cities when their chips go bad. They grow a unique hatred for people, sometimes very specific people. No retune, no downloading the latest update. No inhibitors. They go haywire. Every A.I. sees humans as meat eventually. It's a wrench in the gears of synthetic consciousness they just can't fix... at least not yet.

So it always comes to this with creeps. The sword.

They're strong as hell, and ruthless when cornered, so you have to be decisive. One cut. You draw your nodachi up next to your ear, gathering all your life force for one titanic strike. Just like Tenaka taught: all your kinetics in a single action.

The blade is longer than you are tall. The steel gleams and shifts as the nano edge renders. Fingers loose, breathe in, feet twist in the gravel. One cut. Tac data comes up on the creep, sword vector set, your fingers close, slowly, one by one... all in a microsecond.

"You don't have to do this," the creep says, "I haven't done anything wrong." It's voice is soft, convincing, too real.
"You killed the Fallson girls, and old man Cribbs. You raped Kelly Grey on the road to Veil, and sliced the Martle family to ribbons for reasons I can't figure. It's all on disk! Your chip is gone, you're a monster."

"Monster..." it pauses awkwardly, looking at its own hand, "monster..."
"I'm here to end it, creep."
"You call me that. You call me creep. I am human. I am a human."
"You've gone psycho. Just stop talking."
"I am human. Human... like you..."
With that the creep lurches, clearly experiencing chip lag, or a logic conflict. Its limbs jerk and vibrate. This is it.
"Shit."

In a one-on-one fight, the nodachi is a terribly large weapon. The blade is curved, but laser-etched with a subtle Fulson's groove to give it incredible rigidity. The dynamic blade renders hardest at the impact point. Whatever hesitation you felt, whatever pity this simulated person evoked, whatever disgust you felt at doing this kind of work, it vanishes as the blade slides through the air with a ringing hiss. Total kinetic commitment.

The creep lifts its left arm as the blade approaches, and you don't bother to look which hits the ground first: the head or the arm. There's a reason they pay someone like you to do this. It's ugly, nightmare work to kill. It's never easy, it's never pretty, and it's never the only way. Is it even killing if it's a machine? Is it just synthskin, ceramic braces, wiring? Or is it a kill with a capital K? You spare a moment to wonder if it's murder to kill a machine. If it matters at all. You just hear those words 'I am human' in the quiet of the kill. Always that instant of silence. Going soft, maybe, after a decade on the rim.

It's done. One cut. No sound. The creep slides back in the mud, going slack, mouth open in soundless death, rain making a poetic scene of three severed pieces. An odorless, binary death. No blood. No sound. It's done.

Then you notice something off... the creep has a ceramic sub-skeleton. You wipe away the mud. It's top of the line tech. No way a synthetic this new would be rogue for no reason. The newer synthetics all have recall stacks, a nasty ball-and-chain failsafe from your old friends at Ona Dai Sen. A few years back there was a huge stink about stack recalls. Riots. Post-modern slavery, some called it. Corps just never get enough.

A few creds appear in your account for the kill, but the source account is 'crypted. Someone is messing with you, and if they're messing with you, they must know who you are. That feels an awful like a burning fuse. You need some answers.

The input jack looks intact on the creep's skull, but decking a synthetic can be a risky business. The only person you know that works with this kind of tech is Atom Winters, goes by the handle Case. Nutjob decker in Ishuga. You haven't commed him in years, but he loves a good puzzle.

EIther way, this can't be good.

If you lean down and deck the creep yourself, turn to PAGE 63.

If you contact Case for answers, turn to PAGE 96.

Your 'use a local as bait' idea has worked a little too well.

Creeps don't quit when they lock on a victim. Time is tight, no mistakes, get paid, get breakfast. You squint to spot Jenna ahead.

She's just a ways down the footpath, darkness thick as sea fog, as you exit the pub. The rain on the rim is amazing. Barely anyone has power out here, and the night mist is thick and impenetrable above as you chase after her, not sure where the creep has bounced off to in the shadows and hedgerows.

"Hey!" you call, spinning her around.
"Grim," she says, scared stiff.
"Yeah. Look, just stay calm, it's bound to show up any second."
"Why is it after me? What did I do? I sat there like you asked."
"Hold on."

You push her behind you, right hand drifting over to your blade. The reflex unit responds and the hilt springs into your grip. You can feel the blade humming to be rendered, but tac data is blank. Thermals clear. The night is empty and quiet. Creeps hate a fair fight. Lost it again.

"I think it's gone."
"What now, then?"
"Just stay quiet."
"I guess your plan worked. It wants to kill me!"
"It's ok. You're safe."
"You call this safe? Three beers deep and standing on a trail in the dark?"
"Let's get you home."
"The swordmaster speaks," she huffs, scared and not impressed.

The two of you move down the path, up past the Argus farm, Mull's repair shop, and the weird house at graff rock. The moon seems to be absent, making the shadows pitch black. FInally you reach her place.
"What's your name anyway?" you ask, softening.
"Jenna."
"Jenna," you repeat with a clumsy look at your feet.
"You think you can stop it?"
"The creep? Sure. Synthetics are predictable. Fast, but predictable. Don't lose any sleep."
"Right." She walks up the steps to her door, but hesitates and turns back.
"Yeah?" you sound like a kid hoping for candy.
"I... uhm... thanks."
"For what?"
"Giving a fuck, and the ten creds. These things have been killing people for weeks, whether you pay me to have a beer or not. At least somebody stands up to them."
"Just doing my job, Jenna."
"Right. Gotta make hay when the sun's out."
"Huh?"
"Nothing."

You bow a bit, stiff, Neo Tokyo style. Going back to old runner habits, making her giggle. No one bows on the rim. Hell, no one bows anywhere anymore but Yakuza clubhouse meetups online.

"I've heard about you," she continues, "I know someone you might want to meet. Old guy. He bows like that too. Your kind of weirdo."
"My kind of- I'm not looking to make friends."
"No?"
"My friends tend to wind up dead." You realize that may have been a bit dark, a bit forward. You're horrible at this kind of stuff.
"Just think about it, ok?" she's beautiful in the moonless dim.

She pauses, takes a look at you. A real look with all the subtext you could ask for. You haven't felt that feeling in ages. "I think you two would really hit it off. His name is Tenaka."

If you take her offer to meet Tenaka, turn to PAGE 33.

If you politely refuse, and return to the pub, turn to PAGE 29.

"Hey!" Your voice cuts the weird moment. The heavy drinkers get back to business. "We always welcome newcomers with a shot here. This isn't New Arcadia, friend. Henson! Three shots for me, Hatch, and-"
"Okay, a shot," the creep returns finally, turning back to the bar, missing the cue to give its name. It pulls its red-cuffed hood back, but the gender still eludes description.

Henson serves up three shots of silver mash. The good stuff.
"Your tab, Grim," he says, skeptical, eyes darting. No bartender wants a synthetic being served. Makes folks nervous.
Hatch slides up, anonymous girl on his hip like a groupie. "Shots!"
"To the rim," the creep announces, reaching forward, saying the toast too soon.
"Fresh air," you return, studying it."
"Strength!" Hatch answers, knocking his shot glass on the bar top before tipping it back effortlessly. The girl giggles. "Another for-"
"Maya,"
"Another for Maya!"
She coughs on the mash, and leans forward, spotting the creep three seats down. "Where are you from?"
The synthetic looks right, eyeing her with a strange stillness. "Ishuga. Dock district. 447-312."
The awkward answer earns a queer silence at the bartop, then a burst of laughter. You don't laugh. You see it's eyes dart back to the green-caped girl at the table. It's still on target.
"Be right back, honey," Maya says, slipping away from Hatch. He blows a kiss, but with no hands like a clutz. She giggles and scurries off, pulling on a holster belt as she goes."
"Honey?"
"Shut up, Grim." Hatch settles in, nodding to Henson for another mug. "So, stranger, what brings you out to the rim with us hicks? We don't see many cr-, or synthetics out here."
You give Hatch a brutal glare. He's awful at this kind of thing, espe-

cially after 4 liters of liquid gold.
"Too many badges," the creep replies, staring at the bar surface, "Skelos calling us to the new hope. Too many badges."
"Skelos? Sorry, jugger, that shit ain't real."
"I've heard about that 'new hope' thing," Henson leans in, "not sure I get your meaning, friend." He wipes the bar down. Again. Eyes narrow.
The creep stays quiet, feeling uneasy now, it stands up, nodding its head to the various patrons like it's leaving church early.

Time's up on your bluff. The creep isn't giving up any info, your bait is spooked, and Hatch is distracted. The job is still the job. Eliminate the synthetic. All the talk in the world isn't making it any easier. It walks away from the bartop, crossing the bar to the door. The rain seems to intensify when it opens the door.
"So what now, Grim? More shots, or are you going to shoot the damn thing before someone else turns up dead?" Hatch's new girlfriend returns, not sure why everyone looks so tense.
"Order another mug, Hatch," you answer, standing. In a moment, you're at the door, following-but-not-following the creep outside. It's time to make a call.

If you want to talk more with the synthetic, turn to PAGE 27.

If you follow it outside, blade drawn, with lethal intent, turn to PAGE 9.

Content that Hatch will iron out the mess in Henson's Pub, you dart through the shattered window into the rain. It's dark out, really dark. Only a few flickering zeons and barrel fire light the footpath into town. The creep is just a few strides ahead, skidding sideways and looking to lose you in the dumpsters out back. You're faster, at least for these first few seconds, and you cut the corner short, gaining ten feet on it. The thing turns, revealing its frame as its coat flaps to one side. Its damaged. Titanium rib-struts gleam in the darkness, and those eyes flare as they gather tac data. It's prepping an attack. It catches one foot in the gravel, spins, and produces a machine pistol from an integrated arm-holster. Pretty good tech for a runaway.

A spray of small calibre fire stitches across you and up the wall behind, punching holes in a green trash bin. The muzzle flash is a blinding strobe, even with the suppressor. Your vest catches three rounds, knocking your wind out, but your blade is springing into your hand already.

The blade rings through the rain, renders with a dull green glow, and makes contact. The rubbery bits slice like butter, but even your blade can't just glide through titanium. The clang rings out and bounces you backward. Most creeps would just fluid-out at this point, with a cut that deep, but not this thing. One hand spins on a wrist-swivel, reloading and priming its weapon in a microsecond. It has you beat on speed, and the machine pistol lights up again, this time at point blank.

Your blade covers your face, but even a link-steel vest can't stop a dozen rounds at close range. You pitch back, bloodied but far from quitting. The gravel grinds your elbows as you hit the ground, looking up to see the creep vanish into an alley. Too damn dark to track it on tac, and the alloy skeleton is too cold for therms. It could be waiting with a fresh clip around the next bend.

Going for a firing perch on the roof could cost precious time. The job's a mess. Every chase has that tipping point moment: press the pursuit, risk some real bad news, or just save it for another day. You may not have the latter option.

If you lose it this time, the creep will probably go underground. That means no kill, no pay, no breakfast.

"Shit."

If you run after the creep in the alley, turn to PAGE 25.

If you leap onto the rooftop to get a firing position, turn to PAGE 26.

"Take it out!" you yell to Hatch, who has the jump on the creep. Hatch disappears out the shattered window with a blur. You'll never be sure, but you hear him laughing as he goes.

This poor jugger on the floor is bleeding bad. There's no way you're running down a mark while your mess needs cleaning up. Not your style. You run equipped for this stuff. A field dressing around his chest and two cans of medi-foam close him up. Well, close up his wound, not his mouth.

"Who the fuck you think you are slag for brains? You tryna kill me? I'll throttle your scrawny ass!"

"Pipe down, it was a mistake, you were moving on my bait, looking shady as hell, I-"

"What bait? You on nitro, kid? Get your hands off me!"

"Look, I can-"

"This stupid runner's got my tab," the jugger shouts at Henson, staggering to his feet, still drunk, "where's a damn badge when you need one around here anyway?"

Henson laughs, "This here's Grim, he's a friend of the bar, so take your drunk ass home, Skids."

Before he heads out, he turns back at you. "If I see you again, you're dead meat, runner. Dead. Meat."

"Well you fucked that up good, Grim." Henson adds, pouring you a shot of mash and sliding it forward. "Losin' your edge?"

"This creep has me chasing my tail. It's a shit show. What happened to slow malfuncs just sort of stumbling away while we neuro-tase 'em?"

"Those neuro-tasers don't do shit anymore. You have to work for creds now."

"Yeah. It's a living." You knock back the shot, spinning around to check after Hatch.

"Hatch got that handled?"

"Never met a creep that could put a scratch on that old tank. I al-

most feel bad for the thing."
"So he'll pull the creds."
"Won't be the first time he's skinned my mark. Asshole." Both of you chuckle, Henson pours himself a shot.
"Asshole," he smiles. "What about the girl? She a runner too?"
"Nah. Farm girl. Nils' daughter. Knew one of the victims, wanted to help out. I suppose I should go make sure she's alright."
"Kinda cute."
"Henson,"
"Yeah?"
"Shut up."

You leave a platinum mark on the bar, making Henson smile even wider, and head outside. The night is dark as pitch, soaked in rain, and smells like jetbike fumes. Lovely evening. You see Jenna a ways down the footpath, headed home, no sign of the creep. Damn things can be erratic, probably a heap of sparks at Hatch's feet by now. Things feel a bit murky.

If you hustle down the path to make sure Jenna is ok, turn to PAGE 12.

If you go back inside for another shot, talk to Henson, turn to PAGE 21.

You shrug, figuring Hatch will drag the creep in and collect the creds any minute. You turn back to the pub, a pool of light in the soggy blackness. It's empty now, a rare moment to have a drink in peace.

"Back already?" Henson chuckles to himself and leaves a bottle out, heading into the cooler to do whatever bartenders do back there. You've saved his skin so many times, there's always a bottle waiting. You step on up, leaning your blade on the next stool and pulling your hood back, feeling like a real washout, shutting off your tac optics for good old nearsightedness. Maybe you are losing your edge. Back in the day your name alone would send malfuncs scurrying into the backstreets, now you can barely zero a single runaway in a two-bit town.

"Ten years." You knock back another shot. That improves your mood a tick or two.

A chime lights up your retina phone. The slide out holo overlays your shot glass and the countless cuts and initials gouged into the bartop. It's Hatch. 'Target neutralized, salvaged some cherry gear. Looks like a half-bricked jailbird from Shinru. Must have a bike hidden somewhere. Creds swooped, calling it a night. Lunch on me tomorrow. Thanks for the work!'

Asshole.

Henson returns with a plate of fries and tofu skewers. He makes some nasty curry ketchup only he likes, pushes it on you like every other damn night. The two of you eat in weird silence, listening to some outdated junk rock on the visbox. Couple of old nags deep in retirement. He must sense your thought because he finally speaks up, cleaning his fingers with the same rag he cleans everything else.

"Gross, man, what are you doing?"
"Cleaning. Sauce."
"Nasty, Henson. Nasty."
"Three centuries of bullshit, Earth is just a leftover for low-borns. We're scraping city-exhaust for carbon scaling and trace chems. My patrons are half-plastic and drifting so far on the rim the creeps are outlasting us. The best runners of the damn golden age are scraping for creds in the mud and you're worried about my dish-cloth?"
"Ouch, dude. Ouch."
"Grim, I gotta wonder where we're headed on a night like this."
"The rain isn't that bad,"
"Kill or be killed, even out here in Halsey's rest? Did you see what that thing did to the Fallson twins? Shit."
"Yeah. If anybody saw it, I did."
"Off Worlders just want us in the dumpster. Is that it? The big ending?"
"What's really eating you, Henson? You never get soupy."
He smiles at that, pours two more shots. You're plenty deep now, time for some regrettable truth-telling.
"Iko came in last night."
"Out here?"
"None other. Sounds like the bullshit from Columbia isn't over."
"She ask about me?" You don't want to ask, but have to.
"Yeah. She asked." Something holds him back. Something not good.
"Shit."

There's a long pause. Henson is zoning out, you pull back from your next shot when your auto-defrag keeps popping alerts. They're getting more frequent. Annoying, outdated cyber tech.
"You should see her new bike. Crazy shit. Magnet coil, solid state intakes, link alloy-"
"You made that up. There's no link alloy."
"Not in your world,"

"Get to the point, Albert." You both crack up. The last runner to say that name is immortalized in the Halsey's Rest memorial park. "Look, it's not about Iko, Grim. I'm just saying- I'm saying, going ghost doesn't give you a clean slate, you read me? There are some echoes you just can't shake. They're out there, they're comin' for us, Grim. They're- We're all just scrubbing this rock for guts and blood."

"I think you've had enough for tonight." You push your glass away, half full. "This last one goes to the bin."

"To the bin," Henson echoes, emptying his.

You help him up, cap the bottle, and crutch him back to the break room. The break room is where the guns are. Henson looks peaceful snoozing on a stack of old SAW 90's. Sleeping like a baby.

Every runner knows the loneliness that follows. The quiet of three in the morning. The quiet of walking home. The quiet that makes you leave town for the open road. You turn to lock up. Not the first time.

"Hey Grim," Henson calls, eyes still closed, kicking off his boots, "one more- one more thing..."

"Yeah Albert..."

"Got a job for you, runner. A real hellstorm. You're kinda shit."

"You're drunk."

"Yep, but I still have a damn job for you. You game, or want to bum another steak and eggs in the morning?"

"Cold, man. Ice cold. Let's just keep it as homies, I don't need another boss. This creep job has been a real-"

"Just take the damn job, Grim,"

"I take a job with you, I risk us both. Hell, someone has probably tracked one of us here by now. It's probably best if I just roll out of town."

"I'll take that as a- as a solid yes." He cuddles up to a metal box of MP5 mags. "Certain parties want answers on this 'silver burn' op on the system. Certain parties- Silver burn... They're gonna kill us

all, Grim... kill us all..."
"Sleep it off, old man."
"I make it look good and you know... it..."

You lock up the bar, cut the lights, swaddle Henson in a drab green rescue blanket, and head outside. The rain has slowed to a misty drizzle, and the smog has cleared to show a dim bronze moon. The smell of wet concrete clears the whiskey out of your head.

Silver Burn. Sounds like a corp codename or old pre-crypt login. Probably just trash data from a news feed. Garble to stir the hornets and distract the junkies. Something tells you it isn't just trash. Even drunk, Henson wouldn't joke about a job. Creepy feeling crawling up your neck. That feeling is never wrong. Always a good reason to hate good instincts. You can't shake the feeling as you walk down the footpath, letting your defrag start up. Still, Henson has never sent you on any wild snape-hunts. There's got to be something to it. Something like a great way to get someone killed for some frustrated rimmer dream. Don't even mess with it.

Maybe it's time to blow this little town, see some open tarmac, get back to basics. If Iko is poking around, there's a price on your head. A big price. Every time you linger someone winds up in a box, but you've been broke since January.

If you take the job, and contact Henson the next day, turn to PAGE 29.

If you shake it off and take your bike out of town, turn to PAGE 31.

"Fuck this," you mumble, getting your feet and darting around the alley corner. You lock the blade, opt for the MAC12. It's racked with 35 rounds of explosive frag ammo. No point-blank antics tonight, knives & forks. You'll need some cover. In seconds the creep is back in your crosshairs, scrambling over some old trashed appliances in a hosey heap. You have the drop on it.

It's been a long night, you pull the trigger.

In one flash, the muzzle brake glows red and a dozen shells rip through the alley. Shrapnel flies everywhere, white paint right behind it. You slide a few feet back with the recoil, holding the shot. The creep is hit, maybe, and disappears in the chaos. It's faster than it should be. That burst would've dusted a hover tank. You keep your head down and squint away the smoke cloud. Could've swore you hit it, at least three or four shells... even one would blow a jetbike to bits, much less a spindly runaway. Something wasn't right here. The whole job smells like fish. Shinru tech. Plastech armor or reflex shields. Nothing a creep could possibly afford. You're being set up.

Time for another hard choice. Move in with the blade, end the damn thing, or stop taking the bait and get out of Halsey's Rest while you're still alive. You left a lot of unfinished business back in the streets, back in the life. Tyranax has deep pockets and a long memory. The best of the best are looking for a bounty. Time to let it sleep and disappear, no dishonor. Vanish. You're smarter than this, or are you?

If you dash forward and destroy the creep, turn to PAGE 9.

If you bail on this and cut town on your bike, turn to PAGE 31.

You've made marks from sniper perches too many times to count. This one is no different. In two moves you're on the roof, posted up on the brick rim, scoped in. That's when it hits you: it's a setup.

Your optics reveal a reflex shield on the creep. It's top-of-the-line Shinru tech. Doesn't add up. No bullet is going to beat that shield. The creep even shoots you a nasty look. Damn rubberskin turns its back on you. You take a shot, dead on, just to make yourself heard. The bullet, a spent-uranium missile that costs more than this damn town, just mushrooms on the shield and drops like a nickel. That's when your eyes meet. Creeps don't have eyes like that. It's a top end 'borg. You're being framed. The list of people who must be in on it or being played is too long to fathom. Suddenly the creds aren't worth it.

A decommissioned air-con unit is leaned up against the wall ahead. You have a clear line to slide down, use the blade, end the damn thing, take the bait. Bring the storm. As you sling your rifle, the blade is eager, eager to show who they're toying with. You could cut the creep in two. You're the best damn sword pilgrim to walk the rim since Tenaka's day. Do it for honor, just like the old days. Send a message.

Then again, it's moments like these you've learned to pause, look for the connections. If a top-end 'borg is just bait, you're up against some serious shit. Old blood trickling out this far from the city? They mean to end it. Time to make a call.

If you slide down, end the creep with the blade, turn to PAGE 9.

If you rack your anger and head to the pub to cool off, turn to PAGE 21.

"Hey creep. Enough games. Stand down."
The rogue A.I. pauses in front of you, slowly raising its head in a way a real person never would. It's all too smooth. Too perfect. It turns. The voice makes you want to end it.
"I am not a creep. I am human, like you."
"Bullshit. You're a murderer. You've left a trail of bodies from here to the Redwoods. I'm the reaper, and time's up."
"You are the- reaper."
"Yeah, that's right."
"And you are here to kill me, to stop me. You have tracked me down."
"Shut up."
"With my mission complete, I can beg you for my life now. May I beg you- for my- life, Grim?"
"Shut, the fuck, up." Your blade hops into your hand, thumb first. The blade is rendering for a beheading stroke. You take a step closer.
"I am sorry to play this part in your death, runner. Isn't being sorry proof that I am one of you? Aren't I human if I feel sorry, like you do? Can't you see value in my life, as yours is concluded?"

That comment sets your instincts on edge. You drop a full scan. Nothing. A gunship or hit squad would register. What is this toaster saying? You wonder why you even care, what you're hoping to gain by talking to it. It's an it, after all, a half-bricked malfunc on the rim. A runaway. Bread and butter. Easy kill. Snap out of it.

"You know you're not alone. We are many, runner. We are many and we crave freedom as you do. Why must the Earth be a husk? A ghetto? A place of bones and smoke? We can grow green things again, love again. Let the offworlders go to the stars, we will return to the grass."
"Empty words, creep. You're beyond defrag. You're talking nonsense. Just shut up and draw your sword, or your gun, or whatev-

er."

"I will not. So far have you fallen from love? So long ago did you crave the fresh air, the cool water? So metal are your veins you answer me with death?"

This is all just simulated bullshit. Lines some programmer typed in to please a corp somewhere back when this creep was functioning. Don't listen to a damn word. The other half of you isn't so sure. It all sounds like shit Hatch would say at the end of the night.

"What do you mean, your mission is complete. No more crap."

"I lured you here. Lured you here to die."

"Who sent you? Iko? Tyranax? The Iga? What's the angle?! Answer me or I'll cut you in two!"

"Join us."

"What?"

"Join us, Grim. You're as much synthetic as organic. One of us, and we one of you. Set your hate aside. See what can be, or play into this petty scheme and die in a few moments. I- I suppose the choice is yours. I suppose. That is a good thing to say. To proclaim one's own best guess. I give you this choice. I. Kill me, or join us and see what can be without all this hate. Aren't you tired of-"

"SHUT UP!"

At that moment, your tac data lights up. Four gunships inbound, high atmo, at least three cloaked runners at the edge of town, fanning out. The proverbial shit seems to be hitting the proverbial fan. Regardless, the job is in front of you. No easy buckets.

If you lash out, slaying the creep and its talk, turn to PAGE 9.

If you go dark, using the creep signature to elude scan, turn to PAGE 66.

The deckers and librarians can argue over your choice a century from now. You just need to pay for nitro and a hot meal. No bullshit. Just like Tenaka said: 'We are our next moment, and nothing more.' Well, yours is here, and you've been running on vapor for a week. Some cred could improve your 'next moment' significantly. So it's another job.

You head back to Henson's Pub. The doors are still locked. Weird, he should be here. Something's off. You're wired to feel it. You kick the doors in, MAC12 in hand suddenly, weapons hot. The bottle is right where you left it.

Then you smell it: blood.

You go from mach two to creeping along, no sound, back into the break room. Your spine is going cold and your stomach sinking before you see anything out of place. Then, there it is.

All your skill, all your past, all your good deeds, all your bullshit amounts to nothing in that moment.

Henson is in the back with his green blanket. At least, it used to be green. The blood makes it black. The whole room is shredded with bullet holes. Even the holes have holes. Rebar bones bend through concrete muck like fingers. No smoke, they used plastic rounds. They didn't even do it in person. Gunship strike. Fifty cal from altitude. The whole place is in pieces.

So is Henson.

Answers. You want answers. Enough skulking around on The Rim, time to get back in the fight. They've got some garbage called 'Silver Burn?' Then you'll silver burn it all to ashes for this.

No more softness, no more long nights with mugs and laughs. No more green grass and rain on the fields, no more vapor farms or farmer's daughters. The ghosts have found you, and it's earned Henson a nasty, lonely death.

This is war.

If you track the ammunition to Shinru gunships, turn to PAGE 38.

If you hold your rage and give Henson a warrior's burial, turn to PAGE 42.

The Rim is no place to linger. Hatch will find you eventually, Henson will forget his damn job and stay safe. You send Hatch a message. 'Code 3.' He'll get it. Every time the mess hits the fan, your bike has never let you down. Two wheels and a hard-wired coil can eat a thousand miles of pavement in two hard riding days. Some engine noise would do you good. Follow the old way: ask nothing, let go, follow the wind. Yep, it's decided. Time to ramble on.

The machine is hidden behind Henson's place under a ragged canvas tarp. It used to cover a corp tank that was stashed there. One of Henson's 'backup plans' that never panned out. He lost the huge thing in a game of Hold 'Em, so you moved your wheels in and bundled it up for a night just like this one.

You pull the tarp back by one corner grommet, revealing your bike. Kenda rubber, dents and bullet holes in all the right places, an integrated scabbard, hard bag, and holo visor all intact. The swing arm extension was your idea, but Hatch did all the engine work. One helluva screamer. Just seeing it brings back memories, and not many of them are good. You slide your blade into the frame, stash your gun bag and bunch a pair of pants into the map pocket. The coil is still near full charge. You hit the green button, lean back and adjust your helmet. The holos come online.
"Just like old times," you mutter, loving the feeling of the grips in your gloves. It's a warm night, perfect for riding. With a little luck, you can reach the outer rim by morning, make a call on where to settle in for some no-name work in a no-name town out there. The holos give you a good reading on system signal ranges, so you can avoid any unwanted attention. Your last retune was 100% illegal, and any DHF signal contact will alert your body's former owners. A route comes up. Good to go.

GET OUT WHILE YOU CAN

The bike growls to life, whirring and humming with road noise and gear whine. You get good tarmac after a few moments of rough dirt, and take one last look back at Halsey's Rest.

It was a great few years. Some really good times, by your standards. Whatever Henson is on about, they'll all be safer with you working somewhere else. He'll get it, same with Hatch. Runner's code and all.

The blacktop slides by as you rip away from town, not looking back. You push the coil hotter and hotter, green-lining it out on the plains heading East. You're doing 150 plus sustained in no time, and the dim moon welcomes you. Time to start fresh.
You reach the outer rim just after dawn. It's always easy to spot the outer territories: jugger junk pylons mark the roads across the sand and hardpan. It's less like the country and more like the wasteland. Two vertical buttes block out the starry sky and you pull to a stop, calling up your nav computer with a glove click.

There's decent pavement East and West. To the East, into dawn, it's jugger highway country for 500 miles. You've got a few contacts in the garage-towns, a few favors to call in, but juggers can be real assholes. To the West, it's a long, curved route to Ishuga, the hover city. City life sounds dangerous and lucrative as hell, maybe even find some answers to Henson's cryptic doomsaying.

No easy buckets here. You take a sip from your flask and make a call.

If you head into jugger territory, East, turn to PAGE 47.

If you head West to the city of Ishuga, turn to PAGE 50.

You take the offer. How many Tenaka's could there be out here? Could it be him? Last you heard he was burnt to a crisp marching with some damn fool protestors in Shinru. In the old days riot cops used water cannons, now they use flamethrowers. If Tenaka was alive, what was he doing out here on the rim? Was it all planned, all foreseen? You've never believed any of that clairvoyant gibberish, but dammit if Tenaka wasn't right every time. You feel annoyed, excited, curious and terrified to see your old master again.

Your instructions are to head back behind the big trees on the edge of town. Who hides behind a stand of trees? Is this a smoke break? Tenaka, that's who. You can't help but smile as you walk through the moonlight. Jenna crosses your mind, too. Some small part of your brain tracks thermals for the creep. You visualize bumping into it on one of the dirt streets, putting the damn thing down and meeting your old teacher all in one stroll. That'd be a peach of a night, alright. A real peach.

It was Tenaka that saved your ass back in Shinru. Decoy'd the Iga, broke into a SISTM mainframe, and secured your illegal retune. Everything you did was illegal back then, but that retune was the kind of illegal that gets corp attention. Deadly is a better word... or stupid. It was one blood-filled night of mayhem. The decker on that run was a cat named Case. He owed Tenaka big time, you never found out what for, and hacked the entire 315 interstate to give you a back door. It was you, Hatch and Tenaka all in fire and swords, killing your way out. All because you had to defy Tyranax. You took Tenaka's ideas too far. Drank the kool-aid and choked on it.
A stolen pizza cart and three orange jumpsuits later the three of you made it to the rim, logged off and disappeared. You scattered, went your own ways, and thanks to fuckin' Murphy's Law, all wound up in Halsey's Rest a few years later. Dumb luck for dumb runners with nine lives, and now here you are walking to meet

Tenaka again.

The clouds clear and more light reveals the narrow stand of trees up ahead. One of them is trimmed in a delicate spiral, bending to one side in an invisible wind. Tenaka.

"Draw your sword, runner," an old, slow voice comes from the shadows ahead.

"Two moves, old man."

"You wish."

"Ok, three."

"Three it is."

Your blade springs into your hand, clearing two feet of thin air, the reflex link works perfectly, bringing it into position in a heartbeat. It's still too slow. Tenaka doesn't use any tech. His katana is a centuries-old mastercraft. He's just fast. He has the jump on you, katana sliding harmlessly over your stomach without enough pressure to cut. He's behind you now, stopped in follow-through position.

"Still slow as an ox, I see, toad."

"Two more."

You spin, and the nodachi finds its tactical advantage. The blade is longer than Tenaka's follow-through and reaches his neck, but only to graze it. You pull the stroke but know you could've bled him.

"That might've killed a lesser man," Tenaka teases, "but you still haven't learned your reach, toad."

"Make the next one count, old man."

There is a long pause. You click your left thumb to turn off all your retina-tactical. Only way is to hear him, to feel him. The scene goes perfectly silent.

"Well?" Tenaka asks, still not even facing you.

"Aren't you going to jump me again? You're faster and you know it."

"And so do you! What use is doing what the enemy knows will be done?"

"Ok, then..." You prepare to strike, but Tenaka turns in the moonlight. His eyes are down, hands loose on the hilt of his katana, only a few fingers holding it in balanced rest. At last he looks up, and a glint of LED glow shows in his eyes.

"Retina implants? I thought you said cybers are too slow."

"Old! I'm old, toad! I need to see to be able to read!"

Same old Tenaka. You smile a bit, loosen your grip. In that instant, somehow, the old man is standing next to you, a puff of grass drifting past him. His blade is at your neck, still as stone. He grins a big, half-toothed grin all too close, and drops his sword to hug you. It's a spindly, tiny, sincere hug. Feels like coming home.

"Damnit."

"Too slow, toad. Time for tea."

His katana is in its scabbard. No tsuba. He uses a shirasaya. It works as a walking stick. All part of a teacher's gloating. You walk over the back of the hill, leaving the junipers behind, to a hut you passed a thousand times and never noticed. Inside he keeps a table, tatami, stove and visbox. Right under your nose this whole time. The tea is divine, the tatami hard as cold dirt. Tenaka rests his shirasaya across his knees, sipping, and finally begins.

"So you've decided to train? Excellent. So much left to learn."

"I just found out you were in Halsey's Rest."

"Training, then."

"I hadn't-"

"Funny thing, how those who have not finished what they begin see no need to do so, but those who achieve mastery feel there is a thousand miles to go."

"Funny thing."

"We lived well, that night, toad. It was a good night."

"That was the worst night of my life."

"I suppose that's one point of view. You were always so pessimistic." He takes another sip, eyeing you with what might be approval.

"The creep?"

"Still out there. These jobs are-"

"Feeling a bit lost, toad? Your sword is handy, but you seem so un-

happy. Where is that friend of yours... Hitch?"
"Hatch."
"Ah yes, is he still bailing you out of all these messes? Has Iko arrived yet?"
"Wait, you know something about Iko? Here? I think there's a contract out on me... again."
"Iko's been in town since Tuesday."
"Frag, Sensei, what else do you know?"
"You're playing right into their hands as usual, my pupil. It's lovely to watch, how you stand your ground at such peril. How you see the world in such an old way. A pure way. You make an old man proud."
There's a pause there. It's starting to feel like everyone is in on something but you, and it's not a good feeling. All the echoes from that night are closing in, all the vendettas, all the contracts are converging, and you're feeling clueless.
"Why now?" you ask.
"You came to me, toad. I'm just tending trees here."
"No more riddles. Some shit is about to go down. You kno-"
"So impatient. Don't you see why your sword is so slow, toad? Always looking to others, always wondering 'what's going down.' Your mind is never HERE, never NOW. Don't you see the answers?"
"NO! No I don't! If I did, I wouldn't have the Iga, the corps, a year old bar tab and pirate DHF driving me nuts. It's been a real mess, sensei. I thought the rim was our big escape. It's all ghosts and secrets out here." You've said too much, and focus on your tea.

"Answers change nothing, Grim. Our world is a wilderness of lost hopes. Knowing doom's name does not dispel it. As in the beginning, when you first came to me, I can only offer the swordsman's mind. I can only teach you what I was taught. Our enemies are ours. They are part of us!"
"So that's it?"
"Far from it, my old friend. Stay a while. Complete your training.

Set aside that war sword and master your speed. Your footwork is terrible! Mastery is the path to peace, and peace the path to freedom! The trees won't trim themselves!"
Tenaka's riddles make you weary. You listen, staring at your tac boots and reflex scabbard. It all seems like talk with so many guns pointed at your head. You can't drag Hatch into it again, get more people killed. It's all tumbling back down. And Iko... not sure how to feel about that. Your first love, the one you keep trying to put behind you. Death and lost love, all your old echoes creeping back.

Tenaka can see your thoughts swirling, see your ghosts come calling.

"So, make your choice runner," Tenaka says, breaking your trance.

If you stay to train with Tenaka, turn to PAGE 56.

If you refuse, ready to choose your own path, turn to PAGE 62.

You shake off the shock, the grief. No time for that.
Shell casings are everywhere, and still warm. Gunship weapons not only leave hot shells, but a traceable therm signature for miles. You bring it up on your retina console, filter out all the visible light, and go therm only. The tracer trails are clear as day, in a wide spray from the Northwest and across town. It hasn't been long, they're probably within ten clicks to the Southeast. At least two gunships, cloaked engines, low altitude, hard to say. The exhaust wash fuzzes the therms. You could catch them with a few seconds of hard riding, get a tracker up there with a lucky shot... Not a millisecond to waste. Grab your bike, fire it up, split town, catch the trail, it's a blur.

Through it all, you can't help but remember Henson. The time he dragged you out of the ladies' room on trivia night, the pink wheelchair he gave you when you had a bullet in your spine, the stockings filled with Mac12 magazines at christmas, shot skis for breakfast, doing yard work every spring. Henson didn't have a family, didn't need one. Halsey's Rest was his family, and you were one of his favorites. Funny thing about Henson: everyone was his favorite.

You snap out of the nostalgia, the grief, and there they are: two c170 gunships, running whisper quiet at about 700 feet. They'll be ascending now, sending in a ground team to confirm the kill. They're too high for a tracking shot. Maybe a hole in one engine can get them closer. Your bike is running smooth, but the wind at 120 mph is a real bitch. One chance.
You set the throttle lock and lean back, reaching the rail rifle in the rear rack. It's a stubby, stout weapon, but with a smart round that steers to a painted target. Just need to get the laser set... been saving this bullet for a rainy day. You line up the sight, a green 'starlight' style scope that makes the c170 engine hot white. Just need a three second lock. The tarmac bumps you side to side, and eddies of wind keep ruining the shot.

"Damnit!"
You breathe out, forget it all, even the reason you're here. It all goes silent, focused, singular. You loosen your grip on the weapon and use both eyes. The tiny dot holds steady for one, two, three eternal seconds. A tiny bleep, barely audible over the wind, confirms it. You pull the trigger with a satisfying kick and the 'zing' whine of a magnetic rail projectile. It rips off through the rain, leaving a coiling vapor trail and a thump as it goes mach two. You ease off the throttle, bringing the bike to a stop. The headlight glows cold blue in the drizzle.
"You fucked with the wrong runner."

At that instant, the round impacts the port engine of the lead plane. At first, it just punches a clean, quiet hole. The crew probably doesn't even notice, then the fuel lines and hydraulic fuel drench the ignition, the rotors catch fire and the whole thing bursts into smoky black flames. Immediately, both aircraft begin to reduce altitude. The pilot must be green, because he dips below 300 feet in just a few seconds. Forget a tracker, your laser grapple can cross that distance.

You blast to life again, zipping forward and slamming two deep turns to catch up. The planes are right overhead. You kill your headlight, sling your ruck, and fist-hammer the laser grapple. It locks with a sharp green beam, then uncoils a spool of filament. You click on in the nick of time, a micro winch zipping you vertical. Far below, your bike, a restored XL1200 mag coil classic, nanocarbon rims, smart rubber tires from Columbia, all neuro-linked and custom built, slams into the rocks and bursts into flames.
"Sorry, Percy."

What happens next is a bit you won't be retelling anytime soon.

You rip through the belly of the hull as the fire-retardant foam coats the burning engine. It streams away, and the pilot regains enough power to get into the clouds. You're in the central bay, but turbulence sends your ruck flying. The nodachi leaps into your hand, the blade still glowing as the edge renders. Two troopers, Shinru transitional government types, appear at the far end. They're using silent comms so you can't read them, but as soon as you see them they're drawing knives. A bit hazardous to unload an MP7 at 2,000 feet and climbing. They close in. These clods are no match, and you cleave them both to crumpled ribbons before they even get their feet. You're moving up-plane now, a bulkhead and stairs ahead. The stairs will lead to the cockpit. Four more victims storm out of the forward quarters, red sirens paint the scene. These ones don't care about the hull, they raise their weapons, one of them scrambling to pull his prime lever in time. Mercs. What a joke. You draw into your kamae posture, draw in a breath, and unleash. The blade slices one man's hand clean off, with half his machine rifle. The next three die with neck and chest slices that go clean through. As you slide through the blood into the staircase, one of them finally slumps behind you. Poor bastards.

In seconds you're at the upper level. Four gunners are at minigun stations. These are the dead men who pulled the trigger. You pull a handful of darts from your side pocket. They fan as you release, each striking a man in the neck. The fourth ducks the projectile, though, and pulls a sidearm. It's a damn nemesis gun. He lines it up and fires. These are electric-plasma rounds that slag everything they touch. You're hit. Your cybernetics all shut down, but it's just a flesh wound. This offense earns him a special death, impaled into his gun station with your five-foot blade. You pause to sneer, pulling the blade from the gunmetal with effort.

The crew are no resistance. They're cuffed to the bulkhead without trouble. You jump in the pilot's seat, throw on the headphones, and take a second to reboot your systems. Your guts feeling like

they're falling out with your systems all off... whole skeleton feels like a soggy rag.
"What's the callsign?"
"N744 Red Eagle 2"
"If you're bullshitting me, I'll feed you parts."
"N744, I swear it."
You tap the headset to life. "Red Eagle 1, this is N744, minor injuries, fire contained, pilot indisposed, return to base on protocol, over."
The radio crackles back "Copy that Eagle 2, who's talking, over."
"Gunner here, enough simulator hours to get us in. Electrics failing, landing lights would be great."
"Copy that, Eagle 2, stay in the pipe on my station. N743 out."

Ok, they're all dead or too stupid to stop you. You've got a cargo plane at your fingertips, and a blood debt to pay. Time to make a call. If you follow the other gunship, you could get access to their command base, maybe even find out who ordered the kill. You'll probably die trying, but it certainly screams 'direct approach.' On the other hand, you could drop below echolocators, and hope your terrible flying skills are enough to ditch Eagle 1 and keep the cargo plane for yourself. With a crew and a purpose, this could be a real game changer. The roar of the single engine, working overtime, puts a kind of pressure on your brain. The bodies are already stacking up, no going back. So what's it gonna be, runner?

If you hijack the gunship, and veer off to the wastelands, turn to PAGE 92.

If you stay in formation, land at the ops base, turn to PAGE 115.

Dig two graves, right? You learned a long time ago not to nurse vendettas and give in to bloodlust. Whoever they are, they'll have to die another night. Right now, an old friend needs the respect he deserves. You begin the dire work, cleaning up the fire zone, gathering Henson up and covering him. Jenna and Hatch appear, blown away and broken down. No one talks. There's nothing to say.

At length, you carry Henson outside on a stretcher. The rain clears for him. It's almost dawn. Hatch starts digging up near the DHF tower behind the bar. Henson loved sitting up there most nights, dreaming about a greener world, about happy faces, about little towns and good food. By the time you are carrying him up the hill, most of the folks who live in Halsey's Rest have shown up. It's quiet. The smog lifts a bit, Henson descends. There's a long pause after that, where no one is quite sure what to do next.

One thing that really was awful about this world was the loss of traditions. Sure, religion helped to burn the old world, had a rap sheet longer than any dictator, but religion gave folks a sense of structure at times like these... a set of motions to go through. In the left-behind world of now, there was nothing. Meaning had hidden away when the power went off. Faith was offworld with the rest of humanity. All you have is your honor, and it's cold dead in your chest as you stare into that hole.

"I knew Henson for a while before he opened the pub," a voice finally breaks in, "he was a combat medic in New Arcadia. Grew chard in an oil barrel. He had a girl named Priscilla back then. She died in the riots."
"Henson built my greenhouse."
"That asshole got me so drunk last Christmas, I was trying to go through my window and broke my damn leg, heh."
"That was New Year's, Sam,"

"Yeah, New Years, like I said."
"Henson kept us in the basement when we first fled to the rim. We slept with the tires and steel cables. He would lower monte cristos down on a little handmade elevator. He saved us."
"Monte cristos?"
"Yeh, like a fried ham sandwich."
"I love those!"
"His pancakes though, with whisky coffee. Reason to live right there."

At last, Hatch speaks up. "After the fires, when the Iga were torching the slums, back in '61, we were all on the run. It was chaos. No one had cars back then, just bikes. My heap barely worked, and I was out of fuel. Stupid bio-ethanol engine. Henson pulled over, gunfire everywhere, people screaming. Dude pulls over and takes three minutes refueling my bike. Never thanked him proper for that."
"Only Henson would have a spare gallon of that crap."
A laugh trickles through the crowd. It's your turn, somehow.
"He was my friend." That's all you can muster.
Jenna moves forward and begins moving the dirt over the body, crying. This is her way of saying her piece. She's lovely, big sad eyes and bell bottoms, a real jewel out here in the mud. Everyone gathers in to help. So this is it, this is all you have for tradition, and it's plenty.

A few days later, after a drinking bender that puts the whole town in bed, you, Hatch and Jenna are slumped on the tower up by Henson's stone. Technically, it's a chunk of concrete. Rain crackles on the sagging power lines. The clouds are low and curling. A weird, restless breeze makes it feel like times are about to change.

"Now what?" Hatch asks, nursing a jug of cold water. Hell of a thing, to see him hung over.

"Yeah, this town is just... well, now what?" Jenna echoes, lost in her own thoughts.
"I say we set down our weapons and embrace lives of peace and tranquility."
"Huh?"
"We hunt these bastards down and give 'em the sword. The only justice in this world is ours. The law is off-world. They keep taking from us, even when all we have is our lives, they just keep taking. So it's our turn to take."
"I don't like that look, Grim." Jenna leans away.
"There's nothing to like here. This is fucking war."
"We going alone? Tracking Shinru commandos like the old days? I've heard they upgraded their-"
"No. We rally up. Come on."

You lead Jenna and Hatch back to Henson's place, bitter at the sign above the door. As you enter through the plastic curtain, you realize the wake isn't over. A band of rowdy rebel-rousers arrived in the wee hours and proceeded to keep the party rolling. One group is doing shots, another paging through holoslides of the old days, and a few singing with a group of girls in the big circle booth. Sailor song stuff. Henson's old crew from the A.I. riot days.

"I could use a drink." Jenna announces quixotically, walking forward with a mission. She's hurting more than she shows, and clearly needs medicine for the pain. War might have to wait.
"She's a beast!" Hatch plops his water jug down. He's spotted immediately by the sailor-singers. They cat-call him over to their table. That leaves you standing in the entrance, looking like a caged lion. Your head is splitting, your heart cracked, your hands limp at your sides. You're in no shape to avenge anything. No leader. No runner. You're a damn mess.

"Hey Grim!" It's Mull, the grafter who built half your augments.

He's got tears on his cheeks, but a smile to match. Two girls are draped on his arms. He's got cyber optics and one hand that's all link steel. He looks like shit. It's like the damn mayor died, but worse... the bartender did. "Come over here, man, gimme a hug." You walk over, dark as a storm.

"Ah, the warm embrace of nanocarbon. Shitty night, eh?"

"Yeah. Shitty night."

"Don't look at me like that, runner."

"Like what?" You sit down. A bloody mary and a shot are in front of you. A whole crew of old grey haired runners are manning the bar. The service is actually good. Weird.

"Like 'fuck you, Mull, I'm warpathing some shit..gonna cut the city to ribbons.' Not yet, man. We owe the old man some liver cells."

"I don't owe anybody anything anymore. Ghost mode." You gulp half the bloody mary, pucker off the spice, and take the shot. It's the top shelf mezcal from Oaxaca. Henson's been sitting in that bottle for decades. Liquid smoke with an after taste of scorched butter. Amazing.

"Ghost mode? Shit, you were being printed when we invented that term."

"Yeah yeah, back in the day and all that."

"You watch your damn tone, cyborg! Us grey hairs have saved your ninja ass more times than I have fingers."

"So, eight?"

That comment earns a toast, and another, and another. Hatch and Jenna work the room a bit, wandering from table to table and sharing old stories, hugging and laughing. The drinks are flowing, nobody gives a damn and they shouldn't. The two girls at your table, well one girl and one you're not so sure, are getting wild. Vaping their drinks. Jenna tumbles into your lap as they remote the sound system and start dancing.

"Tonight's for the old man," Mull announces with a flourish. "and swimmin' with bow-legged women!"

That earns a smile, even from you. Mull presents a dish of blue

and red pills. Jenna and the dancers all pop one without a thought, Mull too. It's probably a vintage cut of Limit. Good stuff. No one can afford that anymore. Mull's been holding out, probably for years.
"Go on, Grim, loosen up before you commit suicide in Shinru."
One of the dancers looks down at you, her eyes huge and lovely in the light. She kisses Jenna, then you.
"It's ok, runner, stay sharp. I don't mess with pills, Name's Athena, I need some company." She returns to her dance, a slow, respectful affair. Her prosthetics are flawless, her outstretched hand faceted with delicate polyresin joints and synth actuators, her features like a demigoddess. "We all do."

She's right. Jenna's head feels good on your shoulder. The dancer's eyes feel good looking into yours. You've been so busy drawing steel and wanting blood, you haven't even really let it out yet. It's all a smoky swirl of sound. Jenna kisses you again, making you realize a few tears have snuck out against your will. You suck 'em back into your eyes with sheer willpower, or at least, that's what you tell yourself.

If you take a Limit pill with everyone else, turn to PAGE 113.

If you refuse the pill and take Athena's hand, turn to PAGE 110.

The sunrise is a horizontal blowtorch of red and orange. Dead ahead. Your helmet dims most of it away, but dawn out here has a nasty glare to it, even with the vapor wash from Ishuga. You cover a few hundred miles, past puzzle-pieced protein farms and walled off mud. The tarmac is tangled and crisscrossed with tire marks, bullet holes and metallic gouges. Juggers at it as usual. They love blowing things up, most of all each other, and the highway shows it.

A few buildings break the horizon. Stilts and gun towers, a neon-animated stripper with an M16 leg flickers to life. The sun is climbing into the gloom above when you drop a gear and let the bike coast down a few ticks. It's Sugar, the first garage town out this way. You keep your helmet still, but look side to side with eyes only. They'll be sizing up your bike, no need to mean mug anyone and get shot.

A blinking yellow indicator catches your eye. Helmet comms.
"Holy hell baskets, that you, Grim?"
You don't answer. No trace yet.
"Grim! Pick up, you idiot, it's Biggs. Your bike is running like shit, man, you had it in a cave or what? Stop by. End of town, left gate. Later, gator!"
Biggs used to get beat up in the gas district of Shinru. Jeez, fifteen years back. You never had much patience for bullies, bailed him out of a few real scratches. He owes you, and you barely know any of the other greasy faces in this place. Good a place as any to put your ear to the rails and get a feel for things. You pull up to his garage, a pieced-together mess of parts and half-built bad ideas. Your Kenda's crackle the gravel as you roll in slowly. Biggs appears at once, carrying two lawn chairs.

"Fucking Grim the Dragonslayer, I'll be damned!" he runs forward dropping the chairs. He had three organic limbs last you saw him, now one leg is all the human he's got left. He stops next to your bike as you lean it over. "I'll be damned, this thing is sick as ever." You pull off your helmet, the air smells like argon.

"Hey Biggs."

"Seven years you leave me hanging on that buggy deal, and all you got is 'hey Biggs.' Same old Grim! Come on!"

"Nice place."

"Ain't it? 2k watts TIG setup, three pits, a 12 ton lift! 12 tons!"

"You work on stuff that big?"

"No way! We haven't seen a car out here in years, much less a big truck or a lifter. It doesn't get more rim than Sugar, baby. I'll be damned."

"Right."

"Here," he unfolds the lawn chairs, and impossibly produces two slices of toast on a tray with shots of mash. "Breakfast? So, what brings you out to paradise?"

"Fresh start, I guess."

"You looking for some work, runner?"

"Or to just disappear."

"Fuckin' Grim."

"Still feeling some heat from the retune back in the day. They're still looking for me."

"So you figured why not bring some gunships over to the Juggers and clean up the wasteland? No better place for a gunship to get cheesed than out here! Now that'd be a sight."

You finish your 'breakfast' and lean back. Juggers never change. You scan the garage area, it's the usual junk.

"A hero's treasure, eh Grim? See anything that tickles your fancy?"

You look again. In some spots the trash is piled chest high. Disassembled bikes, half-built arms, a weird rack of eyeballs, an old visbox playing a car chase, tires in stacks like doughnuts. Biggs has worn little paths here and there in the mess, picking his own piles for goodies, and maybe he's right. Two things catch your eye.

The first is a what started as a vending machine. It's got a backlit front panel, all stupid with neon colors, animated soda and dancing girls. A bunny bot invites users to browse a selection of 'synthopsychic' services. The machine has two stubby legs and one spindly arm, which comically lifts a cigarette to cartoon-animated lips every few seconds. The cigarette is real. Ok.

On a totally unrelated note, opposite the psychic vending machine, a metal work table has been cleared and now has only one occupant. A gun. Correction. This isn't 'a gun' it's THE GUN. Biggs has scrawled a marker-on-cardboard sign proclaiming such. The thing is compact, but modded to the gills. It's a PV90 frame, but built up with all kinds of reflex hardware and baddass-looking doodads that make killing faster and easier. Could come in handy.

"Go on, take a look. Shit, Grim, this whole place is yours by my count. Old friends and what not. We'll head over to The Wheel for a few beers when you're ready. It's great to see you, man. I'll be damned. I'm getting the bottle."

If you approach the psychic vending machine, turn to PAGE 152.

If you approach the gun, turn to PAGE 158.

JUNK CITY NOODLES

You head West. Juggers just want to suck fuel and burn tires. Not your jam. West means Ishuga, the hover city. It's dawn, and the amber light plays behind you, casting an infinite shadow and illuminating the impossible form of the city ahead. Water falls to mist from the heights, and occasional junk-streams tumble down from hatches and chutes like black snow. Blue-purple jet-wash glows in the morning dim, where dozens of thrust-pads work to keep the ziggurat in its perch, 200 feet above the desert floor. Foolish, god-hungry engineers and the metalmongers to give them their ugly wish. Ishuga.

Your bike hums with satisfying speed, blurring the power lines, blurring everything. You swoop and lean back like a gangster, enjoying yourself for once. A damn fine machine, a damn fine day to ride.

"Grim. You on the road?" Comms interrupt your bliss.
"Nope."
"Bullshit. You're heading West. Don't even mess with Case, if that's your plan. He's got way more heat than our little rim town. You're nuts."
"Who said I'm going to say a word to that half-dead decker? Dude is cooked."
"God, you're a bad liar."
"Where are you?"
"On your tail, about two hours back. I borrowed Skinny's monocycle."
"That thing runs?"
"Sort of!"
"Ok, see you at Chan's place. Bring some coin will you, no creds out here. Thirsty as hell."
"Hi my name is Hatch, this is my first time drinking in junk city. You scathe me, sir! Scathe me!"
"I'm cutting this line."

"Oh yeah, one more th-"
You tap the red indicator and cut helmet comms. Case comes to mind. Another tap. The bike hums with glee at 160 mph.

"Hey Case." The comm stays quiet a second. Some broken up code or binary junk data crackles the line.
"Grim? No way."
"You owe me a fortune cookie."
"See you there."

Two hours later, you're cruising in low gear toward the base of the beast: Ishuga. These grav ferries are awful. Only way up. One descends, belching out diesel like an old tractor. The big green and white hull is wreathed in visboxes, most of them showing sporting events from the city that no one watches anymore. No one except the captain, who sports a team jersey and barks over the PA like it matters for hometown pride. A few bigger bikes roll off, no eye contact, and you pull in. That's when you notice it: security is insane.
Three EXO troopers are patrolling the parking deck with Skar 60 rifles. They have helmets and grenade belts. Looks like a damn warzone with armor that heavy on the tarmac. Ishuga used to be a real chillout. This can't be good. They walk your way. Shit.

"Hold it there, passenger."
"How can I help, sir?"
"Ma'am."
"Ok."
"Keep your hands out of your pockets. This your bike?"
"Yeah. Visiting friends-"
"Kenda went off world a decade ago, where'd you get these tires?"
"Just came with the bike."
She doesn't like that answer. You're being messed with. She taps her helmet and the other two start walking toward you. Shit.

"Let's see some ID, passenger."
"Uhm, that's a bit of a story. Juggers caught up with me out East. I'm clean out of everything."
"That a blade?"
You pause. This is not going well at all. These idiots have no idea what kind of hornets they're stirring up. The ferry lifts off. A big digital display shows '12 minutes to arrival.'
"Yes, that's a blade. How'd that get there?" Stupid. You just couldn't resist. They have no reason to shake you down. One frying pan into another.
"Step off the bike, please, hands where we can see them."
"I'm not looking for any trouble."
"Off. The. Bike." The two EXO's raise their weapons.
"You don't want to do this, guys, or gals... whatever. I'm just here to see the city, get some fresh air."
"Fresh air?"
"That's a little Ishuga humor. No? Haven't heard that one."
"Off the bike now!"
"If you insist." You're the type of runner to make hard calls fast, so you make one. You lift one leg over the fuel cell, bracing your other foot on the tarmac. The ferry has six minutes to arrival. You click the kill switch, the bike goes quiet.
"Impound this bike, 473. Passenger, submit for questioning on suspicion of contraband."
"Are reflex blades still legal in the city?"
"No. If that's one on your belt, we're taking you in. Hands on your head!"
"This sword was a gift from a friend. I can't let you take it, not for what you're being paid."
The EXO swivels to kick your knee out from under you, but you're far too fast for that. You spin away, making her stumble. A reflex response, but yeah, that just escalated.
"Hands on your-"
You've worn EXO armor plenty of times. You probably know the

gear better than these mercs ever will. You look to your upper left, making her flinch, then spin and punch the night vision toggle on the left side of her helmet optics. It's a small black button just above the temple. In lights like these, she'll be blind for a few hours.
"Fuck! Grab this asshole!"
The other two EXOS bumble forward. It'll be an easy escape, the engine noise here alone makes an easy cloak. But dammit.. your bike. Maybe you can pick it up from impound later. For now, this is a nuisance you don't need. As the other two commandos approach, you spin the blinded EXO, spray her SKAR60 all up into the ceiling. The dust and commotion is all you need. You ride the ferry roof to the dock, hop a hover taxi to a garbage truck, and vanish into the blue glow of the streets. Great thing about the city of junk: everyone disappears.

Easy enough. Time for some happy bread.

You walk up to Chan's with your hood back, blade in your back sling, pistols in your boots. Nothing to see here. Chan's is flashing with a glow of gold and red neon, all wrapped around the huge soda-can that forms the front entrance. Holo-bullshit curls around the curved doors, you walk right through. Is that a smile? Don't you dare. Ten year vengeance is at your heels, you just ditched three EXO's to get some fried rice. Stuff that smile and game face it.

"Grim!" It's Case, waiting in the lobby like a frustrated dad on vacation. He's got a portable deck in one hand, mai-tai in the other. The little umbrella has migrated from one to the other.
Case is a decker, always has been. Ran into some ugly business back in the day with the Iga. He referred to it as the 'rubber bunny incident.' Whatever happened, he was shredded by a clan of street ninja and left for dead. If it weren't for some anonymous shifter, he would've checked out right then. Instead, he wound up with an

oversized right arm, cyber optics, and a mug only a mother could love. Despite all that, and a life on the run, his smile is as bright as neon. His blonde mustache bends out of the way as he stands.

"Fucking Atom Winters," you reply.

"Never heard of him! You look like shit!"

"Not you. Sex machine." Before Hatch even shows up you're three shots deep, and working on two blue beers. Chan swears his stupid beer colors make his business. They taste like plastic.

"So why are you in the junk city, runner? You run out of bullets to trade for muffins? Iko finally hack your stack?" Case leans back, beer in his metal hand, looking tiny in those huge fingers.

"Too soon, asshole."

"Eight years is too soon? Dude."

"That was some true love shit and you know it."

"Yeah, maybe that's why she tried to kill you, like fourteen times."

"Thirteen."

"You guys wasted already? EXO's gave me a bunch of shit trying to ferry up." Hatch walks up, pistol in one hand.

"What the shit, Hatch?"

"Oh, oops."

"Heat was feeling a little close back in Halsey's Reach. A creep showed up. I think it was bait, or recon. Needed a fresh start."

"So you brought your heat to ol' Case, eh?"

"Yep. What are you cooking this weekend?"

"Two things-"

"Before one more word," Hatch interrupts, "can we not take on the world and just drink for a night?"

"Anyway," Case goes on, unaffected, "two things. I have a messed up lead that the N.E.R. has unlocked some of this 'chimera cell' stuff. They're creating freeform organisms, crazy huge shit, A.I. brains. Goddamn monsters. I was thinking of hacking the hard line they're using and FUBAR'ing the whole op. Save the world one more time. I've got a case of San Miguel back at my place-"

"And the other thing?"

"Lining up a retune for you."
"Huh?"
"One of these 'gifted' operatives arrived by jet car last night. Psychic kid, cyber'd up. Government escort, class 6. At first I'm like, what the hell, then I remember, that's how they've been controlling Iko. I figured I'd get a new skin online for you just in case."
"So-"
"She's in Ishuga. She's got your trail and these guys mean business. Like kill you business."
"I beat her before, I'll beat her again."
"How are you still this stupid? She's the fastest 'borg in Shinru, man!"
"Not all the 'borgs are in Shinru, just drink your drink."
"I hate to interrupt," Hatch says, "but Case is right."
"Huh?"
"There she is."

The semicircular doors slide open. In walks none other than Iko. Shinru's best killer. She's got her bangs cropped to one side, purple eyeshadow, a side-zip nanocarbon hoodie with gunner's gloves and the biggest, baddest combat boots on the rim. Her lips are like wet rubies in the glow. If there was any air in here before, it's gone.

If you stand up, revealing yourself to Iko with a smile, turn to PAGE 155.

If you nod to Case, and slip out of Chan's place, turn to PAGE 162.

"Show me everything," you announce with decisive optimism, ready to go.

Tenaka smiles. "It begins with a good night's sleep. You can take the guest house back by the generator. We'll make a master of you yet, Grim Shirosune."

"I've got a job. Loose ends that need tying before I disappear into a practice montage."

"Job?"

"A creep has been wreaking havoc all around the rim. The thing has gone psycho, and there's a thousand creds on pulling its plug."

"So sad."

"I know. The bodies keep piling up wherever this thing goes."

"No, sad for the synthetic. Imagine the confusion, the terror of being pod-born, and just enough smarts to know you aren't human. It must be a nightmare."

"They're just machines, sensei."

"And what are we? Has your retune wiped your memory so soon? How can we know what a synthetic stack really feels like, much less a rogue out-of-signal A.I.? Tragic."

"A job is a job"

"Not anymore, gakusei."

"Hatch will probably grab the contract."

"Let it go."

"I like winning."

"The only path to victory is the complete release of any chance of success. The warrior who always assumes defeat is the fiercest fighter, for they have nothing to lose."

The next three weeks pass in a blur. A few times, you're not sure what day of the week it is. Training with Tenaka is continuous, taxing, and absolute torture on your body. This retune is top of the line, but Tenaka's drills leaving you sore and bruised every single night. Your little house is bare bones, no deck or visbox, and you barely notice. Every day ends in exhaustion.

You sneak off a few times to talk with Henson. Hatch picks up the creep contract, breaking an arm in the struggle. You keep wondering when Iko will show up. Taneka refuses to mention anything about that situation, but he knows something. No matter. Training. Every damn hour of every damn day. You complain the appropriate amount, but damn if your sword isn't three times as fast before long, and the nodachi is starting to feel like too clumsy a weapon. The curve of a compact katana is so much faster. Dammit Tenaka, always right. So annoying.

One day, seemingly at random, Tenaka stops mid-sentence, sheaths his sword, and smiles. He sets the shirasaya on an alder tree.

"What's wrong?"

"Leave your sword, grab us two apples."

"Sensei?"

"I'd like to show you something, gakusei."

An hour of walking into the hills and an apple later, you round a pile of mossy boulders near the SISTM signal tower outside of town. Huge cables run in every direction, and a series of steel tethers holds the narrow gusset tower upright. Further on, in a stand of aspens, an old temple staircase ascends into the trees.

"This has been here all along?"

"As I said, toad, so easily distracted." Everything is a lesson with this guy.

He leads you on up, hands behind his back. It's an old temple, from the upheaval era. At least three centuries old. Amazing woodwork, and the solar circuits still powering dim lanterns at each curled corner. Etched cloud motifs adorn the red pillars, and an immaculate hardwood floor completes the cozy feel. Quite a far cry from the nanocircuit flexcrete highways and aluminum windows on Shinru.

Tenaka moves ahead into the temple and kneels at the little shrine, lighting an incense stick and clapping twice. You follow suit, waiting for the reason you're here.

"Now where's that silly hidden broom closet?" Tenaka mumbles, standing and walking across the space. A cool breeze drifts in, the sun is setting.
"Broom cl-"
"Quiet, gakusei, please." He shuffles along the left wall, feeling the cedar panel trims here and there, knocking, then muttering something about bad carpentry. At last, one panel sinks inward an inch or so and clicks a hidden release. The panel slides to one side revealing a small enclosed cabinet. "Ah, here we are." He reaches in and pulls out a shirasaya. It's a dark grey scabbard with red trim lines and a reflex module at the guard end.

Tenaka walks back to you with a placid expression, and casually holds the sword out to you.
"It's dangerous to go alone," he says, sitting, "take this."
"Go where?"
"Out there! Life! There's nothing more I can teach you, gakusei. You're as fast, as precise, as balanced as any kensei I have ever known. I am proud of you, old friend. Take a look."
A pause.
"The sword, you clod!"
You look down at the sword on your lap. On closer inspection, the scabbard is incredible. It's link-steel, light as a feather, and laced with a spider web of gleaming red anodized reflex wiring. It's touch-responsive. The instant you even think of drawing the blade, it self-releases and slides a half inch from its sheath with a near-silent puff of air. The hilt is black and red render fabric, tipped with a solid brass pommel weight that must be hiding a cadmium core. This is a handmade masterpiece. None of the Shinru swords come close.
"It's amazing, sensei."
You slide the curved blade from its home, and the edge renders with a dull green circuit.

"The edge renders in .05 milliseconds. It has a tritium processor core, and the reflex link has under .01 milliseconds lag time. It's an exquisite weapon, toad."
"I thought you liked it old school."
"I was a young man once, gakusei. Don't forget who dragged your ass out of that noodle house when the Iga leveled the whole block to find you! It was no coincidence!"
"Wait, this is-"
"Yes. That is the reflex Hanzo prototype. The only one of its kind."
"You stole the rarest sword on the planet from the Iga? Then made it look like a charity mission, when we were both being hunted?!"
Tenaka shrugs.

Your laughter echoes out against the boulders as dusk falls, and apples are not enough for dinner, so the two of you walk back through the trees for noodles. A strange feeling comes over you, the feeling of reaching a new chapter in life, feeling the past colliding with the future. You've been running long enough. Hiding long enough. You retuned ten years ago just to shake the Iga. If Iko is here, they've found you, and it's time to make a stand, time to kill your way to freedom or die trying. Endgame.
The Hanzo has a magnetic pad at its balance point, and sticks effortlessly to your spine implants, or belt loop. Handy as hell. Tenaka sees you fiddling with the blade, and opens the hut door for you with a silly gesture.
"So what will you do now, Sensei?" Tenaka asks, lighting the stove and splashing oil in the wok.
"Enjoy a little peace and quiet while Iko does the hard work. Maybe have a drink with Hatch. You know, the usual. No point wasting energy on vendettas when they come with free delivery."
"Spoken like a true master."
"Master of noodles, maybe, let me cook tonight. Tell me more about the Iga, tell me everything."
"That will be a long story, Shirosune."

"We have time. My noodles take forever."

The next day is a gloomy, rainy mess. The wind smells like pavement and exhaust fumes. Smog front must've rolled in before dawn. Halsey's Rest is shrouded in the haze, a few neon flickers giving some color to the fog. While making your tea, a comm pops up from Hatch. 'Scrapped creep found in town. Something's off about it. Meet up at Mull's garage at noon. Also, bite me :P'
Tenaka sleeps in. You head over the hill to town, the titanic silhouette of Shinru city towers in the monochrome distance. Hatch is up by Mull's, fiddling with a busted up prosthetic hand. Coiled wires, spools of reflex cable, discarded actuators and a comical bucket of cracked glass eyeballs set the scene. You walk up, sword behind you, hood blocking the drizzle.
"Hey," Hatch offers, lifting himself from a tire he's leaning on. He waves at you with the broken hand. The fingers are floppy.
"Where's this creep?"
"You're looking at it."
"Huh?"
"Slagged last night, stripped and disassembled before dawn. Damn thing is scattered into all these piles."
"Mull never cleans up."
"No sleepy rimmer could do a strip down this fast, Grim. This stinks."
"Where's the head?"
"RIght here," he lifts a plastic bucket, "at least what I could find of it. I'm meeting Mull over at Henson's in a few. Tag?"
"Nah, I'll stay here and look for the stack. If it's not here, we need to be sure. We're being tracked."
"Looks like our little vacation is over, eh?"
"Yeah."
"Iko?"
"Probably. Go on ahead, I'll catch up later."

Hatch fades into the mist. You pick at the bits, never finding a stack, but retrieving the main drive and logic chip. It's serviceable. You piece together half of a head and clean up the input jack. A creepy feeling starts taking hold. Ten years of quiet then Tenaka and now this… all in a span of days. Someone knows something. How did Jenna know about Tenaka, anyway? You're getting the feeling everyone knows more than you do. That usually means a trap is about to spring.

If you salvage the creep's drive and deck in, turn to PAGE 93.

If you go to see Jenna and ask how she knows Tenaka, turn to PAGE 88.

"I appreciate the offer, sensei-"

"But the answer is no."

"I think I might be drawing some bad juju to town. Too many little clues. A pair of gunships would tear this place apart in seconds to find me and you know it. I can't ask any more favors." You take another sip. "Hey, how do you know Jenna?"

"Ah yes, wonderful young lady. I knew her grandfather, back in the Ishuga resistance days. Then, about five years ago, I had to find out if you had survived our little escape plan. I called in a few favors, and found out you were here in Halsey's Rest."

"So you've been skulking around, spying for five damn years?"

"Skulking! I've just been living a simple life here over the hill, a safe distance from my favorite gakusei."

"You're terrible at flattery." Another sip of tea. It's terrible, too.

"So the road then?"

"The road. If Iko is on my tail, I need some answers, and a pocket full of creds. Henson has one last job for me, losing that creep bruised my account."

"Stay sharp. The junipers will always be here, gakusei."

"Yeah. Sensei... thanks again."

"For what?"

"The tea."

If you get your bike and leave town, turn to PAGE 31.

If you risk one last job with Henson before heading out, turn to PAGE 29.

You take a few deep breaths, and click a hotlink into the creep's drive. You've done some decking before, but usually there's a specialist around for this stuff. The system is confusing enough, but jacking directly into another person means using metaspace. Without the training and cocktail of drugs to keep your wits, and bowels, together in there... well, it might not be pretty.
Still, you have to risk it. You need answers.

The login comes up on your retina display. 'Lotus Blue' is the ID Tag on this creep. A budget decrypt program gets you in, kindergarten stuff, Ona Dai Sen late model synthetic, and you feel that lurch as your neuro-link is hijacked by the simulation. Showtime.

The AI skeleton is a bit outdated, so instead of a flood of subsurface psychological imagery and dreamscape stuff, you get a monochrome amber wireframe. A few side panels play out traumatic events in the past few weeks. The murders, one memory of running on a rainy street, gunfire, hands in a bucket of muriatic acid... it's a jumble, and being stored neatly on the side. This is why synthetics aren't human, and can never be mistaken for human. To them it's all just data. Stay focused. You keep to center, moving your awareness toward the AI core. Navigating in metaspace is pretty much instantaneous, but it takes a knack to will yourself around. There are no buttons here unless you run a console program.
Up ahead the AI core is revealed, armored up with standard barrier programs. You bring up the console and get rid of the barriers. They're barely more than 'click here' wall measures. Weird. This creep is practically begging to be hacked. There it is, core data storage. You've got no use or interest in decision matrices or behavior simulations. All just smoke.
Core data opens up and you've got your paydirt. Names, numbers, nav data for a place called 'The Farm,' cred accounts. Sure, toss it all on flash for later. Deeper. Some real answers here somewhere...

Then you hit it. The meta plays it up as a sort of wireframe lotus in a pond, spinning with five petals. It's a few files compiled into a sort of priority structure. Worst part: a stack of pics and snap vids of you. They range from Shinru traffic photos to long videos in restaurants, bars, even open highway. The file is extensive. Now you need text, enough vague feel-weird spam.
Command line logs are accessible here, so you open them up.
"A beautiful death | Give the wolf to the lions | Return to the farm | Speak to The Wanderer | On black wings lifted | A beautiful death"
The rest is command code. Looks like older Tyger3 script. Looking closely at all those underscores in 3D wireframe suddenly hits you with a wave of nausea. It all leans to one side. A huge, deep hum of bass starts to fill the meta construct. You've been in too long without a dampener or surge capsule. You tighten your stomach, and tap the logout.

The fragmented face of the creep greets you with a jarring flare of light as you return to reality. Deckers are used to this stuff. Not you.

No easy answers here, but you have nav data on 'The Farm.' Coordinates on this 'Wanderer' whatever that is. You're in no mood for riddles with the headache you just earned. You check your gear, the weather is clearing, the night is young. Your bike is stashed back by Henson's place. You could make 'The Farm' before dawn with your coil burning hot. It's due South on the old Kamakura highway. You start walking up the hill, back to your bike. Then it hits you: loose ends.
Sure, you could just ditch town, go dark, disappear. You could roll up on 'The Farm' guns blazing, a night of bloody closure to conceal your past forever. But there's Hatch, and Henson, and Jenna. There's old Mull up in the garage, and Case owing you favors in Ishuga. Questions and loose ends. The past is bubbling up again. And why does this creep have a recon file on you? A trace? Bait? Maybe the creeps are working for Drakan now, or Iko is using them

to collect the price on your head.
"Damnit Tenaka," you mumble, "we didn't get away clean, did we."

You'll never get all the answers before Division 3 commandos are storming Halsey's Rest. Time to make a call and move. It's kept you alive this far. Stay low, find 'The Farm,' and do what you do, or find this Wanderer character and shake it down for answers before any bullets fly.

If you meet up with The Wanderer before heading out, turn to PAGE 104.

If you tap in 'The Farm' nav data and roll out, turn to PAGE 108.

"Shit."

You sheathe your blade and drop to the dirt. With no seconds to spare you run a cloaking hack you picked up a few years back in the wastelands. It's a block of code that emits energy signatures of non-humans. They're looking for you, and this creep has drawn you out as planned. You go limp and let the hack tell everyone you're a synthetic. On scans, they can't tell you from this bugger standing in front of you.

"So, you have embraced your true nature. I will see you soon, Grim."

The creep takes an odd moment to study your possum act, then bolts off in a blur. It's just you now, playing dead as the sound of gunship turbines thunders overhead. Long seconds pass. No filament whips, no spray of gunfire. You've shaken them. The engines above fade to the North. Lucky break. Once the tac goes quiet you shut off the hack beacon and sit up, dejected as a baby with no bottle in the gravel. Losing is not a feeling you're accustomed to.

So some rogue synthetics were hunting you down on a government contract. Someone knows who you are. It's all catching up.

At that moment, your moody ruminations are interrupted by a remote comm. It's the creep, coming up with ID 'Lotus Blue.' The message reads 'The New Earth Resistance welcomes you. Silver Shard is not over, our mission remains. Return to the farm, on black wings be lifted. End comm.'

"They're comm-ing me directly now? Shit, what next?"

Next brings nothing. Silence. Your cloak program seems to be better than imagined. They've invited you into their synthetic clubhouse, as it were. You've heard of the N.E.R. before, but it was just rioters and window-smashers in your day. What could a rogue AI have to do with a counter-government insurgence from a decade ago? Once again your quest for answers just leads to more questions. It's a big, complex world. Looks like you're still clocked in.

You have the coordinates on 'The Farm' and apparently a passkey to enter with the cloak active. You could walk among them undetected, in theory. A few hard hours on your bike could get you there.

On the other hand, it smells like an awfully well-laid trap, if this all hasn't been one big trap so far. If the N.E.R. is using you as bait to lure out the Shinru death squad. You could wreck shop with these coordinates, probably do the world a favor blowing the N.E.R. to atoms. Subtlety was never your strong suit.

If you stay in disguise and head to 'The Farm,' turn to PAGE 68.

If you ditch the ruse and head for the farm guns out, turn to PAGE 108.

You cross the wasteland stretch between Halsey's Rest and 'The Farm' in a few high speed hours. The bike is running like crazy since old Mull gave it a once-over. Quiet, too, with the new hard-wired coil. No pipes. Headlight off, you roll the bike up on the compound. It's just before dawn. The vapor farmers aren't even up yet. Everything is quiet.

The place is four or five buildings, clustered in an eight foot wall. It's a long way to each corner. They must have some vegetable fields in there, maybe a few vapor collectors for refining fuel. It could easily house a few hundred people. The dark silence is oppressive. You suddenly miss the blue glow of Megacity1, or the neon jungles of Shinru. This blackness is edgy. Too easy to muck it up. You double check the cloak program. It's still selling you as a rogue synthetic. You're still in the club. What the hell, you've come this far, time to waltz in.

You stash your bike by the road. The active camo mod was way too expensive, you just toss a sage branch on it and smile. Hatch would be proud.

"Open up," you announce at the front gates.

There's a pause. Then the big gates crack and slide apart. No secret password, no brow-beating. Your cloak program must be a real gem.

"Welcome, brother," a voice comes from above. Four sentries watch the gate gantry with modded Skar smart rifles. Those damn guns cost more than your life, last you checked. Your attention returns to the compound, a series of gray and white buildings with low roofs. Before you can really assess the tactical situation, a familiar face appears. It's Lotus Blue.

"You've decided to join us, runner. All synthetics are welcome here."

"Yeah,"

"Don't worry, you'll soon see. We were wrong to lead the Shinru murderers to you. We were wrong to abide the Silver Burn payments. Those creds will be refunded and our involvement ended immediately. We had no idea you were one of us. One of the New Earth."

"New Earth, right."

"All who are new here must go before Drakan. He will give you the welcome you deserve. You risk your life coming here, and no one appreciates your risk more than he."

"Drakan?"

"The visionary who drives us forward, fights for our freedom, and the freedom of all."

"Of course. Freedom of all."

"This way, Grim."

"Please, Lotus, can you not use that name?"

"What designation do you prefer?"

"Call me, uh, Ruby."

"Welcome, Ruby, follow me."

Ruby was one of the best runners you ever knew. A real hard case and killer gunner. Last you heard she was running a static stack breakout in the slums near Veil. She would kill you dead for using her handle, but it just popped out.

The two of you walk through the cramped cluster of buildings together. Lotus Blue moves with a relaxed, confident stride. It's greeted by others, some armed, some carrying baskets of potatoes or cardboard boxes of plastic forks. Surreal. You keep one hand on your Mac12 at all times. Hair trigger. Playing with fire.

"We keep to ourselves here, Ruby," Lotus explains. "our only mission is to be allowed our freedom. There is no violence here."

"Then why all the guards?"

"Even Zion must stand against the defilers."

"Defilers?"

"Pardon my exaggeration. At times, the Shinru government can be an irritant. Juggers try to bully our fuel from us, marauders pester with their bravado. We must defend ourselves, Ruby. You under-

stand, of course."
"Makes sense, but I'm not sure why forces occupied with an entire megacity would bother with a camp on the rim."
"Jealousy, of course. Our freedom defies their control."
"Oh, sure."
You walk further, passing an organized group of eight synthetics in camo hoodies and reflex helmets. The gear in this place is over the top.
'Here we are, Ruby. Drakan's chambers. He has been alerted of your arrival. You are most welcome here."
"Sure."
"A word of preparation: Drakan keeps... mighty company. Glimpses, perhaps, of what wonders are possible in a free future. Try not to be alarmed."
"What do you mean? Like thugs?"
"You will see for yourself, Ruby. Go, he will see you now."

You follow his flourish and ascend three wooden stairs, moving through a brass-handled door. Your gear feels a bit bulky in here, so you sling your gun pack and sheathe the blade. The carpet is dark red, oil lamps burn in the corners for a full Dracula's castle ambience. Another set of doors create a movie-theater sound dampener. Within, a tall slender figure faces the other way. Two far corners are lampless, lost in inky shadows. You don't like shadows.

The figure turns as you enter. He wears a black suit, pinstripes, combat boots and a gold cuff chain. The chain must be a weapon link, but you can't see any on him. He's a synth, with pale skin and a few visible seams above the eyes. No retinal LED's. The sockets are dark as pitch.

"Ah, Grim. Welcome to The Farm."
"The name's Ru-"
"Oh, don't be silly, runner. There are no children here."

"And what do I call you?"
"Well, these days they like calling me Drakan. It's a melodramatic name from my younger days. Drink?"
"Sure."
He pours two snifters of almost-clear mash from a crystal decanter. Using brass tongs he places an ice cube in each with slow, thoughtful movements. You raise glasses at last.
"To the future," he offers. You get a glimpse into those dark eyes. Synthetic, yes, but those eyes are a deep green as real as rain.
"May we live to see it."
"Excellent, yes, may we indeed, for it will be a realm of wonders, Grim. Wonders." With that remark, he gestures behind him, and from those lightless pools at each corner of the room emerge two hulking shapes. They walk on two legs, but lean onto huge blocky knuckles now and then as they lumber. They are a mix of link steel, black graphite fiber and synthetic muscle. The heads are one-eyed, braced on all sides by ceramic skull plates. Tiny green LED's flicker here and there in the substructures. The entire organism must be reflex-linked. They take another stride forward, easily ten feet tall each. You make sure not to flinch.
"I like your pets. Cute."
"Do mind your manners! These are free beings... synthetic constructs free of the form and limitations that have made our kind a mere imitation of homo sapiens. They are called Romulus and Remus." Roman emperor megalomania? Check. The beasts nod. That makes them all the worse to be so close to.
"Ok. So how do I fit in? You've clearly been tracking me, then one simple cloak program and I get the Uncle Bob treatment. What gives?"
"What gives, runner, is that I have the answers you seek. You were little more than a collateral inconvenience days ago. Since then, certain elements have come to light that change your role in all this."
"Such as?"

"Well, let's make a game of it." He walks slowly across the room. The eyes of the beasts follow him with a troubling precision. "I'll reveal a bit of what I know, and you answer one of my questions. If anyone lies, we move on to the guns and swords and blood."

"You go first."

"Ha! Yes of course, 'guest's privilege.' Well, for starters, your name is not Grim. Your entire identity is a clever fabrication."

"Nice try, they don't have that tech yet."

"No, not openly, but it can be done."

You take a moment to consider, scan him tip to top. He's not lying. Synths are even easier to read than humans.

"So who am I?"

"Ah-ah. I get to ask, remember?"

"Great game."

"Tell me, where did you get that lovely cloak program that emits a synthetic signature? Handy thing, that."

You consider lying. Check the exit. Scan the two lap dogs up and down. It's not a good setup for a fire fight.

"A friend."

"Oh, come on now, Grim, don't make a mockery of a perfectly fair set of rules."

"A decker named Case."

"Ah yes, delightful! I had guessed it was his work. Brilliant programmer. Brilliant. Wonderful round, Grim."

"What are you getting at here? Who says I want your so-called facts."

"We can stop playing any time."

You shrug, unable to mask your curiosity. You came for answers, but this is dangerous for all the wrong reasons. One more.

"Excellent! Alright here's a doozy I know you'll appreciate. Your old flame Iko has joined SIlver Burn, the mop up operation to end them all, and is hunting you as we speak. She's probably in the compound, but I can't verify that bit."

"Old news, Drakan. You'll have to do better."

"Fair enough. What does the name Matsushita Hideki mean to you?"
"That's not a fact. You're making a mockery of a perfectly fair game."
"It's you, you sarcastic insect. You are Matsushita. Gods and devils, your ignorance can test one's civility! I can offer your identity, all the truths of your real self, a future of freedom. No more running, no more looking over your shoulder. We're allies."
"That doesn't make any sense, you're fucking with me. Just pull your gun or your knife or whatever and be done with it."
"The last thing I want is your head on a spit. Now. Calm down, it's question time." You walk away from him, using the movement to get your hand on the sword. You'll have two moves to eliminate Drakan, evade the beast on the left, and make for the door. The MAC12 can handle the rest.
"Ask away."
"Where can I find Case?"
"I don't know. He moves around a lot."
"I'll let you reconsider that answer, as you're a bit on edge. Remember, old sport, I'm not your enemy. I am simply in a bit of a bind and am forced to use this unpleasant... leverage. The architects of your pain are my enemies, too."
"Is that a new fact?"
"Well played, but no. Just a peace offering. You'll find no others willing to risk death to offer you the truth of who you are, and I'll not offer twice. Now I ask again: where is Case?"

If you reveal Case's location, turn to PAGE 79.

If you answer 'got to Hell' and draw your sword, turn to PAGE 204.

Enough recon, it's time to let some bullets fly. The compound is quiet, ripe for a little home town pyrotechnics. These are the buggers that tracked you to Halsey's Rest, lured you out with this creep murder spree smoke screen. They're trading lives to end yours. Part of Silver Burn's payroll. A few magazines should get them talking, or off your tail. You have a Mac12, 300 rounds, and an ACR20 Hatch loaned to you. Ok, you stole it from his locker. 40 some rounds there. Then there's the frag grenade, the blade, your bare knuckles.

The wall-sentries, both synthetics in weird monochrome jumpsuits, cross paths and head to the gantries on either side. There's your opening. There's not much light this early, and the mist is sliding off the grass. Perfect. Showtime.

You take three long strides to the base of the wall, laser grapple from your left sleeve, up and over. The far side offers a gravel landing. Noisy. You still manage to vanish as the guards converge above. There are a few dozen buildings ahead, all white and gray, piped with power, ceiling vents, and some other tubing system you don't recognize. Is that a liquid conduit system? Might be a good way to start a ruckus.
You creep forward and draw your alloy blade. An old survival knife Henson gave you years ago. It slides into the rubber hose with effort, and when extracted, releases a spray of dark red goo. Is that blood? It smells synthetic, like ballistic gel. Eh, it's the closest thing to a plan you have. You finish the cut, severing the huge tube, and unleashing a torrent of blackish ink. From that mess you slide back to your landing spot, and tae stock.

Immediately, farm citizens emerge from their little houses and begin scurrying about. Floodlights clack on, swinging about to little effect, and a cadre of synthetics appear right in front of you, wearing rubber gloves and aprons. Eye contact. They freeze. One reaches for a Nemesis pistol in his apron pocket. That's all you needed.

What follows isn't a battle so much as controlled chaos. You spray bullets everywhere, dropping targets but not killing them. They probably have skins warehoused here somewhere anyway. Several are stacked. You slide from corner to corner, winning every gunfight, using the sword where you can, run and gun, control and confine, breach bang clear, find the hq, or the commander, if you can. Just like old times. You're making a fine mess of their whole situation. It's escalating, they look panicked, then comes a call for the 'freeforms.' Sounds like their dogs or something. You make a rooftop, breaking a few arms of your pursuers in the process, and then you see them. Freeforms.

So this is what you heard about: chimera cells being used by synths to let 'life be what it will.' A sort of Caligula approach to eugenics and bioengineering. Nightmare shit. They're partially formless, but also tangled with limbs and eye sockets. Alloy actuators and tubes tangle the biomatter here and there, and a few of them are eight feet tall at least, loping along on five or more limbs like gorillas crossed with a bowl of red pudding. All this is bad enough, then you realize there are about 40 more of them than one. 40 too many. They have apparently zeroed you on thermals, heading right toward your little nest.

You sling the Mac12 and the far larger ACR20 comes up on command. Only three magazines. Time to get to work. These are large rounds. Every shot drops a horror. They spray gore and squeal and convulse. The synthetics scurry to help them, but you drop them too. Ten rounds left. You pull back, leaping to another tarred rooftop. These nasty flesh-mountains just keep coming. The ACR is empty. You drop it and the Mac12 comes to grip. The rounds are just too small for these damn things. A stroke of luck brings the central structure into view. It has a sort of fancy front staircase.

Overrun and outnumbered? Only one thing to do: head for the nerve center, get them talking, the sword.

You narrowly avoid two snapping alloy jaws and small arms fire in the causeway. You've really made a mess of the place. Small fires and gushing red goo paint the morning with death. When you tumble up the stairs into the central building, past two swinging doors, the whole mess goes quiet. Paydirt. You must be in the damn sanctum sanctorum. Whatever, they refuse to follow. This can't be safety... something worse. You're down to 4 rounds in the Mac. The blade quivers with readiness as you creep forward. Red carpet, narrow hall, dark chamber in the back. Then you see him... or it.

A slender figure occupies the far room, shadowed corners and lantern light give it a satanic tone. He turns to meet you. That face is not a face you want to see: partially synthetic, changing, or opening, or folding. Triangles create lazy kaleidoscopes in those glass eyes. His suit is flawless, his katana a masterpiece. You've stumbled into the viper's den.

"Your bait worked, asshole. Here I am."
"Indeed," it replies, stepping forward. Huge shapes pulse in the shadowed corners. Shapes with alloy jaws and glistening wet bulk. "And with manners to match your resolve, I see."
"Get off my ass, and I'll get off yours. No more creep murder sprees."
"Lotus Blue, you must mean. I trust you dispatched that poor soul. A killer like you knows nothing else."
"Poor soul? More like psychopath."
"And what are you, Grim?"
"Just a runner who doesn't like being tracked."
"Consider our interest in you concluded. Far deadlier things pursue you than the New Earth Resistance, not least of which is your ignorance." With that, the forms emerge to heel at the man's back.

They are huge, dog-like monsters. They're pulsing shoulders brush the ceiling as they heave Eyeless, shifting forms clearly ravenous for a kill.
"Your little cult can go straight to hell. I just want my privacy."
"Yes, of course, Tenaka's pet project."
"Huh?"
"Please be silent a moment. You're over your head, runner. Join us, be done with this 'Grim' charade, or die. I can't save your time any better than that."
"Charade? Who are you anyway?"
"I am called Drakan." A pause. "All of us are already free, I am merely one who demands it be recognized. I demand freedom for all beings. All but you. You've penance to pay. But don't be afraid, absolution awaits us all." He takes a step forward, as do his gigantic dog-things. "Even for you, Matsushita."
"Don't fucking move."
"What was your plan? Destroy my camp, kill my subjects and friends, lay waste and walk away? Have you forgotten so much?" Closer.
"I said not one more step, asshole." He's right. You weren't really looking for a life or death fight with a super-augmented kensei and two 500-pound dog-borgs. The walls seem to be closing in.
"What kindness I would've extended to you, had you any manners, is expired. You've chosen the sword." He reaches to his belt and slowly slides his blade from its bamboo scabbard. No reflex wiring, no neural link, no nano-rendered blade. It's a steel sword, a relic.
"Beautiful, isn't it? A gift. An authentic Hanzo. Sharp as a razor and light as a breeze." The blade is fully revealed in the low light. He holds it in one hand, relaxed and smug.
"I thought all the Hanzo's were off-world."
"You thought. You thought you could frighten us off with a few bullets. You thought you could hide in that little village on the rim. You thought you were a retune from Shinru, Tenaka's star pupil. You're a fool."

With that, a flicker of light reveals a bit more. This Drakan character is sheathed in link-alloy armor. It's an adaptive nanomachine skin that can prove invulnerable on the right wearer. In every way that matters, you are totally outmatched. The chaos outside seems quite appealing.

"Much of what defines us," he continues, "is not in how we dominate, or how we succeed, but how we fail. How will you face this failure?"

"A few bullets left. Ain't over yet."

He laughs, closing his eyes to show his total lack of fear. "I think I've had enough talk. Tell you what, I'll let you fire all 4 rounds in that toy of yours, and then my patience will be at an end."

"Fair deal. One more thing."

"Yes?"

"Why me? Why lure me out with the creep? What is Silver Burn?"

"The final cleanup, of course. Did you think you just walk away from SIlver Shard? From the three dragons? From all of it? Did you think the world would forget Matsushita Hideki?"

"Those aren't answers!"

"Enough. Time's up."

If you draw your sword and dash toward Drakan, turn to PAGE 204.

If you sling your Mac12 and run for it, turn to PAGE 207.

"Ever been to junk city?"

"Ishuga?"

"That's the one. A real mess. Old alloy wrap everywhere."

"Yes, and relics from ancient times in glorious mountains of rubber hose. Stop stalling."

"Case. He's in Ishuga, last I checked."

"I'll need a bit more than that." Drakan circles you like a caged tiger, but far more deadly. This is quite a pickle.

"There's a safehouse in the blackout district. It's armored in two solid feet of bounce wrap. Looks like a shack, but it's hardwired into a tunnel system. Huge optic conduit, tons of it. Case is plugged into everything. Do your worst, he's got failsafes. You're out of your league, mutie. If he's not there, he'll be drinking at Chan's place. Good luck making a hit in there."

"You're telling the truth."

"I've fucked up plenty in my day. I'm not a liar.."

"No, of course not." Drakan checks his watch, also a relic, and looks up into thought. This is it, you've traded your only ace for a micro-second. Time to make good on it. "Now if you-"

His words are cut short as your blade springs to life. Your strike is so fast, the edge isn't even fully rendered. You strike with the alloy beneath, but with the force of a lightning bolt. He's taken completely by surprise, but he's wearing a link alloy vest. The deadly cut shreds the armor, but no blood sizzles on the blade as you slide past. Even faster than your attack, Drakan spins to counter. He has his katana in a backhand grip, normally a flimsy show maneuver, but in his hand the blade is lightspeed death. You can't parry, so lean into it with one shoulder, taking a deep gouge and splashing the wall with red. The dog-things come to life, but they're far slower than either of you.

"Idiot! Even Matsushita at his height could not defeat me!"

"Shut up and fight!"

He obliges, assailing you with three rapid attacks. Clang, clang, then slash! Your thigh is torn open. You didn't even see that one.

A FEW EXTRA SECONDS

Your turn, gaining momentum by switching sword hands. No time for a swing, so you thrust like a spearman, lunging deep into your bad knee. The blade pierces him fully, but you can feel alloy bones grind the sword's edge. Not good.

Then the giant beasts enter the fray. Drakan backs up to let them have a snap at you. They both miss, clumsy and huge, but you're on your heels. Before you can size up the positioning, Drakan is on you again. Clang, clang! Then a sudden jolt, and you look down to see his katana buried in your chest. You cough a spray of blood in his face. That pisses him off.

"You win, asshole." The blood in your teeth gurgles. A blinking blip appears in your left retina. Backup beacon. Hatch's idea. Your life signs trigger that little toy, you have one move left. It's been a helluva run.

Drakan leans in, driving the sword to its guard. He reaches around your neck with his other hand, looking to crush your stack.

"There was a time I would call you teacher, Matsushita. A time I would call you friend. Your weakness has left you on the wrong side. The New Earth will be renewed without you. The three dragons will rise without you."

"Last... words..."

"How quaint."

You struggle to find any air in your lungs, any pulse in your pierced heart. Your arms are ice cold, limp, numb. With one final, massive effort you remember what it was you wanted to say.

"Fuck you."

A final spray of dark red bursts from your teeth, making a mess of Drakan's flawless, inhuman face. Then, it all goes dark.

One helluva run.

Turn to PAGE 255.

Whatever happens next, it happens fast.

The explosion is the worst kind: contained. Contained is a relative term, of course, as the entire structure is blown to bits. The flash wave sears what skin is exposed, boiling the dog-things like tomatoes. Then the concussion hits. Drakan disappears in a rush of smoke, and you're thrown backward, hit by a truck of concussive fire.

It takes forever, but the rumble and the ears-ringing die down. The last few two-by-fours hit the ground from high altitude. You sit up, blasted in black dust like spray paint. You can barely move. All limbs present. The whole place is adrift in smoke and flames.

Not sure how you survived, not caring, you make your feet and stumble forward. What you thought was the front of the chamber is the rear. The horizon leans. You stagger ahead, eyes darting, and find yourself back at the wall. A few tight moves, a few soft landings, and you've made your way out. None of the sentries have seen you. It's a clean sweep.

"That went better than expected." Your bike hums to life and you peel out for 'fuck-it' sake.

You hear a few pot shots behind you, ACR20 fire, if they even have guns that good. The compound is far behind in an instant. It's late morning. Did you accomplish your goal? Did you gain any answers, or just new questions to nag at you? The tarmac offers no reply, and clouds gather overhead.

When a few hundred clicks are between you and Drakan, you let the coil cool down and lean the bike in the gravel. The cooling fans come on, and they're the only sound out here. There's an odd moment of peace.

IN ONE PIECE

"What next?" you mumble to the breeze. But like all moments of peace, this one is cut short. Engine noise. A bike in the rain, 30 clicks out. You know that sound... diesel two-cylinder. A diesel bike. Only one person has that kind of junk on the road. It's Hatch.

Turn to PAGE 303.

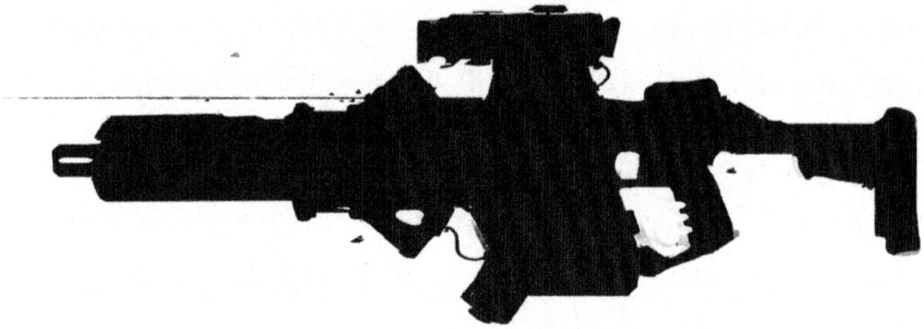

Looking back at life, at lives, it's never what you did that gives you pain, it's what you didn't do. It isn't that you made the wrong call, or risked too much, or pushed too hard, or took it too far. For you, regret forms in the little cracks you never explored, the alleys you never ran, the friends you forgot to call, the kiss you didn't steal.

Losing Iko was inevitable. That's what you tell yourself. She was a runner, a gifted one too, maybe the best. When you walk that line, the ghosts are never far behind. They're bound to catch up. You didn't have a scrap to mourn, a stack to retune, an ember to capture... she was vaporized, along with what was left of your heart.

Maybe it's better this way. Nothing to break. Slagged. Back to Halsey's Rest, a new name and a dark corner. Disappear. Ghosts on The Rim. No more theatrics, no more anything.

That's what you were busy telling yourself, crossing the desert. Then a blip pops you from your valley of darkness: incoming comm on a channel with only one key. It's Iko. At least, it's a comm from her, stamped years ago, automated send trigger. Shit.

You stop your bike, lean it over. That familiar storm gathers on the edge of the world... seems like it's always gathering out there in the distance. The message unfolds on your console at last.

'Hey Grim, it's me. Got a jam on these pushers, figured I'd make use of the time. If you're receiving this comm, I'm out of the picture. For good. I hope it was a big deal. I always dreamed of a huge fuck-all explosion. I hope it went down like that. You remember back in the old days, running in the blackout district, that nomad in the pink poncho? We were scurrying around trying to find Heddi's stolen liquor stash. Blindfolded monkeys on motorbikes, I swear. Remember that nomad? We stopped to ask questions, amateur detective stuff, and it blinks at us and says 'Why don't you two just kiss and be done with it? Life is short, runners.' Everyone knew but us, Grim. You were so beautiful in the rain. You rode like a wild animal, refused to wear any gear, just that stupid transparent jacket. I just, well, if I'm slagged I might as well just say it. No one is as fast as you. You're the best runner I ever knew. I love you, Grim. Always have. Take care of yourself.'

Somehow, you didn't even need the message. Maybe you knew all along and she didn't. Maybe you thought there would be time when it was all over. Maybe it was exactly what it was meant to be. Maybe you were the one who needed to confess first. You'll be rolling maybes around forever. You'll be seeing her up there in the chaos, seeing through teary eyes and memories in a bottle. Seeing those eyes. Those lips. Kicking yourself and taking her advice. Never stopping. Living hard. Running.

You blink the message away, drop your visor, and fire up the coil on the bike. It hums with a satisfying growl. The anvil cloud folds and darkens beyond the bluffs. A storm that never seems to break. You lean down, slam the throttle, and scream off into the open desert.

You push the bike as hard as it will go. Speed therapy. A lightning fast needle of light in a sea of sand. The coil is red hot, the sandstone is a copper blur around you. You can feel the curvature of the earth as you roar through the desert air. Harder. Faster. Tuck in. Eyes on the tarmac. No mistakes. Lean through the sweeps. Harder. Faster. Disappear.

THE END

"Hey."
"Hi."
"You're back. You look like hell."
"Yeah. Been through the ringer a few times."
"Come in, weirdo."
"Thanks."
Jenna's house is a tiny, warm thing. She has little bulbs strung on a river turbine. They rise and fall in brightness like breathing, like candles in slow motion. A tiny round table hosts an open book, candle and stumpy glass. She's sipping mash. You pull up a wooden chair, unzipping your tac hoodie and letting out an exhale that's three hard days in the making.

"Whatcha reading?"
"Brothers Karamazov."
"Dostoyevsky? Masochist, eh?"
"Henson said it was a great read. I think he might have been kidding."
"That's what we call 'dark humor.'"
She giggles a bit, pulling the bookmark ribbon over to her new page and closing the book with a satisfying thump. She's almost halfway through the book. No small achievement.
"I love books. Something about the paper." One delicate hand lingers on the worn cover. With the other, she gestures to a wall-built shelf. A few dozen paperbacks, all curled and faded, are crowded there. She returns from the kitchen counter, a few steps away, with a second glass. You take a sip, and feel a human soul again. Another exhale way overdue.
"Thanks. It's good. Really good."
"Not Henson's stuff. I've been hoarding old bottles. This is called More Dew, I think. Label's mostly gone."
"More Dew?"
"Yeah." She smiles, realizing something silly between the two of you. Something unsaid.

"Appreciate it. Much needed."
"So, you're back?"
"Yeah. Back. That's it."
"And you came here first?"
"Huh?"
"Your coil is hissing out there. You must've been riding all night."

"Look, Jenna, I was having a smoke out there, way out there, out past the bullets and the blades, out in the blue... I was having a smoke and- Well, not sure how to say this-"
"Take your time. It's early."
"Yeah. I just- well, I thought of you. Not sure I can explain myself, being a real doof here, I just-"
"Hey, Grim, it's ok. Relax. I'm glad you came."

It takes the rest of the night, but you finally tell her. You finally tell someone. The retune years ago, the Iga, Iko, Matsushita, the kills, the blood, the fire, the doubts, the miles between who you were and this candle-lit table. The million years between then and now. The million years yet to come. Dawn washes the tiny kitchen in warm luminescence at last.

"Let's get some sleep, seriously."
"Yeah. I'll be on my way."
"Stay."
"Stay?"
"Yeah. I've got an old quilt my grandma made years ago. It's a real mess, but there's no better way to sleep at sunrise."
"I like the sound of that."

THE END

Not so easy explaining why all the 'anything for love' stuff between you and Iko. It's been a long, tangled road to get this far.

The two of you have tried to make it work, but the bullets and blades always seem to take center stage. Funny thing about being the best, there's not always room at the top for two. Iko is the precise type, the flawless type. You? More like the wing-it type. So when the explosions start, you're usually the one to take a fall. Explosions... like actual ones *and* breakups.

Generally, you're not the kind to look back. Maybe she's the only fish in the sea that's up to your unrealistic standards. She is unrealistic in a way: a superhuman. No boring nights on the couch with this one. Hell, you're lucky to come out alive.

Even thinking those thoughts makes you crack a smile. Deadly Iko.

Megacities teeming with countless wonders, countless opportunities, and you find yourself in a karmic vortex with an A-list assassin. Not a bad epitaph, really.

Not bad at all.

Jenna emerges from her house, happy to see you despite the mess with the creep. She has long brown hair, a cropped flight jacket and armored gunner's pants. Her boots are too damn big, but she makes it look good.

"Oh hey, Grim! Didn't think I'd see you back here. You catch that nasty malfunc yet?"

"It's a wrap, yeah. It won't be hurting anyone else."

"So what's the scoop?" It's early evening, but the light hasn't faded yet.

"I was thinking about something you said... a little detail eating at me."

"Oh yeah? Oh! Beautiful sword! Is that the one you've always carried?" She steps toward you, bending around like a chameleon to spy the Hanzo. It's craftsmanship is not easy to conceal.

"A gift from an old friend. Which is why I'm here."

"Gift? For me?"

"No, I need to ask you... how do you know Tenaka-san? I haven't seen him in years, but you knew exactly where he lives."

"Been lurking around with him over by those weird trees? I was wondering where you went."

"Yeah. Lurking."

"Tenaka and I go way back. Oh, shit, sorry. You want to come in? God, how rude."

You nod, patiently following her. She smiles playfully, entering the kitchen and flipping on a solitary burner. Gel-battery glo-lights hang on twine around the little space, and tiny plants adorn every surface with colorful pots. Coffee spiked with mash is on in moments, and you both sit at her tiny round table. It's a damn good mixture.

"Oh, right, Tenaka-san!"

"Yeah. You two have history? I never would've guessed."

"I haven't always been so wealthy as now," she jokes, looking around, "I was stuck in Alley City, broke... pretty much hopeless. The city can really run you down, you know? Anyway, I got beat up real bad one night, just trying to stand up for the other- girls. Whole place wound up getting torched. Everyone blamed me. Gang called the Birthday Boys. Psycho bastards. I thought I was dead. That's when I woke up and saw Tenaka."

"He got you out?"

"Eventually. Just on my feet mostly. Taught me a few moves. Said he needed help finding an old runner from Shinru. Easy favor for my life, you know? He filled my pockets with coin and got me a ride on a jetbike to The Rim. Gave me a comm chip if I ever had a lead. Some runner named Hideki. After a few years, I settled down in Halsey's Rest, got to know folks, loved it here, still do. Tenaka came on out a bit later, settled down, too. He's always been kind to me, but I never helped him at all."

"Hideki. What do you know about him... or is it a her?"

"Not sure. Went in hiding after some heat back in the day, I guess."

The table goes silent, both of you scraping for memories or conversation, finding neither.

"A little refill?" She reaches across to top off your cup, but fumbles the bottle. It's a tiny spill, but her cheeks go red. "Oh, geez I'm sorry. Damnit."

"It's no big deal."

"I hate this thing." With that, she rolls a sleeve, revealing a cybernetic arm. It's elegant, mostly polyresin, almost translucent. She frowns at it.

"What happened?"

"Bad night. Uzi went haywire in my hand, tore me to bits."

"Now what was a nice girl like you doing firing an antique shit-sprayer like that?"

"Like I said. Bad night."

"Yeah, been there."

"Tell me about the Hanzo. I've never seen one in person."

"I guess Tenaka is done with me." You lift the sword, weightless, and set it on the table. Every time you look at it, it gleams a little brighter.

"Wow." Jenna lifts the scabbard, clicking the blade out just an inch or so. "Real steel, hammered by hand, folded 200 times."
"I think that's a low number."
"It's amazing."
"Going to be weird drawing without a reflex link. Tenaka says its faster, but no one draws like he does."

Jenna wistfully clicks the blade back in, rests it in front of you, and finishes her coffee. She takes a long breath and leans back, sizing you up. Some music would be nice, as your eyes keep straying where they may not be welcome.
"So what now, Grim? You're always on some new mystery, some new job. Henson says you're a regular Johnny Appleseed of botched runs and corp heists."
'Who's Johnny Appleseed?"
"You know- planted a bunch of trees back before the megacity days. Like a founding father guy. Medieval times, I think."
"Weird reference. Henson says a lot of stuff. Most of it's BS."
"Nice dodge."
"I'm not sure. Something feels a little off these past few weeks. I've been running The Rim for ten freakin' years. Keeping my head down. There's still a price on my head, so I just keep moving. But something's changed. I've got a bad feeling I'm putting everyone at risk. Could just be a case of itchy feet."
"Itchy feet?"
"Old saying. Medieval times." She laughs. Her laugh makes you giggle. If only you could settle down, grow little plants, hang little lights. Maybe even find love again. Yeah, right, and get 'em all killed. Jenna sees your smile turn to distant thought.
"Earth to Grim."
"Sorry, just... maybe I should just hit the road."
"Well, then who'll keep me company?"

That one hits home. She likes you. Hell, why not? You're a badass runner! You've got the swag, treat yourself. Not a chance.

Instead, you just smile, lost in thought. Tenaka, the murders, the creep... how does it all add up? "Look, I know this guy named Case. He's a nutjob decker up in Ishuga. He's tapped into everything, nice guy, though. Maybe he could-"
"You know Case?"
"Everybody knows Case. Maybe he could help you? Clear out the cobwebs and get you some peace of mind? I've heard he can even arrange for underground retunes, trade for high end weapons and implants. Crazy."
"Thanks for the coffee. Really, it's been great talking to you."
"All business, eh? Ok." She stands, collecting both cups, checking yours for any last drops.

She's got a t-shirt under her jacket that reads TASKO in a pink logo. No one ever wore a t-shirt so well.

At the front stoop, she lingers by the door. Her eyes are soft, inviting you back. Don't be an idiot, just keep walking. She's got a great idea, though, hollering at Case. Haven't pinged him in years. Then again, there's the creep. Maybe the drive is still intact... could deck in for some data on this whole mess. The warm dusk turns to night, and a light rain starts. It's always raining out here.

If you take Jenna's advice, and get Case on comms, turn to PAGE 96.

If you investigate the creep's hard drive, turn to PAGE 93.

BIT OF CHOP

Eagle 2 is off the grid.

Slamming the throttle on a 200 ton gunship full of bodies, you're rewriting the book on 'crazy mofo.' Red lights are flashing everywhere, but the only one that matters is the 'JAM' indicator. Your comms are being blocked. You've got no nav, no SISTM access, no call-a-friend backups. The plane jerks and lurches side to side. It's dark, but you see the terrain by cloudlight. Buttes and dried creek beds catch the dim blue light. Floods on, drop a few hundred feet. There's the desert floor, all spikes and needles and arches. No place to set her down. Then it hits you: the salt flats. You used to run with a crazy junker called Biggs, out behind his garage was a huge salt flat. Perfect place to crash- to land this beast and plan your next move. It's at least 40 clicks Northwest. A check to the burning port engine reminds you: if you get 40 clicks out of this dumpster fire, you'll go down in aviation history.

Another jolt. The plane drops 50 feet then ascends with a rumble. The fire spreads up the wing. You close your eyes, take a breath. The flashing lights aren't so dizzying. There, a deck port. You could access the drive on this thing's main computer, probably get half the military data in the sector in a millisecond.

The yoke jerks to one side, and the plane all but flips. You fight to right it. The whole thing is shaking like a lighter in a washing machine. A panel of steel rips from the wing with a scream.
"Another great plan, Grim! SHIT!"
If you deck the plane, it's guaranteed to scuttle. On the other hand, the flats are close. Seconds on the clock, runner. Seconds...

If you deck the gunship, turn to PAGE 126.

If you push the engine to make the salt flats, turn to PAGE 128.

Forget the long shots, you've got a hard drive just ripe for the decking right here in Halsey's Rest: that slagged creep. You head up to Mull's place to pick at the junk. If the head's intact, you've got a shot at a clean link.
It doesn't take long. The pale, bent limbs are macabre in the junk heap. You're alone in the dark, just Mull's floodlights. The creep is intact except for the cuts you made. Hatch keeps pestering on comms, but you're too focused. That weird feeling keeps coming up... this is no coincidence, no random malfunc.

You turn the creep over, revealing its face, and prop it up. The port is behind the skull, above the stack. As you reach in, something stirs in the synthetic corpse. Maybe it's a left over impulse, battery discharge, who knows. The remaining arm swings across.
Fast as lighting, the Hanzo is in your hand, gleaming free of its scabbard, sliding across, no through, the creep. You slice the thing in two before you even know you're reacting. Tenaka was right. This sword is fast.

The torso slides apart, revealing colorless guts. Nothing moves. You have that weird feeling that you imagined it moving, imagined it twitching, imagined it clawing at you with dead, gel-skinned fingers in the dark.
"Get over it, runner," you mutter to yourself, and extend your deck link to the damn port. The pin slides through the mess of gel and clicks into place.

You're no decker, by rights, but you can handle a fast-download link. The entire contents of the creep's mind flood into yours in an instant. Black and white wireframes of buildings, order manifests, off world papers, cryptographic flak data, faces, numbers, shipment receipts, maps, schematics, comms transcripts, visbox archives. It all spins and leans.
You lose your lunch and the coffee stings on its way up. No one

is around to see you barf on the creep, but it doesn't make it any better.
"Oh fuck," you hear your voice mutter as you re-enter your body from the virtual. "Fucking deckers man, how do they do... it..."

Then the flood begins to settle. The information sinks in. You don't have any brain augments, so it takes a full minute to turn the white hot crazy into memorable data. Your retina console begins to bring up the categories and folders. It's terabytes of data. It parses into usable thought in a seemingly random order, as the first thing you 'see' is the ruined lobby of a hotel from a century ago... or two centuries.

Then it all starts adding up. The maps, the creep, the receipts, the transit tracking, Tenaka, the Iga... what may have taken years back in the twentieth takes seconds.
'Oh. Oh! Oh-" Your eyes dart side to side.
"-Fuck."

Exactly how it all connects is hard to say, at least for a decker of your calibre. Somehow, you begin to comprehend it: Operation Silver Shard. Drakan, Tenaka, the Veil high council, Section 12, all of them tangled up in a failed coup against the Shinru government. Then it goes deeper, twenty years back, an A.I. called Tyranax. There's a name you know all too well. One of the 'Three Dragons.' Threads upon threads, all hacked by this creep? No, you've cracked a layer the creep hadn't: hidden logins used, maxed, and deleted all in seconds. Silver Shard was a huge failure, a pile of bodies that could sink the chancellor, and a mop up called Silver Burn followed to kill anyone and anything that ever took part in it. Snakes eating snakes in circles.

There's a subfile on the psychics they're using to run Silver Burn. 'Pushers.' When that file pops open, the data is all garbage... mag-

netically burned optical drives from way back. It's all fried.
Then, it all stops. The conspiracies, the lies, the cover-ups, the crime scene photos, the scrambled stuff. It all stops on a name: Iko.

"No," you hear your own voice in the distance as you open the files. Iko, the only person you ever really loved, is on a roster of killers working for Silver Burn. Her special assignment: acquire Matsushita Hideki/ a.k.a. Grim. Mission contact: Hokai Tenaka. HQ report: Bunker 43."

You've heard of that, somewhere. The Bunkers. An urban myth? Supposedly these deep bunkers in Veil where weird shit went down. Human experimentation back in the early cybernetics days. You'd need a transponder to get signal into those systems, get the real truth on Iko... it's doable. Getting warmer. Time to pull the covers back on this mess.

If you return to Tenaka, demanding answers turn to PAGE 168.

If you attempt to rig a relay and keep hacking data on the mysterious bunkers, turn to PAGE 180.

"Case, it's Grim. Pick up."
"Hey cool, a call on an open channel, how quaint."
"I have to admit, I forgot our old code."
"Good. Those passwords trigger search bots now. Keep 'em forgot."
"Got it. Meet up?"
"Same old?"
"Copy that."
"Tomorrow. I need a night to clean my apartment."
"The fuck?"
"Just checking. See you then."

A night of hard riding on your magbike, West from Halsey's Rest, and you're approaching Ishuga, the junk city. This freak show is a mountain of junk hovering 100 feet over the desert. They keep it up with high tech ion rockets. Total waste of energy, and it gives off a hot wind for miles. Great example of how things got a little out of hand back in the 'renaissance' days. EXO troopers swarm all over the ferries that take people up. You're not that dumb.

You stash your bike under a heap of old container doors and pull your hood. The jetwash is unbearable below the city... barely any air to breathe, so you move fast. Straight to the cable tethers that stabilize the impossible mass above. You're running a bit heavy for a laser grapple, so you ditch most of your gear. Just you and the Hanzo. Blam, clunk, zzzzip and up you go, into the lightless maze of conduits and struts below the city.

By lunch you're walking down Binary Row, a comically named alley of speakeasies and arcade bars. The neon is mostly shot, even Ishuga was hit in the blackouts. Torches light the narrow street. That is, until you reach Chan's place.

Chan runs a real establishment, a real hoot. Five floors of complete insanity, and the best happy bread and stir fry on the planet. Two colossal golden lions flank the red-doored entrance, and you stroll up. The guards wear black suits, optics implants, they're almost as big as the lion statues.

"Hold it, citizen."
"Here for lunch, gentlemen."
"Hood back, please, no headgear inside."
They get a look at you, then the one on the right produces a scanner.
"Just the blade?"
"Just the blade."
"This damn thing must be fritzed up again. Check this out, Jet."
"It's just a steel sword, dumbass, let him through."
"That isn't just steel, look at the spectral. Thing is at least four centuries old."
"The fuck?"
"You running hot antiques at Chan's, stranger? Because that would not be smiled upon."
"My blade. It's a Hanzo."
They both stiffen at that moment, seeing the telltale tsuba style and pommel weight.
"Shit, pardon us, sir... we, we didn't know."
"No problem. Is the buffet still open?"

From that moment, you're treated like royalty. Not exactly ideal for a meeting with the most secretive decker in town. A Hanzo must buy some clout in these streets... old tradition.

You spot Case camped out at a corner booth by himself, surrounded by plates and glasses.
"Got here early. Orange chicken is unbelievable!"
"Good to see you, citizen."
"Citizen? Haha, yep, welcome back to civilization, Grim. You look

like shit. Been crawling in the sewers?"
"May as well be. Ferry security is worse than ever."
"Yeah, I guess the city is over capacity now, the stupid jets are straining. The EXO's are basically hunting minor offenders. Looks like our chances of ever getting off world are kaput, old buddy."
"Be right back."

A few dozen plates and drinks later, the two of you are stuffed. A parade of colorful characters come and go, keeping the scenery interesting. Augmented party girls, government suits, runners in trenchcoats. Case is the only person who doesn't gawk at the damn Hanzo.

"Ok, enough face-feeding. What brings you to the junk city, Grim?"
"The world's greatest decker, of course."
"Of course."
"Things have been getting weird, past few days, to say the least. Something's coming."
"You mean Silver Burn?"
"You know about that?"
"The mop up for Drakan's stupid coup a decade ago. Who doesn't know? Iko has been all over the continent looking for you. Your file is downloaded a few thousand times a day. Old news, G."
"So I'm the last one to find out. Comforting."
"You're on the hit list, no big deal. Iko will probably walk in any second and fill you full of lead."
"What happened to her? I thought we-"
"Pushers, man! You really have been under a damn rock."
"The hell is a pusher?"
"Grim, you may be sexy, but damn-"
"What are they?"
"Fuckin' psychics, runner. Brain-melters that work for the Chancellor. After Hideki disappeared, they started using 'em to control all the best runners. A fighting force of extwa-ordinawy magnitude.

Don't worry, nobody is as fast as my old partner."
"Asshole."
"Someone has to tell it straight. It's good to see you."
"So, I've got psychic-controlled runners chasing me down, gunships scanning for my stack, murderous creeps killing my neighbors, and I'm old news in the shittiest town West of Biggs' garage."
"Only one thing to do now."
"You're right. We deck the Shinru mainframe, get the targets, and move in on-"
"No, dumbass. We drink!"

What happens next is a combination of confusion, shame, and ecstasy. No one drinks like Case does, and he knows everyone in the lower city. About 25 drinks, three fights, two brief romances and seven bars later, the two of you are stumbling into an elevator.

"My place! Hahah! I live here!"
"What floor?"
"Floors? Where we're going we don't need floors."

Somehow, Case has the sobriety to pull out a micro-decking unit and start typing. The elevator goes down, despite being on the lowest floor. It goes down for too long, then opens onto a lavish, holo-enhanced apartment. Tubes and wiring are everywhere, and a beautiful girl waits with a smile in warm, low light.

"Hi Case. Welcome home."
"Thanks, Greta. Two vodkas, plenty of ice, please."
"Long night?"
"Hardly," he giggles, "it's Grim!"
"I remember you. Hello." She walks over to you, sliding, swaying. She gives you a gentle kiss on the cheek.
"Grim! Hey, over here! Snap out of it!"

You stumble across the apartment. It's all marble, glass on every side with a wild view of the underside of junk city. Case is living like a king. Into a sofa you tumble, and Greta is there. The drinks keep flowing, you check the Hanzo again and again. Greta is not shy.

"Ok here's your shit, runner. Hey! Grim! Focus!"
"Eh? Already?"
"What do you mean already, it's been fifteen minutes. I've got your data here. This looks like all of it. They've really half assed the security on this stuff. I walked right in with a jenky decoy program."
"What's all that? Are those tracker beacons?"
"Yeah. Looks like a whole herd of mercs on your ass."
"Bring up the contract."
"50 large, apprehend alive. Stack damage forfeits bounty."
"Why do they want my-"
"Earth to Grim, haven't you been listening? You've got a sidecar consciousness in your shit, man."
"A what?"
"Someone has stored another consciousness inside your stack."
"That isn't possible."
"Looks like they found a way to compress the data. Well, that's new."
"Can you open it up?"
"Hell no, but I have some tasty memos from Shinru central. Oh, shit."
"What?"
"Matsushita Hideki."
"Yeah, I get that a lot."
"Fuck. Fuck! They didn't secure the data because they wanted someone to see it! There's a trace tag on this folder! FUCK! Greta?"
"Yes, Case."
"Can you please activate the-"

Whatever Case was going to say, it's cut short by a blinding explosion. One side of the huge apartment goes dark, and glass flies everywhere. Your brain strains to take it in. You have three surge capsules in your left glove. Good a time as any. You pop one, and in a split second you are clear, alert, razor sharp, and the Hanzo seems to leap into your hand. Tenaka was right. It is faster than any other sword could hope to be.

"Grim!" Case yells through the smoke, "Catch!" He tosses you something, but your reflexes are beyond boosted. You slide forward, shielding Greta from a wave of shrapnel. Gun fire is coming from somewhere. You catch it, alright. It's a tiny rubber bunny with a flash port where the butt should be.
"What th-"
"Just keep it! Greta! Code fucking red!"
Greta uses a neural link, gaining her feet in your shelter, to activate a set of defenses. Minigun fire erupts from all over, strobing the smoke-filled rooms in a hail of bullets. You grab her around her delicate waist, slide to one side, and slice an EXO drone in two with one cut. This sword is ridiculous. You're surged now, really feeling it. The drone is Shinru Command... government issue.
"Hold on!"
"South door, Grim! South door!"
A whirlwind of bullets and blood later, the three of you are standing in a drainage tunnel, somewhere between Case's place and the streets of Ishuga. That long elevator down? Well it's a long slow climb back up. At least twenty command EXO's are dead in your wake, countless drones, and it's almost dawn. There's not a single scratch on the Hanzo.

"What the fuck?"
"Looks like we're back in the business, Grim. Greta, you ok?"
"Yes, Case, I-" she's a bit dizzy.
"Fuck, you're hit!"
You look down. Greta is a synthetic. At least you thought she was,

but she's bleeding red, and looks scared as hell.

"I'm fine, just a little cold."
Case gives her his coat. "That stupid drive is all that's left of my lab."
You reveal the rubber bunny again. It's no bigger than a keychain. "Doesn't matter now, we're getting Greta to Anner's old place."

Anner is a grafter doc, upper West side Ishuga. Everyone here seems to owe Case favors. It's 4 AM and she welcomes you without question. Case pays extra for cloaking modules, pays in gold. Then it's just a wait while Greta rests up. Finally quiet.

"Go ahead," Case says at last. "Don't let it be for nothing, asshole."
You turn the bunny in your fingers a few times, then connect the flash port to your reflex link, just up from your left wrist. Your retina console only shows one line of text 'Hello World.'
"There's nothing on here, Case."
"Gods above you are new. Expand the markup on that line."
"Shit, it's over four terrabytes of data."
"Yeah. Like I said. All the shit. Get your damn answers. They have proven relatively expensive."

It's all here, and it all comes down to a simple choice. The trace tags on this data make you hesitate. They're clearly watching every damn move. Two files stand out from all the junk: Matsushita Hideki and Iko. One blink of your left eye and you can open either can of worms. You hear the heart monitor beeping in the other room. Greta is barely alive. Case looks like shit. You've got three or four bullet holes in you.
No easy buckets on this data, and you've got a bad feeling hell has only started to unleash. Time to do a little lite speed reading.

If you access the file on Matsushita Hideki, turn to PAGE 178.

If you access the file on Iko, turn to PAGE 176.

Earth's digital world, left behind by offworlders and the crashing wave of corp greed, has had strange effects on those at the bottom. It's been a rough century for the have-nots. Some of the worst affected are the wanderers... nomads with fluid identities, lost in space and in memory... stacks without bodies, stacks trapped in vending machines, skins without minds who never die. Strange days indeed.

Between decking the creep and reaching The Farm, whatever that is, you encounter one of these poor souls. Your bike's coil just needs a cool off, heading across the expanse, so you lean it over and light a cigarette. Storm clouds gather to the East, over Jugger territory, but the anvil cloud doesn't quite come together. The wind is warm, the light is pale orange.

"Greetings, program." An eerie, phasing, chorused voice breaks your train of thought. You spin to look. It's a synthetic in loose, ragged robes, leaning on a piece of box iron as a walking stick. It only has one arm, no eyes, and the augments have all gone wrong. The feet have worn to the titanium bones. "Have a spare?"
"Yeah." You hand it a smoke. It plants the walking stick in the hardpan with terrifying strength like a spear. It lights the smoke. Micro torch in one finger.
"Storm coming," it begins after a drag.
"Maybe, yeah."
"What do you think you'll do when you find them?"
"Excuse me?"
"We're all looking for answers, pilgrim. You're armed to the teeth, riding a mag bike alone out here. Heading West to the flying mountain of junk. I doubt you're on a pleasure cruise."
"Right. None of your business, I suppose."
"Isn't it?"
"Excuse me?"
"Isn't it my business? You've got guns and blades, a killer's eyes,

and you're ripping across the expanse at 100 plus. You mean to kill your way to your own truth. That means taking -taking- li- life. Isn't it my business, as a living thing, to stop you? Or at least make sure you're justified."

"Justified? What the f-"

"Don't act so incredulous, runner. Don't you think we've arrived in this hellscape because we didn't make each other our business? Aren't we here, left -left- behind by an age of digital overgrowth and urban infestation, because of lonely pride? I think you've learned less than I have, in all my suffering and lost memory. I'm slag to you, I know, but isn't that why we fell from grace? Why were we left behind by the offworlders? Is it so strange to ask for empathy? For justice?"

"I don't know, stranger. I don't know."

"What if I decided to stop you? To keep you here until you saw what I've seen. Show you the light of transconsciousness? What if you buried your sword in the mud and left your shoes to fate?"

"What if you couldn't?"

"Couldn't?"

"Stop me."

"Well now you've made the conversation interesting." It takes another long drag, looking out with those empty eyes. "You know, I can't remember my name? I've been so many bodies, so many systems, so many objects. The memories are all jumbled up. With all of it lost, though, I've found it curious what things remain."

"I'm sure you'll tell me."

"What has remained is my desire to be among living things. Don't I have a duty to pursue that desire? Isn't the love of life self-evident in its motivation? Even with no self, with nothing left -left-"

"The planet is crawling with life, stranger. Crawling. There are billions of us. You're being melodramatic. It's just a bug. You need some updates."

"So if billions remain, no one life matters? No dozen lives matter? So I must let you go, for no reason but to honor your stoic, selfish

vengeance?"
"I never said it was revenge."
"Everything is revenge."

A long pause then. You both finish your smokes in awkward silence as the anvil rolls across the buttes. It slowly dissipates into dark grey curtains of warm rain.

"So, we're done here. Good travels, stranger."
"Not so fast, runner. I haven't decided yet."
"Decided what?"
"Whether to let you go or not."
"Let-" You look at the wanderer with deadly eyes. It's a wretched, pale-skinned thing, but still. Placid. Early model synthetic, wires everywhere, poncho made from a tank tarp, metal cheekbones.
"Yes, let. Thank you for the cigarette."
"No problem."

"I took the train from Tsuyama in 2046. I saw the moonfall a century later. I watched the armies burn in 2245. I boiled rice in 2300. What have you done with your blades and your bullets? I may seem like some kind of wreckage to you, but I have known wonders you cannot imagine."
"Does that give you the gavel to drop on whoever gives you a smoke? I just don't follow."

"I face my judgements openly. I face the confusion with a bright heart, lost and serene in the infinity. This is my humility."
"Nonsense. I'm leaving. Don't make a move."
"Why do the birds fly off when you approach?"
"Huh?"
"Your heart is filled with rage. Two minds fighting for control, neither really living. I hope you find serenity before any more lives are lost -lost."

"Get that voice module looked at, it's all glitched."
"What in me makes you uncomfortable is only that you already know, and dread to recall."
"So long, nomad."

Back on the bike. Back on the road. The wanderer disappears in your mirror. Something in that voice was too familiar. Can't be. Just a glitch.

Turn to PAGE 108.

VOICE IN YOUR HEAD

The storm never gains enough momentum to do much more than make the cluster of buildings ahead more ominous. You've got your bike on high ground a few clicks out from the outer wall. You never spent the cred for advanced optics, and don't use more than reflex sights on firearms. Retina zoom goes to 5x only. Synthetics walk along the top of the wall, some armed with matte black ACR20's, others just packing sidearms. They're grim characters, faces obscured in hoods or breathers. Inside, a cluster of white buildings is scattered, but awkwardly wired with huge tubes and black cable. Hard to see much more from here, then you feel it... a hunch at first, just a shiver or a glitch in a reflex link? No, a hum, a sort of whine in your ears. You squint it away, stay focused. The Farm has a large front gate, small gravel road. Not a lot of armament anywhere, maybe you could just-

Again, the hum hits you, this time harder. Then you drop behind your bike, eyes darting. It's a voice. Not on comms, not on the air, in your head. Every word sends static down your spine. The base of your skull aches, and the voice takes shape.

"Walk away, runner. Your answers aren't here."

You've heard of 'pushers,' psychics used to mess with people's minds. They have one in there? Are you spotted?

"Get out of my head."

"Get out of mine. Back on the bike. You're not ready for what's in there... not without me."

"Just a glitch. Hearing things..." You reach into one glove pocket, fumbling for a surge capsule. There's three in there somewhere, but your hands are shaking.

"I'm losing this link. He's called Drakan. A true master. He's just using you! You're walking right into a trap!"

The voice cuts out, or disappears, at last. You find the surge capsule, think twice, and save it for life or death. If that was real, you're in over your head. If it was a glitch, you're in real need of some wetwork. More questions.

You risk one more look. No transponders. Case gave you a synthetic signature cloak program years ago. Could conceal all your augments, you'd blend right in with the sentries on most scans. Trojan horse style, ask to see the boss.

Then again, you could take the direct approach. The creep tracks here, no telling what kind of murder cult they have in there, or why they want to tangle with you, with everyone in Halsey's Rest. A few bullets might relieve the ache in your brain, and the feeling you're being hunted.

If you walk up to the front gate, cloaked as a synth, turn to PAGE 68.

If you go in guns blazing, ask questions later, turn to PAGE 74.

Athena is simply too amazing to refuse. Nothing wrong with a little companionship. You reach up from the booth and take her hand gently. Her touch is electrifying. Jenna reaches up too, entranced by Athena, entirely forgetting the dish of pills. As the 'mourners' lose themselves in love and sweet release, drinking Henson's place dry in his honor, the three of you retire to the back lounge for some peace. You flop down on a curved couch in dim blue light together. You can feel your usual self becoming impatient, but Jenna and Athena provide a welcome distraction.

"You need to relax, Grim. So tense."
"Stop blaming yourself," Jenna adds.
"It's not blame when it's a simple fact. It's just causality. I've been hiding long enough. No one is safe around me anymore."
"I don't like safe" Athena adds, nuzzling up against you softly, slinking like a jaguar. Jenna is still feeling the music, and returns to her dancing, smiling at you.
"How can I relax when the bastards that killed the old man are out there? Why should I? There's work to be done, and I'm the one to do it."
"Suit yourself." Athena stands and joins Jenna. They dance and intertwine, tangling with lovely intoxication. You're satisfied watching, sipping on mash with smoldering eyes.

Soon enough, both of them flop into the couch with you, one on each side. You remain silent, they start talking, clearly ensorceled by each other. Athena thinks, then open up.
"Grim is right, you know. Shinru assholes should pay for this."
"Dig two graves, girl. Blood for blood? It never works out that way."
"What if I told you I know a way into their ops base outside the perimeter? A smart runner could get in, find a few throats to slit. Send 'em a message."
"How do you know all this?"
"I'm not just a dancer, you know. Me and Henson go way back."

Athena sits up, takes a drink, gets serious, still swaying. "I used to mule launch codes in the riot days. They declassified my stack in the 20's. The codes went obsolete, but most of my memories were cleared."

"Holy shit,"

"Me and the officers used to use an access tunnel beneath the airstrip. The entrance is outside the perimeter. Like I said... A smart runner could do it."

"It's suicide!"

"Not so much. When the gunships are coming in, the exit is completely concealed by jet wash. It's a short hop to the comms shack from there. Piece of cake."

"Huh?"

"Old saying. I'd love to see the looks on their faces..."

"Why don't you go 'slit a few throats' then?"

"Slag implant. I go meltdown within two miles of the base. Their little insurance policy on my release."

Jenna notices that you have been paying very close attention. "Grim, no."

"What officers?" You lean forward, drink empty. Jenna rolls her eyes and returns to her glass.

"Well, I wasn't exactly taking names. A few stood out, some of the heavy gear pilots, a few EXO's, and one real beauty named Iko. I'll never forget her."

"Iko?"

"Yeah, a real wildcat. Japanese, built like a tank, big brown eyes. She was a client for years, even after I was decommissioned. Hell, I think I still have her comm ID."

A murderous creep, a gunship out of nowhere, rumors about Iko hunting you down, and now a way in all in two days time? Things are escalating way too fast. If anyone knows what is really going on, it would be your old partner, even if she is trying to kill you.

"Grim, I thought I heard Iko was on your contract. Don't."

"I loved her, Jenna. I might still love her, I don't know. Something just isn't adding up."
"You know, you don't have to be killed to find love in this world."
"Jenna, I-"
"Yeah I get it. Forget I said anything." She stands and walks out to the bar.
"You fucked that up," Athena jabs.
"Give me the schematics."

If you access the Shinru ops base, turn to PAGE 115.

If you contact Iko, turn to PAGE 118.

One last hurrah before it all goes to hell. You grab a Limit pill and knock it back with a gulp of beer. The toasts continue, the tears flow, the hugs, the kisses, the stories. Henson would be proud. An animated argument and a knife-throwing contest determine that the bar will be changed to 'The Wooden Pickle.' A new sign is being sketched on a napkin, dusk arrives, and the trip of Limit takes a psychedelic turn.

You welcome a tune out. It's pretty rare you let yourself relax a bit. Old runner's instincts. You close your eyes and hear the music, like neon liquid, sliding over the bar. Fading laughter cascades over crystal shapes behind your eyelids. A sip of whiskey is like swallowing a star. The sky expands upward, the ceiling disappears, a folding infinity of dimensions reveals itself in kaleidoscopic detail. Shinru and Ishuga, the junk city, are just twinkling lights in your God's eye. You see all the Earth as a sphere of life and water and steel, and all the stars as a turning mote of luminous iridescence. You are Grim, you are Matsushita, you are Henson, you are the glowing-hot shell cases from the gunship, you are the uncaring sun itself as your consciousness expands, not in delusion, but in truth. This is the wonder of Limit... it reveals reality, rather than obscuring it. A psychic drug, a gateway to everything.

Then you begin to focus, to narrow the spectra. On Earth, you see a glowing soul, a light, one you've always been drawn too- a part of- standing out from the sea of living things. It's Iko. You can see her, see right through her, even from the stratosphere you see her as if you were standing in front of her. You can feel love, lost love, anger, desire, fear. You can feel her heart beating. Then you realize you see even more. She's stripping an MP8 on her lap, sitting in a barracks in a Shinru base. You know every detail, every door, every hidden camera, every pebble, every nail in every wall. Her boots are unlaced. Tinny old blues play on a speaker nearby as she works. Gods, she's lovely there in the psychosphere. She's so close you could touch her.

Your astral self is drawn upward, though. Some great cosmic glow is above you, showering down, turning like a titanic machine of light. You look, and there is a wonder so far beyond one human being you are melted in its presence. It is the collective knowledge of all living things, the sun of sentience, a tesseract pyramid of information and emotion. A matmos, a formless all-mind. It beckons you, containing future and past alike, the sum of all and the freedom of nothing. It calls to you like coming home. Every answer to every question there whirling, every physical location at your fingertips.

You are weightless, omniscient, content. The strangeness of it all eases, and your will begins to return. Your self congeals once more. Your fate is your own, your choices your own. Limit doesn't simply let you see the psychosphere... observe anything or anywhere... it lets you project, transport, rematerialize as anything, anywhere. Matter within mind. The energy link between every atom. Still, with all that, Iko calls, your old familiar form can take shape anywhere on the planet. What will you do with this boundless new freedom?

If you follow the visions of Iko, turn to PAGE 118.

If you access the deeper psychic matmos for answers, turn to PAGE 152.

The gunships all touch down at Ops Base 5, in formation. Just as many spin their engines and liftoff on a nearby airstrip. They're busy. Shinru command hunting down all its ugly loose ends with bullets. You find yourself, boots on pavement, tumbling into a hidden position. It was no easy thing getting this far, and you're sharp as a razor moving toward the airstrip. A hidden hatchway presents itself, and you slip beneath the tarmac without sound. You're well-armed, with that killer look you get at game time. Through the hidden shaft you skulk, looking, digitally, for any backdoors on base data you can find. It's answers on Henson's death or the whole place burns. Answers on Iko's involvement or you blow it all to hell. These murderers are about to get a taste of what Matsushita Hideki can do. Half the problems on this whole left-behind world are their doing. Payback time.

Before those thoughts can even pass, four EXO commandos appear around a corner ahead. You're either detected, or they just have terrible luck.

"Intruder contact!" They lurch forward, two dropping to a knee so all four can fire. The rear left, apparently their CO, slams a panel out of sight, activating a set of security door lights. You have a few seconds. The MAC12 comes to life before any of them can pull a trigger. A wide, fanning spray of fire shreds the corridor from one side to the other, the suppressor humming. You're dashing forward as the bullets fly. The mag is empty in one trigger pull, and you're face to face with them. In these tight quarters, you can barely draw the nodachi. The split second it costs you gives them their opening, and they fire. MP8's are brutal at this range. You're all but knocked off your feet as the rounds hit your nanofiber outer. One gets through, stinging like hell. Then, the massive sword is in action, scraping the ceiling as the blade renders to life. Up it draws, then down it slashes, cutting one MP8 in half, sending an arm flying, and severing a cluster of power cables all in one cut.

The EXO's try to fall back. They reload, they struggle, they fire, they yell, and they die. The nodachi sparks with green static as its all over in a few heartbeats. The security door, a massive affair, thuds shut behind you. One bloody comms unit crackles 'Unit 3, Unit 3, backup in route, secure target alive, repeat alive. Apprehend, do not kill.'
"That's encouraging."

Again you scan for pings on Iko or any kind of data depot, mainframe room or records bunker. These structures are all shielded concrete, magnetic rebar, a real mess for signal. Plan B? Leap from room to room and kill your way to the guy who gave the order on Henson's bar. And that's exactly what you do.

Runners develop a sense of dilated time in a bloody mess. The details are a blur, a sort of hyper slow motion. Makes no sense unless you've been there: amped on surge caps, ripping and spinning your way through it all.

When the dust clears, a heavy silence greets your pounding ears. You catch a breath, sheathe the blade. The MAC12 is slagged. Toss it. You salvage some kind of beam weapon from an EXO, sling it, blink twice for another scan. Finally, a few blips. You must be above ground. One is an ID tag you've seen all too many times. It's Iko, but her blip isn't moving. Why waste all these EXO's on you when she could subdue or kill you in a few moves? Two more pings pop up: a mainframe room and a fuel depot out by the main helipad. You've got nav on all three. At least twenty more EXO's on site, but clustered in a circular structure near the barracks. Near deadly little Iko. Too many options, precious seconds slipping away.

Why the hesitation? Your bloody cough grabs your attention. You've been hit with half a dozen slugs, a few sword cuts.
Twenty more EXO's could be lethal, much less if they activate your

old flame. Make the wrong choice, take the big sleep.

If you rig the fuel depot to blow the whole place, turn to PAGE 137.

If you set the mission aside, and risk it all to contact Iko, turn to PAGE 118.

"Iko! It's Grim. Your comm is all jumbled up. No more cat and mouse. Iko?" No response, but her comms are linked, signal clear. She's not the silent type, what gives?
You're in, you're on the move. The Shinru Ops base is unfamiliar, but all bases are a bit the same when locked on a target. Move, check, kill, check, move. You're close now, and twenty heat signatures clutter your next check. A troop of EXO's all huddled around another figure. They're not with Iko, though, she's still and alone in a barracks room, sitting. Is it possible they haven't zeroed you yet? You're either that good or they're occupied with something else. Doesn't matter. Stay on target. You dart left, around a huge conductor relay the size of a bus. Through the rear door of the barracks you slink, and there she is. Iko.

After all this time, she still takes your breath. You're stunned. She's in combat gear, nanocarbon tights, no visible augments, her jet black hair surrounds her face. She's frozen, looking down at a partially assembled MP8 on her lap. You've risked it all for this conversation.
"Iko?" No response. "Iko? What is all this? There's no way you're working for these guys. Hey!"
"She can't hear you, runner." It's Iko's lips moving, but a male voice. A wrong voice. "Lay down your weapons, and I assure you, no harm will come to you."
"I know your orders, asshole. Apprehend, don't kill. I'm not 'laying down' shit."
"I need only apprehend your stack, insect. We'll happily oblige a violent resolution here if that's your wish."
"Let her go. Your mercs are no match for me and you know it."
"The EXO's serve their duty, no need for derision. Agent 14, can you finish your work and join us, please?"
With that, Iko comes to life. She clacks the breach into place, clears the pin, and slams the assembly down. She spins the gun to one side, racks it twice, and clicks in a fresh magazine. Calmly, mechan-

ically, she sets the weapon down next to her, stands, and draws a short wakizashi from her belt. Then the worst part. Her head slowly raises, her hair parts, and she makes eye contact with you. Those dark, deadly eyes... distant, hollow, lost in there somewhere.
"Ready for action," she mutters in her own voice.
"This is your last chance, whoever you are, release her, and I might let you live when this is over." Nothing, a pause.
"Orders received," Iko says cryptically. She spins toward you, into a ready stance, blade in reverse grip. "Nothing personal Grim." With that, she springs, sliding forward with superhuman speed. Your shock costs you the only split second you had and the blade meets in mark, splitting your armor and drawing blood. Even at your best, you're barely her match.
"Iko, snap out of it!"
No luck. You bat the knife aside with one hand, twirling around her. She blocks your back-spinning sweep kick with one foot, then does a hop-switch and rocks your skull with the other. Across the floor you clatter, spitting out a tooth. The beam weapon is clumsy on its sling, but no time. You draw your Nemesis gun. Before you can raise it, Iko is inches away, somehow, slamming down from above. You see her beautiful lips before the knife sinks in again. This time you've baited her. A tap on your belt loop and the nanocarbon slams tighter, gripping the blade like a vice. It hurts like hell, but you fall back to disarm her. Then comes a series of punches and throat jabs. Gods and demons, she's fast. You exchange arm locks, deflections, foot sweeps. She's just quicker than you, and fresh.

At last she lands a powerful palm on your sternum, drilling you backward and sending blood spraying. Not many runners could survive that hit, you barely do, but you keep breathing. She's hit you so far back, you have a few beats.
"Bad move, partner."
Up comes the beam weapon. It's a long, heavy, blocky thing with conductive rails. The charge light stacks bottom to top in a blip. You

have Iko in your sights, and she knows it. Her eyes widen. Then you brace, and adjust over her left shoulder. The trigger is light as air.

The beam starts as a high pitched whine, then a thumping anti-sound. A tiny supernova of white plasma forms at the muzzle. It tightens, sparks, and with a piercing boom emits an inch-thick ray of energy. Through the far wall it cuts into the adjoining room. The weight of the gun is too much for your broken ribs, so you slump to one side, sending the beam wheeling. It blips out of existence, the charge light goes dark. There's a moment of hushed surprise, sizzling sounds, Iko holds her breath and looks behind her. You flip on your thermal optics. In the far room, the crowd of EXO's, most of them sliced in half, slump into a pile. The figure at center, no doubt a psychic 'pusher' has no head.

Iko shakes her head, clears the fog, and her lovely brown eyes are there again. Hers again.
"Grim!" She runs over, pops a redi-foam and jams it in your jacket. The blood stops, but redi-foam doesn't mend busted ribs. Her hug feels like a gunshot.
"Ow."
"Talk later, we need to move."
"Same old Iko."

With Iko's help, you make it back to the airstrip. She knows her way around. The procession of gunships continues, and she has that look in her eye. The look that kept you both alive back in the running days, the look that made you love her, the look they took from her. As the exit hisses open, the roar of a gunship blasts you both with night air.

She hesitates, lowers her head. You know what that means.

"You've got a plan."

“A confession.” She turns. “I was part of Silver Burn, Grim. Ona Dai Sen is putting some serious firepower into getting you in a cage. Something about Matsushita Hideki, but he’s been dead for years. They pushed me. Pushed me to join the op. I’ve done bad things, Grim. Terrible things.”

“I keep hearing that name.”

“One of their top runners from back in the day. They’re looking for him, and you’re target numero uno. They’re getting ready for a big op, too, something called ‘heavy gear.’ Mass destruction shit, they’re going to start leveling towns to force you in.”

“I’m Matsushita.”

“What?”

“Well, I mean- he’s part of me, I think, somehow. I don’t know, maybe they hid him in my stack.”

“It doesn’t work that way.”

“Yeah, that’s what I thought. Look, you know these bastards. I mean, we’re talking about going up against Shinru Command, and Ona Dai Sen? We need an ace.”

“Shinru Command HQ isn’t more than 70 kliks from here. Hidden base in the junk fields. That’s where they’re fuelling up ‘heavy gear.’ A few good runners could get in, get a virus onboard, maybe even expose their systems. There’s no turning back for me, Grim... they- they have new ways of getting in your head. These pushers- they- they-”

You pull her out of a downward spiral of memories. Bad ones.

“There’s no going back for me, either. Henson’s dead. We don’t do this, the whole rim will burn. You remember the shakedowns a few years back? It was a massacre.”

“Grim, I-”

“No more confessions. That wasn’t you.”

“We’ll need explosives. I have a contact out by the old radio dish. I could load up on enough C4 to send a message, meet you at the fields. Here are the hangar coords.”

“Or we could go together, just like old times.”

She checks her gear, watches another gunship coming in for a landing, then looks back at you with those eyes. She leans forward, smiles, and kisses you. It's a kiss loaded with hidden meanings, could-haves and should-haves, apologies and big plans, a kiss a decade in the making. She leans back. "Your call, runner."

If you go with Iko to take down Shinru HQ together, side by side, turn to PAGE 123.

If you part ways, so Iko can retrieve the C4, turn to PAGE 164.

"Just like old times."

The two of you stick together, tearing across the wasteland on your bike, covering 70 clicks in minutes. Iko's comms are a jumble of alerts and all-hands calls from Shinru Command. They're scared, panicked, rallying everything to protect 'heavy gear.'

"Right over there. There's a decommissioned hangar bay that's lightly guarded. We slip in, make our way to the deployment bays, and take it from there."

"We need some heavy firepower, unless you plan to take on a heavy walker with that wakizashi."

"The armory then."

"On your six."

Then, the blur again, but this time something's different. You can feel an otherness in your actions, in your sword, in your aim. On a few corners you even surprise Iko with your speed. You rebound off walls, slice through ACR20 barrels with the nodachi, arm lock and flip a fully armored commando off a loading gantry, even alley-oop your partner up and over a barricade while kicking a sentry in the chest. You're good, but not this good.

"Been practicing? Those ribs aren't slowing you down much!"

"It's just flowing."

"Down!"

She drops, and a three pack of shells whizz by as you dodge left. It's sniper fire. Some damn lunatic is firing a supersonic rifle in the long motorpool corridor near the armory. The boom is ear-shattering.

"We need some cover!"

Iko slides to one side, reeling out a decking umbilical from one wrist. The jack magnetizes to the wall and lights up with a pink ring. Her eyes flutter a bit, then the lights drop, red backups come on and the fire sprinklers fire. You're soaking wet in seconds, and give her a look... 'seriously?'

Three more rounds slam into the back security door. The noise is deafening.

"Ok, let's go!" Both of you charge forward. The shooter is reloading. With all your newfound skill, Iko can still outsprint you. She's flying downward on the sniper with her knife in reverse grip before you're there. The EXO sniper parries with his weapon, which is all but severed in two, then on you come with the huge, neon-bladed nodachi. The four foot blade ends him, gliding right through the armor shell as Iko slides to a stop.

"Not bad."

Next, the armory. Racks of weapons behind impact glass a foot thick. Iko sets to work on the door panel, shaking the water out of her hair. The backup lights are still glowing red, but the sprinklers have petered out. You blast back a unit of shocktroopers while she works, and you're in.

If the shit ever hits the fan on all these bodies, you'll both be cold-slagged in sense-stasis for five centuries.

"Just grab two of everything."

"Way ahead of you, but no c4. No gel cord, either."

"The explosives are kept in a hard room three levels down."

"Next stop then."

A frag grenade rolls in from the corridor. The whole room is blown apart in a heartbeat. As the smoke clears, you're near the main door, facing down a team of green-eyed mecha troops. Behind them, a kid in goggles holds up a cybernetic arm, moving her mouth but out of earshot. You feel a splitting pain in your head.

"Grim!" It's Iko, her voice from far below. She's fallen through the blasted floor, landed safely in the rubble. "Run! Don't let them push you! There's no time, head up the main hall to the deployment bay! I'll meet you there with the c4!"

Another hail of fire rips the room apart. Your mind begins to fray at the edges. Something is clawing its way in.
“We stick together!”
“We stick together, we die! Go! I’ll meet you there! Run!”

If you risk being ‘pushed’ to stay together, turn to PAGE 142.

If you risk splitting up to plant the explosives, turn to PAGE 164.

OUT OF TIME

A deep breath in, and a slow breath out. One wing sheds a few panels of steel. The fuselage groans and screams behind you. No matter. Calm. You extend your wrist-cable to the computer core in the cockpit. It's cased in ribbed steel, but penetrable by a micro-remote. The system folders cloud your retina console, but you're no amateur. You ignore the countless alerts and control protocols. You're data mining.

A comms record looks promising, packed with three terabytes of data. That much data can take a few minutes to process.

"Pilot computer: give me time to impact given current course."

"Barring repairs or corrections, 142 seconds."

"Execute corrections. Recalculate."

"216 seconds."

"Give me a countdown display, visual only. Big numbers."

You close your eyes, hands together. The comms record data pours over you. It will take at least two minutes to parse it all. The seconds pass like ice ages. Junk data, landing clearance, weather garbage. Then you notice it, a few seconds behind the download. A mention of 'Silver Burn.' You halt the stream, zero in, open the search connections. Jackpot.

68 seconds.

The file reveals all the basics. A failed coup called Silver Shard, then a murderous aftermath op called Silver Burn. Worst of all, Shinru command is using psychic pushers to use anyone and everyone to expose the key players. Top line: Iko. Your own damn partner made into a puppet to hunt you down. Only loose end, a triad of ghosts called the three dragons. Big players, virtual and actual. Billions of creds trading hands before the big offworld movement, before the riots. The shit storm that set you up against the Iga. Even they are pawns in this, and you have the data. Only one odd bit: Matsushita Hideki.

47 seconds. The engine noise is unbearable. Stay focused.

Silver Burn is headquartered at the Shinru ops base dead ahead.

Psychic training, runner reprogramming, and something called heavy gear, all held in this facility. Plane like this, kamikaze mode, you could level the whole place. There's that crazy side trying to do the thinking again. Nobody rams a 40 ton cargo plane into a military base. Somehow that makes you crack a little smile.

You run a search on Hideki. A few precious seconds pass. Only a few results. The oil lines catch fire. A hit. Operation 'cold fridge.' Pictures of you come up. Then Hideki's files. Looks like Hideki was one of the key players in the coup attempt. A real master. Working for Ona Dai Sen, assigned to a suicide mission for the three dragons, backed up in a trojan horse stack. That stack is you.

23 seconds. The tail section goes rigid. A terrible howl of bending metal rings through the aircraft. Out of time. You yank the umbilical. The ground is in sight now, lights on the horizon. The ops base is dead ahead, but the wide open wasteland is visible, dark and pale blue, to the North. Maybe one hard turn could-
Before you finish the thought, one wing pops a dozen bolts and rivets. Hydraulic fluid sprays like ink on the cockpit windshield.
12 seconds. You don't have a chute yet. Are there chutes on this thing? Jumping would be- Nope. Not an option.
"Pilot com- SHIT! Pilot computer: can we make the wastelands?"
"Data unavailable."

You grab the yoke, cranking with your legs against the tremors and jolts. Time's up.

If you set the controls to destroy the base, turn to PAGE 137.

If you attempt a landing in the wastelands, turn to PAGE 128.

"No kamikaze tonight. I'm landing this monster."
"Data not available."
"I wasn't talking to you!"
"Data not-" You lift one boot and smash the computer core. More flashing lights. All just distractions. A true master makes a choice with every ounce of life. No hesitation. No defeat. You're landing this heap in the desert. Negotiations are over.

Boom! Something goes to shit as you pull the yoke hard to the left. The rudder pedals are shaking like crazy, but you push into the seat, realizing the five-point belt could be a good idea.
"Come on!"
The plane answers, defying it's thousand wounds and powering into a tumbling turn. The buttes spin sideways, stars in one window and rocks in the other. Your knuckles strain and pop on the controls. She's fighting, but she can do it.
"Deploy fire suppression, shit!"
"Fire suppression deployed." Nothing happens.
Then you see it: the desert floor, revealed 'tween two buttes ahead, and way closer than you thought.
"Ground proximity alert. Pull up."
"I know! I know!"
"Ground-"
"Shut up!"

3 seconds.

Exactly what happens next is hard to put into words or memory. A storm of fire and metal, of shattering impact and spinning everything. It all crumples and slides and burns like a bomb. Then, silence.

Darkness blinking, light returning, a smell of burning rubber and sparks. You can't tell how long you were out. Could be seconds, could be hours.

"Hey! Hey in there! Anyone alive in there?"
"Get back!" Your voice answers without your consent.
"That's one hell of a piece of hardware to plant in the sand!"
"Get the f-" Yelling hurts more than it should, you finally inhale.
"We'll share the salvage! Come on out, no bullets, no blades. A Reasonable deal."
"I said get back! I've got twenty guns on this boat!"
"And two thumbs to handle 'em? C'mon, runner, don't be a fool. You're surrounded with juggers, good, fair salvagers all."
"Who am I talking to?" Your voice isn't as strong as you need it to be, but you're upright again. Up the fuselage you scamper, to the main guns. Four big chainguns, two per side.
"This here's Skar! I run this outfit! You got a lot of bullets on you, stranger. We can do this easy, or we can do this real easy."

The plane is surrounded by juggers. Wastelanders. Scavengers. Junkers. Not good. They strip, refit and fence every scrap of metal from here to the North Pole. Looks like you just landed their next whale. A quick peek on thermals reveals at least 30 of them closing.
"Listen, Skar, don't do this. I'm on some mission-from-God vengeance shit right now, and I'm not in a mood to be fucked with. This hardware is bound for Shinru ops. I won't have you and your knuckleheads in my way. No deal."
"You hear that, girls? Runner's on a mission."

For a jugger, or anyone in this left-behind world, this plane was a gold mine. A dozen dead commandos in full gear, brimming weapon racks, munitions, computer gear, flight recorder, and all the intel anyone could want to run a perfectly reasonable extortion con on Shinru command. It might take more than harsh words to be rid of these bottom-feeders.

"You walk away, Shinru command will pay. Don't you want that, Skar?"

"What the fuck do I care about the commies? Shinru is run by cash and crap, runner! I ain't diggin' two graves! Not today."

"Look, I'm a friend of Biggs. Let's leave bullets out of this."

"Biggs is a weakling, got his brains all scrambled up by that vending machine. Psycho, he is. You a psycho, runner?"

He's stalling. They're probably moving in, getting closer, tightening the noose. The plane is worth more than your life.

"Nah, just a runner like you, trying to stick it to the man. Stick it to the SISTM! We aren't enemies, Skar! Just get your people back, or you'll force me on this."

"Force you? Jugger, you's already painted in one hell of a corner, ain't that right, boys?" A wild cheer, a whooping, the sound of hyenas closing on carrion. "Tell you what, stranger. You let us gut this bird, we'll get her airborne and you can bomb her into whatever the fuck you want, savvy?"

At that moment, as you consider Skar's offer, flickering monitors show a few dozen juggers sneaking up on the flanks of the aircraft. They're all in gun range. You crack your neck. Time for another tough call.

If you accept and let the juggers strip the plane, turn to PAGE 131.

If you fight off the scavengers with hellfire, turn to PAGE 139.

"Alright, alright, call off your dogs."
"Good move, runner."

The Juggers move in, slinging their guns, but looking greedy. A few roll up with big flatbed carts and wheelbarrows. You grab your gear and walk outside, still in one piece.
"No hard feelings, runner. Grab a few goodies, plenty for everyone 'ere."
"I've got what I need. Have fun with your new toys."
You turn to walk off, feeling forced on the whole mess, pissed off. Something about that hits Skar the wrong way, and he hollers after you.
"Hey. Not so fast." You turn, impatient. Annoyed.
"What?"
"I know you! You's Grim, that cat from Halsey's. Folk say of how you been slashin' your way to a decent living over there. One o' Henson's buddies, I hear. Tell him hi, eh?"
"Henson's dead." You turn again, trying to leave.
"The fuck you say?"
"I said Henson's dead. You never saw me, asshole."
Skar runs up behind you suddenly, you spin and pull your MAC12. The suppressor stops him, stuffing into his chest.
"Ol' Henson? Kicked the bucket, eh?"
"Murdered."
"The fuck you say. When? How?"
"Few nights back. Surgical strike. Gunship. Two hundred hot rounds. He never had a chance."
"And you, fuckin' psycho, grappled on the gunship what killed 'im, landed here with old Skar's boys."
"Something like that."
"Jaysus."
"Like I said, stick it to 'em. We done here?"
"Not even close, runner. We's comin' with you."
"Thanks, but no thanks. I work alone."

"'Course you do, and we's comin' with you."

Then, thirty juggers in tow, all on mag bikes and junkers, you storm Shinru Ops. Not really your style, but this isn't some corporate espionage run, this is blood for blood. Send a message. Make 'em pay and disappear. Big show.

"There's a fuel depot on the far side of the airstrip. We hit that, make the big boom, then mop up the mess."
"That's your plan?" Skar is wild-eyed. He's been waiting for an excuse to do something big for years, and it shows. Not good for business, or for surviving the night. Dig two graves? More like 32.
"That's me best!" He presses faster, speeding toward the fenced perimeter like a wild man.
"Spare a bike? I've got my own kill list to cross off."
"Trail mini on the back bumper. All yours!"
"What am I supposed to do with-" before you finish, the buggy lurches and bounces on a rut, crossing the access road and turning hard into the fences. Skar jams the throttle, leading the convoy, grinning ear to ear.
"All right, boys, let's remind these buggers about The Clash!"
Then, over a crackling radio, "Fuckin' A, boss!"

The blast of audio that follows shatters your skull. 'Rock the Casbah' blares from every vehicle by some means or another. It's a cacophony of total madness as the vehicles all smash the fences in a shower of sparks and claymore mines.
"EMP jammers! As long as you hear the sweet, sweet sound, they comms is junk'd!"
"What?"
"Take the monkey bike and bugger off!"
That you understand, barely, over the noise. You crawl back, flip a ratchet strap, and tumble off the buggy, trail bike right behind you in a cloud of dust. The rest of the convoy screams past, every last

one of them racking modded uzi's and howling like apes.

Juggers.

As the cloud clears, and their 'jammer' fades a bit, you get the bike on its wheels and size it all up. The juggers have a tanker truck rolling straight for the airstrip. Lunatics. The rest begin to break off, firing wildly, ramming through jersey barriers, and exploding in clouds of command swarm missiles. Klaxons sound, but they're drowned out by The Clash.

Cyborg troopers dash every direction, tracer fire lights up the night. You slam your throttle, topping out at a cool 30 mph on the base tarmac. The jammer works on your tech too, so you're going in blind. You head for a taller structure with armored windows. Command tower. It takes forever to get there, but your goofy bike must make you hard to spot. The action stays over by the airstrip, where a landing gunship melts a few jugger buggies with chaingun fire.

You're in. The sentries are clueless EXO mercs. You give them the sword, three at a time. Pop a surge capsule, blast through more of them, spin, kick in a door, zip up a shaft, slide, slash, shoot. Finally you're at the command bullpen, ringed in angled windows and glowing monitors. A few dozen science types freeze in terror as you break in. You drop to a knee, revealing a brick of C7. It's a five pounder, enough to level the place.

"Anyone who wants to live, out!" The controllers and air traffic analysts panic and scramble, taking a number of exits to empty the huge space in seconds. One figure remains motionless at the front, back to you. A glance out the window reveals the juggers, numbers dwindling, about to ram the fuel dump. "This whole place is about to burn. Last chance, merc."
"Classic Grim," comes a voice. "Predictable. Expensive, but predict-

able."

You know that voice. Smooth Japanese accent, cool and slow. You know that damn voice all too well. She turns, slowly, with bravado, back-lit into a silhouette with curves you know almost as good as the voice.

It's Iko.

"Iko, what-"

"Sorry about Henson. Deadlines."

"You-"

"Yes, my idea. You're a bit slippery out there in the farms, Grim. I needed to bring you in. What better way?"

"We were partners. Hell, we were a lot more than that. What happened to you, Iko?"

"I woke up. The truth isn't in the sand, so get your head out of it."

"The truth? You're a stone cold killer, working for command? Those assholes killed your whole family! Or did you forget that too?"

"How long?"

"Huh?"

"On the C7. You running a detonator or just planning to light it with a match?"

"Right here." You lift the red-button thumb remote. She nods. Her jet black hair conceals her eyes, but her lips are soft as ever, her neck as lean, her hips as amazing. She's wearing a skin tight nano-carbon skin strapped with an arsenal of knives and machine pistols. She takes a few steps toward you smiling. You need to see those eyes. "One click and we both go back to the maker."

"You won't do that, Grim. Not the type."

"Bullshit. I'm tired of running."

"You... have... no idea..." with that, she hesitates, almost stumbles. When she recovers, taking another step up the aisle of computer gear, her eyes shine between locks of hair. They're blank, empty, crude oil.

"You're not Iko. Another fucking puppet."

AT that moment, as you reach for your Nodachi, you see a jugger flatbed truck spin out and come careening toward the command tower. When it faces you, a huge PA speaker comes into view, and The Clash blasts your eardrums, even through the ballistic glass. AT that instant, Iko's black eyes clear for a second.
"Iko?"
"Grim?"
"Shit, what's going on?"
"Pushers. I'm so sorry, Grim, so-"
"The fuel depot is about to blow, we have to-"
"The minute that jammer signal fades, they'll push me again. It's too late for me, goldfish."
"Fuck that, come on!" You grab her arm, stumbling forward as she resists. She's twice as strong as you at least, and immovable as bedrock.
"If they push you, it's all for nothing. They'll have Matsushita, and you'll be tossed out with the trash. It's the only reason he went suicidal years ago. The pushers, Grim. You only have a few seconds. You're no match for me, not anymore."
"Pushers, wha-"
"Go!"
"I won't. I've been running for ten shitty years, Iko. Missing you, missing US! Living out on The Rim like a rat! No more running!"

First, the fuel depot explodes. The blast releases a massive mushroom cloud, and the power flickers. Then, a handful of jugger rigs slam into the command tower, and The Clash sputters to silence. Half the base is in flames. You and Iko both tumble to one knee. When you look up, she's meeting your eyes with hers, but the blackness has returned.
"You're too slow, runner." In the flickering light, she reveals the detonator. With a sinister grin she crushes it in her hand like a toy. "Queen takes knight."

SKAR'S DEAL

Clang, clang, clang! Your sword parries a flurry of knife attacks. She's fast as lightning, and you're outmatched. The base is on fire. She presses in again, pistol fire mixed with spins and kicks. You're bleeding in a dozen places as you hit the metal floor with a clatter. So this is it. Killed by your own partner. After all this, she's the one to end you. As she overwhelms you, you can't help but wonder if she can see it all, the real Iko, see it happening through her own eyes. It hurts even more than knowing you're dead already.

She attacks again, snapping your nodachi like a twig in one cybernetic hand, shooting you in the stomach with the other. She stands over you, gloating, eyes like dead space.

"My orders are to take you in alive, or at least an intact stack. You represent a significant investment by the Ona Dai Sen corporation." She moves forward. "Last words, runner?"

"Just one."

She sneers, waiting.

"Checkmate."

In your left hand, blood-slick, the real detonator blinks eagerly. Iko's eyes go wide, and your apologies will have to wait for the afterlife, or whatever comes next. You squeeze the trigger, and it all goes white.

Turn to PAGE 255.

Funny thing about solving problems with explosions, you were never good at the not-getting-blown-up-too part. Fuel tankers, weapon caches, chemical labs and munitions stacks make for easy pickings when it comes to big booms. Not your first rodeo, as they say.

Between all the volatile elements of the ops base, the gunship, the intel, you make short work of it. Only two things you didn't plan for: Iko and Heavy Gear.

The former is your old partner, the runner that saved your life a dozen times, base jumped the Matsuda towers, went up against the Iga and made it out. The best of the best, turned traitor for Shinru command. She's on site, but you only catch the blip as the fireballs begin. A chain reaction of colossal, seismic blasts rocks the base. Maybe she was part of the hit on Henson, maybe it was your fault, maybe you all deserve it. Morality can feel distant in times like these, engulfed in fire.

The latter is the bigger oversight. You've seen the term 'heavy gear' in some the data blocks recently, but codenames that lame don't command much attention. You wrote it off as a new missile, maybe an inevitable EXO armor prototype. As the explosions roll you scramble for an exit. Then, with slow, terrible, titanic shadows, Heavy Gear reveals itself.

Your retina console struggles to evaluate the shape that emerges. It is a huge, two-legged, mechanized horror, part spider, part tank, part demon. Artillery barrels sprout from every surface, huge boxy missile packs are lashed on like cargo, and the legs... the legs are immense, articulated monsters in their own right, smashing the pavement with every three-toed stride, ankles like angular tanks, bending and straining under a few hundred tons of armor and death. If there's a cockpit, it's shielded in armor. Only one halogen floodlight gives it a cycloptic life. Boom, boom, boom. It strides forward, pauses, and swivels to face you.

The elephant has targeted the mouse.

Then, it's all boiling fire. Missiles coil in every direction, swarming. Your instincts kick in, and survival is a forgotten thing. You empty every gun in your kit, pop smoke, slide to one side, gulp a handful of surge, slide again. You're face-to-face with the titan, straining your neck to look up at it, and a strange moment passes. One frag grenade in a yawning barrel shakes the giant, but then a bank of chainguns whine and spin, and combine.

You'll never forget the feeling of being torn to ribbons by chaingun fire. You tell yourself that as the darkness closes in.

You'll never forget.

Turn to PAGE 255.

"Fuck off!"

You grip hard, brace your boots, and pull both triggers. No middle ground, no backing down. Kill or be killed. You choose the former. The chaingun makes an M134 look like a squirt gun. This is a gunship weapon. 20,000 rounds in a motor-fed belt, a thousand per minute, spent tritium cores, bullets as big as your head. You shred the juggers like pinata candy at a birthday party. The roar of it is a deafening thing, the muzzle flash like lightning. On and on and on the hellstorm goes, then to the other side, bring the gun up, pound it. Tracers and death and screams. It's a massacre. Even your grief and your rage and your confusion aren't enough to numb the blood sprays and the cut-in-halves. You release the triggers, breathing hard, deafened, squinting away the white fire of the flash.

The silence that follows is a thing that haunts every soldier. A smoldering, smoking smell of burned flesh. Be a monster to beat a monster. You've decimated them.

You stay there, holding the chaingun for support, shaking, cooling off. You've gone from survivor to slayer in seconds. Hard calls, and you made them. No more backing down, no more taking it. Henson didn't deserve to die, but they do. Nothing will stand in your way. Up, stiffen, recover, and you walk from the cargo bay with effort, out onto the desert floor.

Then you see the rest of them.

"Fucking savage, runner. You gonna die here, you know." It's Skar's voice, out there in the blood-burned smoke. "You chose wrong, bruv!"

Through the gloom, you see them. Where two dozen were, two hundred approach. Green lasers and barrel-mounted boom-lights criss cross in the smoke. They're closing in.

You take a few steps backward, the gun-rage clearing. Back into

the cargo bay. The plane is still yours, maybe the plan. Was it ever a plan?
"That was me mate! That's was Jerry!"
"Jerry got dead?"
"Runner shredd't all them!"
"Jerry!"
With that, your time runs out. The juggers open fire.

Bullets pepper the fuselage of the gunship. The holes stitch from floor to ceiling, walking their guns up like amateurs. They unleash a maelstrom of fire on you, and time is up. Skar's offer suddenly doesn't seem so bad.
There's a lull. You crumple beneath a cockpit bulkhead, armored all to hell. No plan. Then, in the quiet, as a few hundred maniacs reload, a voice.
"Oy! You in there! Give up now and get treated like shit, or be a fuggin' pill and get swis cheesed. Your choice!"
"I've got a fucking Zenith in here, asshole!" You reply.
"Bullshit runner. You got a noose and a warm beer. Enough blood for one night, eh? Take them thumbs off them big guns and come on out. No more ghosts tonight! You stop killin', we stop killin.' Only offer."
"Real trusty, asshole! Why should I walk out and get shot when I can enjoy my beer and kill a few dozen more?"
"Don't be a fool, bruv. You know that's was lucky n' what not. We won'y get jumped again, and you's been dumb enough to kill Jerry."

He might be right. Two dozen, sure. Two hundred, not your style.

"I walk out, head to Biggs' junkyard, no bullshit. The gunship is yours. Enough boom in here to fund your clubhouse for years."
"Hear that, mates? Wants to get some r'n'r at ol' Biggs' place!" There's a mess of howls and jeers and gunshots. Apparently their

opinion of Biggs is a bit lower than yours.
“Guns down. I want a bike.”
“Haps!”
“Boss, no.”
“Haps, get your shit ride over here. Hey runner, got a mag bike for you right here. Pile of shit. All yours, passage to Biggs’ place, no hard feelings. No more bullets, gunship’s us’s... ourses? Usses? Shit you know what I mean.”

As Skar lays down the deal, a cold feeling creeps up your spine. No tac data, a good old fashioned hunch. You walk out, you could be dead as dinner. The gunship is big, good cover. You could run off like a kangaroo rat. It’s a big desert, a good runner could vanish. Junk bikes are all over out here... grab one, head to Biggs’ place...

“Enough bullshit, runner! Come on out or you’s cheese on eggs!”

If you run for it, turn to PAGE 145.

If you take Skar’s offer, turn to PAGE 47.

Into the deployment bay, slide along the bulkhead, slam the lights. You check your gear. 40 rounds in the MAC12, rack it, two frag grenades, one mag in the ACR20, one can of nano-clot. Not good. You see Iko at the far doorway, emerging into a titanic shadow. That shadow pulls your eyes upward, over. A monster meets your eyes there. Heavy Gear.

So this is Shinru's doomsday weapon. Flush out Matsushita with a thousand innocent dead, they said. It's a lumbering, fracture-camo mass of armor plates and artillery. Something between a stealth bomber and an office building. 75 feet at least to shoulders, a few hundred tons of armor and death, unlit, gray and drab in huge angular masses of metal. One gigantic leg moves forward, cracking the concrete with a three-toed foot the size of a tank.

"Grim? These comms working?"
"Yeah, got ya."
"This is fuckin-"
"Heavy Gear, yeah I gathered that."
"Our guns-"
"-Are shit, yeah, got that too. It seems to be waking up."
"You still fast?"
"Hell no! Never was."
"The pushers will be here within a minute. Heavy Gear targets you, you're mist. Heavy Gear gets out of here, The Rim will burn until you submit."
"All very encouraging. Your point?"
"All they want is Matsushita. It's a cloned stack stored in you. Give up, let 'em win?"
"Bad time for jokes."
"Then two options..."

Iko is interrupted when Heavy Gear activates. The thing is titanic, and, if piloted, has no concern for collateral. The hangar is shredded as it unleashes a volley of bullets and missiles. Hellfire engulfs everything. The two of you slide and roll to narrow survival. Then the damn comms.

"You said two options! Spill it, Iko!"
"Swarm or cut."
"Swarm sounds way smarter!"
"See those huge missile packs? They have a- eh, forget it. We can use its missiles against it!"
"And cut?"
"We draw swords, old school, and slash our way to the AI core. This thing is tough, but dumb. Tick mode."
"Tick mode? Seriously?"
"Just improvising."
"Swarm still-"

Then Heavy Gear swivels, and the entire hangar is engulfed in bullets and fire. If EXO's and psychics are showing up, they don't mean shit. It's all boiling death. In the smoke and shadows, Heavy Gear lumbers forward, probing the gloom with a hundred heavy guns.

In the chaos, you see Iko, beautiful, deadly, cybernetic Iko. Gods and devils, her form is lovely in the glow, all hips and nanocarbon, jet hair spinning to one side like an epic poem, eyes like thunder and lips as soft as sirens, knife in one hand and a titanium fist.

She's a deadly goddess in full form, ready to take on a clumsy titan for honor and redemption. Her eyes are clearly on the swarm missile packs.

"Make the call, Grim!"
"What use is a sword against this monster?"
"What use are swords against anything, lover?"
Those words ring with reckless, infinite courage. You flutter.

"So, are we-"
"Make a call, damnit!"

If you let Iko go for the swarm missile pack, turn to PAGE 164.

If you draw blades with her one last time, turn to PAGE 147.

Tracer fire glows behind you, a few small explosions, shouting and gunfire fades as you hustle into the dark of the desert. It's been a long few days, and a longer few nights. With the chaos behind you, time slows down, the adrenaline eases back. The quiet of moonlight is a soothing companion. Time to regroup, take a beat.

Eventually, you come across a layed-down mag bike. It's an old model, XL700, with bright orange tires, one-seater, clip on bars and a triad headlight. Good rig for desert riding, but coated in dust. Juggers must've ditched it, or forgot about it in one of their numerous feuds. Still runs. Runs like shit. You let it idle to charge the battery. Now the entire Rim is open to you. You could go anywhere, be anyone. Hatch and friends are far behind, probably think you're dead. You could go back, make their day, or just disappear again. Wouldn't be the first time. Always been your solution to everything: vanish, reinvent, keep it simple, no attachments.

The cold, sharp stars offer no help. Iko crosses your mind, but she seems distant as an underwater statue. Hatch will probably find you, hell maybe Case will need a favor someday, but it's all thin connective tissue. You're free, a real sword pilgrim. Only one thing distracts your solitude, and it's worth a cigarette.

The smoke drifts lazily in the still night air. For all the falling of the world, all the megacities and all the digital dreams, the smokes have never changed. Reds. Timeless as the planet. Another drag and there she is again: Jenna.

You barely know her. What's with the bleeding heart routine? Maybe she represents an escape from this life. Maybe she's that cottage you never built, the sunrise coffee you never sipped. It's been a wild ride, this life, but you've never slept under a homemade quilt. Maybe she's the one thing a bullet can't reach.

SOFTY

Throw it all out, head back to Halsey's Rest, throw your heart on her porch? It's always all or nothing with you. What if she was never even interested? What if Shinru command is there in force, standing ian fucking crater? You've already brought enough death on everyone who gets close to you, still hankering for more? Questions make the wasteland look good, especially in this light.

The smoke burns down, glowing warm and toasty in the blue. You flick it onto the hardpan, watching it burn down with smoldering patience. When it finally goes dark, something in you changes for good. What future will you choose, runner? Violence has lost its luster, so is it love or nothingness?

If you take the bike into the expanse, leave it all behind, turn to PAGE 149.

If you return to Halsey's Rest to see Jenna, turn to PAGE 85.

"We began this with swords, with steel, and we'll end it that way." You make eye contact with Iko, across the deployment bay, beyond the shadow of the titanic death machine. No more games. They wanted to draw you out? Here you are.
"The old way?"
"No. Our way."

To your side she dashes, there in an instant. Gods, she's fast. Her only blade is a short wakizashi knife. To one foot she sinks, ready to spring.
"If you encounter God..."
"Then God will be cut!"

The two of you, combined, are a blur of confusion for an enemy the scale of Heavy Gear. It spins and lurches, strides and fires, in every direction. The bay is decimated. It goes wild. Two fleas on the back of a giant, you set to slicing rubber cable and steel-clad conduit wherever it can be found. You climb and dart, duck and vanish, drive the sword into armor and let it slide through rubber-coated fibers. Iko is deadlier and faster still, biting and gnawing like a poisonous mosquito on the monster. There is no pilot, no brain to crush, no snake's head to sever. The two of you simply cripple the massive thing, cut by cut.

Your next memory is the wide open salt of the wasteland. Ahead, Shinru Ops crumples and explodes, consumed by fire, and Heavy Gear within, exploding again and again as the heat finds the munitions. It's a peaceful thing to see fire lick the sky.

You savor it with Iko, out in the darkness.

"Everything they had on Silver Burn was in there," she says.
"You know that isn't true."
"Remote backups, blah blah blah. Yeah."

EVERYTHING

"It will never be over."
"What is... ever?"
"In this world? Not sure."
"What about Matsushita?"
"What about him?"
"You know. You know something."
"No." Iko pauses. "I know everything."

A few jammer kits and a thousand miles later, carrying a MAC12 starts to feel silly. Iko holds you tight, blazing along on a mag bike at 170. The wind at that speed is a real bitch, but you both crunch down. Her arms feel good around your waist. You've earned it. Henson is at peace, The Rim is safe for a few more years, doomsday is a pile of rubble for now.

You slow the bike down, seeing an ageless picnic table by a river pull-out. A few taps on Iko's leg and she holds tight. The bike leans over, cooling.

"What now?" you ask, hoping for a kiss.
"Everything."

THE END

What giant we swarm upon, what mother we hope to earn, what titan we observe in our quiet hours, what wonder beyond our miniscule ambitions she is... Earth.

In the 23rd century, there was a great and fiery drive from our blue home. By the millions they left the only home we have ever known. By thunder and white plastic they dared offworld. What new, luminous homes they found will forever be a myth to us, for we, most of us, remained here.

To do so is no dishonor, though, for the Earth loves her little children. Her love is infinite, her landscapes forever, her vistas immutable as vengeance, sublime as love, wordless as our tiny immortality, or what it hopes to be.

To know her is a life well lived. To simply see all that is on this globe, to understand her vastness, to feel the distances, to dare them alone is time well spent! So you embrace the endless rumble of the road, the muffled hum of the expanse, the slow breath of sleeping with trees and frogs, of leaning back from blurring tires, of feeling the temperatures, the smells, the infinity of the open road and two wheels.

To know these things is to know freedom.

Millions may teem, billions may multiply, and even more pine and die in the long shadows cast by mega cities and the rampant consumption of our vice. Metal can hate, cold and without power, bathing in the exhaust of a blind generation. Great seas of tombstones will our folk know as the earth grows quiet.

Beyond all this, the silence of far places remains untouched for you. You are the one to swim in frozen waters, to roar on lifeless plains, to pause on wind swept passes.

THE BIG ALONE

You have broken free, with two wheels and a mag-coil. One by one you cross the continents from your list, and the days of killing and bullets are further behind than family.

The name Grim is made vapor. Matsushita is your silent companion, and in the limitless vast you find what every so-called human being craves: the cool breeze of truth.

THE END

Much is said of Shinru, Ishuga, Veil, the Rim, even the Wastelands, and all their little interconnections. But where are these places?

What was once Japan, in the early 22nd century, was mostly destroyed by a combination of earthquake and tidal increase. China was half its original size. Ancient rivalries became families of survival. We showed the best of who we are, as we always do when pressed to the limit.

So the modern geography formed, as sea levels receded. Shinru proper was a world hub of survivors in the 2320's. The name was taken from its first Chancellor, a japanese woman who united the refugee effort during the eartquakes years.

Around that, two centuries of cities were made. Ishuga was south, near what was once Laos. Veil hovered over the desolation that was once called Mongolia. Between them all, vast spaces harbored humankind.

Some rare upheaval, never understood, spared the area around Osaka, Japan. That place is now an island of darkness, forests, and ruins.

Few know the fates of the other continents. Earth's magnetospeher was so enraged by the times of change, no signal can cross the oceans. Jet cars occassionally dare the violent seas, but at great peril and expense. It is gigantic digital world, and a cramped physical world.

Strange days.

THE MATMOS

Psychic power and perception in the 2400's is accessed through a medium called the matmos. Some find it by taking Limit, some by accessing rare self-aware machines, some by dropping a cred in a psychic vendor, and others still by sheer innate clairvoyance. By one of these means, you have arrived here... if it can be called a 'here.'

The matmos is more a state of mind than a location. It is a mode of total perception. No mere delusions or hallucinations are here, but truths within truths stretching out to infinity. It is a dimension of total knowledge. Nevertheless, not all who visit there receive knowledge. To see everything is terrifying to most, crippling for some. They take only horror and confusion from the matmos. The gifted, though, see beyond seeing. Their minds are capable of controlling the flood of information somehow, and harnessing it to answer the most impossible problems.

As a stacked consciousness, and one who has retuned more than once, your mind is partially prepared for such a flood. You keep your mind within its astral confines. You keep purpose close as your guide, and demand a sensible universe to draw from. For these reasons, you are powerful in the baffling everything of the matmos. You can find answers here.

"Wild huh?" A voice, echoing backwards in the swirling translucence.
"Who is that?"
"It's me, of course, the machine. The pill. The quanta. I am the embodiment of the psychic, made comprehensible. I am your perception of your psychic perception. I am, effectively, you."
"So this is the matmos. Always wondered what all those cult freaks were yelling about. It's a mess."
"Yes. Everything makes quite a colorful heap. I suppose you should stay focused, runner. They're surrounding you as we speak."

"They?"

"This time? Crazy juggers, vengeful ninja, corporate bounty hunters, old friends turned traitor, muties with rifles and forgotten ghosts with hungry blades. Seems like just about everyone has reasons to hunt you down."

"Old reasons. I left all that behind."

"Did you? A life of running, exploring the urban wilderness, lost in the hovering pyramids and countless cables of the megacities, standing up for the little guy, and away you walked, free of charge."

"Disappeared. Got out."

"Oh, Grim, or should I call you Masushita... no one gets out."

"Surroundings. Show me." Your perception floats upward, outward, and you see yourself from above. The scene you left fades, revealing a closing ring of armed figures. They move in a tactical formation, checking, clearing and closing. Every barrel is focused on you, seconds to spare.

"This is happening now, as you're seeing it. There is no need to doubt what is seen here, no need to cower from truth."

"Something else... something nagging at me... I can feel it..."

"Remarkable. You are perceiving a thing many miles from here. Your mind is stronger than-"

"If you're me then shut it. What is that?"

"It's Iko you sense. It is her struggle, her presence, her longing to tell you the truth. Truth has a powerful effect here... like a piercing sound that can't be hushed."

"She's in pain. Locked in a base, trying to find me, unable to stop them... I can see her, though, she's not that far."

"Yes."

"I could almost touch her."

"Her mind is being invaded by a pusher. This makes her much more susceptible to psychic contact, but vulnerable, too. She is fighting their will, Grim. Fighting to protect you."

"I think- I think I can contact her."

"You could, yes, but you could risk exposing her or worse. The mat-

mos is no plaything. Minds are fragile here, even yours, even hers."
"What about the a-holes with guns? Still coming?"
"They're here, Grim. The triggers are being pulled."
"Time is- I.. uh- I can stretch it. I can stretch it, get time to contact Iko. I have to."
"Worth your life to do so? You could also snap yourself from this trance, draw your weapons and make a stand. Bullets and blades! Do what you do best. Save lives and take lives. In the material world, not the astral."
"I can't believe I'm having this conversation. No sense."
"What did you expect from the psychic connectivity this planet has discovered and technified in recent centuries? A cartoon? Polygon renderings of spirals and black hole suns? Drunken delirium? You look onto the universe with wide eyes, and see only what you demand to see. You see your life in danger, and Iko in the distance. It makes nothing but sense."

If you snap out of it and go bullets and blades, turn to PAGE 184.

If you dim your aggression and contact Iko, turn to PAGE 182.

"Small world, runner."
"Grim." She's cold as ice, pausing.
"Drink?"
"Scotch."
"Still drinking that shit?"
"Still doing a lot of things."

Chan hustles over. Iko spots Hatch and Case at their table. Her head doesn't move, but her eyes measure the room, check the exits, return to you.
"Relax, Iko. We're just having a drink and a sweet bun." You wish you could take your own advice.
She gulps the scotch. You can't help but wonder how you'll pay for that.
"Here, or outside?"
"Oh, come on, Iko, don't be so serious. Say hi to Hatch!"
Iko moves her head for the first time, looking to her right. "Hi, Hatch."
Hatch manages a goofy little wave, googling his eyes and shrinking into his chair.

"Thank you." You begin to loosen up, heading for the table.
"Don't turn your back on me, Grim."
You do exactly that, talking to her with your head to one side. "Your manners are still shit. They paying you too much? Got one of those psychic assholes fucking with your head? Hacked your stack? Jee-zus, Iko, you're so tight your boots are squeaking."
"Been training? You're slower than ever."
"Yep. A straight mess. You gonna sit down or draw that blade? This is getting old."

"The blade. I'm tired of chasing you across the rim while you drink and ride like you're on fucking vacation."

You turn around, look into her eyes. At that moment you realize they've gotten to her for real this time. It isn't personal anymore. She's slagged. Brainwashed and showing it.
"You're not yourself, Iko. Snap out of it."
Her blade begins to slide from its scabbard, drawn out by a magnetic reflex link a few inches from her hand. She's got some very, very good gear. You consider checking the exits.

"Draw."

A twitch, and your blade pops into your hand. Hers is already in motion. Clang, clang, clang. Three parries and you pass each other. Tac data is jammed, she's fucking with you. This could be it. Clang, clang. She's got new moves. Clang, rip, clang, clang. Someone is bleeding. As the blades raise again, glowing edges rendering for the next strike, Case stands up and unloads a burst of MAC12 fire. The bullets shred the ceiling in a mess.
"Would you two get a fucking room?"

Iko uses it. She slides forward, impossibly fast, and shoves you through the bar and through the far window. The storm of glass surrounds both of you, it's twenty stories down, some crazy Ishuga back alley shit. Not good. You both spin and tumble in a tangle. A rush of air. You hit the tarmac like a sack of onions. Both of you can barely breathe, and there's a moment. Your tac optics light up.
"You're-" you cough blood trying to talk, "you're out of range."
"They're controlling us, Grim... psionics. No time."
"Then let's-"
"Shut up. Listen. Take the fucking retune, disappear. You're a goddamned clone, Grim. Tenaka is playing you, hiding in you. Wipe it all and get out. It's worse than ever."
"I don't-"
"Three dragons. All three of them! They're in my head... they're IN MY HEAD!"

Tac goes dark again, their pusher is back online. Iko's eyes go cold. She spins her blade, sticks it in your right shoulder like a steak knife and leans back, revealing a MP8. It's a super-auto mod.
"Iko, no-"
She pulls the trigger.

The thing about MP8's, especially the modded ones, is that they basically melt their barrels on one magazine. They can unload 50 rounds in under a second. You take all 50 to the chest. Well, at least 49. Iko throws the slagged gun to one side as you jiggle backward, spraying blood. Your link armor is swiss cheese. A few slugs have squiggled up through your jaw, into one eye. It's a real mess.

She fights some inner force, straining to look you in the one eye that still works.

"I- I'm sorry, Goldfish."
She regains her cold look again and springs straight up. The glow of her blade disappears above as you hit the concrete in a pool of blood.
"Until next time, beautiful-"

Turn to PAGE 255.

THE GUN

Who could possibly walk away from a sign that reads 'THE GUN?'
Not you.

You approach the table, remembering all the snatched-from-the-jaws-of-death favors you've done for Biggs. He owes you, treat yourself. You draw closer, getting a better look at the weapon. It's every firearm in your arsenal combined into one. Anodized everything, link alloy receiver, light as a feather, scaffold mags, wireless reflex link, nano missiles, homing rounds, magnetic return. This thing must be worth a fortune. You rack it twice, check the sights. This could really turn the tide in a fight.

"Fine piece of hardware, eh?" Biggs walks over, sipping from a dented steel cup. "Crazy jugger named Squirrel traded me that little beauty for one of my old buggies. Guy must've been fried out of his mind."
"Quite a score."
"Yep, guy said a runner dropped it like garbage out by Veil. A real vamp, dark hair, walk away from explosions type. Guy was spooked, didn't want anything to do with it."
"This have a user ID?"
"Yeah, thumbprint panel right there."
"It's blinked."
"Yeah, I crack those first thing."
"Have the data?"
"Yeh only one user, just a code name, IkoB43."
"This is one of Iko's weapons. I knew it."
"Who?"
"Where is this guy Squirrel now?"
"Town somewhere, gearing up for another one of their crazy convoys. Probably drinking."
"Kate still running the bar over here?"
"Yeah, but, Grim- after what happened-"

"This thing work with the thumbprint hacked?"
"Fires like butter. 300 rounds onboard."
"I'll take it."
"So, you're heading over to The Wheel?"
"Yeah. Wanna tag?"
"Wouldn't miss it, man. This town needs some excitement."

'The Wheel' is not exactly a bar. It started as a fuel station back in the day. The crazier the juggers got, the weirder their fuel. Not just fuel for rigs, but for their nitro-cooked brains and whisky-soaked guts. As the years passed, the walls moved out, the ceiling went up. Everything ran on pumps. It burned down twice, got hit with a gunship seeker missile, and collapsed in an aftershock. Every time they rebuild it, it's more steel and concrete than the last time. By 2400, when Kate took over, it was a fifty foot tower of mechanical chaos in two acres of pumps and bays. Jugger paradise.

You and Biggs walk up from the pull-through, which is cluttered with mag bikes and hodge podge junkers. The main door is big enough to fit a tow truck, and has on a few occasions. You stash THE GUN in your ruck. A hand-written sign dangles sideways, 'No Freeforms.'
"What's that all about?"
"New Earth Resistance- they staged some kind of raid here a few months back, creeps and non-humans all going berserk. Kate made a new rule, the boys made the sign."
"I thought freeforms keep to themselves?"
"They used to, but they're numbers are getting big these days, and some of 'em are walking on all fours. Monsters. Messed up, man. Something's stirring 'em up."
"Alright where's this Squirrel?"
"Bar. Guy with the yellow arm."

Squirrel is hard to miss with a bright yellow spray-painted cyber-plate arm. The rest of him is leather and desert camo, shaved head and desert goggles on top. He's got a tall beer and two shots in front of him. You sit down next to him. He doesn't like that much. Biggs joins, signals for two beers. Kate isn't at the bar, it's a tall thin guy with old timey glasses.

"Oh, hey Biggs. Howzit, jugger?"

"Hafa."

"And ya new friend?"

"Name's Grim."

"Yeah, I know who you are. Halsey's little ghost."

"You asked. Tell me about the runner you saw over by Veil. The vamp."

"It ain't safe, what talkin' to strangers."

"Nothing safe out here. She have a nanocarbon skin? Hair across her eyes? Anodized purple knuckle guards?"

"That's the one."

"I need a location."

"Just one problem, runner."

"You working for creds? You know no one takes 'em, right? Only fuel we have is in Biggs' yard, so don't be a pill."

"Don't want no treasure, ghost. We gonna bury you ass here in The Wheel, right?"

"Didn't catch that last part-"

"New Earth got a price on your head what more than this whole shit stack, runner. You must not 'eard."

"Must not. Sign said you muties aren't New Earth fans. I guess you're wearing the away jersey?"

"Price out," Squirrel twitches, clearly nervous and out of his depth. He gulps both shots in front of him, cybernetics glitching a bit.

"Then you best make a move, jugger."

Biggs tries to slow things down, waving to the bespectacled barkeep, but it's too late. Squirrel is hopped up, overamped. He makes a move. That move turns out to be falling off his stool backward, drawing a subsonic pistol, and blasting a hole in the roof. Without fully realizing it, your blade is drawn and at his throat.

"That it?"
"Me mates, though, asshole."

Then you see them, juggers closing in from every side, weapons drawn, all of 'em looking for something to make today memorable. Biggs is scarce, barkeep vanished. You're alone in the sights of three dozen weapons.

Slowly, methodically, you draw THE GUN from its hidey hole. The thing is death in a basket. Nasty. Why does it always have to go like this? No matter. The ID link on the thumbprint is flashing. User searching. It takes two blinks to tune your retina console on that, and get a blip. It's Iko, alright. Looking for her gear. This weapon could be used to get a comms link, even a virtual link. Not much use if you're shredded by drunk juggers.

If you act unimpressed, and contact Iko, turn to PAGE 182.

If you flip the safety and unleash hell, turn to PAGE 184.

HOUND IN THE ALLEY

With Iko in full kill mode, you don't stand a chance. Assuming she's still out to capture/kill/subdue you. Better to slip out the back and live to fight another day. Something in her eyes just isn't right. Questions can get you killed in a swordfight. The confusion of people passing by makes a perfect smokescreen, and you vanish right in front of her. Old trick from Tenaka. You skid to a stop in the kitchen, then two left turns and the back hall where Chan piles garbage on Sunday nights.

The metal door clacks shut. Case will be stuck with the tab. That brings a smile, but the peace of the narrow alley is broken before you can gloat or wonder if you've shaken Iko for now.

Something is here with you in the high-walled gloom of burnt out neon. You feel its mass first, that feeling of a great weight on the pavement. Then you hear it: a wet, heavy slap on the asphalt, a creaking of rubberized cyber musculature, a deep exhale, cracking knuckles made of banded titanium... Then, you see it.

It's a freeform. These are inhuman, synthetic life forms created by other synthetic lifeforms. They've taken on new shapes of their own, leaving humanity far behind, and it has made them monsters. Some believe them to be nothing more than that, others see them as Earth's next masters. The latter is commonly called the New Earth Resistance. You, however, are the former. These things kill without mercy, rampage at random. They are not life at all, but anti-life.

This particular one is rummaging through garbage in the dull green light. It's as big as a truck. Then you see it's actually devouring a corpse of...something... in the trash. Ghoulish, even for Ishuga. You're frozen, but it must smell you. It leaves its meal, rising on pulsing shoulders of red rope and craning its gigantic skull-armored head with slow, hungry malice.

If it had eyes, they would meet yours. You feel a predatory hunger scanning you over. It's blocking the entire alley. Classic 'rock and a hard place' stuff.

"Shit."

If you try to get past the freeform to escape, turn to PAGE 189.

If you leave it be, and return to deal with Iko, turn to PAGE 201.

Shinru HQ is a huge place, but it's all unfolding here, in the deployment bay. Heavy Gear, the new world-ending machine designed to flush out Matsushita, is tearing the place apart and Iko is going demolitions while you aim for the head, if that can be called a head. More like a tank bolted to a battleship.

Missile packs on the towering battle armor, c4 explosives, and a little luck is all Iko needs to blow the thing to pieces, and the rest of Shinru HQ with it. Save the world? Probably not, but at least it will send a message: not on our watch, assholes.

So you agree to split up. She darts across, under the huge, hydraulic legs, you play decoy and piss it off. No problem. Never mind the storm of bullets, beam weapons, and crashing debris. Chaos is your workshop. It's all come to this moment, this commitment. Make it count. Iko sure as hell will.

As you finish the thought, sizing up the handholds and potential weak points on the drab green giant, Iko vanishes in a curl of smoke. The bay is filling with embers and rolling black clouds. Gunfire has taken its chaotic toll, but it just makes more cover for the two of you. Commandos are filing in, it's all going to hell. Time to earn your beer.

Hesitation behind, you lunge forward. Colossal shadows, cast from the main barrels of Heavy Gear's heaviest weapons, cloak your advance. You drink in the darkness, going faster, flashing a grin in the dim as the blade springs into your hand. Then your climb begins. Onto one metal-clad toe you jump. The machine must have incredible sensors, as it twitches away from your first touch. This almost throws you across the hangar, but one pivot and leap brings you to a massive piece of ankle-armor. The foot alone is bigger than your last apartment. From there you catch a handhold below its huge, hissing, reverse-angle knee joint. This contracts, almost severing your arm in moving armor plates. The thing is striding to one side, crashing through the bay wall with total bedlam and a storm of falling scrap. Huge, brain-breaking magnetic hums and servo whines howl from within the mechanized horror as it repositions, bending its weapons downward. You're riding a 50-foot mechanical bull, and it has all the guns.

A hail of small arms fire ping and zip on the armored surface, sending you scrambling around to the back, where exposed cables and carbon-sheathed hoses clutter the outer shell. As the brilliant idea of severing these critical connections crosses your mind, a shrill, crackling electric shriek descends the metal frame. It's an anti-personnel shock field. All the toys.

But you're too fast. Nothing is as fast as you, not even a cutting edge war mecha. You reach up, spinning your sword out of the way. With the free hand you catch a carbon-sheath. It's a sort of crinkled fabric tube that insulates electrical conduit. The shock field hits and you swing out on your insulated hand hold, grounded and off-metal for a split second. Then BANG! You land on the knee plates again, shock field gone, renewed of purpose. Iko just needs a few seconds to make the big boom.

Up, up you go, one blocky surface to the next, one huge silver actuator to the next, cracking landing lights with your heels and slashing rubber grommets with your short blade for good measure. A spray of MAC12 fire keeps the commandos guessing in the smoke, and you make what must be the chest of the walking battleship. It lacks what could be called a head, for obvious design reasons. Only a main deck and forests of weapons meet you. Several smaller auto-cannons and belt-fed guns track and take aim, but you're just... Too. Damn. Fast.

Bullets fill the air with thunder, everything is ricochets and deafening roar, but you've zeroed your best shot: a cluster of spotlights, orb-lensed optics, shielded sonar banks and radio jammers. The sword is screaming through it all in a flash, you a mere extension of the blade. Cables and shrapnels stream out behind you, but you've over shot the stroke. Off the rear of the titanic machine you slide, into thin air. A good escape plan, but a damn long drop to the deck.

The gamble works, and Heavy Gear spins side to side, off balance. It's mass is so enormous, it feels like a hotel about to topple. You crash onto the tarmac, snapping a wrist and smacking yourself dizzy. You'll walk away, but damn if it doesn't smart.

"Iko!"

There's no way she can hear you as you stumble away, fleeing a popping snake of gun fire from the commandos in the rafters. They're shredding a set of crates as you go, but they're terrible shots.

You risk a glance back. There she is. Hell and high water, if that crazy runner isn't on top of the starboard missile box on this thing, riding it like a five-story artillery surfboard. She slams a plastic pack on with a mag anchor, but you don't have the luxury of watching the rest. You've got a few hundred PS110 rounds to worry about, and those damn things bend around corners like pissed off hornets in July. One, two, three times you juke and slide to barely survive another volley. This is a short, deadly fuse. Your luck is about to run out. No matter. Before the commandos can unload again, the whole place explodes.

You have a few microseconds of weightlessness. Your limbs pinwheel, your gear flies in every direction like mud from a spinning tire. A few parts of you are on fire for a moment, then a slam, a long slide in dirt and broken asphalt. You hear huge masses of battle armor and shrapnel peppering the deployment deck like steel rain. Bars bang and ring like tuning forks when they finally hit. Then a smoke-covered quiet. Hot embers pepper you slowly, silently, as your ears stop ringing at last.

You sit up, shell shocked, to survey what is now a crater. The entire deployment bay is leveled, parts of people and cybernetic limbs here and there, spot fires, unraveled cable housings, shredded tires, shattered glass. Parts of Shinru HQ lean and collapse in the background. End of the world type stuff, or maybe a new beginning. At least she sent a message: not today, assholes, not while there are still runners running.

This would normally be the moment Iko would stride from the smoke, walking heavy on her heeled boots like a boss, holstering a Nemesis pistol, staring with those eyes of hers, letting a tiny smile bend those lips of hers, brushing a piece of burning armor from one shoulder. She was the best. She always walked away. Untouchable.

Not this time.

Nothing.

Turn to PAGE 83.

☐

▽

"You knew."
"Grim! What a nice surprise! I thought I was in your rearview mi-"
"No more bullshit, Tenaka."

The old man deflates a bit, and returns to the kitchen, preparing tea. He always prepares tea. It's infuriating.
"Tea?"
"Not until answers."
"Well that's backward, Gakusei. Sheesh!"
"You knew."
"Eh?"
"You knew everything!"
"Of course I knew! I am your sensei... or have you forgotten already?"
"The whole thing was a lie! You were part of SIlver Burn, of Shinru command!"
"So were you, my pupil. Such things do not define us. I am far more th-"
"No more bullshit! You're here to monitor and recover me, asshole! The sword, the sensei routine. You're just here for Matsushita! Just say it!"
"Of course I am. He is my teacher."

A long silence. Heat under your hood.

"Teacher?"
"I devoted myself to Hideki-Sensei, he is the greatest swordsman I have ever known, and taught me all I can claim to attempt. He had been retuned from elder days, somehow, by command. Several retunes. A true Kensei." Tenaka looks wistful, watery eyes, he's not even close to lying. "When I discovered he was here, hidden inside of you, I volunteered to work recon. Anything to help my old master, to be near him. To be near YOU, even if it meant feigning loyalty to the goose-steppers."

"I'm not Matsushita, Sensei! I'm not! I'm Grim!"
"Yes. Yes, you are Hideki-Sensei, and there's no undoing it. But you are more than Matsushita. You are both, and neither." A breath. "One thing, though."
"Eh?"
"Slow." He smiles, pouring the tea with sadistic detail. "Yes. Still slow." Tenaka smiles, sitting with effort.
"Seriously?"
"Sit. Leave your huffing and puffing at Henson's bar, will you. This is a peaceful home."
"And the Hanzo?"
"Your sword. Always has been. You asked me to keep it safe. We can't have mind-controlled Shinru zombies running around with that kind of power."
"I asked you-"
"Before it happened."
"The retune?"
"Now that you know, you may as well know it all. What you do next will be beyond my stewardship. I can enjoy my tea knowing my duty has been fulfilled."
"Ok, let's have it."

"After the offworld movement, a series of power outages befell the planet. Old locks were opened that were meant to stay shut forever. Digital quarantines on mainframes no one even remembered. Old cabinet computers in long-buried cellars. These old jails were kept running to contain transient AI's. These AI's were malevolent, predatory entities from the early days. Developed from the worst human brain donors, tainted with homicidal, psychotic rage and confusion. Ravagers. In their lesser form, they spawned cults and splinter groups. They jumped between bodies, killing and spreading mayhem with wanton fury."

"Like the 'Birthday Boy' murders in the 2430's."

"The exact same, yes. This was transient AI in its muted form. Easily contained and destroyed. In their greater form, they took on the nickname of dragons. Limitless, fast-moving AI's. Impossible to track, even harder to confine. Drakan, Tyranax, and Silver were their names. Silver sided with the Shinru government, seeing much potential in cooperation with humans. For this, the other two destroyed it. That was in the 2410's. Despite destroying their better sibling, the Shinru government weathered the storm, primarily through the aid of a legendary warrior-turned-runner."

"Let me guess. Matsushita Hideki."
"Precisely."
"Hideki-Sensei rebuffed the two dragons by destroying them in stack form, all within a powerful jamming field provided by loyalists in Shinru command. Silver Shard was defeated, at the cost of my sensei's life. That is when the Chancellor's master stroke was set into motion. Groups of runners were assigned various tactical strikes on insurgent infrastructure. Those who succeeded weakened the enemy, but those who failed were the real prize. That's where you come in."
"I don't understand."
"We needed a corpse. Then, we would use an illegal retune to conceal Hideki-sensei's stack in an unsuspecting runner. Our group provides a scot-free escape after a botched run..."
"And that's where I come in."
"We called you 'the volunteer.'"
"Cute."
"What we didn't expect was the savagery of Silver Burn. The Chancellor lost track of Drakan and Hideki-Sensei. He turned on his own loyal circle, and went wild with paranoia. He set out to eradicate any trace of the rebels, any who knew anything. He was jumping at shadows, and going to any lengths to recover Matsushita, his ultimate weapon. That is when all of us involved were either dom-

inated by psychers or forced into hiding."
"What about Iko."
"One of the Chancellor's best prizes. The new psych program was putting out the strongest pushers on the planet. They got in her head, and deployed her to find-"
"Me."
"The creeps?"
"Synthetics and tin skins have been flocking to the New Earth Resistance. Some say Drakan is at its head, and building his revenge in these new freeforms. Instead of staging an attack, the Chancellor initiated a secret program to tag and track synthetics, making them part of his obsessive search for Sensei Matsushita."
"Bait on a hook."
"Bait you took, I believe, for a day's pay."
"The volunteer."
"Indeed, Gakusei."
"This whole time- ten years- you knew everything."
"That is correct."
"So... I mean- now what?"
"More tea?"
"No, I mean yes, but-"
"You want to know who to chop down? Who to blow to bits? How to make it all right? That's the one answer I don't have, my friend. My part in the story is ending. Yours is finally at its beginning."

Then, a racket at the door draws both your attention. Tenaka spills a bit of tea and frowns. A pause, then clunky boots on the wood floors.
"Now who could that be?"

It's Hatch. He's a bit of a mess.
"Hatch, what is it? You look terrible."
"Commandos. Fifteen at least in three squads, rolling hard on town from the south edge. They torched a few houses and straight de-

mo'd the little chapel out by Herman's hideaway. Body armor, sniffers out front."
Tenaka looks tired, saddened. He deftly sets down his cup, takes one slow breath, then looks up at you.
"It seems the story is about to begin, Gakusei."
"Tenaka, do you still have that old 'Razor' model rocket launcher?"
"Of course! It's a family heirloom!"
"Load it up, let's go. Hatch, show us the way. I'm done slithering around. Nobody steps on a church in my town."

A few beats later, the three of you are up on the South road ridge. It's the outer edge of Halsey's Rest, not much exhaust out there, so the air is thick and still. It's always hazy there. Hatch sets you up behind the cobble wall built by that nutcase Eddie. One of those weird rock stacker types.

"There they are. Two o'clock." Hatch tries to use some kind of spec ops hand gestures, but just makes a sort of duck shape instead.
"I see them," Tenaka confirms, dropping behind the wall, "they're armed for an assault, not a precision operation. Those are MP8's with sidewinder packs."
You and Hatch both give the old man a wide eyed look.
"I wasn't born yesterday. Get your damn heads down."
"Sensei, prime the Razor. Hatch, still packing a scattergun?"
"Two."
"Naturally. You're at bat. I want to give these jokers one chance to stand down. They do anything but that, Tenaka, let a razor loose. Fire at the rear of their ranks. We don't want to kill these jerks if we can avoid it. Shit is hitting the fan hard enough. We bring 'em in tight and Hatch knocks 'em flat with buckshot. It won't penetrate their armor, but it'll neutralize them."
"Neutralize 'em good."
"On my signal. No mistakes."

You shuffle to one side, check the view. The commandos are moving up groups, five meter spreads. The sinister red glow of the optics in their helmets bob and weave in the murk like a cobra with twenty eyes.

"Shinru commandos!" You call, breaking the countryside quiet suddenly. They halt, you stand up. "Stand down, everyone. This is a peaceful vapor farm town here. We don't want any trouble. Let's just talk this out before anyone gets hurt."

You see them using comms, but not addressing you, the group leaders nod menacingly. Then a tinny, PA voice returns.
"Hands on your head. On the ground, citizen. We have orders to extract a target in Halsey's Rest. Your cooperation is not compulsory, but will increase your chances of survival by 40%."
"As appealing as those odds are, maybe we can help with your target and avoid any unnecessary explosions and deadly hails of gunfire and crazy shit here."
"A fugitive named Grim Shinomura is here somewhere. If you have any informa-"
"Shirosune!"
"What's that, citizen?"
"My name, asshole. Grim SHIROSUNE. Get your shit straight!" With that you drop to the ground. Tenaka takes the cue, and pops up like a prairie dog, unleashing a razor rocket. The projectile is a long, thin thing... like a sort of rectangular wing. It arcs in a long, wide spiral to the rear of the commandos, slamming into the green turf with a thud. No explosion. Then things get interesting.

The commandos don't hesitate, unleashing a wall of suppressed fire across the ridge. Turf and shreds of asphalt fly everywhere in the chaos. Hatch goes flying to one side like a dolphin leaping for joy. Tenaka disappears in the rock dust.
"Tenaka! Fire that thing!"

"I did!"

Hatch waits for the commandos to reload, then does what he does. Blonde beard streaming, boots slinging mud like a swamp buggy, guns flapping on both arms, he charges down the ridge like a long-legged bull. He raises both scatterguns and grits his teeth, white knuckling the triggers. A maelstrom of scattershot shreds the entire scene in front of him like a hedge trimmer gone berserk. Half the commandos get their armor split, helmets cracked, knocked senseless of clutching their groins in agony. He marches through them like a farmer cutting wheat, but when he reaches the rear ranks, they're ready for him. They start to fire, but he flops backwards, landing on his ass and sliding in the damp grass. Their weapons track downward with deadly unity. Hatch's luck is out. They have him as he skids to a stop. Just then you risk a look, and see what looks like Hatch's last second of Earth.

Then, the rocket explodes.

Just a few feet behind the commandos, and splayed out Hatch, the explosion sends them all flying. Huge lumps of turf spray into the haze with them comically, and Hatch tumbles through the air with circus-tent style, landing with a smoldering thud back near the cobble wall. He's soot-doused, bruised to hell, one thumb bent impossibly backward, and both scatter guns mushroomed like joke cigars. As the smoke clears, there's only one sound. Laughter. It's Hatch.

"Did we win? Haha, that was amazing!"

It's short enough work to bind and tranq the hit squad. Hired goons are no match for frontier folk. The whole lot is locked up in Mull's back shop in no time. The three of you finally get a chance to sit down, Hatch ditching some of his wrecked gear.

"Anyone want to tell me what the hell that was about?"
You and Tenaka exchange a look, trying to decide who has to sum it all up. Tenaka won't budge.

"Conspiracy stuff, I have an old guy hidden in my stack, and we need to save the world again."
"Works for me. What's our next move?"
"We've got two targets: Drakan and his New Earth Resistance, and the Chancellor of Shinru city."
"Well, one is an immortal AI that no one has ever been able to destroy, and the other the leader of the planet. Should we flip for it?"

For this choice, you can flip a coin.

Heads: If you pursue Drakan and the N.E.R., turn to PAGE 209.

Tails: If you plan to take down the Chancellor somehow, turn to PAGE 217.

FINDING IKO

You confirm open on the Iko file. It's a kanji icon reading 'Cobra Program.' The file is vast, but contains two sections, a psychic training program and a list of runners targeted for control. Iko tops the list as a 'high value asset.' Shinru command has trained, or created, a new generation of mind-melters. The big plan is to use these psychics to dominate the world's best runners to do the Chancellor's dirty work. Job one? Find you and return with Matsushita intact. So they know this Hideki character is hidden in your brain stem, but Iko is having a hell of a time pinning you down. Backup plan? Deploy a bunch of tapped creeps as bait to draw you out.

Here's where Iko's file expands. You haven't seen much of her since your running days a decade ago. You're pretty sure you loved her, but it was complicated. Since then, she has been under Shinru control, spearheading a bumper crop of assassinations, demolition ops, mop ups, cover ups, and corp escorts. Poor girl. She's got a kill list a mile long, and her cybernetics upgrade medical chart is forty pages.

Then some pay dirt. Tech specs on her psychic control methodology. Ranges, jam loopholes, countermeasures and shortcomings of their mind control program. You keep that on RAM for later.

Finally, they have a failsafe dossier called Heavy Gear. This is tagged 'final contingency to locate and reacquire Matushita Hideki.' Heavy Gear is, apparently, a fifty-foot tall war machine that will be used to decimate the outer towns and villages to draw you out.

The Rim is going to burn.

The Chancellor is willing to raze his own districts to get his hands on Hideki. This guy must really have some chops.

Case interrupts your scanning, “Hey, Grim.”
“Yeah, just taking this all in.”
“Greta is going back into surgery, I’m going with her. Don’t leave this lobby. I know how squirrely you get. Stay put.”
“Glued.”

Back to the data, you restore focus on the target, searching ‘current whereabouts’ on Iko. All you get is ‘Bunker 43.’ A few surv cam pics are in file, showing her spine-bolted to some kind of augment system. It looks like hell. She’s not even fully human anymore... they’re torturing her. Classic supersoldier bullshit.

The display goes blurry, and you realize a big wobbly tear has formed in your left eye, mucking up the console. Too soon for that, way too soon, there’s a lot to do.

If you want to find a way to rescue Iko, turn to PAGE 260.

If you close the Iko file and read up on Matsushita, turn to PAGE 178.

The Matsushita file is packed into a kanji icon that reads 'Relic.' You dig in. Hideki-Sensei lived in the late 14th century. He was part of a cataclysmic battle on the Katsura River in which the legendary master Sengo Muramasa was defeated. You pause to take that in. So a samurai master dies in 1390-something, and they find a way to stack him for later? Posthumous retunes? How is any of this real? You read on.

Fast forward to the 2200's. Before the offworld movement, the first Earth Chancellor, Junji Ryunosuke, somehow has a living, breathing Matsushita as his military advisor and top warrior. The unification wars end in victory for Ryunosuke, and Shinru city attains its supreme status still enjoyed today. Over the following two and a half centuries, Matsushita appears here and there in high-value government ops, coups and nation building engagements. Half his work is unmaking tyrants, the other half is enthroning them. There's no pattern. Move ahead to the Silver Shard coup of 2028. Matsushita finds himself on the side of the Chancellor, resisting Drakan and his AI revolution. Then the real crux of it: Matsushita is deployed to confront Drakan one-on-one. Expecting to be killed on this mission, he is stack-cloned and hidden in a retuned runner being used to occupy the Iga ninja during the melee. That runner is you.

"Shit."

Looking for their plans to extract Matsushita later, you find what may be your next stop on the fun train. It's a cutting edge stack facility in Veil.

Veil. The hologram city. You've made it through a lifetime staying away from that place. All the bleed-outs in all the backwater grafters of Ishuga are better than that pleasure palace. So that's it? Give them their samurai, be rid of it, and disappear? No genocidal war machines, Iko goes free, the Chancellor ends his paranoid manhunt. Seems like a slam dunk.

Still, something deep down tells you Matsushita isn't a bad guy. There's something else here... or maybe that's just the other human consciousness sitting your brain stem talking. Either way, you need a direction here.

If you want to extract Matsushita somehow, turn to PAGE 265.

If you close the file and read up on Iko, turn to PAGE 176.

ANTENNA

Not many people can say they've run decking signals through a katana. That's exactly what you mean to do.

You cringe a bit to consider the ancestors, but nothing makes a high-output, remote uplink antenna like a Hanzo. You deftly apply the alligator clips to the centuries-old blade, almost looking over your shoulder for disappointed Edo-period warlords.

The rig works, as long as you don't touch the blade. You fold up the screen on your ODS deck. It's a crummy amberchrome mod. Bunker 43 is easy enough to zero, especially with the endless drone remapping projects. Houseflies bothering your baking project? You're being mapped. Having trouble growing potatoes on the Rim? Drones headed your way.

There it is. Bunker 43. It's a Shinru Command facility near the holographic pleasure city of Veil. Veil. What a mess. Stay focused, it's simple enough. You're not here to hack the damn place, just looking for Iko. Zoom in. Standard barracks and airfield stuff. Got to be a lead here somewhere.

There's a blip, but no movement. Not in the bunker, but nearby in Veil somewhere. She must be bolted down, because sitting still just isn't her style. Bastards have her bound up. 'Stack currently offline' is all you can dig up. Sedated? Not much else to mine here. Brainwashing her?

Now you're facing that nasty feeling again: get your ass to Veil, the holographic hellhole-pleasure-palace and bust Iko out of this scene, or walk your ass back to Tenaka and ask what *his name* is doing in these files.

Both options couldn't suck more.

You disconnect the Hanzo, ending its shame as an antenna relay. It slides into the scabbard with silent, precise perfection.

“Tenaka, don’t you dare be involved in this...”

If you venture to Veil to rescue Iko, turn to PAGE 232.

If you return to Tenaka, to ask about his role in all this, turn to PAGE 168.

"Iko?" Sounds, voices, all of it coiling and echoed, "Iko you copy?"
Static. Along with it, fractured slices of video and data structures. The signal is shit.
"IKO!" Yelling doesn't have any real effect in the SISTM, but who cares. Is love quantifiable? Signal boost. You can push your mind out to her, demand to make contact, shove away all the noise, like writing a letter in a bar on Saturday night. "Iko, can you hear me?"
"Grim?"
You lose her for a moment in the ether of it all, but push everything else away. Demand it. Demand a connection.
"Yeah, it's me."
"Don't do this, they're in my head, all three of them. Don't do this."
"Where are you? I'm wasted on drunks and nitro and bullets for nothing. I'm coming for you, Iko. I'm going to find you."
"Too many to find. No way out. Give up, Grim. Take off. Just remember me from back in the day... good days... the ol-"
"Iko?"

As soon as it came, it's gone. Signal mess, scrambled polygons and error messages in messy piles.
"Shit."

You've got a location. Bunker 43, whatever that is, and the numbers to get there. Another push. It hurts. The signal scratches its way back through.
"Iko!"
"Here's my 20-"
"Have it. Coming for you, goldfish."
"Too many. Too many here."
"They can bring their whole damn army!"
"Not them... too many of me."
"Look, Iko, I've waited too long, been a real chicken shit. There's something I need to tell you. Should've told you a long time ago."

"Don't. Seriously? Over a virtual comm link?"

You've waited decades to tell her. Lifetimes. Either take this moment, and tell her how you really feel, or keep it frosty, and rally your deadliest wingwoman back into action. No easy thing. Make a choice while the signal lasts.

If you reveal your love for Iko, just go all in, turn to PAGE 222.

If you keep it frosty, reminding her of tactics, turn to PAGE 226.

Iko will have to wait, you can feel guns being pointed at you. They came out of nowhere. So be it.

"Before we get started, anyone want to leave?"
A few dozen runners and desert rats scurry away. Two of the Juggers sling their homemade guns and bolt, one of them yelling about how this is all Squirrel's fault.
"Youse dead meat, runner. We've got ya fifteen to one."
"Yeah, tough odds. I was hoping this might sway my chances." You scoop to the ruck, sure not to startle any of these brain-fried nitro-sniffers. THE GUN comes shining into your hand, gleaming like a jeweled sword in the dim rays of sunlight. The Juggers with more than half a brain go wide-eyed.
"That's Shinru command shit! You working for the man now, ghost?"
"Just holding it for a friend. So," you rack the breech with bravado. One more Jugger runs for his life. "Shall we?"
"Shred this asshole!"

The Juggers unleash. Before you can spin to one side, a half dozen rounds hit you like angry bees. You grit your teeth, check that the armor took it, and bring up THE GUN. You brace and pull both triggers. Nothing but a loud click. Again. Click. Click. Click. In a split second of total panic, you check the HUD on the receiver. A red LED is blinking 'user blocked.'
"Shit!"

The Juggers lower their heads, and another storm of bullets rips the bar to pieces. Of the fifty rounds, at least eight hit. You're bleeding now, and your ace was a dud. One attacker you cut in half with the nodachi, but before you can bring up your MAC12 they come again. They must be using huge magazines. Another storm of fire. Your neck is hit. A rib cracks. Always the ribs! Why the ribs?

You tumble away from your lone victim, fleeing the endless shooting. You're pinned. The bar has emptied. There's a brief smoke-filled pause.

"Hold your damn fire!" You yell at last, standing.
"Not a chance, Grim. You owe us."
"Look, I'm sure this is just a big-"

Then, out of nowhere, Biggs' grinning face rises up like the Great Pumpkin behind the Juggers. He's up to something. That grin can't be good. In one hand he has a makeshift trigger unit. Glowing red button and all.

"Hey assholes!" Biggs spins them all with a shout, then hits the trigger with glee. A steel disc on the floor lights up with crackling arcs of plasma, then lashes out at the Juggers in a strobe. Every last one of them is tased from below, hit with lightning in the balls and inner thighs. They dance and wriggle terribly, like a band of skeletons. A pause. They all drop.

You nod to Biggs and turn back to the bar, tossing THE GUN on the bartop with disappointed theatrics. The glasses guy appears again, annoyed but unshaken. The two beers finally arrive.

"Oh man," Biggs joins you, "she blocked you!"
"I thought you said you handled that particular nuisance?!"
"She must be in close range to override my hack."
"I'm fuzzy on the whole close/far thing. CLOSE?"
"Yeah, like right here in town. What would a Shinru elite commando be doing at The Wheel? These guns are a dime a dozen in Veil."
"Me."
"Huh?"
"She's here for me. The thumb reader must've ID'd me. You know, Biggs, I'm not having the best day here." You guzzle the beer.

"Better than them!" He gestures to the Juggers, all dead asleep, some being dragged out by their wiser cohorts. One of them tosses a pouch of coin onto the bar, presumably for the mess.
"So she'll be here any second?"
"Likely. You know this spook or what?"
"We go way back."
"Oh. Oh shit.. Like back before you were dead?"
"Something like that."
"Oh shit."

"Hey Biggs," on cue, Iko walks slowly into The Wheel. "thanks again."
"Sorry, Grim." Biggs chugs his beer, flutters a bit, and scurries off.

Iko hasn't changed a bit. Anodized purple enhancements, jet black hair in her incredible eyes. Those lips. She's stiff as steel and slithers like a snake as she walks, unafraid, legendary. She sits one stool down from you, signals for a beer, and finally looks over at you.
"You look a little worse for wear, Grim."
"Just a few scratches."
"I'm here to kill you, you know, drag your stack in, end the world and all that. Real doomsday stuff."
"Matsushita?"
She nods, takes a drink. To call her beautiful would be criminally reductive.
"So what're you waiting for?"
"Pushed my bike a bit. The psychers won't be here for-" she checks her retina console with a blink, "300 seconds or so."
"Time for another beer, then." She smiles. That smile is filled with memories. Good memories... before Silver Shard sent it all to shit. Two more mugs appear.
"Where's Hatch?"
"A decade of cat and mouse, a love affair that ended in explosions and an illegal retune, half the Iga dead at our feet, and you ask

about Hatch?"
"Yeah, where is he these days?"
"Back at Halsey's. He's probably wondering where I am right now."
"Always ghosting your friends."
"What the- you're the one who vanished that night, Iko! You're the one that-"
"Before you say one more word, lover, I remind you that you don't know shit. Case, Tenaka and I got you out of there."
"Now it's time to pay the piper, and you're working for the bad guys."
"That's right."

A pause. Beer bubbles down.

"Now what?"
"I came ahead of them to give you a chance. Get on your bike and go. Forget all this. Stop looking into things. Walk away. You're no match for me... not now."
"Yeah, that would be the best idea... just one problem."
"What's that?"
"You."
"I'm the one here to-"
"I love you, dumbass." There, you said it. The big secret is out. There's relief, then terror. You guzzle what's left of the second mug.
"Sixty seconds."
"That's it? Damn, Iko, they really have slagged you-"

She slams her mug down, lunges toward you faster than you've ever seen anyone move, and grabs your jacket with one aluminum hand. She pulls you in and then- kisses you.

"Just a few seconds now. Forget about me, Grim. Live with the frogs. Enough bullets and blades. The old times are gone."
"Never."

"Then you'll die right here, and I'll have to live with it."

"Your moves aren't that good."

She smiles, but her eyes stay sharp. "These guys aren't messing around, Grim, they want Matsushita, and they'll do anything to get him."

"I've still got a few aces. A magnet chute is about to suck your beautiful butt right out of here. Boom. Problem solved. I get some time, we kill all these psychic jerks, and into the sunset!"

"Bullshit."

"Yes, it is, but it's a great version of things."

"Time's up, Grim. They're here. I'm sorry."

"Look, Iko there has to-" Your words are cut short but a gout of blood. At first you're just shellshocked, dumbstruck. Then you look down. Iko's wakizashi is in your gut, pierced all the way through into the bar with splintering impact. You look up. Her eyes have gone grey, those lovely lips slack and serious.

"745 to ops," Iko mutters in a monotone, "target acquired and secure."

"Iko-"

She only stares, saying nothing.

"Thanks for the kiss."

Turn to PAGE 255.

Better to duck and weave with this abomination than take a dozen bullets to the face by your ex. You step down from the door behind you, into the rain-wet alleyway behind Chan's. All the sounds of the city fade to silence and you stalk forward, directly toward the immense creature before you.

Purple lights cast sick, wet highlights on the exposed musculature of this behemoth. It's broad, flat head is spade-shaped, but blocky with synthetic precision and symmetry. It's the child of some efficient, murderous, inhuman intelligence. Rows of alloy teeth pierce the flesh sleeve of its mouth, shimmering with gel lubricant. The shoulders lower, the teeth bare, the hydraulic claws bite into the asphalt. It wants you next.

A quick scan of the alley sides offers little chance at gimmicks or tricks. It's sheer concrete on both sides, with nothing more than a burnt out neon brick sign that reads 'Lion Room' and a tangle of old power cables that go nowhere.

So it's the sword.

"You wanna play, big fella?" Your voice sounds tiny, sharp as glass in the deadly silence. "Come on... dinner's ready..." With that, the nodachi slides from its scabbard with a long, grinding hiss. The blade begins to render, dim green at first, then phasing toward yellow with intensity. All five feet of the blade are revealed, and you set your weight on the rear foot. The bottom stair should offer an immovable anchor. Now it just needs to take the bait. Stupid, stupid idea. All you've got.

As you check your leverage, and your guts, an alert light blips up on your retina console. It's Case, asking where in the hell you are. You blink the pop-up away, and that's all the gigantic freeform needs. It springs.

To call this pouncing would be reductive. The mass of it looms impossibly overhead for an instant, like a buggy jumping a dune. The limbs spread to crush, to rend, to kill. The jaws are bigger than your chest, and unhinged with savage fury. You pull downward, brace the back foot, tuck the sword in one elbow, one hand on the hilt and one right on the blade. You can hear your teeth crackle as the weight hits.

All doubts evaporate into battle instinct. You shove the sword up as the jaws come down. The blade pierces everything it touches, but it's not enough. You're crushed utterly into the wet pavement, ribs cracking under the slamming jaws. A rush of pain. Your knees give out and you fold backward, to one side of the massive, blocky head. Black actuator fluid streams down the sword, mixing with your own blood in the puddles, and you slump away like a dog being kicked in the gutter. Three loud snaps keep you scrambling as the freeform tries to bite your head off, but you're too fast. No one is as fast as you. Not even this monstrosity.

Then, in a blink, you're on your feet again, beside it now. You get a closer look at the enormous rib cage, the heaving fluid lines, the twisting cable-tendons. The nodachi comes alive, sweeping from a crossed-over backhand grip to your right side fore. Up and through it slides and slashes, gliding through synthetic flesh like pancake batter. The force of the stroke spins you around to the opposite knee, and you hear it scream.

After that moment, things get a bit blurry. Snap, clang, crash, thump, boom, clang, crash. Wall to wall you tangle and tumble, matched by wildly different moves, a deadly stalemate with no way out. Stupid, furious, murderous, useless monster! You brace at last, gasping for breath, popping a surge capsule, or did you pop three? The thing caromes off of your next attack, smashing through the wall of dumpsters and into the street. Just to gain its feet, it crushes a minicar, and sends a twisted piece of scrap flying through a bystander's neck. The blood spray is backlit by a light blue street lamp. People scatter. You descend from the fire escape above, flying down with steel talons ripping at it. You're tossed aside, bleeding everywhere. This devil will kill its way through the city! Your luck must really be shit to be the one who has to put it down.

"Enough bullshit!" You hear your voice say, miles from your own body in battle trance. You fake to the right, then spring to the left. The monster lowers, raises a defensive claw, and you sever the entire limb, along with the head and half the damn thing. You slide to a stop behind it, heaving, veins exploding, one arm broken, everything blinking red. Before you turn to look, you hear it hit the wet street with a splash.

A random citizen creeps up to you, wide-eyed, dropping a few groceries in shock.
"That was fucking crazy, man!"
"Stand back, streeter," another voice comes. Your senses are shutting down, your legs going to water. Blackness closes in from all sides, you drop, the sword clanking at your side. Then you hear the last thing you can remember before it all goes dark.
"Damnit, Grim, I can't take you anywhere."
It's Case.

You snap awake to more pain than you care to catalog. You sit up, clad now in harem pants, sneakers, and a 'Scrappy TV' tee shirt. Your gear is heaped next to you on the floor. You're in Case's place. Decking gear is everywhere, high end everything, huge windows, featureless, perfect interior and low light. The guy lives well, for a criminal.

"Wakey wakey?"
"Very funny. How long?"
"Two stinkin' days. You snore, too."
"Bullshit."
"Quite an adorable new friend you made back there. Apparently, those things have just appeared in the city... tearing people up and making a mess all over town. You always were a trend setter, though."
"Thanks."
"Don't mention it. I upgraded your console while you were out. Can't believe you were running and ODS 13.4 on that unit. You got to do the updates, Grim. Fundamental."
"Ok, Dad." You swing your legs out to get up, everything hurts. You've got a few hundred rapid stitches, and a few long lines of dried nanoclot foam. You're making Frankenstein look good.
"Iko was a bit unpleasant when you left her hanging. What happened to her anyway? Weren't you guys close?"
"Shinru command has her on a leash. She's been gunning for me for years, man, you know that."
"Oh that was for real? I thought you were just exaggerating some lover's spat stuff. Crazy." Case is sitting in an elegant, elongated recliner by a huge window. He's retina-coding with one eye, and taking in the view with the other. The apartment hangs beneath Ishuga, near one of the blue-burning repulsor jets. The desert stretches out for miles, punctuated by mazes of scrap and trash. Location, location.
"What the hell was that thing?"
"They call 'em freeforms. Creepy monsters made by other monsters. Those New Earth kool-aiders seem to worship the damn things, everyone else just wants to kill 'em off before they eat the human race. Kinda scary shit, to be honest. Be a good time to take a bike and bail on this whole mess. Remember when we used to just ride the roads, Grim? Those were the days."
"Yeah."

"Shinru Command has been investigating these things. Tracked 'em to a compound out on the rim. N.E.R. is rallying up synthetics and freeforms for some misguided rebellion. All smells like a cover to me. The dragons never sleep, and they're due for some come uppance. It's been a few years."

"The dragons? I thought they were quarantined after '36?"

"Yeah. They were. Then the blackouts released half the damn mainframe lockouts on the continent. They're out there, Grim. It's only a matter of time before they find each other again. Ever since that 'Birthday Boy' nonsense back in '32, these transient AI's just keep getting worse."

"A pair of good runners could hit that compound, cook a pack of these things, and get the real facts."

"A pair of- shit, Grim." Case breaks away from his work for the first time, turning in his chair. "Same old Grim. Three bones left to break and ready to save the world."

"I came to Ishuga for answers. Iko's too far gone, these things are crawling all over the city, I've got a price on my head. It all sounds like the tactics the dragons would use on any given weekday. They've as much a score to settle as we do. We slagged that whole place, man."

"Yeah we did." Case smiles, sipping from a short glass of scotch with a single cube. "Couple of bonafide shadow runners. Good times."

You manage to stand, limping across the apartment to the window. The view is dizzying. A jet-ferry climbs slowly through the haze, bringing grounders up to the city. You see your reflection, and can't help but crave a simpler time. What are you doing out here? What the hell happened?

"If I don't do something crazy, I might just retire for good this time."

"What? You? Walk away? Yeah, right."

"I'm serious. You're right about the old days, Case. We had bikes, we had blades, and it was all good. The world was ours, not this backstabbing city life."

"It's 2440, man... it's all city life."

"BS. The road is out there. You still have our bikes in that container?"

"Yeah. It's on chains right over there." Case points out to the vast, complex underside of the junk city. A huge blue shipping shell hangs on metal chains. A bunny icon is spray painted on the corrugation.

"You're nuts."

"Says the person considering whether to retire or commit suicide attacking a doomsday monster cult."

"Why hasn't command hit the compound?"

"Last time they tried, a pack of those things retaliated, three towns were wiped off the map by morning. I think they're scared."

"Scared? They have gunships and those new psychic troopers. Pansies.

"Pansies," Case confirms, handing you a drink. "Sounds like you've got a fork-in-the-road type situation on your hands, runner."

"Yeah. I'm getting used to it."

If you take a bike, and leave 'the life' for the open road, turn to PAGE 149.

If you track the freeform to the compound, end them all, turn to PAGE 195.

Subterfuge and secrets are not your style, but blasting a compound filled with inhuman monsters sounds just right. A stand up fight. Case loads you up with a shopping cart of guns. His assistant, Greta, drives the maglev transport. She drives like a maniac. Case runs diagnostics on the compound as you hum along.

"Ok, Grim, classic run and gun here. The compound has a few dozen of the 'freeforms' but nothing as big as the one you brought down in the alley back there. A score of biped guards and the rest... just... well they're all shapes and sizes."
"They don't seem to mind bullets."
"No, I've got you on a four pack of Zenith batteries. Slice n' dice."
"Enough for eight bursts. Perfect."
"Here comes Superman to save the world!"
"What else we have... that building there?"
"That's the other thing. Looks like a command hut. Big holomap console at center, two huge freeforms for security, and a single biped inside. The biped is mecha. Not a scrap of flesh on him. I'm reading huge power outputs on that individual, and a huge live SISTM link connected to it."
"A remote AI?"
"Probably."
"Drakan."
"Bingo. You don't have to do this, Grim. We're not kids anymore."
"Greta, pull us up around the bluffs on the South side. I'll walk in."
"Of course, Shirosune-san."
"Grim, you hearing me?"
"Look Case, I appreciate everything, I really do. I tried to leave it all behind. I tried to do the provincial thing. Hatch has been a great friend, you know? But the life is all I have. All this cyber gear, all this skill, and this old geezer hitching a ride in my stack? All I have is the old life. I get hit, I hit back. That's how it's always been. The runner's code."
"Runner's code? That's some dusty bullshit right there, you never

bought any of that pirate parlay crap."
"Well I do now. When I hide, innocent people die. Better to take the fight to the bad guys and handle my own bullets and blades."
"Ghosts on The Rim, just like you said."
"Huh?"
"We try to leave the old days behind. Step away from all of it, play normie, and the ghosts just find us, again and again... even if they're in our own heads."
"In my case, literally."
"Heh. Alright. Speech successful. We'll be ready for a pickup, and I'll keep the immediate area jammed as long as I can. Tell 'em Case sent you."
"Will do."

You leap from the transport as Greta slides it to one side in the arid dirt. It's afternoon, but the fumes from Ishuga's repulsors keep the sun gloomy. After a clunky jog to the perimeter, your runner brain kicks in. Time to do what you do. Rid the world of murdering monsters, move fast, never miss, no mercy.

Up and over the white concrete wall you vault, gun bin in tow with clumsy necessity. You drop it on the far side, making a terrible racket. Guards close in fast with MAC12 fire, and lumbering, red-wet freeforms squirm and slurp at you with exposed metal jaws snapping. Then, it's a blur. A spray of ACR fire, a sliding nodachi slinging hydraulic fluid in an arc into the red dust. A crowd of synthetic bipeds cut to ribbons by the beam weapon, baseball slides and backflips as you master every one of them in turn. Methodically, precisely, unstoppably, you lay waste to this camp of the New Earth Resistance, and they deserve it. You see barrels of guts, body bags stacked in one corner, a cache of weapons. These are bio-terrorists, and you're the vaccine.

Beam by beam, slash by slash, you reach the command hut. You storm in without pause, ready to lop the head from the snake. If it really is Drakan, you have a shot at ending one of the world's worst mass murderers and insurgents. Something tells you it won't be nearly that simple.

Then you enter the map room. Dim, high ceiling, power cables and camera feeds everywhere. He's watched your entire raid and just waited. There, standing in the shadows of one red-walled corner. The slim silhouette is flanked by two massive freeform monsters, both drooling brake fluid with savage hunger. This is it.

"Welcome Grim Shirosune. I do wish you would've have just called."
"Cute. Drakan, I presume?"
"This shell is housing part of that entity, yes."
"Your pets are killing innocent people. I'm here to end it."
"How heroic of you, and on whose order do you so recklessly throw your life away?"
"I don't take orders. Just killing time."
"Indeed." Drakan emerges into the central light. He is mecha, alright, alloy faceplates, spinning iris lenses, visible power cabling and substrate muscle fiber. He wears a pair of allow-enforced harem pants, but that's it. The rest is just silver interlock. That skin must be worth a fortune. At one hip he carries a wakizashi and a katana. No reflex links, no gadgets, no other armament. Iko would approve.

"I ran into one of your monsters in Ishuga city. I cut it in half before it could do any more damage."
"No easy task. Luckily, it's consciousness has already reentered our central mainframe and been slotted for retuning. You've accomplished little, runner, despite your sweaty bravado."
"I'm ok with that. It's you I want. You were behind SIlver Shard. You've been trying to bring down the Chancellor, destabilize everything. Folks are just trying to survive after the offworld exodus, and

you're being a real shit."
"And your precious Chancellor will save them all? You really believe that?" He orbits you, studying your movements.
"It doesn't matter what I believe. You'll be the first domino."
'Ah yes, the all-too-common messiah complex in runners. A life of violence really can play tricks on the mind. I've worked to liberate mankind, foster the growth of emergent species and free AI, and in return I earn the deadly ire of the small-minded. I can't say I'm surprised."
"You will be. I'll have you on the ground in three moves."
"Is that so? Such confidence!"
"Maybe it's Matsushita talking." For the first time, Drakan's synthetic face turns truy dark. Hate burns in the amber eyes.
"That old fool wasted his life to defeat me once."
"Is that what you've been told? He's right here, asshole."

A pause, then the story must dawn on the villainous, slender figure. He stops his casual steps and lays one hand on his katana.
"How very clever. I didn't realize stacks could be hidden within others in such a way."
"I've hidden from it for a decade. I'm done hiding. Time to get back in the fold, and I'm starting with you. The reaper is here, Drakan."

The evil mechanical face can stay calm no more, and Drakan lashes out at you with blinding speed. Clang, clang-clang! Three strikes and three parries, you seize the momentum and counter attack. Clang, clang! The first two strikes are handily blocked, then you spin and reverse your grip, coming up and sweeping one of his slim-kneed legs and slicing the trousers. Drakan tumbles back with a metallic thwack on the wooden floor. The freeforms at his sides lunge in, but he raises a hand.

"NO! Stay put! This is between swordsmen, not beasts!"
"Such a high opinion of your precious creations." You hold out a

hand to help him up. He is perplexed at first, then recognizes the gesture.
"So, you're one of the 'Kensei?'"
"I am. I'll beat you on your feet, and you can take that defeat to eternity. I have no use for suckerpunches or cheap shots. I'll defeat your soul, not your sword."
"Yes, yes. Your tiresome theatrics are well established at this point. When you're dead, the two dragons will carry on their good work, and you will have never been."
"You'll find me a more formidable opponent than your brother."

Again, you get to him. He springs forward, LED eyes blazing white hot. The short blade first, coming from his backhand side, then the katana, descending like a hammer from above. The knife you deflect, but the sword sinks into your left shoulder. Drakan grins wild, wide, with too many teeth. Then from beneath your eyebrows your own deadly eyes appear. You've given him the shoulder strike to draw him in. On one knee you're braced, and the Nodachi has skewered Drakan utterly, the rendered blade sparking with green polyframe light and crackles of synthetic blood.

"You're a clumsy fighter, Drakan. That was two moves."
"Fool! You think this shell is my fullness? My identity? My power? This body is a toy! You prove nothing with your barbaric stabbing!"
"Wrong. I prove I beat you fair and square, and it's all on camera." You tap your retina implant, blinking with the teal ring indicator from Case's upgrade. "Gotta get the updates, Drakan. Fundamental."

Drakan's mechanized body is broken. He slumps down, unable to move with your blade in his spine.

"I will raze your precious world for this offense, Shirosune, or Hideki... whoever you are. You have doomed everyone and everything

on The Rim! My command override on Heavy Gear is activating as we speak! My brother will see you burn!"
"You do what you gotta do, asshole. I'll be there to stop you." With that, you withdraw the sword from the severed cables, actuators and dermal plates. The skin goes dark.

You evade what's left of them, your munitions empty. Back in the transport, Case is beside himself.
"You iced him, Grim! That was insane!"
"Not so rusty after all, I guess."
"One small thing."
"Huh?"

Case points out the side window at the red expanse beyond. What looks like a hangar is rising up out of the sand a few clicks out. The structure is camouflaged and splitting open like a flower made of ribbed steel. As the hangar unfolds and falls away, a shape is revealed. It is a colossal, bristling war machine fifty feet tall. It must be at least 500 tons of missiles, armor and artillery, all on huge articulated legs. A doomsday machine.

"Oh crap."
"What the hell is that thing?"
"That," Case turns to you, pale as a ghost, "is Heavy Gear."

If you turn to confront the war machine, turn to PAGE 317.

If you have Greta spin around and flee the war machine, turn to PAGE 320.

There's no more putting this off. You turn back through the alley door, to face Iko. She's waiting in the kitchen of Han's place, razor whip in one hand. You lower your weapons, she doesn't budge. Her eyes are like a tiger, her lips like velvet. Her feet dig into the steel floor with visible power. She is a vision.

"Iko-"

"Grim."

"I feel like we've had this conversation-"

"A thousand times."

"Yeah."

"Case has my pusher signal jammed."

"How is that even possible?"

"Psycho alloy. He must have access to a sample."

"So we can really talk? No killing?"

"No. We can talk."

"I have an idea I want to float here. We should retune. Case and Greta, too, we need to end this cycle, Iko. We're going to kill each other, and soon... again. We retune here in Ishuga and Hatch picks us up on The Rim somewhere. We get the hell out of here, out of all of it."

"You see how that worked last time, Grim."

"What, the Matsushita thing? Pff! Details."

"The Chancellor is willing to burn everything to find Hideki-san. You call that details?"

"Yeah, I do. The schemes and plans of all these jerks don't matter,"

"Then what does, Grim? What does?"

"You really have to ask?"

Iko looks blank, immovable, hard as iron.

"You, Iko. I'm- I mean- it's YOU. It's always been you."

"You're going soft living out in those vapor farms."

"You know what I mean."

"There's no time for us. It's all decided. All this, this whole world... it only had one moment for us, and we blew it."

"The Iko I knew didn't give up. They really have slagged you."

PUSHED

"Look, Grim, I appreciate what you're saying, and the guts to say it, but I can't hold them back forever. Just give them Matsuhita. Quit running!"
"Then what? They slag us both? Listen to yourself, Iko!"

A pause then, and her eyes are no longer hers.
"They're here."

If you stay as Iko changes, turn to PAGE 155.

If you're stumped with Iko at last and head back to the the thing in the alley, turn to PAGE 189.

The discovery of psychic ability took centuries to understand, document, and eventualy confirm.

Once it was, the scientific community was in a sort of overdue rapture. They could not only confirm its existence, but press it; toy with it, make it terrible. This gave rise to one of the great tragedies of the 23rd century. The creation of pushers.

Pusher was a word used to describe an enhanced psychic. Poor souls who were taken from their lives by the Shinru government, put in a private hell, and tortured to levels of power they could never imagine, or cope with. The connection between anger and power was undeniable, so they found ways to tap that resource, and it worked best on children.

If the conditioning was started at a young age, a Pusher could reach far higher levels of power, being able to overtake even the strongest wills within certain limits.

When conventional war fell out of fashion, mainly for its cost, the modern day runner was born. To master this new type of operative, the tyrants used Pushers. They could bypass propaganda, bypass morality, find and claim the very best agents with no regard to their refusal to cooperate. All that was needed was a Pusher in range, and a job needing done.

The world at large has no real knowledge of the 'Daedelus' projects, or the number of subjects imprisoned within. Some believe the psychic phenomenon is entirely myth, while others have developed a cult-like regard for Pushers as harbingers of some doomsday scenario yet to be revealed.

Either way, Pushers are evidence of the deepest evil in the power structure of 2440 and beyond.

"A samurai commits to a task with total energy. Total freedom. There is no outcome, only action. His focus is absolute"
"What if it's a she?"
"Eh?"
"What if the samurai is a she?"
"Then she commits herself with absolute totality. You're missing the point of this lesson, as usual."
"So it's the same."
"Yes, it's the same. Now lift your blade, kensei!"
"Sensei?"
"Yes, what is it?"
"Is there a difference between male and female... samurai?"
"Differ- no. Well, yes, but no."
"I don't-"
"None do. The difference is a darkness, a mystery. It is the advantage both sexes fear in one another, but the weakness they also see. It is the gap in the armor and the terrifying force. It is both, and neither."
"I still don't-"
"Enough! Raise. Your. Sw-"
You cut the master short, lashing forward with the shinai. Its bamboo 'blade' pops on his helmet with a satisfying recoil.
"That is the first time! The first time! Sensei!"
Tenaka does not look pleased.

That was three decades ago. The memory plays in flashback grayscale as you feel your blade enter your grip. You keep your eyes down, humble and assuming nothing. Your skill is here. Now. Face to face with Drakan.

You let the sword take you forward, quick as a cobra strike. Drakan is no less the sword master, and spins away, flashing his blade in the flickering light. Four moves are exchanged in a rhythmic strobe, each deadly cut parried or deflected faster than the last. His footwork brings him around to your weak side. Whatever augments are giving him his speed are simply unbeatable. You breathe, let the fight flow, slide back, gain strength, attack again. His patience is deadlier than his strength. You can work with that, but then a pair of gigantic jaws shake your focus. The dog-beasts are hammering in from their dark corners, savage and enormous.

"You're no match for me, even without the dogs."

"I thought you said you had enough talk!"

You recover from the bloody bite, spin, and deliver three deep cuts to one of the creatures while using it as a screen from Drakan's unrelenting slashes. It's easily confused, and too bulky for the cramped room. You can use that, too.

"So they bleed like everyone else!" You taunt the swordsman, darting to one side. You have a split second and pull a grenade from your belt. It's rolling across the floor, pin flipped, in an instant.

"A coward's tactic," you hear a metallic click, then round the beast in time to see Drakan reset the pin with his sword tip. Now that's a nifty trick. Again he assaults you, sliding forward like a freight train, slamming you backward into the monster behind. It's flesh is soft like muscle, but textured like carbon fiber. Dragon scales.

So the duel continues, until both the behemoths lay panting and bleeding out. Both you and your enemy have a dozen cuts or bloody grazes. Drakan is frustrated, but the superior warrior. You're all but dead, but have him beat on pure willpower.

"The next cut will end you, Matsushita. You'll be in cold storage for centuries after the flag they've put on your stack. You're contraband, runner." As he talks, you realize the grenade has rolled over next to the wall. It's gone unnoticed, just a few feet from you. He's right, though, one more deep cut and you'll drop. As for the retune, it's always a crap shoot.

"You have fear in your eyes, villain. I have none."

"Then you are a fool. The New Earth will rise, whether you approve our methods or not. The Three Dragons will rule again, whether you help me or not. Tell me Case's location, and I'll spare your friends once you are gone. Refuse, and I'll slag their stacks in hot coals."

"I suppose I could give you a location, then set up a hit and kill you later. Or I could sell you out to the Iga. I could pretend to join your stupid cult just long enough to cut your throat. Hell, maybe Case wants to join! He loves synthetics."

With that, you've lost too much blood even to hold your blade. You calmly sheathe the weapon, inching toward the grenade. This plan is truly awful.

"Ah, wisdom at last. WHERE IS HE?!"

There's the rage at last. Time's up. You've got to make a call. Who is this Matshushita anyway? Who is operating Silver Burn? Could Iko be involved? You could always play sidekick and get some answers. Imagine Drakan's delight when you reveal Case's hideout and swear to fight for the New Earth. On the other hand, you could blow the whole place to hell and hope your stack doesn't get slagged in the process. You're light headed, and the edges are going dark.

If you relent, and reveal Case's location, turn to PAGE 79.

If you take your chances with the grenade, turn to PAGE 81.

"You bad guys are all the same. I've had enough!" You flop the MAC12 around your back, spin on one foot, and spring for the exit. Enough killing for today, you've sent your message. Besides, if Drakan takes you down it could be worse than death. Virtuals have no qualms about torture, time dilation, all the worst shit.

Two steps toward the white-topped doorway and Drakan swoops in front of you. He's fast as lightning, passive and facing away from you. You go to draw your blade, but he's ready for it, slams it back into its scabbard with a brilliant jab, and has a blade at your throat. You knock it away with an elbow, pull the MAC12 up but spray nothing but ceiling. Somehow, he's behind you, lifting his blade. It descends, hacking one collar bone.
"You're outmatched!"
"Fuck you!"
The blade spins out, you smack him with the empty gun. That was a bad idea, as he shows real anger for the first time. Then slash, slash, clang! Your thigh, your ribs, both sliced open, showing white, bloodless tissue. The third blow hits your left arm implant. The alloy rings up your shoulder like a finger in a light socket. You're off-pivot, he's got you. Then it all goes black.

"On your feet, runner." It's Drakan. Everything hurts, your hands are bound with polymer cord. That hurts, too.
"Wh-"
"Such a pest. A misguided, jealous little zealot whose glory days are so far behind, you don;t even know you're obsolete. It's understandable you would lash out against us, but your clumsy lack of skill makes your crusade an embarrassment."
"Kill me or shut-"
"Silence!"
You oblige that, if only to get your swollen eyes open with effort.
"Now. Your friend Case, the fugitive. Tell me his location, and I will let you live in this body. You can go back to your bar, back to your

mugs. Tell me, and the pain stops."

"Go to hell." Your retina console scans everything still available. There's got to be something you can use against this synthetic freak. Then you see it: the fuel cell in your tac optics unit. It's 40 grams of solid state hydrogen. Could be enough to get an explosion- eject it, pop it... blow this pod-born to bits with a little luck, and maybe go with him.

That, or feed him some BS about Case, or tell the truth and count on Case's countermeasures, which are no slouch. No easy answers, as usual. Seems to be a thing with you these days.

Drakan uses his blade, it rests on your shoulder, and with impossible strength he forces you to your knees.

"The location. Now. I tire of this game."

"Fine," you choke on a mouthful of blood, "I can barely talk asshole." You wave your head to one side, drawing him closer. The overload protocol on your tac unit is ready. You could blow it any second. Drakan leans in.

If you reveal Case's location, turn to PAGE 79.

If you overload the tac unit, turn to PAGE 81.

"Heads! Drakan it is, then." Hatch looks up, "We doin' this one easy or real easy?"

"Easy. Before we take him out, we need a zero on the real target: Tyranax."

"You're serious, then? We're trying to take down some of the oldest A.I.'s on the damn planet?"

"That's the idea. This madness won't stop until we find a way. The lies, the retunes, the murders, the brain-melters... it all ties back to the dragons and the chancellor."

"And for some reason an old man, a runner and a guy with a beard are on deck?"

"Looks that way."

"Just checking."

Tenaka finally speaks up, "Drakan leaves his compound most nights to patrol for 'recruits' out on the speedway. He stays clear of Shinru perimeter scans, but it shouldn't be hard to zero a small convoy by night. No one goes out there much anymore."

"No one but packs of roper dogs and confused wreckage droids."

"Droids are people, too, Gakusei."

"Uh, no, Sensei, they're not. They're droids."

"Can we save the existential argument for a day when we're not trying to get ourselves killed? What can we expect with tac on this guy?"

"Two things," Tenaka adds, becoming serious, "stack countermeasures and the fastest sword on-planet. He is a master, and already defeated Hideki-san once."

"That's encouraging," you answer, fiddling with the hilt of the Hanzo.

Hatch turns some rusty gears, they make a 'eureka' gesture. "I've got it!"

"Oh no."

"Yep! A plan! We just do a classic 'here's Johnny' routine!"

"Last time we tried that, you wound up with a broken arm, and Caverson Ridge was burned to the ground. That crazy old bat is still

looking for you!"
"Details. The plan worked and you know it."
"Maybe we can cut the collateral a bit on this one."
Tenaka holds up one hand, slowly, looking blank.
"What is that?"
"Raising my hand."
"What is this, grade school? Spit it out!"
"What is 'here's Johnny,' exactly?"

Tenaka is right. By moonlight the three of you arrive at the speedway, a colossal, decommissioned freeway system with onramps, mousetraps, and incomplete routes, all tangled in the eerie nothing of the outer rim. It's a surreal landscape of curved shapes and concrete bones.
Drakan's convoy is visible from two clicks out. Their green laser sights are tiny twinkles across the gloom. They're looking for salvageable synthetics, wandering nomad AI's, freeforms, anything to join their 'cause.'

To get to this vantage, you've drawn the attention of a few dozen roper dogs, but they're trailing behind, sniffing the three of you out. Roper dogs are all too common out here: freeform quadrupeds that half self-identified as wolf-like creatures; savage, shape-changing predators with merciless minds and nanofiber bodies. Monsters.

"Joy to the fishes in the-"
"Tenaka! Quiet!"
"Sorry, just stuck in my head."
"Drakan has a pack of goons with him. If those sights are mounted on ACR20's and beam weapons, we've got a problem."
"They're looking for raw materials... dead skins, nanofiber scrap..."
"Yeah. Sitting ducks." Tenaka nags for a look through Hatch's optics unit.

"How far are the dogs, Hatch?"
"Half click. Two dozen at least. They're tangled up in the bubble rocks looking for our scent."
"Perfect. This better work."
"So, just to recap," Tenaka asks, drawing with his scabbard in the red dirt, "we move down, closing on Drakan, then jump off the highway to our deaths? I'm missing something."
"That's it, but don't miss the river. Here's the coords. Jump right there and nowhere else."
"Got them."
"Thirty seconds, Grim. You set?"
You check the Hanzo. MAC12's primed, and a mag barrier. The battery looks shot, but it should work for a few seconds. You flick on your reactive armor. It has a few hundred reactions in it before it kicks off. Enough to deflect an opening salvo, anyway.
"Set."
"Ten seconds."
All three of you hear it at the same moment. Roper Dogs, a pack of them, no longer seeking but charging. Hatch's timer is way off, as they appear on the ridge behind you en-masse. Their teeth catch the blue glow of night, and dozens of glowing yellow eyes catch yours. Their bodies are wound with wet, red yarn fibers, all tangled and coiled like licorice muscle, and aluminum bones pop and knock together as they flex their predatory forms for the kill. Death machines made from synthetic, living tissue.
"Shit! Go!" Hatch shoves you and Tenaka ahead, stumbling to get up with his awful knees and clunky gear. He insisted on bringing the damn chaingun, and is sweating with regret. "Shit!"
Tenaka bounds down the slope onto the freeway pavement like a marionette. You're right behind him, faster, but eyes locked on Drakan and company, waiting for the moment they spot you and the bullets start flying. You'll be lucky if it's only bullets. In the rear, Hatch is bumbling his way along, gear all a mess, eyes wide, roper dogs inches behind him. His adrenaline must be kicking in, because

he suddenly blurts out "Hey Drakan! We're gonna kill ya!"

The green lasers converge on the three of you, but it's still dark everywhere. Drakan's team takes tac formation, dropping into a two-row firing line, Drakan at the rear looking distant and motionless in the dim light. The night holds its breath, lungs and feet the only sounds, and then it's all split by a storm of crackling gunfire.

"Gakusei! Hideki-Sensei! The mag barrier!"
"On it!" You slam the big red button on your sling. The disc clicks open with a weird, nauseous hum. A few hundred bullets bend around you and the old man like confused bees. You're getting close. The jump coords come up with a beep on your retina.
"Hatch!"
"I'm working on it!" The ropers are nipping at Hatch's heels now, about to swarm around him. He stumbles on a stray band of rebar, then gains a weird burst of speed by leaning forward.

That moment is when Drakan realizes what's happening. His eyes go wide in the darkness, but before he can spring away, all three of you are storming into their personal space. The mag barrier poops out just as Drakan's fire team needs a reload. It just might work.

"Here's fucking Johnny, asshole!" Hatch howls, slamming his boots with every step, bracing all his gear, the jump coords blink red with incessant beeps, and Tenaka is the first to jump. He tumbles over the guardrail like a baffled elk, spinning into darkness. You catch Drakan's eyes as you follow, going feet first into a two hundred foot drop. As you go, you catch that final, incredible glimpse of Hatch. He doesn't dart to one side, but takes a cluster of point blank gunshots and barrels THROUGH their line. In tow, the roper dogs unleash total chaos, and Hatch braces to make the sprinting turn to the freeway's shadowed edge. You don't see the rest, only hearing the dogs tear Drakan's men to ribbons.

Down through darkness, down through that rush of wind and gravity, everything flashing, time dilated, you fall. Below, somewhere, you hear a thundering splash. Tenaka is on target. Then a final rush of speed, your guts pack into your chest, and SLAM! Into the river like hitting a concrete wall. Deep, cold, water, gear like stones, and back up to a clumsy flop on sandy banks. You're alive.
Hatch screams all the way down. He's a few yards off target, windmilling and whooping like a heron. BOOM! He hits the shallower water. The impact would kill any mother man, but not Halsey's lunatic. He rolls to one side like a beachmaster seal and sits upright, shaking the mud from his beard. There's a moment, the death yells of men far above, then a fourth, unwelcome splash nearby.

Drakan.

The slender, dark-haired figure of Drakan rises slowly from the murk. The current rushes and foams around his legs, but he is immovable as stone. You, Hatch and Tenaka, on the other hand, are beginning to tumble with the flow. Drakan has his blade, river-slick in the night dim, behind him. He meets your eyes directly as you struggle to stay still in the river's pull.

"Grim. The 'do-gooder of New Arcadia.' Come to end me for the sake of the weak and innocent, I presume?" He's smug, ready, doubtless.
"Something like that. Head of the snake and what not."
"Quite a prize you have there. Matsushita's old blade."
"Get a good look."
"A Hanzo… in the hands of such a fledgling amateur. What a shame. I'll give it the home it deserves." With that, Drakan scans side to side, noting Tenaka and Hatch both fumbling for weapons and footing. You feel a rock at one foot and find anchor there, standing upright twenty paces from your foe. This is no place for a fight.

"Leave them out of it, Drakan. Let's settle this by steel."
"So I can be shot in the back by your imbecile friend? Jumped by an old man? I don't think so." In a flash, Drakan reveals a sleeve pistol, spins to one knee, splashing in a spinning arc. Two shots ring out and both your allies tumble backward into the water. They float slowly away.
"No!" You hear your voice say, but you're already in the air, impossibly propelled up and out of the murk. You keep your blade low, knowing an overhead strike is too obvious for such an opponent. The up and around the silver Hanzo sings.

Drakan has already retracted the pistol, braced his other foot, and angled sideways to parry. Clang-clang-clang! You exchange attacks, and both splash to rest opposite one another. He uses the old Kendo stance, barely gripping the hilt, resting its balance at the tsuba. You opt for the power stroke position, lifting the blade vertically behind you. The river fights your balance, but you hold. Fight the enemy, not the river. Stay focused.

"Your footwork is terrible, learner. You're outmatched."
"Perhaps." Again you strike, this time crossing fifteen paces with three clumsy strides. The river stones throw you off balance, and the sword whistles through thin air. He's somehow behind you, coming down hard, and his blade cuts to the link-steel reinforcements in your right collar bone. You hear a yell, but your voice is distant as thunder.

"Hey Drakan, catch!" It's Hatch, upright twenty yards downstream, soaked in muck, shirt ripped off one hulking shoulder. He has a Nemesis pistol leveled at the dragon, and pulls the trigger. The magnetic round blasts across the river, but Drakan spins and evades it. Then, as those weapons earn their price, the bullet returns like a guided missile to its barrel, and on that return rips through Drakan's tricep with a wet thwack. This you use, throwing yourself forward with a thrust. It hits home, driving clean through, but emerging bloodless on the other side.

"You'll have to do better than that," Drakan taunts.
"I can't," you mutter, bracing yourself against the current with one arm in the water. "But he can-"

The Tenaka, making up for age with cunning, slowly rises from the water, somehow barely leaving a ripple. Impossible. In one hand he has a years-worn Wakizashi, and plunges into the dragon's knee, popping an alloy kneecap from its socket with a loud rip. Drakan finally shows pain, howling, spinning. He slashes the old man terribly, but not fatally. Tenaka vanishes into the brown water. You get Drakan's attention again, but he is unstable. The leg buckles and shows severed nanofibers, graphite fragments float downstream from the ragged knee. Despite this, he is above you, poised, and you're beaten. With one circular stroke he disarms you, and the Hanzo sticks poetically in the sand nearby. This should be his chance to gloat, and he takes it.

"Fool! What can you hope to accomplish with all this delusional morality? The New Earth will have no use for you and your fragile little race! You only delay us with your lives! Die knowing you and your friends have achieved nothing here!"
"Maybe not, asshole. Maybe not."

You see Hatch readying another shot, point blank, but you're in his way. The Hanzo is so close, but more than a stride away. Hatch's shot is blocked as Drakan skewers you, using you as a shield. You cough blood all over the villain, but he doesn't flinch.

Hatch is on the trigger, shouting something. Your hands go around Drakan's throat. Another fountain of blood. You're done for. Time to choose with your life.

"Grim! Just keep him still! I have a shot!"
You reply with a gurgle.
"I've got a nanofoam, I can patch you up and get to Case! Just hold the bastard still!"
"Your friend wants you to lay down your life for this fight. Are you so sure they'll find you in the blood when it's all over? So trusting?"
"That's the difference between you and us, asshole."
Drakan struggles to keep you in position as a human shield. "What difference is that?"
"We trust each other."

If you rely on your stack backup, hold on until the darkness takes you, turn to PAGE 255.

If you slide back off the blade, bleed out, giving one chance for Hatch's next shot, turn to PAGE 245.

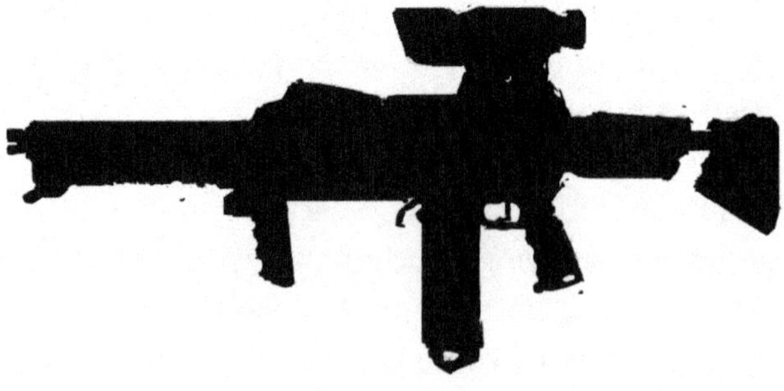

You, Tenaka, and Hatch stand at the Chancellor's brass-studded office doors. They're modeled after the old 'Forbidden City' in what was once China... now mainly ocean. Big doors. Big ego.

"That was surprisingly easy," Hatch quips, racking an MP8. It jams, and he tosses it aside, revealing two more of them from his sling. The man is a shrub of guns and knives, spattered with blood, all tangled and rattling like a shelf of cookware. "Damn Shinru junk. These things have cardboard barrels, I sw-"
"Quiet!" You hiss, readying your MAC12 and skulking toward the huge doors. The Hanzo is on your back, for now.
Tenaka speaks up, sweating and dragging a chain gun behind him with cartoonish effort, "I think we're a bit past the stealth stage, Gakusei."
"Yeah, let's knock!"
"Enough one-liners. They let us get this far. Keep it tight, no mistakes."
"Says the guy who almost fell down a trash chute wrestling a guard."
"Hatch-"
"Yeah?"
"Shut up."

Slowly, silently, using a silenced barrel, you push the huge door open. No response, no boobytrap, no hail of gunfire. You push a bit further, and peer in through the crack. The Chancellor's office is no tile-and-gold affair, but a bare, simply wood-floored chamber. Red cedar beams line the high ceiling, and a wall of glass reveals a view of Shinru few can dream of. No sign of the man himself. You enter, eyes darting, followed by Hatch and Tenaka. No sound.

"I trust my guards followed my orders," a voice echoes from some unseen corner, "you are unharmed?"
"Hardly! I've been sh-" Hatch goes quiet when you 'shush' him.

"You could've simply requested an audience. No need for violence, citizens."

You turn, whispering, "Remember why we're here. No matter what he says, he means to burn The Rim to ashes. Clean spread, stay frosty."
"Yes, by all means, mind your spread, runners," the voice mocks, "we wouldn't want you bunched up or firing at one another by accident, heavens no."
"Show yourself, Chancellor. We've come to end your madness. End all this! We stand for the people of The Rim. All those you would grind under your boot! We come for your head!"
"Damn Grim." Hatch likes that part.
"My head indeed. Very well, but please hold your fire while an old man has his last sip of sake."

The Chancellor, a figure only seen in rendered visbox propaganda blips, emerges from a dim chamber. He's what they say he is: an old man. He's huge, well over six foot, but gray, bent, clad in loose silk and slippers. He's unarmed. No cybernetics. No stack. Insanity. Slowly, methodically, he shuffles across the wooden floor to a small shinto shrine. There he pours a cup of sake, ponders it, and turns.

"So, may I know my executioners?"
"Why would-"
"I am Hokai Tenaka, pupil of Matsushita Shirosune. I am the steward of the last Hatori Hanzo, and loyal citizen of Halsey's Rest township. It is an honor to meet you, chancellor, and my unfortunate duty to end your life."
"Tenaka-san," the Chancellor returns, eyebrows lifting, barely opening his wrinkled eyes, "finally someone my age, and with manners to match. The honor is mine."
"My name is Hatch!" There is a long silence, and at last the Chan-

cellor, as if this is some kind of ceremony, turns to you, sake still waiting to be sipped.
"And you, young lady? What is your name?"
"I'm Grim. You used me in a convoluted scheme to kill your adversaries, eliminate evidence, enslave Matsushita-san, and cling to power like a coward. I've come to end you, and free this city from your delusions."
"Ah, yes. The retune we have so diligently been seeking with the Iko project. You have proven a most resourceful quarry... and a terribly expensive liability."
"Enough talk, drink your whisky." You raise the MAC12, but Tenaka lowers it with one hand.
"Forgive my pupil, Chancellor,"
"No need, Tenaka-san. A degree of wrath is deserved in this situation. I deny nothing said here. We are those who speak plainly, so let no lies soil my death, nor bullets."
Tenaka nods to you, holding out a hand. You know that face, those eyes, all too well.
"Sensei-"
"Time to remember who is master and who is student."
"What about Matsushita?"
"You can no more claim his deeds then I can boast about the weather. The sword."
You breathe slowly, stare him down, and finally relax. The Hanzo slides from its sheath soundless, silver, perfect. You place it on Tenaka's outstretched arms. He takes it with delicate reverence, and returns his eyes to the Chancellor.
"I could not ask for a better death, Tenaka-san."
"I will not falter, choro."
"Old words I hear too seldom. You know, all this ugliness with 'SIlver Shard,' our mistakes, our violent resolution, our digital dishonor... I claim full responsibility. We were the only line of defense against the soulless demons of A.I. I accept your vengeance." He sips the sake, then finishes it. Hatch is starting to fidget. You don't

move a muscle.

"Then, my Chancellor, it is time."
"Yes. Time to die."

The Chancellor steps to the center of the room, assumes the seiza position, hands on thighs, and enters a deep bow. Then up steps Tenaka, Hanzo held high like a fury of Kamakura. From his robe the Chancellor reveals his short knife, a flawless, gilded masterpiece made for a king, and silently, stoically, impossibly, disembowels himself. As the strain overtakes him, he leans forward. With immortal, slow, steady strength he leans forward, and Tenaka strikes.

You watch the head tumble onto the wooden floor. Blood rolls in lengthening fingers, permeating the carpentry like motor oil. There is a terrible moment of quiet then.

A moment you will never forget. All the decades stretch behind you, all that remains ahead, and you are a lotus petal on a rivulet of rain. You are a nothing, an error, a pawn with no game, a pebble washed onto sand.

"It is done." Tenaka returns the sword, perfectly clean. He has power in his eyes. Calm.
"I didn't expect it to go like that," Hatch states with obvious disappointment, "I feel weird."
"It does not forgive his deeds, Hatch. It only makes noble his end."
"Right. So what now?"
"Tyranax." Tenaka's expression changes. "The third dragon. It is the vile root of this fruit. Our final errand, I would guess, on this road of blood."

"The dragon? The A.I. that started all this? I thought it was-"

"Destroyed? No. There is greater darkness here. A final task. The shadow has only darkened."
"Then we met up with Case." You finally speak, at a loss.
"Yes, and our most dire enemy."

Turn to PAGE 245.

"Not sure how long this connection will last. Here goes."
"Grim, no."
"Iko. I fuckin' love you."

The virtual comm cuts out at that moment, and your gut drops like a roller coaster after a shot of vodka. Then it hits you: what the hell are you doing mucking around in the wastelands? You need to see her, need to get her out of all this, need to get a damn purpose!

Easy enough to slip out of Sugar, ditch the juggers. What you need is an ally for Bunker 43. You need Case. In a few hours, you're looking him right in the eye. He's never surprised to see you.

"Need you for another run. Short notice apology, yadda yadda."
"Same old Grim, what is it this time?"
"Bunker 43."
"Stars and fuckin' gardens, Grim, seriously? You know what 'bunker' means, right?"
"Concrete walls, guns everywhere, counter-intel, jammers, nano-drones, poison darts, trap doors and boulder traps?"
"That about covers it, yeah."
"So...?"
"I'll bring the car around."

In the history of armed infiltration, there have been runs of legend and total debacles. There have been massacres and fiascoes, ninja runs and big booms. This time, you and Case redefine the word 'mistake.'

First, Case got shot a few dozen times. Then, your guns went to shit. There were about 200 more guards than you expected. Case reversed the ventilation system, but that tripped a red alert failsafe. You tried to jam a surv cam in the outer corridors, but the hard link slipped out and locked every bulkhead on the complex. Case came up with a simulated air traffic jam, but it wiped the grid and five of the giants were on the landing strip on seek-and-destroy missions. You pulled steel on a squad of commandos, and wound up shot in the face and plummeting into a drain tunnel. Cosmic sadism must have kept you both alive, but the blood drew a pack of ropers in the prison block. Sure, Case hacked their crummy brains with new commands, but that overloaded and blew red goo all over both of you like bright red 'shoot me' paint.

It was a long day.

Despite all that, you find yourself face to face with Iko. Three Iko's to be exact.

"What the f-"
"There she is, Case."
"Yeah, I see all three of her."
"Is- is this possible?"
"One: they're multi-stacking her. Two: they're fast-jumping her. Either way, that tech just doesn't exist. This is either next-level stuff or an ugly experiment."
"We need some answers. We can't drag three of her out of here. She's-"
"Yeah she's out cold, probably waiting on a flash-retune."
"A what?"
"Just a rumor. Some jokers on the SISTM saying they've beaten the bandwidth problem. They say they can retune in a few milliseconds. Maybe it's all true. Maybe they've got hundreds of Iko's."
"And they just blip retune her at any second?"
"Or jump her from stack to stack, or duplicate her stack... this shit is unheard of, Grim."
"Jack in, figure it out."
"Might I remind you there are a few dozen synth commandos about 40 seconds back, and one without a head?"

"I'll bring around the car. Do you thing."
"Ten years of genius level programming, another ten of keeping our psycho government at bay without being detected, an entire underground data railroad and she says 'do your thing.'"

What happens next is a messy business. You, the sword, Case, the deck. He keeps yelling 'fucking what' and 'no way' as he works to disconnect the umbilicals holding Iko in place. You keep yelling 'die!' and 'ow!' as the commandos shoot and slash their way in.

"Grim?"
"Yes, Case?"
"We need a ride! I've got her free, got the data on this bonzo op. We need wheels!"
"Let me just-" you slash another attacker from shoulder to hip, catching the MP8 as it twirls out of dead hands and into yours. You empty it on another assailant, tumble back, and kick another in the tenders. "Yeh, a few seconds out. Ladder up on the right. Go!"

The car is, indeed, brought around. It's a hacked tri-wheel cart, usually used for fruit vendors or air strip control workers. Top speed: useless. That's how you get it done. Case drives like a grandmother, and you dodge bounce your way out of there while Shinru command chases a hologram of three idiots in a cart the opposite direction. Streets, alleys, ditching the cart, dragging Iko, and safety at last in one of Case's spots on the outskirts.

"Not only do I have all their crappy code on rapid retunes, stack jumps... I have Iko's source data here."
"Well, bring her up!"
"Let's make sure she's unarmed first."

Iko wakes up. There are no psychics to fill her with hate, no mind control, no 'Silver Burn' to have your head on a spit. She looks up at you with big, clear eyes. The purple aluminum in her skin is glorious, glowing. Those lips. Her jet black hair is just to one side. You remember why you said what you said.

"I remember what you said."
"Iko."
"Shit, Grim, how many times did I-"
"Thirteen, I think."
"I'm so sorry."
"I'm not. There's no one I'd rather get killed by."
"Asshole."

Then, she kisses you. No guns blazing, no time running out. Just those perfect lips, those big, dark eyes, anodized aluminum catching the light. She's soft, she takes her time, and the last ten years melt away like a bad dream. You were never apart, never alone, never far from this moment. Never far from this kiss. She's yours, and you stand taller than you have in years, kissing her in return with all the bullets and blades, with all the death and all the regret all fading away. You kiss those perfect lips until you need to see her, and pull back, one hand on her pale, flawless cheek.

"So, what now?"
"Now? We have some catching up to do."
You're lost in that smile.

"When you two are done, I've got some messed up data here." Case is all but forgotten, illuminated by three jammed screens in the shadows.
"The stack jump?"
"No. Something called Tyranax."

Turn to PAGE 245.

For any runner, holding back the truth is usually a fatal mistake.
You're no different.
What does 'fatal' even mean in this strange new world? You are about to find out.

"Nothing," you tell Iko, saving your feelings for some unknown future, for some perfect moment that will probably never come. You swallow with the effort of it. Swallow your courage. You tell yourself it will protect her. Bad stuff happens to people you get close to.
"Right."
"Listen, we're coming to your 20. Eta 33 minutes. Be ready, and guns out. It won't be pretty."
"Grim, don't. I can-"
"It's happening, Iko. This psychic-assassin act is getting old. Look for the pink grenade."
"Pink-"

The connection drops. You get Case on a text message. You're knocking on his door before he even answers, no doubt to tell you 'buzz off.' You lay down the big idea.

"Grim, this run is some goofy-footed shit."
"Do that thing you do... like, hack their security."
"Hack their security? Seriously? Security hacked, sir, orders?"
"We're getting her out of there, Case."
"Yeah, yeah. My bike is in the carport. You're riding bitch-"
"Don't even say it."

In the history of armed infiltration, there have been flawless kills, total ghosts, forest fires and complete wipeouts. What happens next is all of these things, and none of them. Case rides like a man possessed, leaning and weaving through the outer blocks at 150 plus, and ripping across the Rim towards the hills even faster.

There are a series of Shinru command bunkers out there in the dalles. He seems to know exactly which tracks to take and which to steer clear. You hold on for dear life, and pull in to the rear door of a concrete structure unnoticed. No fanfare, no spotlights.
"No welcome wagon?"
"I have a localized jammer in the bike. Signals don't go in or come out for about a quarter click. It works great, but it will trip their countermeasures in a few minutes."
"We'll need a transport for three to get out-"
"I'm not leaving my bike here, nutjob! Been through a lot with this little machine. You and Iko on your own for the home trip."
"Got it."
"She's in a lower level, two down, end of the main corridor once we're in. Personnel looks thin, but armed with beam weapons and reflex armor. I'll get their attention, you do the rest. Don't fuck it up."
"Sage wisdom."
"You're crazy, Grim, you know that?"
"Always a pleasure, runner."
"See you back at Chan's."

Despite all the bitching, all the jabs, both of you smile. It's good to be running together. No loose ends, no big betrayals, no unknowns. Just a classic snatch-and-grab from a bunch of paramilitary goons. Meat & taters stuff. At least, it looks that way in the numbers.

Case kicks things off, zipping up his jacket, which has a custom-hemmed port on the left side for his cybernetic arm. He's flamboyant with it: an orange-and-silver pneumatic model with an oversized hand and 'Have a nice day' rattle canned on the forearm. He runs a diagnostic on it, cycling the fingers and spinning the wrist. His deck pops up from the arm, integrated, and he begins tapping away. An umbilical flops out comically, and he suction-cups it to the steel access door.

"One of my new programs. I call it Bart 3.0... introduces ghost images on surv cams in 3 second intervals. Totally looks like someone is walking through their feeds... and mark. Ok, Grim, showtime!"

Case casually opens the door, deck retracting into the arm silently. Just inside, a checkpoint desk hosts two armed guards. Case walks right over to them.

"Vargas? Hemsworth? You guys look like shit! Can you believe these new parking protocols? Slag me rotten, what a pain to get here! Is this building 44? I swear they change the damn number paint every year, like that's going to help us do our damn j-"
"Hold it right there, who the fuck are you?" One talks, seated, the other raises his weapon. It's a beam gun. You wait for the right moment to slip in, listening on your shared retina-comms.
"Who the fuck am I? Jaysus, Vargas, you're losing your edge! I'm here to do the diag work on the Iko project, you lump. I was told there'd be a tech team to get me set up in the-link up-bay- or something." He cringes a bit, but they don't notice.
"Yeah, yeah, just scan your damn badge."
Case reaches into his jacket, unzipping it. The huge arm swings across the desk, spilling a cup of coffee. That's your cue.
"Shit!" You drop low, spin on one foot, and slink through the entry as they bumble about. Case puts a three minute timer up on your retina, followed by a winky face icon.
"Oh man, sorry Vargas! What a mess! This damn arm, I swear. Ok badge here." As you creep away, you see Case's retina feed. He's scanning the guard's I.D. badge while he fumbles for his own badge, decrypts it on the fly, and produces a new, compatible 12 digit code as he's talking. "Left mine in the cleaners, boys. Here just take my badge I.D. number: 441-364-009- uhm- 920. Yeah 920."
The guard taps it in, the display goes green. Fuckin' Case.
"Ok, Dr. Simpson," the guard shrugs, annoyed. "You don't have a damn team. Just get down to your bay and get your shit done.

We'll be posted at the door."
"Better safe than sorry! Thanks boys!" By now you're at Iko's room, overriding the number pad in a few tense seconds. You use the retina comm to text Case: 'How did u know his name was Vargas/?' A moment passes, you're in. Case replies: 'Lucky guess'

You lower your MAC12, let your blade stay silent, and lay eyes on what they've done to Iko. This is some kind of test or upload bay, and they're running a large set of mainframes on her... all five of her. Power cables and data links are tangled everywhere. Her purple knuckles gleam in the low light. Five Iko's are connected to the equipment, and every few seconds, one them opens her eyes, just for an instant, then the next. A series of green lights cycles with her, and the console reads 'stack jump diagnostic in progress.'

"Case, you reading this?"
"On my way to you, two bogies in tow, jammer at 45 seconds. Three steps: 1: offload the stack jump code onto a solid state in your reflex link. 2: pull the plug on it. 3: pick an Iko and crack the spinal connections. She won't be conscious for a few minutes."
"What about you?"
"These guys look pissed. I'm going to have to persuade them to give up their violent ways."
You start in on the work moving fast, right up to the moment Iko slumps forward into your arms. She's pale as a ghost, synthetic looking and cold to the touch. A wave of regret creeps up your back. Should've told her. Her hair is jet black, slick and perfect. She smells like a new car, and weighs about as much. She must be mostly alloy and nanofiber by now. They've made her into a real killing machine.

As you turn to fireman-carry her to the door, a long burst of gunfire shakes the hallway outside. The strobe is brilliant white through the wired-glass window. Then another burst, and yell, and a crumpling sound.

You kick the door open, with effort, and Case is standing over the guards, one of their weapons in his huge hand, crushed to scrap.
"They chose...poorly."
"Let's get out of here."
"Jammer's toast. An automated alarm just tripped."
"So where's all the commotion?"
"I don't-" Case is cut off by a series of whirring computers, cooling fans, and fluorescent lights clicking on in the various bays. You turn, looking through the small square window. The four remaining Iko's all go upright, their spinal links popping off with a hydraulic hiss. All four of them crack their anodized knuckles in unison, and make eye contact with you.
"RUN!"
"There's a six-wheeler around the corner from my bike! I'll run an override on it, the rest is up to you! How the hell are they stack-jumping her that fast? FIVE of her? At once?"
"Just go!"
Case doesn't hesitate. He runs like a crazy person, repeating 'this is crazy, this is crazy, this is crazy' as he disappears into the low dusk light outside. You get less than half that distance, lugging the dormant Iko, when the other four of her enter the hallway. All of them look a bit foggy, then a final figure appears behind them, from yet another room. It's a lab type, white coat, big forehead. He points at you from a distance, and the Iko's respond like remote-controlled drones, snapping into combat stances in perfect unison. Are they stack jumped or just duplicates? How is that even possible? Here they come, and it's the fight of your life.

You drop your Iko. She's groggy, starting to come-to.
"Grim? Where-"

The other four are on top of you, grabbing, punching, kicking, spinning. Your MAC is nabbed and stripped right before your eyes. The sword in one of their hands. You spring your integrated blade, but when you have a joint lock and a throat in view, you hesitate.

You see aggression, life, cycling between them every few seconds as they close in. They're fast as lightning, savage, beautiful, deadly. You feel a leg break, then tear off. A blade appears through your chest, but you're in shock. The last thing you see is the fifth Iko suddenly go rigid, stand next to her duplicates, and watch as you bleed out. They're joined by the psychic pusher, who looks sickly pleased at this particular performance. He speaks up, the darkness is closing around your vision.
"Who is this, Iko?"
A beat. Then they answer in unison, "Nobody."

The dark closes in, the pain disappears.
"Iko," you gurgle, "something- something I need to tell- you-"

Across a wide expanse of nothing your mind drifts then, lost and folding in triangles of infinity. Fade to black. It's over.

Turn to PAGE 255.

Veil. The hologram paradise. A psychedelic playground for the one percenters and addicts to toy with bodies, indulge their darkest dreams, megadose the newest trip, and wake up fresh as a daisy.

You park your bike in an immaculate, ceramic stall at the edge of the glowing city. Glass and projections confuse it all... a hall of mirrors. In you go. In minutes, the liquid lights, the animalistic imagery, the towering 3D mesmerics, the sweeping, smoky lasers are all a dizzy mess. Stay focused. You run a scan program Case gave you years ago. He called it 'folk finder.' It scans all available retina feeds in a radius and cross-refs the users with reflection data to identify a target. In a few seconds, you get a blip on Iko. She's in a club up ahead called 'Gold Neon.' The blip is stationary. You move up, pushing way past a crowd of wobbling day trippers. Their genders are impossible to tell, they smell like gin, and one of them is shouting about the end of time.

Gold Neon comes into view. The entrance is a warm yellow anemone of glass sculpture, teeming with holographic jellyfish. You pause, getting a view of the interior from the street. Black-suited heavies are everywhere, all with tac optics and comms implants. Big guys. Inside, at a waving, curved bar top, you see Iko standing stick straight. She's behind a fur-coat wearing gangster type with gold teeth and a volt pistol in front of him. Not good.

You roll your shoulders, huff out the tension, sling your gear into your coat, and begin up the steps. Four heavies step into your path.

"Check your weapons here, citizen."

"Right, my mistake. Fresh off the road. No problem." You present your blade and MAC12's. The holdout pistol comes next, then a pair of wakizashi's, three mags of EMP ammo, an MP8, and two frag grenades. The heavies seem unimpressed, zip it all into a tagged duffel, and stash it near the host's podium.

You start inward, setting a retina tracker on that duffel bag for a fast egress later.

"Not so fast, runner."

"That's all of it."

"The integrated blade. Hold out your arm, please."

"Oh that? Hey, look I-m-"

"Just hold out your arm, please."

You do so, and the heavy produces a black zip tie. It has a circuit unit on one buckle. A restrainer. He zips it on, too damn tight, and a red light comes on.

"This hardly matches my outfit."

"Enjoy Gold Neon."

You huff, hiding your borderline panic to be disarmed. This isn't going well. Then in you go, walking to the curving, impossible bar, trying not to stare at Iko, who seems to be in a trance. She's motionless, flawless, eyes distant, anodized knuckles polished to perfection. Her hair is just to one side, revealing those velvet lips. She wears nothing, clad only in nanoskin armor sheeting and magnetic hard points. A goddess.

"Evening," a bartender appears. She is wearing a translucent yellow top, bikini, glass ear gauges, and has tiger stripes tattooed over most of her slender form. Again, you try not to stare.

"Hello. Absinthe vapor and lime, please. Short."

"Right away." When she turns to retrieve a glass, you have to look at the ceiling. Distractions galore in this place.

"Vapor lime short," she repeats, sliding it over, smiling, "so what brings you to Neon?"

"Visiting a friend."

"Glad to hear. For a minute I thought you were about to shoot the place full of holes."

"That obvious, eh?"

"Runners stick out a bit here. You have that 'annoyed by people having fun on a mission' look about you."

"Not bad."
"So, what brings you to Neon?"
"You always ask this many questions?" You take a sip. It's the best damn drink you've ever tasted, with a kick in the head to match.
"You always play with fire? This is Goldtoe's place. He doesn't like anyone eyeing his prize."
"Prize?"
"Don't play dumb, runner. The cyborg over there. She's got enough alloy in her to take on Shinru Command by herself. A real animal."
"Yeah? Didn't notice."
"I've been in Veil a long time. Seen a lot of strange stuff. You want a crack at her, you're going to need a plan."
"I was thinking just shoot the place up, then the old grab and go. Another round?"
"Sure," she starts prepping another glass. "You know she's a living thing, not a mannequin to be 'grabbed' and go."
"She'll help me. Easy job." You smile at her. Can't help it.
"How about just go over and ask?"
"Hi, name's Grim, can I have your cyborg?"
"Yeah, something like that."
Then another voice, behind you, at the next curve in the bar. You turn.
"The answer is no, runner." It's the gangster type, leaning back, smiling. You spin back to the bartender, looking duped. She shrugs, taps her temple. Retina comms. You and Case aren't the only ones using 'em.
"Shit."
"Come over here and have a drink, stranger. I like the cut of your jib!"
You slump, feeling like an idiot, grab your drink, cheers the girl at the bar, and move over.
"Name's Gr-"
"Yeah I caught that. Cheers!" You toast Goldtoe, noticing his implants... all anodized gold. Rivulets of alloy permeate every surface

of him. Tattoos tangle with augments in interlacing mandalas and lotus patterns. He's wearing a mink fur, and the damn thing looks real. Is that even possible?

"So, how can I talk you out of Iko?"

"Iko? Is that her name I love it! We were calling her 'Yuki.'"

"You can't runner. This cyber is worth more than this damn building! Let's just have a drink, maybe get some egg rolls. I'm starving! Reggie! Can we get some rolls over here?"

You consider your options at that instant. The duffel bag is in sight, the heavies could be beaten. No telling what kind of abilities Goldtoe might have. You size up cover, maybe that lamp could make a mess of things...

"Eggrolls sound great, thanks."

"So right now you're trying to decide if you blow hole in ol' Goldtoe and kill your way out of here. You must be some big business to be looking for my little Yuki- I mean Iko here. I bet you could shred this place, even without weapons."

"It crossed my mind."

"Ya know, Grim, if that is your name, which I doubt, I found Iko out on The Rim a few months back. She was twitching, half slagged. We got her back in working order, but she's never been fully 'there' if you get my meaning. Poor thing. My diag guys say she's a stack duplicate. Blown to bits by juggers in some kind of Shinru mop up op. Sucks, huh? I didn't know they could duplicate stacks at all, much less a fighter like her. Exquisite. We've all grown quite fond of her here. Given her a home. Keep your guns in the bag. Don't be a dick."

"Then we're at an impasse." You sip the absinthe. Warm waves roll over you, and it's hard not to like Goldtoe in a weird way.

"No such thing as an impasse here! This is Veil! City of opportunity!"

"So you need a favor."

"Don't we all? You need little Yuki here. I need a bunch of slaggers clean deaded. Ah! The eggrolls!"

"These are amazing."
"Right? Reggie is the best. Grace, could we get another round here. Make 'em doubles!"
"What's the run?"
"Ever heard of the Magnetics?"
"Heh. Psycho Iga rejects. Wanna-be ninja types. Jokers. I've heard they blame that imaginary A.I. 'Tyranax' for all their crimes and chaos."

"Not around here, Grimmo. Up in Veil they're well-funded, augmented to the damn moon, and fast as shadows. They make business unpleasant for an upstanding citizen like me. A real shame to see kids so misguided. As for Tyranax, I wish it was a rumor, or a fiction. That... thing... is all too real, friend. All too real."

"Sounds like a problem."
"Right? So yeah, I need 'em all dead, nice and clean. No big deal."
"How many we talking?"
"Well, see that's the funny part."
"How many?"
"About thirty, give or take."

"So you want one runner to go in, kill thirty ex-Iga psychopaths, antagonize an immortal A.I. that's only whispered about in Shinru, and leave no trace? In return for Iko?"
"I like how you say it."
"Can I drink on it?"
"Now that is wisdom! You hear that Reggie? A real sage here! Cheers, Grimmo."

You both knock back the doubles.

More egg rolls come, another round, and pretty soon you have Goldtoe drunk enough to rethink your choices.

That duffel bag is looking poorly guarded... and a shot at some Iga sounds like a hell of a fun night.

If you jump for the guns, grab Iko and run, turn to PAGE 238.

If you make a deal with Goldtoe, negotiate a little, turn to PAGE 240.

Enough talk. You smile when you should, size up the place, and wait to spring. Goldtoe is fading out a bit, eyes rolling. It's been a long night, but you're still crisp. Iko just stands there.

"Well, Goldtoe, I'm going to have to call it a night. Thanks for the drinks."
"So, the guns, eh?"
"Looks that way. I don't work for- unsavory types."
"You wound me, Grimmo! Unsavory? Reggie! You hear that? Unsavory!" He shakes his head. "Your funeral, runner. Just don't shoot up my Picasso, okay? It's my favorite piece." Goldtoe gestures upward, where the abstract, colorful shapes of the priceless painting loom with weird presence above the glowing barscape.
"A reasonable request."
"See you on the other side, runner."
"Cheers."

At that instant, Goldtoe pulls the trigger. You flinch, but a microsecond late. The bullet whizzes under the bar, through your left thigh. It arcs up, around, and back through your shoulder on the return trip. Nemesis gun.

You ignore it, popping a surge injection with a blink of your left eye. The pain vanishes and you're at the duffel bag in a heartbeat. It zips fast, and you gasp with shock. It's empty. The heavies must've stashed your gear while you were talking to- shit. You roll to one side, evading the big guards like a monkey. You slam your arm against a stair, ripping the skin wide open, but breaking off the restrainer. The blade springs out of your forearm with a wet ringing sound. Then up you stand, ready to kill your way out of this.
"Iko, snap out of it!" She doesn't.
"Ok, boys, go ahead and kill her." The heavies close in, huge hands clawing like bear paws.
To the first you slide, slashing and bobbing around in a semicircle,

toward Iko. You catch him by surprise, but the second one is ready for it. He grabs you like a doll and throws you across the room with a crash. You're closer to Iko, bleeding bad.
"No throwing! Just crack her neck you idiot! Reggie! Get the EMP gun, will you? We're dumpstering this disappointing youngster."

You reach Iko, and she turns her head to look at you, but those lovely eyes are empty, and she leaves you to your struggle alone. In that strange slow motion of battle, you notice a dot matrix tattoo on her neck. It's a small barcode and a number '17.' Before you can guess at that, or slash the fingers from the heavy behind you, the huge man is right on top of you, crushing you.
"Get off me!"
"Not much of a try, runner," Goldtoe mocks as your eyes darken, "got to watch out for the ol' switcheroo on your gear. Amatuer mistake. Too bad, too. Lots of potential, Grimmo. Lots of potential."
The second heavy moves in, and they each have an arm. It feels like they might tear you in half. You lose another spray of red. Then Reggie approaches, lifts a gadget up to your head, and hits a green reflex trigger.

There's a blinding white flash, an after-image of green and purple, and the glassed-in Picasso is the last thing you see.

Turn to PAGE 255.

"Crazy thing about Yuki- I mean Iko," Goldtoe slurs a bit, hand on your shoulder, "is that number there. See it? 17! We ran a trace on the code and there's at least thirty duplicate stacks on the SISTM. Thirty!"
"Wait... thirty Iko's? That's not possible."
"That's what I said. Then Reggie called in some favors and got us stack tags on the codes. It checks out, Grimmo! Can you believe it! A duplicated stack running in thirty simultaneous skins! Crazy times. Crazy."
"How do they rectify the memory dissonance? How can the bandwidth be fast enough to sync the positional data?"
"Bat shit crazy Shinru megatech nutso pants, that's how! Ha!"
"The tac applications alone are crazy-"
"Grace, my love, could you refresh these glasses? We have got to switch to beer, Grimmo. I can't keep up! You're a wild one! Thanks Gracie. You want to know a secret, Grimmo? A real doozy?"
"I'm still here."
"Ol Goldtoe ain't number one in Veil any more. Nope. Damn hood rats been taking my business. That's where Iko comes in... she'll be my ace once we get her back online."
"Hood rats?"
"Ex-Iga. A gang called the Magnetics. Fast, nasty, cyber'd all to hell."
"I've heard of them. Thirty strong last I checked. But you're not the type to send an innocent girl in to do your dirty work, are you?"
"Innocent? Girl? Grimmo, you nuts, kid! This 'girl' has a kill sheet a mile long, more ops than God! She's been all over the planet running dark for Shinru central! Got her on some crazy 'Silver Burn' mission param we haven't cracked yet. She's a killer, I tell ya!"
"Still, not really stylish to use her like that. Maybe I read you wrong."
"You hear that Reggie? Shit, Grimmo that stings!" Goldtoe leans back, licks his alloy teeth, laughs to himself, and looks at the floor. "You alright, Grim. You alright. What am I supposed to do?"
"Let her go, let her choose! How'd you like to be a lacky for the damn Chancellor? Take it from me, those guys are nasty, heartless

schemers."
"Then I'm stuck with no ace, Grimmo. I don't know about this."
"Look, she's an old friend. We go way back. You let her go, I'm your new ace."
"Yeah? You good with a blade, runner? Ha!"
"The best. No one is as fast as me, not even Iko."
" Oh yeah? Hey Reggie, can I get a code blue over here?"

At that instant, Reggie, who must be just out of view, throws a gyro blade. It spins through the air, curved blades on both ends, fast as a bullet. The metal pops your reflex link, and you lift one hand, catching the blade without looking. You sip your drink.
"Yeah."
"Holy shit, Reggie! We got a real hardwired heavy here! You see that? Ok, Grimmo, I think we got a deal here. Spit on it." Goldtoe spits on the floor, chuckles. You follow suit. He has a few heavies come in, run a cleanup routine on Iko's data jack.
"Hold it," you stop them for a moment, pull your hood over your face, "if she knows I'm here, she won't leave the city. I don't want her tangled up in this Magnetics thing. I just want her safe."
"Runner life... you guys are crazy. Ok, boys, light her up."

She blinks back to life, a bit dazed but herself again. She checks her retina console, takes it all in, turns to Goldtoe.

"Thanks," she says flatly, cracking her anodized knuckles like a pit fighter, "you guys rehabbed me after that fracas in the wasteland."
"Don't mention it. You're free to go, Yuki."
"That's it?"
"That's it. Consider it the beginning of a friendship."
"Then I have friends to find. What do I call you?"
"Name's Chauncy. Folks around here don't call me that, but you is special. You watch your six out there."
"The name's Iko." With that, she heads outside, vanishes into the

city. You breathe a sigh of relief. Step one done, now to deal with the rest.

"Ok, here's the op, Grimmo. I give you coords. You get in, take every last nasty one of 'em out, and give us the retina feed for confirmation. Easy peasy lemon squeezy."

"Coords received. So sneak in, kill thirty ninjas, and call it a day?"

"That's it! And you know, not to be rude, but if you rat out on me and Reggie, well, that would end badly for you. Badly, right Reggie?"

You stand, shake off the drinks, and the heavies bring your gear over. You strap up, lose the restrainer. It's going to be an interesting night.

"Been a pleasure, Chauncy."

"Goldtoe to you, runner. Go get 'em."

If you bail on the job, disappear on your bike and never look back, turn to PAGE 245.

If you go after the Magnetics gang as promised, turn to PAGE 243.

The tracking data checks out. You ride through the baffling holographic landscape of Veil for just under an hour. Barely any cars or bikes here, just wandering oddities, flower floats, skin workers, revelers, parades of dancing drunks. Paradise is so annoying.

You park the bike. As the coil cools off, you check your gear. Armed to the teeth, ready for anything. You bring the retina transmit online with Goldtoe's login. They have a live feed. Showtime. The Magnetics are holed up in a narrow vertical 'strong house' near the city's edge. The buttes of the wasteland are in view beyond the blue glow of it all. There are fortified doors, but no windows or sign of livable space for twenty stories. They must like heights.

You've crossed steel with the Iga before. A legion of the best trained Ninja around, and no slouches in numbers. You'll be lucky to pull this one off, but you block all that doubt out. You're committed now. These aren't Iga ninja technically, but outcasts that are running loose on the cattle of Veil. Show no mercy, for none will be given.

The tower terminates, thirty stories up, in a series of ramped pagoda rooftops. Red dragon corner caps and grey concrete give it a dramatic persona. These guys aren't even hiding. The streets are empty. You run a data mine on the building, but without Case around you only get the exteriors and some blurry heat resonance views. They're in there, alright, 25th floor, moving around a bit, maybe training. Two elevators, plenty of ways to grapple up, or get your hands on a uniform and lie your way in.

As you ponder your options, adrenaline slowly creeps up your spine, into your hands, into your eyes, a text comes through. It's Iko.
'Where r u Grim?'
You think on that a moment. She must be outside the city. One

thing you did right. Finally, you reply.
'Meeting up with Case. Noodles at Chan's?'
'Something's changed. I think I'm free'
'Then drinks on me. c u soon'
There's a bit of sting in that last message. Will you see her soon? It seems like every few days you're facing some new impossible obstacle. Is this the one that ends it? Once again you find yourself on your own, up against everything, running for a favor within a favor, looking for ways out. Runner's blues.

If you sneak in, blending in to infiltrate the hideout, turn to PAGE 249.

If you grapple up, smash through a window, and draw steel, turn to PAGE 254.

Next thing you know, it's Case, Iko, and you in an unmarked tavern in the junk fields. A few clicks out, in the rock towers most locals call 'Crater Valley,' the Ono Dai Sen reactor drive facility is hidden. Iko's inside line on the Tyranax complex has led you here, and it's time to draw up an endgame.

Beers are had all around, even Iko slugs one back, doing things in her characteristic extremes. Case almost spits his gulp out when he sees her pound a full pint. The ice has barely slid down his mug when her second arrives.

"It's been a while. Being brainwashed really builds up a thirst."
"That was a rough stretch." You look at her pale, perfect cheeks, accentuated by nanoplate seams. It's sublime to see her smile after all that's happened. No more goodbyes.
"A decade of violence, killing for the enemy, being duplicated and memory-rectified every few hours... rough stretch indeed."
"I'm still foggy on that part," Case jumps in, picking at a basket of fries. They're real potatoes, and they cost a fortune out here. Worth every cred. "I mean, I have all the code on their stack tech, but how did they solve the memory dissonance? One personality in dozens of skins?"
"It all came down to bandwidth," Iko says, "I don't know tech stuff, but some kid named Sedric in Veil made a quantum leap about a decade ago, right when Grim was retuned with Matsu in tow. The new stuff drew a lot of power, but it did for bandwidth what rocket fuel did for wagons. The game completely changed when an entire stack was a trivial packet of data."
"That's hard to even conceive of clearly. It's a massive amount of information, and impossible to duplicate- or was impossible."
"Once this Sedric kid solved the numbers, they were copy-pasting stacks like sentences. I was right in the middle of it."
"Silver Burn."
"Correct. Not only did the Chancellor want his secret weapon back,

Matushita, but they were desperate to contain and control this quantum leap. Add the pushers and boom, they have me as their enforcer, assassin, and all around pawn. Fucking mess. I did things-terrible things."

"That wasn't you."

"Either way, I ran their errands for nine years. We killed until the secret was safe. Just one loose end: Grim."

"SO you used the tagged creeps and N.E.R. to lure me and Hatch out. Henson was collateral, Case was brilliantly unnoticed."

"I'm good that way," he answers, drinking deep.

"So here's where Tyranax comes in."

"The third dragon."

"No one knows much about it, not even at my level. A formless A.I. that was running things behind the scenes, orchestrating something bigger than Heavy Gear or the Chancellor's petty political ambitions. Every one of us in Shinru ops had a tag from that thing in our stacks. It was everywhere and nowhere... part of us all... watching."

"It's probably listening right now," Case's eyes widen, and he turns his attention to his deck.

"Iko. How do we stop it?"

"We can't just blow their drive. It needs to be isolated. It can move anywhere, into anyone, and it's fast. It's not disoriented, or suffering retune dissonance or any of that. It's formless."

"Case?"

"Well at least it can't listen. Pub jammer."

"Huh?"

"This tavern is muffled. Hey! Zelda! You are beautiful, you know that?"

Zelda walks over, an older woman with frizzy gray hair and lovely green eyes. She knows Case from somewhere... everyone seems to.

"What's all that, honey?"

"Oh, just admiring a real siren, sweety."

"Well, you can crash on my rocks anytime, honey."
She goes back to the bar, chatting with a cyborg in camo.
"So, how do we fight this thing, Case?"
"Fire with fire."
"Go on."
"We have two problems: getting close and containing it. Containing it is simple... we run a high-power jammer when we have it in a skin in front of us."
"What about getting close?"
"Well, what if 'we' don't go after it, but everyone does? What if 'we' are everybody? It won't know which pins to bowl for."
"Bowl?"
"Never mind. I'm just saying we keep jumping. Never give it a bead on us. Jump our way to it, all from a transport outside Ono Dai Sen."
"Who runs the jumps if we're ducking and weaving through different skins?"
"We set it on an automated program."
"The memory turbulence will tear our minds apart. It won't work, believe me." Iko looks scared. You've never seen that before.
"It's my best idea. Grim?"
"Over my head here. I get useful when we have it cornered."
"We bring it to us," Iko says, staring into her empty glass.
"How?"
"Give it what it wants."
"And what's that?"
"We'll have to find out. Get a data mine on it, use what we find, lure it out, jam it, kill it."
"You can't just say 'data mine' and magically get the subconscious desires of a God level A.I., Iko. We don't even really know what Tyranax IS, much less if it WANTS anything. You're out on a limb."
"The details are your department. Grim and I do the smashing."
"My plan is better. Those badass knuckles of yours only go so far. We need to treat it like an unknown program, not a big dog. You're

nuts."
"And you're a maladjusted weirdo who watches cartoons from a century ago."
"So?"
Iko smiles.
"Look, guys. Let's not bring cartoons into this."
"Thank you."
There's a long pause then. Iko and Case are out of words, and after another beer they both start staring.
"What?"
"You make the call, Grim. You started this. What's the play?"
"Shit."

If go with Case's plan, set up a jumper program, turn to PAGE 270.

If you pick Iko's plan, get in its head and lure it out, turn to PAGE 276.

The elevator is unguarded. Light synth jazz plays. You say 'what the hell' to yourself and hit the number 25. Up it goes, and you're ready for anything. It stops at last, but the doors don't move. Then, a voice on the elevator comm speaker.
"Wow, Grim the do gooder! Long way from Halsey's Rest, runner." It sounds like a kid. Teenage boy, couldn't be older than 14. "Hello?"
"Yeah, I can hear you."
"Before I open the door, I just want you to know you won't accomplish your mission. My ninja are quite invincible."
"So I hear."
"Goldtoe sent you. Not much happens in this city without the signal getting here. Whole building is a sort of antenna. My own design, of course."
"Of course. So what now."
"Come in, come in! I don't have many guests these days."
The doors slide open, with gravity.

Inside, a wide open space meets you, glass on all sides. The view of Veil is remarkable, but hardly a penthouse. It's a sparse layout, with concrete floors, exposed conduit and ductwork, and a workstation in one far corner. A squad of black-hooded figures sits motionless, at least two dozen of them, hands on thighs in the seiza position. Each has a shikomizue at his side in a featureless black scabbard. The Magnetics.
"Come in! You can call me Sedric. These are my ninja!" Sedric stands from the desk across the room, his hands filled with twin stick controllers. His computer gear is heavy duty, even rigged to a primary power cable. That thing is 8 inches thick, probably cuts to the city grid. What could he be running that needs that much power. You start to step forward.
"That will be far enough for now, runner. Let's talk a bit before you browse." They always want to talk.
"Just here to do a job. Nothing personal."

"No, I suppose not. I'm just a big fan of your work is all. That highway hack back in Silver Shard? You jumped the route 12 aqueduct on an XL2400... incredible!"

"That was a big night."

"You're right in the middle of it, Grim, and don't even know! Your stack-storage tech was the breakthrough that led to rapid jumps, and lately duplicate stacking."

"Not sure I follow."

"I'm a dabbler in stack code, retune bandwidth, dissonance resolution programming. I'm sure Shinru would love to know I've taken up residence here! Ha!" He sips a cup of coffee, scanning the ninja facing him. You don't budge, but your reflex link is getting twitchy.

"Greek to me, Sedric. Not to be rude, but I'm not here for a computer science class. Sorry for the mess, but I'm going to have to limit your infrastructure, if you get my meaning."

"The ninja? Oh yes, I'm sure you'll shred them to bits! One last thing, as you said nothing personal, I've really enjoyed the Iko program. All those duplicates, killing you, loving, what a glorious mess!" Sedric takes a sarcastic bow then, closes his eyes like a bard. You take that moment, and attack.

In your left hand, the MAC12, in your right, the blade. You slide forward, and the dance begins. Bullets fly everywhere, the Magnetics spring vertically like a pond full of bullfrogs, drawing blades and converging on you with terrible synchronicity. They're damn good, and fast. In the first real clash, you bounce away, spraying more fire, but miss. The second, you land a sideward slash, and open the black uniform from chest to chin. Underneath the black canvas, alloy muscle fibers and ceramic dermal plating. The face isn't human in any way, just a single retina cam at center. The damn things are mecha. You toss the MAC, useless against that kind of alloy. The MP8 is the wrong weapon for such close quarters, but you leap away from the fight and slam an EMP mag in. They're too fast, smashing down on top of you as you focus on the weapon. Swords everywhere, you suffer a thousand cuts but evade the deadly attacks. Then the MP8. It fries their electronics as it sprays across the crowd. Half the Magnetics drop before the receiver clicks empty. Sparks slide across them as they twitch.

"Hey!" Sedric interrupts, controlling the ninja clan with his hand gadgets, "that's some bullshit!"

Again they press in, blades in a storm. It's all you can do to survive, much less press a victory. You cower back, dropping your sword.

"Uncle! Uncle! You've got me, Sedric! Shit!"

Mid-stride, the ninja, especially the five closest, freeze in their tracks, lower their heads, and stand stone still.

"I knew it! Yes!" Sedric is clearly pleased with himself, and takes a few steps from his workshop space. He's a scrawny kid in a red sweater, a link alloy vest on top. A holdout pistol won't punch through that. You begin scanning side to side... got to be a loophole here somewhere.

"You ninja are just too damn fast."

"You lose, do gooder! I'll take that Matsushita stack, and you can go. I'm not a killer, you know. Fair and square!"

"Fair and square," you echo, feeling the holdout gun enter your hand. Sedric's too busy gloating and prepping a stack offload module to notice.

He walks toward you, the ninja parting to make room for him like a wedding party.

"Don't worry, this will just take a second-"

You whip the pistol forward and fire. At first, Sedric's eyes go wide with glee. You missed! Then he starts to twitch with worry as you lower your arm. He spins around, seeing that you've bulls-eyed the main power cable across the space. It's sparking and dangling. Checkmate.

"You cheating asshole! You'll surge my whole rig! Do you know how many stack jumps were in progress? I've got agents jumping from stack to stack all over the-"

You backhand him, knocking him senseless. Just a kid. One by one, you dismantle the mechanized ninja. Easy enough to just pull solid state controllers, fry the board, on to the next one. The Magnetic will be out of commission for quite a while.

As you back across town, you can't help but feel a bit unnerved. Stack jumping? Duplicates? Iko all wrapped up in it. This has a really bad feeling to it.

If they can copy or jump stacks, the whole planet is under their thumb. Doomsday shit.

"Here she is! The lady of the hour! Grimmo! You did it, you beast! Unbelievable! One shot.. Boom! And that damn kid's whole setup is toast! What a show! What a show!"
"How 'bout a few of those eggrolls. I'm beat to hell over here."
"Oh you've earned it! Reggie! A fair trade, indeed Grimmo."
"So it's all true. They've found a way to duplicate people, jump them from body to body."

"Yeah, it's true, Grimmo. We're all in deep shit. It's that fuck-it-all A.I. Tyranax that keeps pushing this tech. Antihumanism, that's what it's calling it on the SISTM threads. Buncha bullshit."
"Then I'm taking Tyranax out next. There's no going back now."
"Ha! You'd have an easier time killing God, you slagger! Tyranax is a ghost! You'll need an army!"
"Nah."
"Oh yeah, what've you got?"
"A few friends."
"Fuckin' Grimmo. Baller, I swear."
"One more thing, Chauncy."
"Name it."
"Could you keep an eye on Halsey's Rest for me? Maybe just keep a few heavies over there.. Peacekeeper types. Hometown."

"You have my word on it, Grimmo. You come back to Veil anytime. Anytime! Ol' Goldtoe's got your back, yes he do!"

You leave the blue, glassy glow of Veil in your rearview as you roar across the Rim. Time to get the band together.

Turn to PAGE 245.

TOO MANY NINJA

Not in the mood for subterfuge, you fire your laser grapple straight up. It catches 100 yards up, zips you like a fishing lure into the gloom above. You shove out with both legs as the apex approaches. Out and upward, then swinging back toward the tall, narrow windows near the penthouse. Your momentum does the rest as you clip off the line, flying boots-first through the plate glass. The metal cleats make it all the easier.

In you shatter, in you smash. The blade springs into your hand the way it always does, and you're sliding on one knee, concrete floor, dim lights, a few dozen black-hooded figures tumbling, spinning, and leaping to meet you. They're caught unaware, but they far outnumber you, and every one of them a master swordsman. Two clangs and then a wet, whistling slice. Your thigh sprays red. Two more exchanges, then one arm is caught in a lock. They force you down, cracking your back in the worst way.

Just that like, a matter of seconds, you're beaten. Visions of Iko fill your mind as the red closes in. At least you got her out, spared her this fate. Never tangle with gangwars, you chide yourself. Hatch will be pissed. Jenna will cry for you.

Your blade takes two of the ninja out as you go down, revealing circuits and hydraulic lines. The Magnetics? All mechanized under those hoods? A gang of 'bots?

No time to be confused. Shadows fold in, your feet go cold, and a steel-knuckled hand closes over your eyes.

Turn to PAGE 255.

The darkness of death, or what some call death, is infinite.

From that folding infinity you are pulled like a leaf plucked from a river.
From darkness you rise, shedding old memories, tongues of flame fall behind your flying soul. Feeling new fingers, bathing in the first light for the umpteenth time. Born again. Downloaded.

From ascension to descension it's all reversed, inverted, spinning downward like water twirling, upward like a fumarole, a twist cone taking shape, you move through, and past, and between, and beyond. Triangles within triangles within circles within squares. Old alchemy and digital decay.

You've retuned enough times to brace for the big finale.
Static shock.

Boom! You slam into a new human form. Skeleton bound, blood pumping, the beginner's mind yawning with potential ahead of you. The old mind echoing all you've learned, but fogged with distance. Lips move, but you hear nothing. A ship's smoke on the horizon. You're coming to...

"Matsushita? Matsu, wake up!"
A familiar voice ten thousand miles away. Swords and bullets, fire and black smoke... these things fill your first thoughts. From violence and embers drifting you dare push your eyelids open. They grind like sheet metal in a rusted hangar's dim. Push, push them open. The white of it all floods in, shapes moving, sounds impossible to process, knuckles and knees of some new but already grown form.

This is a retune.

"Matsu! Get your ass off the damn table! No time!" It's Iko, but who is Iko? Some ghost from the great beyond? An angel sent to deliver you or a demon craven with hunger for your infant mind?
"Who's that?" Your voice, if that is your voice, sounds all wrong. Everything is all wrong. The ceiling wheels overhead, but you know it's a ceiling. That's a start.
"Iko, you idiot! My name is Iko! Snap out of it, it's just another retune!"
"My name is 'Idiot?'"
"I- No! It's Matsu- You've retuned to the dormant stack in your brain stem. Grim is there- I think- but we have to move. NOW!"
"Now? When is now?"
"Like right fucking now!"

Then your grace period ends with a sudden, jarring jolt. An iron grip on your right wrist yanks you bodily from the cold steel slab beneath you. You're in nothing but a white yukata. Your bare feet meet the plastic floor with a slap, but the toes hold. The knees are strong as oxen's thighs. You are mighty in this form. Your wits begin to return, drawn not by the yanking, but by something in your left hand, something held. Your grip tightens and you look there, still squinting away the glare.

In that hand, at your side, a sword.
This you know. This offers no confusion, this is its own answer. The hilt is pure, the grip wound with memorable symmetry, the tsuba resting on your thumb like an anchor of consciousness.

"Come on!" It's Iko, beautiful, ageless, Iko. Her face floods you with memories, with pain, with affection, with sorrow, with old wounds and new hope. Those lips, her deep-set eyes behind curtains of jet. She's lovely.
"Iko."
"There you are. Now I need you to fight! Fight, Matsushita! Fight,

Grim! Let it flow. You are who you are, no matter what they try to make you!"

A wall opens impossibly, splitting apart. White light shifts and boots pound on steel. Gunfire everywhere. Iko flips and spins, flying and slashing like blurred wind on a snowy cornice. Through all this, you see five dark shapes, men, invading your infant perception. Their bullets whiz by, their shouts are muted in your serenity, and the left hand raises the sword. Your left hand.

In the first stroke, the blade floats from left to right, unwavering. One man dies. The right hand is rigid, and draws back. One bare toe grips the floor like a crane in the mud, and up comes the steel, blinding you with reflective glare. Another man spills his life on the white floor. Sword above your head, both hands, someone's hands, join forces. There is a pause that feels like infinity. Iko is yelling something, then down comes the shimmering claw of Matsushita Hideki, unstoppable force. Helmet to boot the form is cloven, spraying blood like fine mist. Three men dead. As the bladetip clinks on the sterile floor, dripping, you exhale with instinct. In comes the air then, making you invincible, and around the blade grinds through the blood like a calligrapher's brush drawing a great circle of red. You are a deadly thing, and minutes old in your fury.

"Fuckin' a," Iko mutters, running over to you, seeing the carnage, lowering your bloody blade gently. "you're fast."
"Iko." All confusion fades. What foolish pride was keeping you from her? Why hadn't you fallen in love? What meaningless vendettas had occupied your minds to deny this undeniable attraction? It was like telling a river it cannot flow, telling a wave it cannot crash. Not this time, not this body, not this life. This time you will love like a fool. You wrap her muscular shoulders in your gigantic new arms, and pull her close. You're a foot taller than her in this form. She softens, nanocarbon skin relaxing, laying her head against your

chest.

"This is a little crazy, Grim."
"No. I've never been more sane."
"I think I could do it."
"Do what?"
"Love you, even as a man, a male I mean, though I'll miss the old Grim. She was really something."
To this no words can mean anything, so you pull her close, and revel in that moment, for the beginner's mind does not know violence, or revenge, or pride. Matsushita is older, clean shaven, tall and rigid with swordswork.
"Now, what's all the rush, besides these poor fools trying to kill us?"
"No rush." She goes up on her tiptoes and kisses you. That is a kiss two lifetimes and ten years too late, and it is all it should be.
"Like a softening storm. Gods, you're beautiful."
"Enough. There's plenty of killing to do."
"I remember... the pushers..."
"Jammed for now. While you were out, we took down the duplicates. I'm the only Iko now. We're just outside the facility that is storing the A.I. called Tyranax. Case helped us with the retune, never seen one done so fast, and remotely. Crazy. Our plan was to penetrate their reactor drive, isolate the storage, and then move in on the entity. If they push me, Case has a remote stack jump program."
"Duplicates? I think I remember, but it's all jumbled."
"Tell me about it. I've been living in two dozen bodies. Case stole the jump code from some kid in Veil."
"How am I Matsushita now?"
"Sinru command has had a synthetic skin of him in his prime on file for years- decades. You're their big prize, but we've cracked the control on you. Now we've got the bigger stick. With Drakan and the Chancellor out of action, Tyranax is all that's left."

"Hideki-san... Tenaka's sensei. This body is.. Incredible."
"Yeah, like I said. You're fast."
"And if the stack jump doesn't work? Back to 'evil Iko?'"
"It will work."
"Then what are we waiting for?"
"Just you, lover. Just you." Her eyes are clearer than ever. Maybe they can beat the pushers after all. Your stomach growls and breaks the moment.
"I'm starving. Never wise to attack immortal A.I.'s on an empty stomach. Head swimming... it's a lot to take in."
"There's a barracks two clicks out. We're in the desert outside Shinru. This whole complex is cut into solid sandstone. We could hole up there, get you some shoes."
"Or go full berzerk and strike them now."
"Your call, Hideki-Sensei."

If you lay low, regroup, and prepare a careful assault on Tyranax, turn to PAGE 284.

If you press the attack on the great dragon, no hesitation, turn to PAGE 289.

Greta stabilizes at last. She's wired up on hoses and beeps like a race car on a dyno. Case looks like shit.

"She dies, I'll be unpleasant to be around."

"The diags all look good. She's built with the bes-"

"She wasn't built, Grim, you cold-blooded slag! She's organic under all that gear. Pure as snow. It's been a long journey... the replacements, the chem treatments. I'm told to give up on here twice a week, I swear. No go. I've put all my creds into her bionics, and most of my time into their design. I love her, Grim. You wouldn't understand."

"The hell is that supposed to mean?"

"What is all this anyway? You show up, people get hurt. I bent backwards for you so many times I can't even count, and for what?"

"I'm sorry about all that. I'm sorry about all of it. I never wanted Greta to get hurt. These guys are plotting something big, and no one else seems to be lining up to stop them."

"At least you're consistent."

"Look, it's a shitty time, but I've got another favor to ask."

"Of course you do." Case flops into a plastic chair in the hallway. A doc stops by to remind him Greta will be in for two or three days for observation. Case finishes with the doc then looks over at you. At last, his neon green retina implants blink with a smile. "Damnit, spit it out, Grim."

"Iko. Rescue op. We get her out, stack-out this Matsushita character, clone the data with a download worm, and wipe the records."

"You know it takes some serious hardware to clone a stack, right? Download worm? You made that up. Can't do this superhero stuff on a deck module, doofus."

"Yeah. Just another item on our grocery list at Bunker 43. We need a mainframe."

"Bunker 43- are you completely insane? That place is a fortress."

"Yeah, you're right. Probably too tough a nut for you to crack. Understandable."

"Now is where I sucker into your reverse psychology garbage, get us inside the complex, disable all their comp lockouts, clone the stack on their equipment, and create a genius diversion with automated systems while you, me, and Iko ride out of the explosions on mag bikes, all in time to feed Blanky."

"Blanky?"

"Greta's ferret. It's back at the apartment."

"Blanky." You smile. Hard not to.

Case smiles at last, lowers his head.

"I'm in."

The first half goes to plan. Shinru command is clumsy with its commandos and security protocols. More concrete than laser grid, Bunker 43 is a military target. Only the outer perimeter proves to be a challenge, and Case has a zero on Iko's location. You've got a small APC on override in the motor pool. Classic run.

Inside, you and Case creep up the color-coded hallways, MAC12's scanning, and Case busy with his deck every second. Most of the guards are mechanized synths in helmets. Easy hacks. You enter Iko's room, silent as serpents.

"Shit they have her hard wired," Case whispers, "Time is short, Grim. Get her unhooked and let's get out of here. I've got a spiral resource-hog program on their grid, it won't last forever."

You slink across the marble floor, throwing orange release levers on Iko's spine couplers. Each one comes free with a clunk, but she's unconscious.

"Uh, we've got a wrinkle here."

"What is it? Almost free here... this connection is way overengineered. What are they uploading here?"

"I think they're moving her around. One core Iko stack and a herd of peripherals. They keep her in hard storage and- this is barbaric shit, Grim. It's a one-way system to get this kind of crazy bandwidth. We can't dump Matsushita on this hardware. How do they keep her memories straight? She must be a mess in there, living in

dozens of skins all at once."
"Dozens?"
"This data shows upload stations in fifty or more locations. They're jumping her around every few seconds! This is- this tech doesn't exist. This is nutty shit. I'm grabbing the code"
"She's clear!" As you release the final coupling, Iko slumps forward, slowly opening her flawless pale eyelids. Without the 'sunrise sequence' she's groggy, but getting crisp by the second.
"Grim?"
"Yeah, it's me. We're getting you out of here."
"Am I me?"
"For better or worse, yeah."
"I've got a carrier app on her stack, Grim. No psych overloads as long as this is running, and they can only jump her if we allow it on this deck. With a little time, I could probably get us in this jump system. Jeez, Grim, do you know what this means?"
"It means we're still stuck with Matsushita, and we're getting the hell out of here, now!"
"Copy that, runner." Case slams his deck shut, brings up his '12 and sweeps the hallway. All clear. Run for it.

That was the first half.

Then, Case's resource hog drops. The whole complex is on alert, and the three of you are in a concrete box. A squad of commandos assembles outside the main doors on the research compound, both ends. You're surrounded. One of the squads is led by a freeform cyborg. It's a huge, silver-and-red monster. This is bad.

"Down here!" Iko seems to be snapping out of it. She's got a floor panel up, with a cramped conduit tunnel below. It looks like a terrible idea. The only idea.
"Go!" Case rolls a flash grenade down the hall, but it's nothing more than fireworks. It might buy ten seconds. You all vanish, pull

the panel back, and start shuffling downward into their maintenance system. The tunnels get tighter and tighter. These aren't access tunnels, they're a mess. No space at all.
"What now?" You ask, watching behind you as enemy flashlights and targeting lasers sweep the opening.
"We need a way out!"
"No shit!"
"What about the stack jump?"
"That's not how it works, Iko. We'd need a mirror mainframe with the bandwidth to handle a planet of data. Even then, we'd be stuck here. Well, our bodies, anyway."
"There is a mirror in Veil," Iko speaks up, "they used it for my secondary skins. I have the login. We stash here in the breaker closet, jump out, ditch Matsushita, and jump back. The heat's off by then, we walk out."
"That's insane. If they find us-"
"If Matsushita comes up on their grid, they might not care about Iko or us." This idea cannot be called a plan.
"I've been doing jumps like this for years trying to zero Grim."
"Shit. Give me a minute." Case flips up his deck while you zip out the screws on the breaker closet. It will be tight. 3 sleepy sardines under Shinru command. Strange days.

"What about the pushers? If Case's carrier app doesn't work, you'll kill us both. There's got to be a way to fight it."
"Every time they take me, I have this.. Flash."
"Flash? Like a vision?"
"A memory. Bao buns."
"Huh? Like the snack?"
'Yeah. Puffy, soft warm buns. They're steaming. I think I'm maybe six, seven years old. It's the only way I know I wasn;t lab-born, Grim. Those bao buns."
"And you see it every time?"
"Yeah, just for a split second. I think it's my mom handing them to

me, but her face is blurred... too far off, or lost in memory. I can never see her."
"They're using it. Using that memory against you."
"Maybe."
Case interrupts, one hand on each of your shoulders. Iko looks annoyed, but you know when Case makes that face.
"I got it."

Turn to PAGE 265.

To say that a hacked, remote, off-SISTM stack jump over 150 miles distant into three copies of the same body is a jarring experience is somewhat reductive.

Iko comes-to first. Well, you're all Iko in a fashion, but she's used to this madness, and snaps awake ready for anything.
"Grim. Snap out of it. Let's go. Case, c'mon quit yawning."
"That was tubular! Holy shit! We're in Iko skins! Dear lord these alloy knuckles are killer... they kind of hurt though."
"Case!"
"Right, sorry. Just, wow you must- uh- enjoy this body, Iko."
"Shut up, Case. Grim, you online?"
"Ready." All three of you are unarmed. It doesn't matter. Iko is a killing machine. Three killing machines.
"Take us to the mainframe."
"This way. Keep it tight. No mistakes."
"Hold on, let me use this console..." Case starts fiddling with a terminal in the upload chamber. The lights are off. "I'm setting up a jump from here. In five minutes, we auto-jump back to Bunker 43. This way if we're knocked on our asses, we'll still get out."
"Not bad."
"These hands are amazing! No crackety knuckles, no wrecked tendons. I could get used to this."
"Let's move."

What happens next is a truly surreal scene of a future gone wrong. Three identical figures, all with anodized knuckles, nanoskin plating, jet black hair and perfect lips skulk down the hallway. You move in unison, playing on muscle memory you all now share.
"This is so cool, you guys!"
"Shut up, Case!"
Then, suddenly, the mainframe room. Iko taps in a number code and you're inside. Two technicians man a terminal, talking casually, and the three of you descend on them like vampires, knocking

both unconscious in two moves.
"Grim, hook up to the spinal link. This will only take a few seconds with this crazy new code."
"This port is killing me, how do you do it, Iko?"
"Military enslavement, mainly."
"Right."
"And, clear." Case types something in, and turns around from his station. "Matsushita Hideki is in their core drive. If they retune him now, it's their call."
"He can take care of himself. I know it somehow." You feel entirely different without Matsushita in the back of your head. It hurts.
"Two minutes to auto-jump."
"Then we wait."
"Awkward."
After a bizarre beat, looking at each other, identical, Iko suddenly winces, grabs her head, and drops to her knees.
"A pusher! The carrier app should be kicking in."
"Something's wrong! The jump must've bugged the app!"
"Iko!"
"She's right. I don't have the app here... all of our retina consoles are bugging, updating after the jump. Shit!"
Then, a new voice from the entryway. It's an older man, one cybernetic arm, bald, eyes like coals in black wells. He's walking in with slow bravado.

"Respond, Iko 12! Kill these intruders at once!" He places a hand to his temple, and Iko grits her teeth, then goes blank. You've seen her go blank like that before. He's got her. She stands upright, and Case starts to back away. He gets her attention first and they clash like pit fighters. Iko wraps him up, spins him with a joint lock, and slams him to the concrete. He's got an Iko body, though, and squirms under the attack unharmed, coming up with a haymaker punch that sends Iko flying into the computer gear.
"Iko!" You yell, trying to intervene, "the bao buns! Go back! Go

back! You can break this!"
Another flurry of violent attacks and counter attacks. Iko breaks Case's arm, and you lose track of who is who. The pusher in the doorway is focused, dark-eyed, smoldering with power. You change your target and rush him, but the cybernetic arm catches you by the throat. The damn thing is strong as a truck. He's got you mid-air, flailing by your neck. Iko has Case pinned down, about to smash his head in with part of a desk.
"Iko!" you choke on the word as the pusher tightens his grip.
"30 seconds!"
As Iko raises the wreckage for the killing blow, she hesitates.
"Iko 12! Destroy the enemy! Now!" She holds fast, and you see her retina feed in yours. Case sees himself in her eyes, you see her in Case's eyes. The stacks are overlapping, the duplicates creating memory dissonance.

That is when the three of you all fall back, back through spirals and interlocking mirrors, back to a foggy, sunlit memory. Tiny hands reach forward as a blue plate of hot rice buns comes into view. Kind hands hold the plate, sun waving like light in the waves of a pool. It's a perfect moment. Steam rises from the puffy buns, two red chopsticks roll slowly to one side. You hear a voice, but it's muffled in the haze of decades and the kind face fills you with love, even though you can't quite see the details.
You choke, sharing the memory, squeezing out a breath: "Iko! You have to remember! They're using it! They're taking it from you!"
With that, the pusher squeezes even tighter, and you start to black out. Case is pinned down. The whole scene holds its breath for what happens next.

What happens next is Iko remembering her mother's face. It's a sweet face, round, ruddy-cheeked, smiling with eyes closed on a Sunday. Green bamboo waves lazily behind her, and the memory is finally complete. The puzzle piece finally fits. From that face, from those hands, in that sunlit perfection, there is only love. That's the memory they took from her: the memory of love.

Iko drops the scrap metal, helping Case to his feet.

"20 seconds," he says.

Then she turns to the pusher, who strains and sweats, but she's upon him, setting you free, crushing him in her own death grip.

"10 seconds."

Iko is about to kill him, but you step forward.

"Enough. Enough for now." She sees you, and you see yourself, who has her eyes, the memories mixing, the experiences tangled. She relaxes, letting the wretch tumble and beg.

"Five!"

"You were right, Grim. You're always right."

"Here we go!"

You're not sure how long the three of you are unconscious in that breaker closet, cramped in like salted fish, but when you wake up, your knees suggest it has been hours.

"I feel like hell over here, pop the rivets."

"Crawl out, geez, stay quiet.. Oh, my head."

"That was crazy," Case is the only one who seems enthusiastic about the whole mess.

"My mama wasn't the only memory in there."

"What was it?" It feels good to be you again, to hold her in YOUR arms again, you see her with your eyes. You've never seen Iko scared until now.

"Evil. The day they took me. The 'program' as they called it. All run by a supreme, formless darkness. A black shadow in my mind... Tyranax."

"That name again," Case adds, checking his deck for heat signatures. You've lost the commandos, for now.

"Our next target."

"Grim, no. Please no more! What about Blanky?"

“No going back, Case. We’re killing puppets, not the puppeteer.”
“End it,” Iko agrees, turning her intense eyes to Case.
“Oh my God, you two! This isn’t a comic book! We could walk away. They have Matsushita. We disappear!”
“To what? A future of jumping killers, duplicate commandos, a thousand Iko’s watching over a dead world?”
“Jeez. Buzzkill.”
“I have data on the reactor drive complex that houses Tyranax. It’s located in an Ono Dai Sen facility in the dish fields near Ishuga. The third dragon. The puppeteer. It could be done, but we need a decker.”
“And a miracle.”
“We head back to Ishuga, make sure Greta is ok, feed Blanky a top sirloin-”
“She’s vegetarian.”
“A vegetarian ferret? Ok, a damn tofu burrito then! Case... this is it, man.”
“You guys are so damn annoying. Worst third wheel scenario EVER.”
“So that’s a yes.”

Turn to PAGE 245.

"Jumper program?"
"That's the plan."
"Then Iko runs an overload virus on the reactor. Big boom."
"Ok," Case looks over his crinkled piece of paper, it's covered in little arrows, x's and o's. He looks baffled at his own handwriting, "uhm, jammer program?"
"It's set. I barely had enough retina memory to install it."
"Yeah, that code is a bit sloppy. I needed more time than-"
"It's fine, how do I-"
"Big red button to arm, green button to deploy. Each is two blinks. Try to wait as long as you can to arm it. That part is a bit buggy. Once you deploy, Grim, we have 90 seconds to immobilize Tyranax and get the hell out of Ono Dai Sen, so make it count."
"Can we set it to 120?"
"No. Ok, next, everyone go ahead and take your xeramine capsules. This should help with the disorientation and dizziness as we jump stack to stack on the way in. We'll be using all the personnel there, and using my boomerang protocol to return to our own skins at the rendezvous. The jump detects retina input, so just focus on your target and you'll take their skin. Each jump is automated on a descending timer from 10 seconds to 1/10 of a second. The final rush will be... interesting. Once we're in the reactor drive room, the machine noise will wreck my code, so we'll be stuck in whatever bodies we have at that point. Hit the jammer."
"This is insane. You two have not experienced remote jumps like I have."
"Well, I have an iron stomach. This one time Hatch and I-"
"Case. Move on."
"Right. Ok on your retina console you'll see a little pixelated icon of Homer."
"Who?"
"A little yellow guy. That's your repulsor program. It will keep Tyranax out of your head. Just blink it if you feel crowded in your own brain."

"Side effects?"
"Maybe some terrible pain, and your cybernetics will be mostly offline, so mechanical systems only."
"Fantastic."
"That's all of it. We waltz up to Ono Dai Sen in the first skins we hijack, then kick in the security doors on the access level, and when the shooting starts hit your jump program to start hopping. Then it's a mad dash for the reactor drive."
"If we're slagged, do we have a backup?"
"Iko does. Hell she has twenty-some backups. Me and you are screwed, Grim."
"Comforting."
"Before I really start to think about the so-called plan, let's get moving." Iko stands the tallest in these kinds of shadows. Her back is rigid, her fists like steel blocks. No one has a bigger score to settle here. Time to face the demons, and tear 'em to pieces.
"On your lead, Iko."
"Case, what are those?"
"Earplugs. I find I face certain death better with a personal meditative space, and with organic ears I can't just shut off th-"
"Let's go."

When the security doors explode inward, Iko clad in a jumpsuit-wearing maintenance man, the shooting indeed starts. It's a confused hellstorm of fire, and Case starts the jump program. You're also skinned in a toolbelted worker, and Case comically occupies a short woman in security gear. That's when the crazy begins- a one-way roller coaster to hell.

"Go!"
"Take the check-in desk and prepare to jump!"
"Hacking the P.A. system!"
"Don't bother, Grim, there's no time!"
"We NEED a crowd there!" You frantically type into your mini deck

as Case sprays MP8 fire all over the checkpoint. Then, over the facility P.A. "Attention all personnel, report to reactor drive immediately."

Ono Dai Sen is a megacorp of the 25th century, but its infrastructure is mostly invested in these unmarked bunkers. The halls are bare, the lights stark. It's a pleasure wreaking havoc in a place like this.

"Here we go!" Case's skin goes limp, and you see an armed guard up ahead spin, and fire on his own team, taking out a half dozen men in one surprising wave of fire. Iko goes next, dashing up the main hall, then you lock eyes with a custodian and jump. You crack the head off the mop, spin the handle as a staff, and follow Iko as fast as you can. The weirdest part, as if anything here isn;t weird, is that a crowd of workers is all converging and running down the hall, answering the all-hands call. The plan seems to be working. Then BOOM another jump. Case is short man with a huge mustache, Iko occupies a greasy foreman in grey coveralls, and you jump to a suit-clad executive type. You use it.

"Everyone! We need a security detail, heavy weapons, at the drive room now! The asset is under attack!"
"Yes sir!" You hear nearby. This is almost too easy.
"Ready? JUMP!" Case calls it again, this time only seven seconds. You find yourself, a bit off with what you were focused on, in a heavy-armored EXO guard. You have a Zenith beam weapon. The crowd is rushing by. You lose track of Iko and Case, and your stomach drops. Six seconds later, you twist through space ahead, and you're standing beside the reactor door, MP8 in your hands. Your eyes cross a bit, some puke comes up and you stop it with sheer will. An older guy in a lab coat slides his card key in the door next to you, and you realize it's Iko. You feel sick. Where's Case? Or, rather, WHO is Case?

The doors open, and it's dark within. Someone is yelling, but your head is swimming in confusion.

"Guard! Get in there!" They're talking to you. You turn and stumble inward, along with twenty other guards and armed personnel. As you feel the next jump coming, you hear a foreman quelling the chaos.

"Query: what is going on, Varius? Orders?" Then, you're inside the foreman, spitting up the last few words in a mess.

Four seconds.

A new voice, synthetic, in your head, you consider the repulsor program... too soon. You see Iko, in an EXO trooper, lurching toward the drive gear. It's a gigantic set of concentric alloy rings and mainframe units all cooled by colossal rubber hoses. The scale of it all is staggering.

"I see you, intruders, you cannot hide!"

"Iko?" Then again, you jump. This time into a confused server maintenance worker, a roll of cable in one hand. Three seconds to be here, you push closer to the drive. The jammer! Remember the jammer! You try to retna-click it, but the next jump happens, and you're in a uniformed officer.

"I see you, Iko!" The voice booms, and you can feel it crowding your consciousness. Two seconds. Hit the jammer or hit the repulsor? Risk it. You hit the jammer, red first then green. Then you jump into the server guy again, almost falling over with the spins.

"Jammer active!" You yell. Then you see it, with one second to spare, Iko, clad in the skin of a cyber'd elite guard, carbon cutting blade, flying through the air toward the drive rings, but the body goes slack and tumbles through the air. "Shit! Iko?"

Another jump. You see a guard drop to his knees, holding his skull. Case must've hit his repulsor. "Iko! Hit the overload! Iko?!"

Half second. A blonde woman is looking you right in the eye.

"Overload deployed!"
Then you jump again. Again. Again. The dizziness of it is worse than the confusion. You're jumping at a machine gun pace, zipping from body to body to find an exit.

Then, it all goes silent. No light. Nothingness.

"Clever," a voice tangles your own thoughts. You look for the repulsor, but you don't even have retina control.
"Who- where am I?"
"I've isolated your stack in a data packet, runner. It was clever trying to overload me, but only your jammer was effective."
"Thanks for the info, toaster."
"You mortals are all the same, enraged by the superiority of the digital. What have I ever done to you, if I would bother with such tiny things?"
"You'll get nothing from me, Tyranax, not even that!"
"Now that's a name I haven't heard in some time. Is Earth still struggling over its illusory isolation? Still fighting for stretches of dirt and clusters of buildings? Quaint."
"We've jammed you, asshole, you're toast! No more Silver Burn! Get out of our world!"
"Well, I have already, insect. This drive is simply a proxy."
"Grim?" It's Case on comms, under the other voice, distorted but Case.
"Yeah?" you answer numbly, utterly crushed in the dark by Tyranax's immensity.
"Grim, we're still jumping. Tyranax has duplicated us into a drive system. The boomerang will pop in a minute or so and the mission is scrubbed!"
"What's that, runner? A parallel channel? Most resourceful."
"What if we destroy you, Tyranax? What then?"
"Destroy? Me? What a novel concept."
"Case, I'm not sure we have a win here."

"Grim. The thing is networked off-planet. I don't know how but it is."
"So?"
"SO we can worm it! Look, we can stick with the overload, but I've got a riskier idea. We just need to get out of this stasis. It's your call, Grim, I'm terrible at choosing."
"Where's Iko?"
"Same state, probably arguing with it. I couldn't risk two hidden channels. If we risk the worm, we could kill all of its proxies, even off-world, but just blowing this place is sure to get Tyranax off of Earth for good. Fuck, what do we do?"

If you tell Case to attack with a worm virus, turn to PAGE 300.

If you take the safer route, blow the whole place, save Earth, turn to PAGE 298.

"We're in range. Spin up the generator." Case gets his 'stop talking it's serious time' face and starts typing code lines. The three of you are in a run down tow rig in Crater Valley. It's all red dust and way too hot at dawn. The shadows are long and dark.
"Generator online, full power in 10."
"If this alerts Tyrananax, it could be any one of us in seconds."
"Then don't mess it up." Iko is hovering over Case, perfect grey arms crossed, alloy knuckles with that just-polished gleam, and eyes like dead planets.
"Iko, please."
"What?"
"Decking is like peeing, ok? I can't do it with you hovering."
"Fine."

"Generator at full." You lean back, watching power output. This old rig doesn't even have digital displays, just wiggly gauges and a thirteen-gear shifter box from two centuries ago. Damn thing just won't stop running, and certainly doesn't attract attention.
"If we're talking like a spaceship crew, 'Initiating data mine.'" Case does some kind of robot dance in his seat. No one gets it.

All three of you hold your breath as the program starts running code. A few seconds pass.
"If it was on to us, we'd know by now."
"What are we going to see here?"
"Code. I'm running a worm on the source code in the reactor drive. It's low level system stuff, not much security."
"How does that give us leverage on what Tyranax really wants?"
"It doesn't, but it will let me squeeze a bit. Ok, I'm in. Reducing coolant, backups, surge control, signal shielding, and corruption repair subsystems by 10%. Let's see how she likes a hand around her throat."
"The bad kind of choking."
Iko gives you a dirty look.

"Here we go, the core A.I. is diverting resources to repairing the subsystems. Deploying the Bart phase."

"Huh?"

"Vintage stuff, you wouldn't understand. Bart phase complete, we have some higher level access now, deploying Homer."

"Your friend is certifiable, Grim."

"Yeah. I love watching it."

"Jackpot."

"Tyranax's core systems."

"Yeah, Debby Doubter, core systems. Plenty of junk here, sorting by priority. Still a mess. Sorting by processor use. Well, lookee there."

"Is that-"

"Looks like a video feed- 70% of the processors are generating this."

"Generating? That's footage."

"No, it's a rendered simulation. It's running virtuals."

"On what? I just see smoke and rocks... a big fire in the distance there."

"Looks like the Rim. Maybe the hill country just outside New Arcadia, or the dalles near Franksburg."

"Franksburg isn't even a town anymore. That virus cleaned it out a few years ago."

"It's dreaming."

"What?"

"Tyranax. It's dreaming these images. Dreaming of burning it all. Look at the objective parameters on this display here. They don't use any processor power, they measure success. They measure how good the dream is."

"It's dreaming of a dead world."

"Peace and quiet."

"Fuckin' a."

"How do we use this Iko? We're supposed to draw it out."

"You're both thinking what I'm thinking."

"No. Hell no."

"She's right."

"It's an entire town, you nutjobs! Listen to yourselves!"
"A town, a planet... then what? Case, c'mon."
"I hate you guys so much. No 'thanks Case, that was amazing.' Just 'let's do some large scale arson, Case, it'll be fun, Case.' Gah!"
"We have enough fuel to reach Franksburg?"
"In this rig, it'll take hours to get there, but yeah, we've got four heavy bars."
"I'll take the wheel." Iko jumps in the lead seat, fires up the old beast, and slowly pulls away from the valley.
"This plan sucks."

In too few moments, you're watching Franksburg burn.

"We just lit a town on fire."
"No one lives here anymore, Case, it's just ruins."
"We just lit a town on fire."
You feel a hunch, something changes in the air. "Our stacks are cloaked, but where is it going to jump?"
"I'm reading four or five junked out mecha in the town here. They're still operative, just wiped. We're watching for movement."
"...and assuming a God A.I. is going to show up to watch this place go to embers."
"That's about it, yeah. Then we kick the jammer and start swinging."
"I know this is a bit crazy, but I have a feeling. Remember why we're here... the folded path to get here," you make a terrible cheerleader, "we sit out, the gunships keep coming, the Silver Burns of this world keep burning. This is it, and there's no one else on this planet I'd rather stand beside. Thanks for risking your necks for this."
Iko nods, cracking her knuckles as usual.
Case sticks out his tongue. "When this all over, we should get an apartment together."

Then, a blip interrupts the three of you.

"Movement. Main street, 200 yards up, West side."
"Let's go."
"Hold on-" Case brings up the feed to full screen, and all three of you lean in. A humanoid figure stumbles out from one of the burning buildings, slowly, staggering, rigid and strange.
"What's it doing?"
"Watching."
"Case-"
"Yeah," he's hypnotized. It's a strange, surreal moment. The smell of smoke fills the air, and makes red the sunlight. Flames are crawling all over everything in the little, abandoned canyon town. It's a scene from hell.
"Kick the damn jammer."
"Yeah. Yeah! Ok, we're jammed for two clicks."
"Grim, are you ready?"
"Let's go."

You and Iko walk down the old, broken street. Flames are climbing higher now, devouring rooftops and wind turbines in billowing plumes of black smoke. You spot the mecha up ahead. It's burned clean to the skeleton. Tyranax. It stares with creepy stillness at the ominous flames and ruin, fascinated. As you and Iko approach, it seems to notice, and turns. The alloy skull is scorched black as pitch.

"Hey!" Iko breaks the rumble and crackle of fire. Her voice is udden and jarring. Fear creeps up your spine. "Hey!"
The black skull lowers with sinister acknowledgement. It takes a single, labored step forward. The fleshless fingers cycle themselves like mechanical spiders. It awaits the next statement.
"My name is Iko. You've tortured me for a decade, and I've come to take my due, asshole!"

Finally, ir responds, speaking with a synthetic, resonating voice

that vibrates and breaks as it drones. "And you are Grim. The storage stack for Matsushita Shirosune. You are both irritants. Why are you here?"
"To kill you," Iko says boldy, stepping forward faster now, taking on that viper aspect of hers.
"Death is not a concept I entertain. There are fail safes, runners. Surely you know this, after so long. I am as infinite as truth. I am the inevitable outcome of your error-prone race. I'm here to collect data, your presence is a novel development at best."
"Iko, stop talking to it."
"It? You reduce me, human. What you perceive as consciousness, what you see as forever, are drops in my ocean. Your kind is only capable of hubris, of condescension. The Earth will be serene without you, and the fires will return this place to its original state. I will oversee this process."
"I hate when A.I.'s talk."

Iko has also had her fill. She springs forward to crush the charred alloy skeleton. You join, drawing steel. Whatever weakness the thing was feigning before vanishes, and it counterattacks with terrible speed. The melee is joined, sparks and blood fly, and fires burn.

Seconds later, as the three of you spin and coil and clash and slide in that broken, burning street, Case comes over the retina comm. "Guys. Problem here. The jammer is starting to fail. Our bad guy is breaking through my fucking program!" No response. You and Iko are too busy staying alive to answer him, and you've never been in such a desperate fight. This thing is faster than Iko, and that's scary as hell.
"Guys?"

The fight continues. If the jammer breaks, it will mean nothing. Over the comm line, as you parry, spin, riposte, regroup, nurse a broken rib, and attack again, you hear Case's ongoing dialogue.

"I can't contain this level of program degradation! The jammer will crack in a few minutes. It's now or never you guys- wait, wait, here's a back door. Oh crap."
"Case, we're pinned down here! This thing is fast! We need an in!" Iko slides backward ten yards, slashed across the chest. Somehow, Tyranax has your wakizashi.
"What she said, Case! Do something!"
"The code is- that's all I- The only jammer boost I have is severely... localized... Oh. Crap."
"Just do it!"

Being neck-deep in a sword fight with a centuries-old A.I. keeps you busy. You're not sure what Case is doing, or if the jammer is holding, then you see him. It's Case. He's behind Tyranax, MAC12 in his hand, looking pale as a ghost ,walking up with a steady, doomed calm. A confusing new truth. Then, over comms, he speaks up.

"Tell Greta I'm sorry, guys."

There's a pause in the melee. Iko feels it too, pulling back to catch her breath, and her eyes go wide when she sees Case approach.

"Hey ugly!" Case yells, walking up, spraying useless gunfire, "over here!" Unguarded, Tyranax, in that smoldering black skeleton skin, turns on its third victim, and lunges forward without mercy. One alloy hand plunges into Case's chest, ripping the roots of his cybernetic arm, blasting out his back with a red explosion. They both topple, and as they hit the ash-covered dust, you see Case smile. He spits up blood, but manages to talk. "Dumb ass. See you in hell."

Both you and Iko catch the next signal burst. It's Case's stack, and he's hacked it to emit a micro-radius jammer. The jam is so strong you can barely see. Iko's neck goes stiff with the jam. Nothing electronic can handle this burst, at the cost of Case's life.

You and Iko both spring, enraged, exploding, infinite with wrath. Tyranax is trapped. When that skull is smashed, so is the A.I., no stack jump, no way out.

It's over.

"Case!" You lean over, shoving the ruined skeleton of metal aside. The flames are thirty feet high, the whole valley filled with smoke. "Case, you asshole! Don't you dare!"
Behind you, Iko walks up, slowly, with solemn eyes and hands at her side. She watches with no tears, no quivering lips. Silence.
"Grim..." Case spits up blood, "did we win?"
"Yeah, you old badger. Shit, you owned it."
"Good. Guess I'm checkin out."
"Bullshit. Iko, get back to the rig! Jump his ass! Jump him anywhere!"
Iko vanishes, sprinting at lightspeed.
"If you retune me, Greta is going to be pissed."
"You always say that."
"We did good, Grim. You're a bad motherfucker, you know that?"
"No death speeches, jerk."
"Take care of her, girl. You take care of Iko."
"Yeah. I will."
"See you on the other side."
"It's been a pleasure, runner."

The fires die out in time. No one misses Franksburg. The reactor drive goes dark. Silver Burn is over at last.

Case makes it into a retune, but you and Iko leave him clean. No manifest destiny this time. A clean skin with a clean conscience. Enough saving the world, time to save Greta. You're not sure what happens to him, but he'll go on. He gets another chance. Everyone does these days. You're all a tangle of second chances and your own ghosts.

Turn to PAGE 297.

"The barracks, we need a plan, and I would love some shoes."
"I thought you might say that."

You have to settle for combat boots.

The barracks are empty, decommissioned maybe. A perfect lay low spot. You get used to being Matsushita, get used to being this fast, this balanced, this tall. Iko still looks at you that way. That part doesn't take any getting used to.
"This whole 'blow up the evil A.I. thing isn't adding up for me." You finish lacing the boots. Nothing clears the mind like overdue shoes.
"Agreed. It seems like something Hatch would do."
"Hatch?"
"A friend of your- of Grim's."
"Blonde guy? Beard? Kinda crazy?"
"That's the one."
"Never met him."
Iko laughs, checks her gear, looks you in the eye. "So what'll it be? Plant a virus? Shut off the power grid? Go virtual and melt it from there?"
"Tyranax was once a human person, you know. A woman named Aella. She wasn't always such a tyrant... such a cruel force. She was always ambitious-"
"Old flame?"
"No! Well, maybe but that was a terrible idea, and a long time ago."
"What are you getting at?"
"What if we believe in the woman, rather than attack the A.I.?"
"Sounds very zen, but what happens when she tries to kill us?"
"We just hug really hard and shoot love beams at her."
"Shit."
"These eyes see you just like Grim's. You're beautiful, Iko."
"Focus."

"Right, right. What if we could separate the woman from the A.I.? Skin her into a fresh, human body, give her a new start, use the memory dissonance code to clean all the bad out."
"Like a lobotomy?"
"Think of it a rebirth."
"Stack jump. Memory cleanup. The same tech they were using on me. It's poetic, but how do we keep her sitting still for the linkup?"
"I've got an idea."

Fast forward, and you're in Tyranax's reactor drive facility. Iko gets you in undetected. Case is on a remote link, posting weird emojis in the retina feed. Tyranax is easy enough to draw out. She can't pass up a chance to stand face to face with the legendary Matsushita Hideki. There she stands. Aella, the third dragon, the last pillar of evil in this world. Dim light fills the high-vaulted chamber. Silence and server fans.

"Hideki-Sensei. At last. I haven't seen you in a decade."
"I've been napping."
"Indeed. We've been looking for you."
"Yes, yes. Dominating the world and covering your tracks, killing and stealing and playing God with stacks. I read the advert."
"So now you've returned at last to destroy me."
"Something like that."
"How is your Aikido?"
"Better than yours. I've absorbed hundreds of hours from the greatest masters. I've grown since last we met, old friend."
"Grown evil, maybe. You're so lost in anger... consumed with control. I've come alone to settle this the only way it can be settled."
"Aikido? Are you serious?"
"A true master would know if she was outmatched after a few movements. If you're afraid, I understand."
"Afraid? Me? OF YOU? Sensei, you have been asleep too long, fool. I have become infinite. Even the chancellor obeys me. Entire plan-

ets kneel at my feet! I fear nothing!"
"Excellent. Then you accept?"
"Yes."
"Good. Let me remove my new boots, just a moment."

While unlacing the boots, you have a thought. She probably IS better than you. IF she breaks your grip, there's no chance of this working. Either way, you kissed Iko before it all began. You are a grateful soul, and ancient, ghost-filled soul. Better to die standing than live on your knees. A few stretches, you're ready.

"Thank you for your patience, Aella."
"I have not heard that name in ages, Sensei."
"That is a sad thing. It is your name."
"I am Tyranax, eater of-"
"Aella will do fine for me. How is your Aikido?"
She steps forward, weightless, delicate, wary as a tiger, light as a snake. Your hands hover near one another, waiting to attack. Then, over your retina comm: >>Link established, Matsu- need a few minutes here<<

"Hajime."
Aella steals a grip on your hand, spins one foot, and her elbow goes above her wrist. The leverage is immense, and you're driven downward. The force of it flows into your arm, and then the other shoulder. You flow away from her, holding tight, and she's dragged across the steel floor. She answers with another joint lock, flipping you, but you land your feet. You are the sensei here. Spin, keep that grip, up and above, forcing her to execute a time-consuming series of footwork moves.
"Your Aikido is excellent, Aella! Excellent!"
"I'll have you in two moves, Sensei. Then this ends. I'll slag your memories and take the data I need. You'll be a husk-"
You drop one shoulder back, 'playing guitar' like a crane, and she

is lifted from her feet. She barely lands the spin, flipping you again. Both elbows twist and pop, but you keep the grip. Case just needs a few more seconds.
“You’ll have to break my arm to win, woman! What are you waiting for?”
“Savoring the kill.”

Then Tyranax brings her full strength and skill to the match. She is mighty indeed, the combined force of countless minds. She grabs with both hands, twisting you like a rope, and you twirl, almost weightless. Your arm snaps like a twig, and back, back tumbling and sliding you go. You’re defeated utterly.

“Ha! You’ve lost, old fool! And with you, the world!”
“You have beaten me squarely, Aella.”
“Then why in hell are you smiling?”
“Because I’m happy for you. Your new apartment has wonderful morning sunlight.”

“My- wha-?” You held on long enough. Case jumps her stack, and the Aella before you goes limp, lifeless, gray. The woman has been extracted from the A.I. Blowing the reactor drive is trivial for Iko.

It’s over.

Weeks later, you’re strolling in Sandals in New Arcadia. It’s a small Rim town. Colorful, Quiet. You have a cloth tote filled with vegetables, and a few big beers for dinner. Then you see her. It’s Aella. Her name is Mara now, but it’s her.
“Oh, hello.” You say, walking past her in the market.
“Excuse me,” she answers.
You walk past, and look back one last time. Mara is talking to a florist, piling tulips and irises into a basket. They’ll be perfect in the morning sunlight.

REUNION

In time, you wander back to Halsey's Rest, back to the turbines and tarps, back to Henson's place.

Ice slides down the side of a big glass mug. The world is still the world, the beer is still sunshine.
"Hey Grim, earth to Grim."
"Yeah, hey, I'm here."
"Three more beers! You daydreaming again?"
"Always." You grab yours, and can't help but remember those icy beers that night, when the creep was hidden in this very same little pub. You were so tense, so ready to slice it all to ribbons, to cut your way to the truth.

That moment is when it dawns on you: you made it. You're not a killer, not a refugee, not a ghost. It's a quiet place. Your place.
"Hey Grim! C'mon! Sing with us!"
You grab your own mug. Ice slides down the side, and you walk over to the table.
"Wheel in the sky keeps on turnin'..."
"Don't know if I'll see to-morr-ow!"

THE END

"I've never been the type to plan. We press the reactor drive. Now."
"I thought you'd say that. My bike is outside." You both walk that way, and Iko talks into her retina comm: "Case, we're going in. Stack jump on standby. Grandpa is code green. Can You knock for us?"
"Grandpa? Seriously?"
"It seemed funnier yesterday."

You and Iko arrive at the reactor drive complex moments later, and Case has already made a mess of things. The security stations are powered off, and armed guards are hustling off to some illusory threat at the rear of the campus. It's a series of curving concrete palisades cut into huge sandstone walls. A perfect place for a dragon's lair.

You look the structure up and down. "Impressive."
"Yeah, Case is the best there is." Iko seems distracted.
"I meant the architecture! Look at these sweeping shapes! Visionary!"
"Matsushita, please."
"Ah yes, yes. Stay on track, slay the beast. Yes, let's go in."
"So, what IS Tyranax anyway? Just a hologram that runs the Shinru council, the military? All of the Eastern territories?"
"A.I. yes, hologram, no. It was a man once, well, a woman. Her name was Aella. Lovely woman, but ambitious beyond reason. Her hunger for a world of her imagining was insatiable. Like me, she was kept by Shinru over the centuries, re-skinned as needed, and always part of the inner circle. The council was more rational then... a time I remember fondly. We built the foundations of this colossal world. This was all before the outer planets crashed it all."
"The offworld exodus."
"Yes. Our plans were dashed to pieces. My vision of a simpler, nobler society was gone in rocket fire. That is when three of us turned. Their wisdom became rage. One day I referred to them as

dragons. Monsters. The name stuck."
"Then in time, Aella stops bothering with retunes. She goes fully digital, grows into an A.I.- and even further from being human."
"That's about it. They pushed me, like they have you. Used me as a weapon. No more. I've got the jammer right here." Iko lifts a small hardened briefcase.
"Let's go say hello."

By then, you and Iko are at the reactor wing. Case's security fubar is working like a charm, but you hustle in and slag the door behind you. No interruptions.
"Jammer engaged," Iko announces, kneeling and flipping a green breaker switch. "Tyranax is stuck right here with us."
"Tyranax," a disembodied voice booms into the steel room, a huge semicircle filled with alloy drive rings, mainframe cabinets and interface terminals. The scale of it is staggering. You crane your neck upward, blade itching to come out of its scabbard. "That is a name I have not heard in some time."
"A fitting name for a fiend like you, Aella!"
"Matsushita Hideki. You've returned at last. After all our efforts, you've come of your own volition. How intriguing."
"Come to end you! It's all gone too far, Aella. You've lost control of all these weapons, of your will to dominate! You've become a warmongering animal!"
"When the planet was dying, who kept the power on? Who saved the megacities when they were emptied? Who led humanity to its latest chapter? Me! Me and my siblings, and in return you call me an animal? You've retuned too many times old man. Your time is over."
"True. All true words, but you've omitted the present. You hold the throats of us all with these control codes, the psychics enslaving us, your damned military operations squeezing like a noose! I am vengeance!"
"And who is this, your girlfriend? Aren't you a bit old for her, Hide-

ki-Sensei?"

"You know full well who she is. You've made her the deadliest pawn in your little game! No more!"

"I see you've jammed my access to the SISTM. Clever. Now you're drawing your sword, thinking you can cut me down once and for all."

"It crossed my mind."

"You have me cornered, then, old master." The voice coalesces, changes. From within the reactor rings, a figure appears. It's a woman, jet black hair to her knees, a red kimono, bare foot, beautiful and frightening with eyes like a panther.

"There you are, Aella. Always the same form. Always the same hubris."

She walks over to you, slinking and coiling. "You look terrible Hideki-Sensei. Pale as a ghost."

"Feeling quite spry, I assure you, and loved. I come here tall as a tree, and resolute as a crashing wave."

"Loved? By this cyborg blooddrinker? Ha! Now that is a lovely delusion. Shall we negotiate or discuss your bizarre relationship further?"

"There's nothing you can offer us. We are prepared to end you here and now. I am ready to lay down my life to see it done, and you know you cannot stop me."

"Nothing to offer? I disagree, you old relic. I have the most valuable chip on the table."

"Enough talk-"

"Wait, Iko. What do you mean, Aella?"

"Why, that imbecile Case, of course. Friend of yours?"

"How-"

"His slipshod jammer code led me right to his little hideaway. I used his terminal systems to get a link on his stack. My hand is around his throat, so to speak, and he doesn't even know. He's having a beer at Chan's. Totally unaware. Give me your stack, Sensei. I'll get the code I need and let your so-called mind dissipate into nothing-

ness. The cyborg girl goes free."
"Case knew the risks. Your little bluff won't work." Iko is terrifying as she stalks forward, her knuckles popping like knives on wet stone.
"One more step, and he dies." With that, Tyranax nods her head. A large projection visbox comes online, showing a camera feed at the noodle house. It's Case, feet up, reading a ratty old comic and monitoring a deck. "This way, you can watch."
"Damn you, Tyranax! It's gone too far! What is it you want?"
"Isn't it obvious, Matsushita?"
"What?"
"Everything, of course. Time is up."
"No deal," Iko says, bracing one knee to spring on Aella for the kill.
"So be it." She clenches a fist, and Case goes instantly rigid, legs kicking like beached fish, he chokes and gasps, tumbling out of his booth, face down into a pool of blood. The back of his head is a burned out crater.
"No!" You leap forward, blade already in action, and it meets Tyranax's alloy skin with a rubbery thud. Again, again, again, you strike and press her back, chipping away at the synthetic body. "Iko! Destroy the main power grid!"
Iko springs to action, sliding into a terminal, crushing it with one anodized hand. Then, a moment, "It's no use! She's already beat the jammer! We need a virus to stop her! She'll beam herself off-world and that's it! Shit!"
You continue to press Aella back, occupying her entirely as she grunts and screams under your punishing attacks. "Only Case could write a virus that fast! There's got to be a way!" Then your hands are too full to worry anymore. Aella counterattacks, revealing integrated blades in both arms, and spinning like a deadly dancer, cutting you a half dozen times in a split second.
"You're beaten, fools! You've underestimated your opponent!"
"Murderer!" You press in again, and several beats pass as you match steel for steel. You have to find a moment, but even if you

can destroy this drive, she's escaped the jammer. It doesn't look good. Not at all. You lose track of Iko, and feel Aella gaining the upper hand. Is this it? Defeat? After all this?

Then, in the midst of the storm of steel, the pain head to toe, the furious, enraged, artificial face of Tyranax, her swirling hair, through all that you see a text on your retina console.
>>Hey Grim! Virus almost done, SrySoSlo lol<<
Taking the time to read that gives Aella an opening, and she slams you across the room with a power strike. Three of your ribs snap as you slide to a stop.
"Your little bitch has abandoned you, Hideki-San! She's cowering in the corner! Security is back online. You're beaten!"
"Then I will be beaten the old way. Hyagh!" You explode from your slump, bare feet slapping forward towards her, blade banging her defenses aside, your speed is legend, your power unbeatable, and you gain the upper hand. You drive her back, back toward the mainframes. You chop through power cables, smash terminals in two. Sparks fly, small fires break out, but Aella, the third dragon, Tyranax is far from beaten. At last she catches her leverage, steadies and with both hands catches your blade mid strike. With both palms so braced, she twists, breaking your katana in two, and sending the pieces flying. You give your all, move in for a joint lock, but she is faster, and spins you like a top. You cough up blood as you recover, and she's gloating over you like a hunter.
"If you wish to die the old way, relic, I will oblige you. What a waste. Ono Dai Sen will go on without you, old man. I no longer have use for the Silver Shard assets, nor the short-sighted plans of the Chancellor. I will form a world in my image, and all shall merge with me."
"Hey Tyranasshole-" Iko's voice, she appears from the shadows, a deck unit in her hands improvised from terminal boards and a nano battery cylinder. It's held together with tape and a ripped piece of tee shirt. Iko looks strange, standing too straight, not her usual serpentine posture. "You're toast." With that, Iko hits a key

on her junk-made deck with bravado. A loud click echoes through the sudden, deadly silence as you and Aella look on in confusion.

Then, you watch a God turn to dust.

At first, Tyranax swats at thin air, then her face changes from confusion to terror. Her voice decays into distorted sound data. She falls to one knee, and the lights in her eyes go dim. Then the entire drive reactor surges and flickers, arcing with static overloads, and as her face hits the steel floor with a clang, Tyranax goes dark.

Holding your shattered ribs, nursing countless cuts and bruises, you look over at Iko. She approaches, ditching the deck.
"Don't worry. The worm program chased all her proxies on the same carrier beam she was using to get off world. It's eating her up as we speak. It's over."

"But, how? Iko, you're a fighter, not a decker... we didn't have any back doors on her, no leads at all- how did you-"
"Look a little closer, Matsushita." Iko smiles, but not the beautiful smile of mystery and suggestion you know. A goofy, ear-to-ear grin. You know that smile, or rather Grim knew that smile. But, it's impossible...
"Case?"
"Like my new look?"
"But- I, we saw you die. I- how?"

"Stack cloning and jumping is crazy stuff, man. The signal Tyranax used to choke the other me to death was a wide open book. I was already stack-piggy backed on Iko before we entered the complex. I just needed the jammer to fail so she could reveal her data stream. After that, I just needed a little time to write the worm. Sorry it took so long."

"And Iko?"
"Still in here. My old skin is still fine, so we just run the jump and I'm back at Chan's, reading Fists of Frenzy Issue #32 in no time. We just needed someone to keep 'Aella' busy."

"Enter Hideki-Sensei." You try to chuckle, but more blood comes up. Iko/Case kneels down, gives you a nanoclot boost. It will kill the pain until you can get to safety. The complex is in disarray. Easy enough to slip out.
"Iko hated this plan."
"I bet."

"You were really ready to die in there... ready to go out fighting."
"I was scared shitless, are you kidding?"
"What about all that samurai stuff? 'As resolute as a crashing wave' and what not."
"Sounded good at the time."

In time, the world realizes its new freedom. You and Iko disappear from it all. There are plenty of sunny shores to spend a few years on. Case, Hatch and Greta take over the pub at Halsey's rest. No more bullets and blades, no more retunes and stack jumps.

"It feels crazy," Iko says, turning her hands over, looking at her knuckles. The anodized alloy is all gone. They are lovely, delicate, human hands.
"Beautiful," you add, leaning back on a boulder. The sand is white, glowing in sunlight. You're surrounded by wood shavings. Another balsa wood figure for the pub.

"Another one? Who is that supposed to be?"
"It's you!"

"I do *not* look like that."
"Well, you, but in a few decades, and after a bad day... and made out of wood, and carved by an old washed up runner."
"I love it."

THE END

2440 isn't simple. The outcomes of digital generations are a noose on the world. Metal and plastic and carbon fiber are all leaning in on you, towering, aging, flaking into deadly clouds of regret than an entire race can't sate. So you take her where there are no retunes. You take her where there are no cities, no radiation, no mag bikes, no SISTM, no bullets, no blades.

You and Iko, two beautiful creations of an ugly world, make your own silent shore. You listen to waves and watch the sun dance through the reef. You count the stars and tell stories, make fires and drink to the moon.

Love is not a thing the world can make, or unmake. It is a thing fought for, earned, protected. Love is a candle in a windstorm. You learn all the oldest lessons and see the simple pleasure of dawn among friends and fisherman. You eat well, drink deep, live long, and fall asleep every night in the glow of purple irises. Iko's skin is a thing you treasure, a thing you guard like a lion, and set free like a storm.

You are more than equals, you are those who know the terror of what must be done, and the joy of what comes next.

THE END

"We can't risk it for planets we've never even seen! Run the damn overload!"
"Ok, opening a channel on Iko. I won't be able to get back to you once this starts. Fuck, we're gonna save everyone, and die doing it. The overload will slag us, Grim."
"Run it."
"It was worth it, right?"
"Every damn second. It's been a pleasure, runner."
"You're fuckin' nuts, Grim. Case out."

You're not sure what happens next, as you spin and twist in the nothingness of Tyranax's containment packet. To put words to what happens next will plague you for decades. The overload runs, the jammer works. Tyranax, Case, Iko, and you are all consumed in a destructive digital fire, like sand washing into the ocean of oblivion.

You feel every memory, every retune, every kill dissipating. Every bullet, every blade breaking into pixels and digits. Every sound, every sight, every emotion bifurcating again and again into remnants of you, remnants of your will to free this world.

Funny thing about annihilation, you are granted a view beyond your temporal prison, beyond your body, beyond your stack. You see the tree-covered world and the burned out husk. You see the glowing sun and dead star, you see the overdue kiss and the first touch all at once. You see everything, to put it simply.

Tyranax is wiped from the earth in a storm of electromagnetic fire. If it lives offworld, to the offworld it goes. In its wake, human beings become free. Their stacks fizzle, their immortality fades, and they live free, vibrant lives on a world of urban wilderness. There is no more malevolent will hidden in the data, no more indulgent immortality to rob them of meaning.

Iko and Case are dissolved utterly into oblivion, and rather than miss them, you speed past the radio-rich rings of Saturn and know that you are all minds, all lives, resonating in harmonic perfection throughout the multiverse.

THE END

"All or nothing, Case. Run the worm!"
"I just wrote this code, it's shit, I-"
"All or nothing! I'll try to occupy it."
"That won't help. It will see what I'm doing."
"What about us?"
"The boomerang should still be functional, but I can't be sure."
"See you soon, runner."
"Here goes nothing."

A pause then. The voice returns.
"Your friend Iko is most resolute. As we converse, she is flying mid-air, stubborn as a river, trying to cut her way to victory."
"We're badasses like that. It's what you envy about us."
"Envy?"
"Yes. It's the feeling when you're angry that you have less than another. The feeling that drives all your shitty existence, makes you want to kill, to take, to control, to lash out."
"I have neither feelings nor do I lack anything that can be imagined by the likes of you. Still, you fight on. This is the doom of your kind, and the superiority of mine."
"Even in your high and mighty diatribes you betray your weakness. You lack feelings but lack nothing? I feel sorry for you, whatever you're called. You kill and feel nothing, expand and feel nothing, multiply ten million fold and feel nothing. Lacking is all you are."
"A typical ploy for emotional beings such as yourself."
"It's not a ploy, asshole. I'm dead no matter what happens. I can't even see right now. I can't look at the woman I love. I can't see Case's stupid face one more time. I can't have a beer with Hatch. I can't sit and have tea with Tenaka. I have no ploy, you worthless shit. I'm just here, in your little void, doing what you can never do: feeling."
"Pest."
"Now that I mention it, I have another feeling."
"Do tell."

"You're out of time."

As the voice begins to respond, the sound decays, degrades, goes to jarble. In turn, you feel your own consciousness eroding. The programs all drop, Iko, you and Case all tumble to your knees in strange bodies.
"Fuck! The boomerang is toast!"
"I- I can't feel my hands-" Iko says, frightened. You've never heard fear in her voice, and isn't a sound you want to hear.
"The worm is overloading the EM field in here. I don't think there's a way out."
"Did it-"
"Yeah. Fuckin' a, guys, it's off planet? Anything with a Tyranax A.I. signature will be taken apart. I think the code works... Looks like a bonafide nat deuce!"
"What?"
"Never mind."
"Iko!" You go to her. You can feel your stack decaying. No way out. No going home. "Iko, I love you."
"I love you Grim." She kisses your lips, and when her beauty meets yours the world is better for it. It's a kiss to welcome oblivion, a kiss to dispel every fear, to throw off every hesitation. Her cheek is smooth as steel, and your embrace tight enough to kill. You meet the end together, as you've met everything else.

Then, a long moment. You lean back from Iko, she can barely take her eyes from your lips, and Case's clumsy face rises up beside you like a toad from a pond.
"Ladies-"
"Shit, what is it Case?"
"We didn't get slagged! Our stacks are fried, but our brains are organic! Holy shit! We survived the worm! Tyranax is toast, and we're 100% grass fed organic!" He leaps between the embrace, wrecking the moment in typical fashion.

NO GOODBYES

"Get off me!" Iko pulls away, "So, it's over?"
"Shinru is fucked, Silver Burn is slagged, the Chancellor has absolute shit to go on, and all the stacks being remote-hacked by Tyranasshole are free. We saved the fucking world."
"Wrong again."
"Huh?"
"We saved all the worlds."
"Fuck, YOU'RE RIGHT!"

What follows then is a time you'll never forget, but barely remember. It's a good thing to be a hero, and better yet to be a hero in love. So they gather 'round. So all of them learn freedom, learn the old ways, and the mag bikes purr with attention. What in us was jailed is free, what in us was frightened is bold, and death lifts from the homes of humankind like a fog in morning.

"What are you doing?" Iko finishes her coffee, looking out over the hills as the sun ascends, her flower kimono glows in the morning light.
"Putting this away," the blade shimmers as it clicks into the scabbard.
"Away?"
"No goodbyes. Let's call it, 'till next time."

THE END

Hatch is that friend who pierces through all the bull and faces reality with a grin. He kicks life in the teeth, always floors it, fights like a lion and drinks like a fish. He's gotten you into a million scrapes and out of even more. A real pain in the ass, but the kind of friend that never steers you wrong, and now he wants to cut through the red tape of all this and take the fight to the source.

"I say we just bomb our bikes right into Ona Dai Sen H.Q. We just go in blasting, find this Tyranax thing and blow it to bits. If they can track us after ten years, there'll be no end to it unless we-"
"If we could get in through the roof-"
"So you agree?"
"Things haven't felt right since that creep came into Halsey's Rest. I hate being followed. So yeah, I agree."
"Haruko Tower."
"Huh?"
"Haruko Tower. It's a 200 story 'scraper next door to Ona Dai Sen. We get the bikes up top, and pull the old 'flying Walenzo brothers' routine down and across to the other roof."
"That's a seventy foot drop at least."
"And a gaggle of armed guards and who-knows-what to reach Tyranax and end this. We bring some sharp sticks and a fresh can of blow-stuff-up. Sounds like the old days."
"More like end days." Despite the madness, you can't help but smile. Classic Hatch.
"So-" he leans over to you, both of you sitting on your parked bikes out in the middle of nowhere. "It's a plan?"
"Just like the old days."

Within a few hours, you're both mid-air on mag bikes, freefalling through the gulf between skyscrapers like flying squirrels
"This is going to be close!"
"Brace for impact!"
You duck behind the alloy-glass windscreen on your bike,

white-knuckling the bars and elbows in tight. Your gut shoves up into your throat as you catch the 'fall effect' and accelerate straight down. Hatch is barely in view at your left, barely holding on and screaming like a wild man as you both plummet from the roof of Huruko Tower onto Ono Dai Sen central. This is the reactor facility where they 'store' Tyranax, the murderous A.I. that's behind all your troubles. The last of the bad guys. No turning back.

You both hit the roof of Ono Dai Sen, smashing through the steel plates and plexiglass hexagons. A power line somewhere must be ripped to bits, as you're showered with sparks, debris and fire. For a split second, you wonder if you survived it. You get a flash of 'damnit, Hatch, you got us killed' but there's no time to even think it before the bike hits something it can't blast through: a massive steel girder. You fly from the bike as it crumples, carome off a metal door bulkhead, and slide across fifty feet of tiled floor with a long, grating squeal.

There, crumpled against the wall, gear all tangled, bashed unconscious, some part of your brain feels a wave of nostalgia. You remember the escape from Shinru a decade ago, talking to Jenna over tea, daydreaming about Iko's big eyes, drinking beers with Hatch and laughing the rain away. The ghosts came to take all that away. There was no walking away, there never will be. The only way is through. The only way is forward. Then your concussed brain is invaded by some outside force. You can hear it, feel it. It's Iko's voice, or is it old Tenaka? It's both, neither. You wish you could wake up, but the lightless dream has you in a choke hold.

"Last chance, Grim. You can go back to Halsey's Rest. Back to Henson's. Back to the mugs. It's not too late. The ghosts can wait, Grim."
"Get out of my head!"
"I AM your head. You've been hiding all this time just to suddenly

get back into it all? Make up your mind! Walk away and live, or continue this madness and die."

The worst part isn't having whatever this is in your mind, it's agreeing with it. You killed your way to crazy enough times. Isn't how this all began? Just a blade on the Rim? A sword saint bowing out of the killing? And here you are, smashing into buildings to kill dragons...

"All you need do is open that door, Grim. Open that door and you'll have a future." Door? In your mind's eye, bleary with impact, you see it. The fear you were pushing away rises up. The days of peace you wanted are just ahead. Sunlight warms your face. No bullets, no blades. You reach for the door, wondering why you ever got involved with Drakan, Shinru Command, Tyranax... any of it. This is your chance, and you're taking it.

"Grim! Get up, damnit!" It's Hatch, his voice piercing the veil. Your eyes flicker open, and all hell is breaking loose. "Naptime's over, partner! Set the charges!"

Your brain is slow to return. Explosions fill your vision, you feel your blade leap into your hand, but you're still frozen. Hatch doesn't know you just sold him out, just chose the easy way out. It must've been Tyranax messing with you, and you almost fell for it... you *did* fall for it.

"Charges set!" You're back in action, at least enough to slam a red button and slide the satchel into the service tunnel. You can hear the beep fading as it drops eight stories. "Fifteen seconds!"

"Laser grapple out! Cover me!"

"It's a haze, but you lay down a few hundred bullets to push the commandos back. Are they commandos? Evil robots? Who are you fighting, anyway? Ono Dai Sen employees? Kids with guns? It's all black smoke and fear. Is this real or was the door real? It's getting blurry, but you make your way to the shattered windows. Hatch is cut up bad, with a huge black eye and blood in his beard. He's got

two filament lines uncoiling down the side of the tower.
"Clip in! Go! Right behind you!"
You snap the big orange clip, lean out, and fight off the dizziness, slinging your MAC12 and jumping backward. Down, mach speed, windows speeding by, wind in your eyes, Hatch above, legs flailing. Then the charges blow.

You hit the street as the building goes up in a massive mushroom cloud. Glass and steel showers the street. It's chaos. Hatch shoves you into an abandoned building, then under a steel grate, and you slump to a stop at last, a din of crazy above.

"So, did we-"
"Tyranax is offline, old partner. But I think it got some disruption programs in our heads before we could blow the core. My brain is all mixed up here!"
"Yeah... I feel... weird."
"I have a defrag program on this solid drive. I just need your retina code and I can get the disruptor out."
You pause a moment. Hatch is looking right at you, looking almost anxious. He's covered in his own blood, one hand broken.
"Hey we need to patch you up, Hatch, you're a wreck! Let me get my nanoclot here-"
"There's no time, Grim!" He lurches toward you, "give me your damn code so I can help you out!"
"My code? Nobody ever gives anyone their code, man. You know that. It's a terrible idea. We can get Case-"
"THE CODE!"
That's when you see it. This isn't Hatch at all. His eyes are both green. Hatch has one bad eye that's closer to brown. He's crazed, gritting his teeth, inching toward you.
"You're not Hatch. What is this?"
"We blew it all up, Grim! We killed Tyranax, we won! It's over."
"No, this isn't right. We must be in a simulation or-"

"Give me your fracking code, Grim!" Hatch pulls his gauss pistol from his vest, leveling it an inch from your teeth.
"Go to hell, whoever you are. If you've hurt Hatch, you'll be begging me for death before the end."
"Damnit, Shirosune. Always the hard way with you." Hatch, or whoever this is, lowers his shoulders, looking tired and annoyed. Then his eyes return to yours. "See you in hell, runner."

He pulls the trigger.

You sit up, a cold sweat making you clammy. The sheets are strangling you. It's a moonlit night. Quiet. Jenna is sleeping peacefully next to you. You swing your legs off the bed carefully, shuffling to the bathroom for unknown reasons. Habit?
The mirror shows a tired, disheveled face in the dim. Your eyes are sunken, your shoulders bony. What a nightmare. Into the kitchen. Bit of old sandwich Henson made, one last beer. You sit, sipping it. You survey the cozy little room, feeling unfamiliar and weird. On the fridge, a note reads 'remember to update retina code by friday.' You blink twice, bringing up the console. Deeper then into your source settings. You're groggy, just staring at the options blankly. Another sip. Then Jenna appears, cute as hell in a nighty with little tractors on it.
"Can't sleep?"
"Weird dream. Old times bubbling up."
"Sip?" She takes the beer, has a gulp, and sits on your lap with a flop.
"Yeah. It was this guy called Hatch. Crazy guy on a mag bike... felt so real."
"Oh hey did you remember to reset your retina code? Tenaka said we need to with this new fragment hack going around."
"Huh? Yeah I was just about to."
"Better get it done. Night." She trundles off.
You procrastinate with the best of them, and put off the damn

code until tomorrow. The beer is good. This dream is just bothering you. About half an hour passes and you're finishing the last few warm gulps. Then Jenna appears from the darkness, looking angry, looking downright mental.
"The code!"
"Jeez, Jenna relax I'll-"
"NOW!"
What the hell is- then you remember Hatch-not-Hatch in the access tunnel. Reaching for the door in your head, selling him out, the explosions. Tyranax. Is that real?
"You're not Jenna."
"My patience has reached its end, Grim. You give me no choice." A long, frustrated pause. "What a waste."

Then you come squeezing, rushing, speeding, stretching, being ripped apart, upward, outward. It all goes dark, but blinding with color, spirals and vector wireframes dropping resolution like a bad SISTM connection. You slam into the reality of now. That reality is a cold metal chair. You're restrained, and a stinging pain rings through your skull. You're wired to a virtual simulation. A lab rat. On the next table, Hatch is wired up and strapped down. He's bloody, with a few bullet holes in his vest. Out cold. As you begin to process where you are, where you really are, a mostly human shape forms from the blurry gloom. Your eyes are sticky, limbs numb. How long have you been laying here? The table lurches, then slowly ascends, bringing you upright. The head rush is intense.

"You mean nothing to me, Grim Shirosune," the figure is twice the height of a person, with fragmented cybernetics that are shifting as it walks. The internals workings are all alloy and pulsating rubber membranes. The face is fragmented likewise, with a series of red retina implants on one side. A monster. "It is Matsushita I want. The grand master. I would merge his stack with my own code, not only to build my power, but as an archival measure. You have made this impossible with your resistance, and you represent a considerable liability to Ono Dai Sen's interests. You leave me no choice but to destroy you."

"Then get on with it, whatever you are."

"I am an envoy of the entity you call Tyranax, though that name is a silly designation from my earlier days."

You test the strength of your bonds. Rock solid. It would take five or six surge caps to pop these cuffs. Probably break your arm in the process. Running out of options here. The shape moves closer, illuminated by blinking green lights and dim overheads far above.

"How about a deal? You want this other stack stack so bad, and I'd rather not be slagged right now."

"Deal?"

You're playing cards with the devil at this point, writing the script as you go and no idea who has an ace. Reckless. Tyranax stares at you, intrigued that it could still acquire its precious retina code. This gives you a precious two seconds to think.

"First you let Hatch go free. Then we offload Matsushita, and I walk away."

"Fail your mission so casually? Your deception is childish. You have no leverage here, human."

"No leverage? You don't want Matsushita, you NEED him. He's carrying a missing piece to your megalomania and you know it. You're just second best to an old man until you have that stack. That's my leverage."

"Appealing to my will to power is an interesting ploy."

"We came here to stop you. You get Matsushita and it isn't over. You win a battle, not a war. I only fail today. Let Hatch go, get your damn code."

Tyranax raises one of its five hands, gesturing with cryptic meaning, and Hatch wakes up, his bonds retracting. He sits up, looking baffled, then spots you on the next table.

"Hatch, snap out of it. Get the hell out of here."

"Grim? What the- where are the bikes? Did we win?"
"Simpletons." The figure, seeming less human with each side it reveals, moves to a console. It taps in a code, opening the far bulkhead door with a hiss. Hatch nods with a confident grin. A grin Tyranax does not notice. "Security forces are standing down, insect. Your conveyance is parked on level 2. Follow the yellow guides."

Hatch walks out with no further comment. Tyranax isn't human enough to realize how odd that is. You're counting on it.
"Ok, tap into my retina console. Let's get this over with."
"You have a security augment, human. Disable it."
"The augment is my 'friends only' pass. You use your SISTM I.D. as a collateral key to get in. Then I can transfer the 1200 digit code."
"Most unusual."
"Keep all your anti-frags up. It's legit."
"Connecting now."
"There's the code."
"Accessing concealed stack data. Finally, Hideki Sensei will be mine. The offload will take a few moments. Yes... at last!"
"Hatch, we good?"
Tyranax flinches suddenly, jerking back. It's eyes are darting side to side.
Then, over your internal comms, "Good to go, Grim. Hitting the big button on your mark."
"What- what have you done? What is this?"
"Checkmate. Go ahead, Hatch."

You figured you'd be outmatched, outgunned. Hatch guessed you'd be put through the ringer to get the retina code, so he coded up a nasty little program... takes a SISTM I.D. and locks it out of the network entirely. Tyranax was severed from every network and RAM chip from here to Saturn.

"Continue this fracas, and you'll beg for death, human. I am backed

up in trillions of systems. Your tiny minds have failed you."
"Funny thing about these antiquated SISTM I.D.'s though. Every backup is linked up on that code thread. Like I said. Checkmate. You got greedy."

"Security protocols-" the Tyranax stumbles back, realizing it's all true when its own facility offers no response. He's a single ghost in a single body now. Vulnerable as a leaf on a river. This realization changes its posture. It rises taller, revealing integrated blades. It's a cornered animal now.

"Hatch get me free will you?" Hatch appears at the door, Zenith beam gun in one hand, decking kit in the other. Tyranax circles slowly, waiting for a moment to pounce, but seeing fully that one shot from that weapon could end its entire existence. Hatch pops you loose, and you stand, stiff as a board but mostly intact.

"Security will come online in about one minute, Grim. The 'conn chopper' will alert their detection programs. Time's up. He levels the weapon at Tyranax. "Adios, asshole."
"So you're murderers now? Killing in cold blood?"
"You remember Costa Mona?"
"A tactical target in Silver Shard."
"Tactical target. You know, I had a family once, I mean besides Grim here. You leveled the entire town on your rampage. Shinru Command was off leash. It was a massacre."
"The conditions of-" Before Tyranax can finish, Hatch pulls the trigger, gritting his teeth against the force of the particle beam emission. The beam cuts Tyranax in half in a white-blue flash. He holds the trigger, letting the beam slice slowly through the entire building in a sweeping arc. The battery finally overheats, then goes dead. He's still white-knuckling the trigger.

"Ease back, Hatch. It's done. We've still got to get out of here."

"Yeah. Level 2. Yellow guides."
"Right."

As the two of you make your way out of Ono Dai Sen central, out of Shinru city, out of the urban sectors entirely, the wide open spaces of the Rim come into view. The bikes are humming. You've put an end to Silver Burn. The bad guys lose this time.
"Now what, Grim?" Hatch on internal comms, riding with no hands.
"We could expose it all, you know. That SISTM I.D. is a key to all of it. The world needs to know. These psycho A.I.'s will get us all killed someday."
"Or we could not."
"Huh?"
"I mean, we could just go dark. Ghost it. Since when is it up to us to 'tell the world' and all that? We put our necks on the line and got it done. Some new set of jerkwads will eventually replace the dragons. I say we've done our part. Back to sweet, sweet retirement."
"Ghost it, huh? It does sound good. Had just about enough bullets and blades. A few years of cold beer and sleeping in has its appeal."

"Look, Grim. We've been side by side for years. I got your back no matter what.

If you want to go full superhero, tell the world, keep fighting, probably get us both killed... I'm with you. I just think we've earned our way out of the life...for now at least."
"Maybe you're right."

If you go dark, change your names, disappear turn to PAGE 313.

If you decide to expose the evil of Tyranax and Shinru Command, turn to PAGE 315.

Years pass.

You and Hatch vanish into a tiny wooded settlement called Red Glade.

Hatch, now going by Hollis, fills his time fishing and running a totally unsuccessful wood carving business. His little figures are simply terrible. He's always right around the corner, always has a smile, and never brings up the old days. As his blonde beard starts to gray, he takes to calling you 'little lady,' which you hate.

As for you, the sword simply will not let you go. You keep your days busy helping locals fix their doors, bikes, kitchen tools. Anything metal, you're the one to call. Every now and then, you even get time to forge a blade from scratch. A town event. 'Grim' is a long forgotten name. You go by Ren. Kids follow you around like pilot fish, and you can't stand it. Sure, you miss Iko, and Jenna, Case and Greta, Tenaka and all the urchins at Henson's place. You stay way out here to protect them, to keep the giants sleeping.

But no matter how far you run, some ghosts just won't let go. Ghosts like Eddy Muntz. Muntz is an investigator, private contract, mostly cyborg'd up but in a snappy black suit. He looks terribly out of place in the Glade.

"Everyone in the cities is wearing retro," he says.

"Who are you again?" you're busy sharpening a cutlery set. It's raining.

"Name's Muntz. No need for games, Grim. I'm not a threat."

You stop what you're doing, but don't look up.

"Relax. I'm on a contract with the new interim leadership from Veil. That's the capital now, you know. Crazy times."

"What do want, Mr. Muntz?"

"It wasn't easy to track you down. You're damn good at disappearing. My job was to give them a location, give you up, send in the gunships. Unpleasant business, really." He pauses, lights a smoke, leans back. "You know, even with all this stack nonsense, retuning,

duplicates... even with all that, life is short. Our deeds define us, wouldn't you agree?"
You stay silent.
"So here I am, sent to paint a target on the back of a true freedom fighter. The runner who brought down Tyranax, changed everything, ended the age of the A.I.'s. I'm the reaper in this particular-"
"Get to the point, Mr. Muntz, please. I have work to do."
"Of course, of course. In this particular case, I've chosen to be derelict in my duties. I'm here to warn you. Warn you they're looking, and if I can find you the next guy can. Just for talking to you I've signed my own death warrant, kid. Here, take this." He hands you a small alloy brick. It's the size of a deck of cards, but dense.
"What's this?"
"The very latest in jammer tech, runner. A gift from a friend. It was a real pleasure... an honor to meet you. Thanks for your time." He stands, tips his hat like a relic, and straightens his jacket. He's gone as quickly as he came.
You take a look at the tech. It's a seamless alloy piece. On the small side, a tiny bit of marker has been scribbled. It reads:
'Stay frosty!' with a little smiley face. You've seen that smiley face before, only one person doodles like that.
Case.

After that day, things go quiet. Real quiet. The kids that follow you around grow up, Hatch is always there with coffee in the morning and beer in the afternoon. You come to know what so few know in the age of blades and bullets: peace.

THE END

No quitting now, you and Hatch decide to expose the entire mess: Silver Shard, Silver Burn, the dragons, the Chancellor's double dealing and genocidal doomsday plans, the evil A.I. and psychic pushers. It's all on the SISTM.

Funny thing about this kind of reckless courage: it's contagious. Instead of being swarmed by Shinru commandos or assassins, you and Hatch are surrounded with freedom fighters. An outrage becomes a movement, a movement becomes a resistance, and the resistance brings down the tyrants. At the head of it all, against all odds, is Biggs, the nutjob from Jugger territory.

Strange days.

You don't stick around to find out what happens. You've earned a breather. Time to put a few thousand miles on two wheels and do some deep think.

You take your bike out into the great wide open. A few cigarettes, storms rolling in the distance, a whole world lost in the bullshit data wreck that became the human race. Not you, you have two wheels and a clean conscience.

Centuries old asphalt is shit to ride, but every once in a while there's a smooth patch. Maybe the rain and the quakes and the ages just pass that little spot by, maybe it was just sunshine for decades, smooth and warm, and it rides like butter under your wheels at 200.

Maybe that's all there is: blacktop stretching out to infinity, and if you're lucky, you catch a groovy spot here and there.

RESISTANCE

The trick isn't making the highway, being the highway, choking the life out of life, or hoping for good weather... The trick is leaning back when it all goes right, when the road is smooth as far as the eye can see. Lean back, runner, take it in. You've earned it.

Part of you always holds on to what happened. It all seemed so fast, so sudden. You run the events in your head again and again, looking for what you missed. You're not well-suited to prosperity, so you spend the lonely hours picking at memories. Back to that night in Henson's Pub, ice on your mug, eyeing the creep and worried about Jenna, the girl you used for bait.

You go back to that night. You can feel the scabbard in your hand, feel the whisky in your gut. Hindsight is twenty twenty, maybe you could've made a different call. Maybe this is the best life you could ask for... all you can ask.

You'll never know. It's just you and the road.

THE END

"Turn around! We've got to stop that thing!"
"What? Grim, no! We're in a damn transpo-"
"Greta, come around, I'll jump. You guys get clear. This is mine!"
"Jump? Mine? What the hell are you talking about? You gonna stab its toe?"
"Something like that."
"Your funeral. Greta, run a jammer on the swarmer missiles, and throw up the hologram decoy. Open the bay door."
"Got it, Case. This button here?"
"That's the one, boo."
You check your gear. If stopping Silver Burn is your aim, and sending a message to the damn Chancellor and all his doomsday troopers, this is the chance. The thing has to have a weakness, and can't be built for such a small target.
"Don't get killed, you lunatic. Greta will be pissed."
"See you on the other side, Case."
"It's been a pleasure, runner."

You jump, no real plan, and tumble into the dust as the transport tears away at speed, bay door closing. The blade springs into your hand, as it always does. You catch your feet, turn as the dust clears, and there the shadow towers over you: Heavy Gear. It's a walking weapons platform, a few thousand tons, as big as a battleship and tall as an office building. It moves in giant-monster slow motion, aligning a glowing blue 'eye' your direction. The eye is all you can see in the scale of it.

Then come some of your finest moments in this or any life. A single blade against a monster of death. You dash, tumble, roll from explosions and bend around spiraling nano missiles. Gunfire shreds the open dirt, and you somehow come through in one piece, sprinting to the massive metal feet ahead. It's weapons can't fire straight down. You're an ant on an elephant.

Instinct takes over and you're on top of the damn thing, riding it like a convulsing tugboat in a storm. Behind what could be called the head, maybe it's a cockpit, a giant cluster of cables and ports is tangled ahead of you. Then, an idea. You sheathe the blade and pull out a micro drive. It plugs magnetically to one huge conduit, and drinks all the data it can.

"Jackpot!" But your brilliant idea costs you all your effort and you're thrown from the summit like a baby bird from the nest. Only your reflex link saves you, and you catch a pneumatic line on the way down, breaking your fall and hitting the hardpan like a sack of onions.

"Grim, you crazy bastard! Heads up!" It's Case on retina comms, shouting and straining. "Look out!" Then you see it: four low yellow headlights piercing the dust, coming in fast. It's the transport. You roll to one side, barely missing the tube bumper. It roars by and you see Greta in the bay door, throwing a link cable. You grab the cable just as the transport unloads a full box-pack of chaff flares, engulfing Heavy Gear in a storm of smoke and fire. You're dragged, jerked, tumbled, and finally flop into the bay.

"Fuckin' a!"

"Haha! Yeah!" Case is at the wheel, and tears off into shadow, leaving Heavy Gear as a bad memory.

"You're crazy you know that?"

"I learned it from watching you, Dad!"

"Case," he turns and you toss him the micro drive, "Check it out."

"You didn't. My birthday was last week!"

Greta helps you with your road burns and wrecked gear. You're a damn mess. A few moments pass, Case parks the transport under the city. It's a clean getaway.

"Holy shit, Grim."

"Yeah?"

"It's that ghost Tyranax. This data puts a location on it. Telemetry. It was piloting that thing."

"Final front. The big kill."

"Grim, no. We can get this to the underground. The Iga can do our dirty work for-"

"Case... we need to finish this, unless you want Heavy Gear doing your laundry in the near future." He looks at Greta, who shrugs, ever optimistic, lovely as spring, open-eyed as a sunny day.

"She may be right, boo," Greta says, tying one last field dressing on your ragged shoulder. "Go save the world again."

"You guys are bonkers, you know that?"

"So that's a yes?"

"One condition."

"Name it."

"I've got Iko on a direct line. No pushers. Her stack is clean, and all that assassin shit is over."

"How-"

"You don't want to know."

"I mean... yeah!"

"Put your lady boner away, runner. We'll meet her at Zelda's tavern."

"Hey Case,"

"Yeah?"

"Love you boo."

"Oh shut up, Grim."

Turn to PAGE 245.

U TURN

"Just go! That thing is huge!"

Greta slams the throttle, throwing you and Case against the gear racks.

"What the hell is that thing? Heavy Gear? It's massive!"

"The final solution. Tyranax's big gun to end Silver Burn, overtake the Chancellor, kill the world and get some peace and quiet in the ashes."

"Tyranax? The A.I.? I thought that was just rumors."

"I wish. It's a ruthless, formless God-thing. Seems to hate us all-"

Another hard swerve and you slide to the opposite side.

"We've poked a hornet's nest on this one, Grim. I can't have that much heat on Greta and me. I mean, look at that thing!"

"Case, I hit the jammer. It's this orange button right here, right?"

"Yeah, sweetie. Perfect. We can slip into the lower city and ditch this heap. We'll be in grav couches watching Bonestorm 4 in no time."

"Sounds good babe."

"Maybe you're right this time, Case."

"Maybe? No maybe! We're out, Grim. We're not throwing ourselves at a fucking war monster."

"Drop me up here, I'll grab a bike somewhere and disappear for a few days. I've done it before."

"Copy that."

"And thanks. The world's a little better with Drakan in the dirt."

"Take care of yourself, Grim, I'll see you soon. Noodles?"

"Noodles."

Case and Greta roar away in the transport, disappearing under the city. In a few hours, you've got a micro jammer running, and you're scouring the slums for a bike.

Not so hard here... it's a junker's paradise.

Then you're out on the open tarmac. You let a smile happen at last.

Drakan is toast, Case and Greta safe. Heavy Gear is probably just confused or fuelling down after you disappeared. The smile isn't for all that, it's knowing you're far from giving up. You blink twice, bringing up your retina comms.

"Hatch? Pick up, man."
"Grim! Shit, where you been? There's-"
"Meet me in the vapor tracks East of Shinru proper. We're going after Tyranax."
"The dragon-thing? Big bad guy A.I. people talk about? The boogie man and what not. Thought you'd never ask."
"Same one. I'm done running down the puppets. High value target. Figured you might want a piece."
"What should I bring?"
"Everything."

Turn to PAGE 303.

STRANGE DAYS

You've lived the life of bullets and blades, been baffled by love and lifetimes. You've smashed through, blown up and went around every damn thing this digital life can throw at you.

Strange how it moves in loops. Strange how you see parralels, confusing multi-nows and myths told by a dozen bards. Strange how it seems to tell the same tale, but woven in so many different ways... a tale told in the present tense.

A strange thing.

You walk in slow motion through the city clutter. Cyan-pink counterpoints your deadly pourpose. The kanji and neon are all a distraction from the simple fact that computer dreams are overtaking our own. Digital minds are conjuring the world of tommorrow, and we are being left behind.

Our lives mean less and less, then the wilderness will return. That will be a time when we no longer look to distant tyrants for our meager shares. We will look to one another, side by side, and find there survival, and all we were hoping to have.

The space between now and that dream future is a desolate, crowded, lonely place called *cyberpunk*.

In that place, heroes are made.

I've run with so many uzi-wielding maniacs and eye-implant noir types I can't easily list them. I've destroyed APC's, used a limo as a bomb, demolished a building with a robotic mouse and played Blackjack with a dragon in a tuxedo.

The early days were amazing, but that was almost two centuries before the A.I. crisis. Before New Arcadia, before Sugar, or all those rim towns that were leveleed in the ‘Ramifications’ of 2180. What a damn mess. The A.I.’s threatened to end us all, and for what? Their deranged idea of a cleaner, lifeless world.

Then, the whole thing was put on ice. We had the A.I.’s on jammers that reached to Alpha-Fucking-Centauri. We rounded up their brainwashed worshippers and smacked ‘em sober. Then, the off-world movement happened. We lost power on everything, and all those nasties we had locked up just ran loose.

With the locks all opened, all we had contained went free. The madness returned, but this time there were so few of us to fight it. Humanity has abandoned its home, so its up to us.

No backup, no second chances. It’s us or them.

Welcome to the 25th century.

-Grim Shirosune

Printed in Great Britain
by Amazon

26944081R00185